The Gráinne Journals

The Gráinne Journals

Robert C Coyle

Basement Press
DUBLIN

First published in Ireland in 1995 by
Basement Press
an imprint of Attic Press Ltd
4 Upper Mount Street
Dublin 2

A catalogue record for this title is available from the British Library

ISBN 1 85594 165 1

Cover Design: Michael O'Dwyer
Origination: Verbatim Typesetting and Design
Printing: Guernsey Press Co. Ltd

This book is published with the financial assistance of The Arts Council/An Chomhairle Ealaíon, Ireland.

Dedication

For my wife Olive. Only she and I know her contribution. For Siobhan, Fiona and Rob, my three reasons for pride.
For Cathleen O'Neill and KLEAR.

Quietus

quietus: *(kwy-ee-tus)*
release from life;
final riddance.
The Oxford English Dictionary

The dense drizzling rain permeated everything. The car, open sided and canvas-topped, gave precious little protection. He sat as low as he could in the front seat, hands dug deep in the greatcoat pockets. The collar was turned up and he kept his chin down.

He was tired watching the erratic passage of the windscreen wipers as they attempted to keep the glass free from the rain. He was frozen to the marrow. Cork and a double whiskey seemed almost beyond the edge of hope.

The road rose steadily, turning and twisting before their slow progress. The engine howled in protest at the never ceasing climb.

A shot. Jerking upright, he shouted, 'Ambush. Stop the car and into the ditch.'

The driver swore and stood on the brakes. With a screech of tortured rubber the car stopped moving and the engine cut out. He hurled himself sideways, landed on his shoulder and rolled across the road. He tore at the holster and clawed the Webley free. The lanyard was at full stretch as he started to fire.

How many times had he impressed on the men the importance of using whatever conditions presented themselves? Weather such as this drastically reduced the advantage of greater firepower. The attackers would be invisible from the road. They could sit up on the hill and pour their fire down at the two cars.

A ragged volley rang out from the darkness and he pressed himself flat. His eyes tried desperately to pierce the blackness, looking for a muzzle flash, anything at which to direct his fire.

He called out, 'Keep down. They're shooting blind. They can't possibly see us. If you see a flash, fire as fast as you can. With a little luck, they'll be too wet to keep it up for long. Any casualties?'

The sergeant from the car answered, 'No sir. How many do you think are there, sir?'

'From the sounds of it, no more than half a dozen.'

Now fire was coming from his ranks. The men had recovered from the surprise of the attack without taking a bullet and were shooting – probably at nothing, but at least it would keep the enemy busy.

Ten minutes passed. Had he thought of it, the rather desultory pattern of incoming fire might have given him pause. The attackers did not appear to have their hearts in it. As if they were waiting for something to happen.

Away in the distance, a whistle shrilled faintly. Silence.

'I think they're leaving. Just keep still and we'll all be in Cork tonight.'

From out of the mist, a soft voice spoke his name. His head jerked up instinctively. He did not hear the shot which killed him, did not realise that it had come from less than ten yards away.

Immediately the firing started again, this time with far more purpose. It was uncomfortably accurate and kept them pinned down for twenty minutes.

Suddenly it was over.

One

'Frank, wake up. Something's happening next door.'

I sat up, blinking the sleep from my eyes. Theresa was standing at the window peering through a gap in the curtains. A sound came to my ears. It was like hearing someone shaking a mat or tablecloth in the garden. The same snapping noise.

I leapt out of bed. Now I could identify it: the sound of flames crackling. 'It's a fire. Downstairs, quickly.'

'It's Mrs Perry's. I'll ring the fire brigade. Go out and see how bad it is, but for God's sake don't try to get in.'

I looked at the clock. Ten past four. The party wall felt hot to my touch. I grabbed my dressing gown and a couple of heavy sweaters. I had a feeling that we might be spending the next few hours on the street.

I ran past Theresa in the hall as she gave details over the phone.

To give them their due, the brigade were in position in less than ten minutes. We stood on the opposite footpath watching them as they attacked the flames. They had our assurance that the house was empty, which, I suppose, made their task easier. In truth, there was little they could do to save the house. The roof collapsed as we watched, sending a mini-fireball skywards.

'Do you smell anything, Frank?'

'A house on fire.'

'No, I don't mean that. There's something else. I can't put my finger on it, but it's there.'

I sniffed. She was right. A distinctive smell overhung the scene. I blew out a silent whistle. Petrol. That was it. The whole place reeked of petrol.

We looked at each other, eyebrows raised. I walked across to where a senior officer seemed to be in charge. 'Would I be right to say that I can smell petrol?'

His eyes were cautious. 'You would be...?'

'Doorly, Frank Doorly. I live next door.'

'Well, Mr Doorly, we have to get the fire under control before we try to find the cause.'

'Fine, but if this is arson, my wife and I have been put in danger deliberately by someone. This house is unoccupied but ours is not.'

'My men's first priority, once they were sure that the burning house was empty, has been to ensure that the fire does not spread. The wall between the houses has been thoroughly damped.'

'Even so, will there be any damage, structural or other, to my house?'

'Nothing in this business is absolutely certain, but my experience tells me that you may suffer small amounts of smoke damage, nothing worse. Is your house insured?'

I nodded. 'You haven't answered my question about petrol. Is the smell significant or not?'

He looked tired and his expression soured. 'Look, sir, I can't be blamed for every smell at the scene of a fire. If you smell petrol, you must draw your own conclusions. Now, if you will excuse me, I have work to do.'

He walked away and I saw the light of the flames reflected in his white helmet.

I told Theresa what had transpired and she shrugged. 'I suppose he's right, Frank. Thank God we're not affected. Can we go in?'

'Best wait till we get the all-clear. I've a feeling that he would like nothing better than to haul us out again. Here, snuggle up. We can try to keep each other warm.'

Time passed slowly after that. We were glad of the sweaters, but after the first rush of excitement the cold crept through us. I tightened my arm around Theresa, feeling the shivers start. My hands and feet were quickly numb, and my eyes watered. Even the end of June can provide seeping chill at five in the morning.

I thought, a trifle ruefully, that Number 74 Greenview Road had assumed remarkable importance in our lives in the last twenty-four hours or so.

In that time, we had, if you like, found Mrs Perry, lost her, and seen her house go up in flames, these flames having apparently been caused deliberately. More than a little outside the usual run of experiences in our tight world.

I had called to the house the night before, at Theresa's insistence. She had met Mrs Perry that afternoon and had been worried by the old lady's frailty.

The conditions in which I had found her had come as a great shock. Our previous contacts with her were of the 'good morning' variety, but we had noticed an air of slightly reduced circumstances which she seemed to tolerate quite well.

Now, however, I discovered that the house was stripped of furniture apart from a settee and cupboard in the one room I had seen. The term 'living room' had taken on a whole new meaning. Mrs Perry slept on the settee fully clothed against the cold. She 'cooked', heated tins of beans actually, in the fireplace on a small spirit stove. The electricity was off, presumably for non-payment, and the coal bunker was empty.

The shock of all this on Theresa was then compounded by her discovery the next morning of the old woman lying on the floor. She had fallen and broken her thigh.

Two unusual aspects of her arrival at Beaumont Hospital were quickly brought home to us when we visited her later in the morning. The staff nurse in whose charge the old lady was asked us to step into her office. She was a stern-looking woman probably in her early forties and I admit that I took an immediate dislike to her. Theresa was clearly not too impressed with her either.

When she had shut the office door firmly, she took her place behind a desk. 'I understand you are friends of Mrs Perry.'

I was quick to kill that thought at birth. 'Not friends. Neighbours.'

She raised her badly plucked eyebrows at me. 'The ambulance men informed me that you had called them.'

Theresa's tone was little short of hostile. 'We live next door and naturally did all we could when we discovered that she had fallen. Apart from infrequent 'good mornings' we really hardly knew Mrs Perry. Did you find any mention of relatives in her handbag?'

The starched veil shook in a silent negative and the nurse leaned across the desk towards me. 'Despite what you say, as you are the only people showing interest in Mrs Perry, I have no alternative but to ask you some questions. You see, Mr Doorly, Mrs Perry was examined by the admission doctor. He first noticed that she was wearing white gloves and when these were removed he found her fingers in a dreadful state. At some time in the distant past, this old woman has been subjected to what I can only describe as torture. Every one of her fingernails has been forcibly removed, leaving severe malformation of the fingertips. Further examination showed scarring of the body by both burning and whipping.'

I was about to launch into my opinion of all this, when Theresa beat me to it. Her voice was low but definitely sharp. 'I've never heard such rubbish in all my life. Do you seriously expect us to believe these...flights of fancy. Surely to God, your first duty to this old lady is to guard her privacy.'

She rose to her feet. 'Come on, Frank. I want to see Mrs Perry.' She looked back over her shoulder at the nurse. 'If you repeat these ridiculous stories to anyone else, I'll report you to whoever is in charge of this hospital.'

So we had gone in to see Mrs Perry, dismissing the bizarre ramblings of the Sister as pure nonsense. The old woman's death a few hours later was only shortly preceded by her request that we recover a box containing her private papers from the house. Her instruction was that if she died, they should be destroyed unread.

The flames had long been extinguished when a Garda approached. 'Excuse me, sir, would you be Mr Doorly?'

I nodded. 'This is my wife.' People say the most stupid things under pressure. Who else would she be?

'I'm told that it is safe for you to go into your house. Could I have a few words inside?'

Theresa led the way and put the kettle on for tea. We sat around the empty table. I checked my watch: five twenty. A kitchen, no matter what cosy memories it provokes, is a cheerless, depressing place to be in the hours before dawn.

Theresa was setting out cups as I said, 'Everything seems to be under control, now.'

The policeman was middle-aged and grey-haired, and a stubble was evident on his square chin. His cap lay upside-down on the table like an abandoned dinghy floating on a calm sea. 'Yes, sir. A bad business. Mr Tuite tells me that you have a theory about the cause of the fire?'

'Mr Tuite?'

'The officer in charge. He said that you spoke of a smell of petrol.'

'I smelt it. My wife smelt it. I asked him if he could smell it. He wouldn't answer.'

'The smell of petrol or other such substances at the scene of a fire is a very strong pointer to arson.'

'So we were right?'

'Maybe so. How long was the house unoccupied?'

'Since about nine o' clock this morning, yesterday morning. Your people should know the exact time. We had to call you to break in. The woman who lived there had fallen. I spoke to one of your men at the time. I'm sure he reported it.'

'Actually he did, sir. Mrs Mary Perry was the occupier.'

Theresa joined in as she poured the tea. 'She died this afternoon.'

'Yes, madam. Very unfortunate.'

'So,' I said, 'vandals obviously heard that she was not there. How did they get in? We heard nothing before the fire.'

'Actually, Frank, I did hear something about half an hour before. I forgot to mention it. Thinking about it now, it was probably a window breaking.'

'We're not too worried about the method of entry in this case. The fire has destroyed any clues about that. Were either of you familiar with the inside of the house?'

We shook our heads. He continued, 'The seat of the fire was most likely in the ground-floor back room. Would you have any idea what was there?'

'Yes. It's the only room that I was in, last night and this morning. The furniture was a settee used as a bed by the old woman, and a wooden cabinet or dresser. There was nothing else.'

'Why would anyone light a fire in an almost

empty room?'

'Vandalism or heat,' I replied.

'Hardly either, Mr Doorly. A large quantity of petrol was splashed around that one room and set alight.'

'So, we *were* right. But if it was not vandals, then who?'

'That's my point, sir. Whoever it was came equipped to burn the place to the ground. I can tell you, in confidence, that this was not a random fire. It was a professional job from start to finish. Now, that sort of people do not come cheap.'

Theresa's voice was full of scepticism. 'You're not trying to tell us that somebody paid to have Mrs Perry's house burnt down?'

'It's early to be sure but it looks that way. Are you sure there was nothing else in the room? This cabinet. Was it locked, did you notice?'

'Not another stick of furniture. She slept on the settee, cooked her meals in the fire grate.' I glanced sideways at Theresa. Her expression was neutral. 'As for the thing being locked or not, I have no idea.'

He stood up and recovered his cap. 'Thank you for your help and for the tea. I'd better be heading back.'

When he had gone, we sat and looked at each other. 'Frank, why did you not tell him about the box?'

'I don't know, love. She said the papers were private. I sort of feel that we owe it to her to keep them that way.'

'Are you thinking that the papers were what the man or men were looking for? And he burnt the house when he couldn't find them? In case they were hidden?'

'Aren't you?'

'Maybe what that nurse said was not so unlikely after all.'

'Now what?'

'We've got to examine the box. We have to know what's in the books.' Having made the decision, we did not rush pell-mell to the task. It was after five and we needed to recover the lost sleep.

We soon found that a smell of damp and smoke pervaded the rooms with party walls. The kitchen, bathroom and box room were the only places free from the acrid, heavy odour.

Theresa made up the single bed in the small bedroom and we settled down, clasping each other, as much for safety as any other reason.

We got off all right and I woke at half-past eight. Quickly, we had breakfast and drove to Mass, returning before ten.

I made a tour of the house, looking for smoke or water damage. I even climbed into the attic. Everything seemed fine, but I was determined to have someone out the next day for a professional assessment.

This done, Theresa made a big pot of tea while I carried the box into the kitchen. I put it on the table which she had covered with a sheet. House-proud to the last.

The box was of cardboard, with the words 'Sunlight Soap' printed large in red. It had been many a year since this container had been used for the first time.

We sat opposite each other and I took a bundle of the school exercise copies from the box. They were held together by an ancient rubber band which disintegrated as soon as I touched it. The thin books were numbered, in this pile, 11 to 20. I delved about until I found number 1.

I leafed through the pages. They were covered in small, angular handwriting, easy to read but untidy at first glance. There was something about the writing. Then I got it. The writer was left-handed.

The ink was black. Each page seemed full, with, in some cases, extra sentences or words being squeezed above the first line.

I looked at the first page and began to read aloud.

Monday, 19 May 1919

Nineteen today. I will start my journal with a short account of my life thus far. My name is Mary Stewart. I am known to my family and close friends as Molly. I was born in Thurles. Father is a doctor and lives in an estate-house owned by Lord Martindale. I have two sisters, Angeline and Martha. I am the eldest girl by four years, Martha being ten and Angeline fifteen. I also have twin brothers Arthur and George, aged seventeen. Our house is quite small with five bedrooms upstairs, not counting the servants' quarters. Mother spends most of her time helping workers' families. We were all sent to England for our education. My sisters are there still. Our school is Rightwell near Gloucester. I hated every moment but the others seem to be happy there. The boys have just finished at Brentwood in Sussex and are bound for Trinity College, Dublin where Arthur will study Law, and George History.

I have come to Dublin to take up a position in Dublin Castle. Father wrote to the Lord Lieutenant and he has been kind enough to offer me the post. This has been my first day. I am attached to Mr Alfred Cope's staff. He is the Assistant Under-Secretary. My duties are to take down his letters in Pitman's Shorthand and type them on a beautiful Royal. He very kindly agreed to speak quite slowly until I have grown accustomed to the work. He is in charge of the Military Intelligence and, as such, writes a large number of long letters. I found that the time passes very quickly and agreeably. There are two other ladies in the office. Both have Army connections. They are Elizabeth (father, Major Browne), and Alice (widow of Captain Smethurst). Alice was particularly kind, sharing her luncheon with me. I was not informed that one was expected to provide one's food. Tomorrow I will be better prepared.

I am living with a friend of Mother's, near

Kingstown. The address is 19 Victoria Crescent. The woman's name is Mrs Kartleigh, but she has kindly allowed me to address her as Aunt Beatrice. Mr Kartleigh is abroad and they have no children. Aunt Beatrice treats me as if I were her daughter and I have a lovely room at the back of the house. I can see the harbour from there and I could sit forever watching the packet steamers arrive and leave. I am sure that many sad and happy moments take place under my eyes. Perhaps I will become a novelist and tell such tales of farewell.

I looked up from the page at Theresa. 'Nothing very earth-shattering about that.'

She shook her head. 'No, but it's certainly interesting. To read about that time after all these years.'

'I'm a bit disappointed, to tell you the truth.'

'What were you expecting?'

'I'm not sure. I suppose I was looking for some clue as to why anyone would burn down a house for these things.'

'We've only read one page, for God's sake. I say, give it time.' 'You're right, I suppose. Anyway let's have a look at the next entry.'

I turned the page. 'Well, she didn't write every day. The next one is a couple of weeks later. Here goes.'

Monday 2 June, 1919
I have decided not to attempt an entry every day. It would be ridiculous. I shall concentrate on days when something interesting happens. Today, I was in the office typing when a young man in uniform came in. Everyone else was busy, so I asked him whether I could help him. He introduced himself as Lieutenant Lincoln. He is the new junior aide-de-camp to General Macready and had an appointment with the General. I showed him in. Alice came to my desk and whispered that he was very handsome. I thought so, but of course

did not say that. Alice was laughing all afternoon. Elizabeth spoke sharply to us and we continued with our work. Lieutenant Lincoln came out of the General's office soon afterwards and thanked me for helping him. Of course I had only done my duty but I thought it very kind of him. He told me a little about himself. He is English, of course. His family live in Hampshire and Dublin is his first posting. He is stationed in the Castle. He wanted to talk further but I had to tell him to leave. Elizabeth was staring at him, looking very annoyed. Later the General called me into his office. He said that there is to be a reception in the Viceregal Lodge tomorrow evening to which Lieutenant Lincoln has been invited. He knows no one in Dublin and has asked General Macready whether I could accompany him. I told the General that I would have to ask permission from Aunt Beatrice and he said that he would telephone her at once. The result of all this is that I am to accompany Lieutenant Lincoln and he will call for me at half-past seven. I am quite astonished by the whole event. What will I wear? My white gown, in which I was presented last year, is quite unsuitable. Perhaps the blue would be better. Oh dear.

I threw the book on to the table. 'For God's sake, it's like reading a women's magazine. Bloody bilge.'

Theresa laughed. 'Well, I think it's great. I'll read the rest of the books. If there's anything interesting, I'll let you know.' 'Right, you do that. I'm going to look at a video. I'll go inside.' That was the start of it.

On the Monday evening, Mrs Perry's remains arrived at the local church. We were the only ones present. At Theresa's insistence, I had undertaken to pay the funeral expenses. When the house site was sold we would get the money back. Sooner, if there was any insurance on the old lady. Neither alternative seemed copper-fastened to me.

The funeral itself, on Tuesday, was a grim affair. Again we were the only mourners. The dreary walk in the summer rain to the graveside settled a deep depression on me. Only a couple of large whiskeys afterwards saved me from the familiar spiral into the depths. I was unable or unwilling to go to work that day and spent the afternoon in bed.

Three days later, Theresa rang me in the office. 'Frank, a big lorry has arrived next door. Three men are starting to pull down Mrs Perry's house. They've a skip and they're dumping the bricks and stuff into it. They've filled it twice already. Will I try to find out who they are working for?'

'Yes, do that. Call back if they know anything.'

She was back in ten minutes. 'They're from a firm called O'Reilly Builders in Finglas. Mr O'Reilly sent them out to do the job. They have to reduce the house to ground level. I asked if our house could be damaged by this but they said that there was nothing to worry about.'

'Have you a phone number for this O'Reilly man?'

She gave it to me and I dialled. After about a dozen rings a rough voice answered. 'Yes?'

'Could I speak to Mr O'Reilly please?'

'This is him.' A man of few words.

I explained my interest in his workmen and asked if he could tell me the name of the owner of the house. He could not. Who had ordered the demolition? An insurance company. Would he give me the name of the company? Trident Insurances Ltd. The address was on the Quays, near the Four Courts.

Trident Insurances Ltd answered the phone promptly. Once again I outlined my problem. On whose behalf had they ordered the work to be done? On their own behalf. The property was covered by a policy issued by them. Who is the owner of the policy? The name on the policy is Mary Perry. Who had reported the fire to them? The police. The name of the officer on the notification? Inspector Ryan,

Broomstown Garda Station.

That evening Brendan Archer arrived just as we were sitting down to dinner. He was an ex-boyfriend of Theresa's and an architect. He had given the house a going-over before I had bought it. He was here to look for any damage from the fire or water.

He didn't come cheaply, but finally expressed himself satisfied that all was well. He irritated me by referring to Theresa as Tess all the time and kissed her far too warmly for my liking when leaving.

The accounts for the funeral and Archer's survey came to almost two thousand pounds.

For no particular reason, Theresa decided to key the diary entries on to the computer which we keep in the kitchen. Her 'job' was typing manuscripts and we had invested two thousand pounds on a set-up which gave her the best word processor and printer.

She had a few writers on her books and they were glad to pay top dollar for the stuff she produced.

When she had started with a plain typewriter and photocopier, she had taken on anything she could get. She was a first class typist and prided herself on the quality of her work. Everyone using her got a guarantee of accuracy. Many's the evening I had spent calling back letters and documents and watching her retype a complete page where she discovered a mistake.

Nowadays, she could afford to pick and choose her clients. On average, she put in about twenty hours a week.

It kept her happy and paid a few bills.

Ah well, enough of that. Back to Mrs Perry's house and my outlay. Two grand is two grand, in anyone's money.

I rang a solicitor friend of mine and told him the story. He said that he would carry out a search on the deeds of Mrs Perry's house that would establish the ownership and give me a place to start. This merely confirmed that Mrs Perry had owned the house since it had been built in 1969. A mortgage on the property had been fully paid off ten years later.

A call to the Guards failed to produce Inspector Ryan. He was away in England and no other officer knew what I was talking about. I left word that he should get in touch when he returned.

For the next two weeks all Theresa's spare time was taken up with ploughing through exercise book after exercise book. I forgot about Mrs Perry and her quaint early lifestyle, until they started to impinge upon my comfort. I began to arrive home from my office to find that I would have to make my own dinner. It was an unwelcome reminder that Theresa had discovered something more important than me.

I must confess that the situation threatened to cause me problems in the office.

Civil-service jobs are looked upon by outsiders as sinecures and that is fine as far as it goes. However, at the higher levels, where politicians need to be satisfied with one's work, more than merely turning up each day is required.

As an Acting Sub-Secretary in the Department of Education, I was in fairly constant contact with the Minister's office. After a couple of untypical mistakes on my part had drawn a more than mild rebuke from Leinster House, I found that I was blaming Theresa and the damned diaries for every little imperfection in the day.

I never got to the point of vocalising my concern. She had shown during our fourteen years of marriage that direct challenges to her position were met with cold fury. I was not prepared to take the chance. In other words, I was afraid of her.

Two

On a Tuesday evening when I walked in, Theresa was waiting for me, her face aglow with triumph.

'You look as if you've won the Lotto. What's got you excited?'

'I think I've found something Frank. In the diaries. And I know who Richard was.' Mrs Perry had called out the name as she died.

'The fancy army officer. Lemon...Langton... something beginning with an L.'

'Lincoln. Lieutenant Richard Lincoln. They fell in love.'

'So what's new? I could have told you that after he first appeared. She obviously fancied him.'

'Anyway, that's only a side issue. There's a couple of entries I want you to read. Take your coat off and come into the kitchen. I'll put the kettle on.'

'To hell with the kettle. I want my dinner.'

'Yes, yes, I'll get you something later. Now sit down while I explain a few things.'

I frowned, annoyed at her enthusiasm. 'How do you mean explain? I can read. And frankly Theresa, its a bit of a liberty not having the dinner ready when I come in. I've been working bloody hard all day and I don't think it's too much to ask.'

'Oh for goodness sake Frank, don't be so bloody pompous. Are you going to sit down or will I just go on without you?'

I threw my coat over the back of a chair and sat. She held a volume in her hand and she went on, 'After the first few entries, she started to get better organised. The writing is even smaller than before, but it flows more. She uses initials instead of people's names, and after the first mention, only the initial by which she calls them. So the Lieutenant became R L and then just R. Her parents are F and M. When any lesser characters appear, she puts in the name the first time she mentions them in each entry. I know it sounds a bit complicated but you'll soon get the hang of it. Now have a look at that.'

I took the diary and looked at the page she had marked.

Thursday, 11 September 1919

I write this in my room at home in Thurles. I am unsure whether I shall be able to make any sense of this dreadful day's events. This morning while in the office, a telegram arrived for me. At first I was embarrassed but then became excited as this is the first such message which I have received. I hold it in front of my eyes as I write. These are the awful words. 'I regret to inform you that your dear brothers have been killed. Please catch the noon train. I will meet you at the station. All love, Father.' I fear that I screamed in anguish at this news. The ladies rushed to my side and Mr Cope ran from his office. I was unable to talk to them but Alice took the telegram from my hand and read it aloud. They became most solicitous and AC brought me a glass of water. A volunteered to escort me to Kingstown and, if necessary, to Thurles. AC summoned a taxi-cab and paid the driver for the journey to Kingstown. In a daze of grief, I allowed myself to be taken to Aunt Beatrice. She sent A back to the office and took command of everything. In an incredibly short time we were sitting in a taxi-cab on the way to Kingsbridge Station. On the train AB secured a first-class compartment and positioned herself at the door, thereby preventing any other travellers from intruding. She settled a rug around my legs and under her encouragement, I closed my eyes. I certainly did not expect to sleep for an instant. The next thing which I remembered was her hand shaking my shoulder and her voice telling me that we had arrived at Thurles. On the platform was F, and as I embraced him he began to weep. My tears joined his and but for AB's intervention, we would have remained thus for a very long time. Eventually we boarded F's motor and drove the four miles to the house. No word was spoken during the journey. On the estate, black ribbons were much in evidence and the workers' homes showed drawn blinds. Everyone who recognised the motor crossed themselves and for the first time in my life the gesture meant more than a silly superstition. These people were signifying that their prayers were with us.

At the house I found a place of dreadful silence. Everyone went about as if afraid that any sound might awaken the black despair hanging unseen overhead. The girls, their eyes swollen from constant weeping, came into my arms and grasped me tightly. F told me that M had been in bed since the news came this morning. I asked for details of the accident which had cruelly taken my brothers from us. He took me to his study and sat at his desk. This is what he told me. 'Arthur and George went out at dawn to shoot rabbits. They did this on most mornings. They were anxious to get as much shooting as possible before the term started at Trinity. I awoke to the sound of many shots. I felt a dreadful sense of foreboding and rushed downstairs, careful not to disturb your mother. She had taken a light sleeping draught last night. By the time I had dressed, a knocking was coming from the back door. It was Mr Bates, the farm manager. He was greatly distressed. He too had heard the gunfire and had gone to investigate. In a small copse on the southern side of the estate he had come upon a scene of carnage. Arthur and George were dead, their .22 rifles some distance away. A group of Shropshires were standing around, laughing and joking. Mr Bates asked them what had happened. The officer in charge, who seemed quite drunk, said that they had been travelling towards Thurles when they had come under fire from the copse. They had returned fire and after some time advanced to the scene. They had found two men, well armed, lying dead on the ground.' F had gone to the spot. The bodies had been taken by the military for delivery to the hospital after investigation of the dead men's backgrounds.

Back at the house, F had told M and the girls the news. He was about to set out to call to the hospital and send me a telegram when a man called at the back door. F knew him well. He was Brendan Dunne, a local poacher. He said to F that he had seen the incident. The boys had been shooting rabbits about two hundred yards from where he had been fishing. He was under the bridge which takes the road over the river. This enabled him to remain unseen during the events which then took place. An armoured car had stopped upon the bridge and six soldiers had alighted. They had apparently heard the shots from the boys' weapons. They proceeded to surround the copse and moved towards it. When they were twenty yards away they had called out, identifying themselves as soldiers. A and G had stood up with their hands raised, leaving their guns upon the ground. The soldiers had run to them and beaten them to the ground with rifles. They stood over the fallen boys and demanded to know their names. G had answered, telling them that they lived here. 'Why did you fire on our armoured car?' 'We did not. We were shooting at rabbits.' The captors laughed at this. 'That is what all the Fenians say. You have five minutes to say your prayers to the Pope.' A replied that they were not Roman Catholic, but Anglican. 'Then pray to the King. He might pardon you. If he does we will tell your family that we are sorry.' With this, and surrounded by laughing men, the boys were dragged some distance away and ordered to stand against two trees. A called out that they could shoot him if they let his brother go free. The men shouted that they did not need permission from filthy Fenians to clear away rebels. At that moment they started to fire. Most of the shots seemed to hit G, and when he had fallen, they fired only a few rounds at A.

On hearing this horrible news, F drove to the local RIC station. His protests were met with blank indifference. At this point in his narrative, F again began to weep. G had received twenty-four wounds and died immediately. A had been shot four times and lived for thirty minutes before succumbing. I put my arms around F and held him. So deep was his despair that I feared for his sanity. M came in and saw me for the first time. She ignored me and rushed to F. They embraced and seemed to gather courage from each other. When the tears had ceased, M turned to me and kissed me warmly. She was much more calm than F. Her inner strength showed through. In a most matter-of-fact tone she related the arrangements for the funerals. Lord Martindale will, of course, be present. The burial in the family vault in Saint Anthony's churchyard will take place tomorrow at noon after a brief service in the church. When we were alone she spoke forcefully to me. F must be dissuaded from attempting to raise a storm over the deaths. If the family become in any way identified with anti-Government feelings, we would all be in great danger. We might even lose our home and our position. I close now as I am tired and ill. Tomorrow promises to be even more dreadful than today.

Friday, 12 September 1919

For the first time today, I am alone. M asked me to remain close to Angeline and Martha during the tearful events. The funeral was sad beyond words. I felt close to collapse as the final prayers were recited. A huge throng was present. When we left the church and the undertakers were about to load the coffins into the hearses, some men from the estate came forward. They insisted that they carry them to the vault. M seemed bewildered but F quickly gave his permission. There was an air of something approaching defiance as we all walked behind. I kept the girls one on each side with my arms holding them tightly. At the door of the vault the procession stopped briefly and six men appeared with guns in their hands. They stood stiffly and one of their number called out words which were unintelligible to me. They all raised pistols in the air and fired three shots over the coffins. This event lent to me a strange comfort. My anguish at the loss of my dear brothers was now replaced by a deep anger. The killers were undoubtedly members of His Majesty's forces, but I cannot believe that the King or any member of his Government would condone their actions in this case. It needs such a tragedy to bring home the ghastly pass to which our country has come. No amount of armed resistance to England can justify the cold-blooded murder of two young men of blameless character.

At the end of this sad day, F called me into his study. I presumed that he wished to give me solace but such was not the case. He showed himself to be as angry as I. When he said that he would never forgive the Government, I told him that I agreed with this sentiment. He said that the men who had carried the coffins from the church were members of a local group from the Volunteers. So also were those who had fired their pistols. These people had approached him later and identified themselves. Far from being of a mind to betray them, he was full of admiration for them. He will do what he can to support their struggle for Irish independence. He said solemnly that as I was the only member of the family working away from home, he needed to know my views on the matter. I am in total accord. He finished by saying that someone would contact me in Dublin. I would be asked to perform some reasonably safe work for the organisation. I kissed him and assured him that I would do all within my power for those resisting the murderers.

I looked up at Theresa as I finished the passage. I met her raised eyebrows with a long stare. 'Well, what do you know? Straight into the lap of the IRA.'

She smiled. 'It certainly shows that her class was treated just as badly as the Catholics. Those two men, they were really only boys, were murdered for nothing. I've never heard of the likes. I thought that the Catholic people were the only targets for the Brits.'

'Of course that's what we've grown up thinking. The locals in Thurles seem to have rallied around. They got their speak in at the right time. The doctor was ripe for the picking and they moved in very quickly.' Theresa frowned. 'It's a bit ironic though, isn't it?'

'How so?'

'Well, with the talks and John Hume going out on a limb with Adams?'

The usual taste of bile which the mention of IRA/Sinn Féin brought to my mouth caused me to swallow before replying. 'You know my views on Adams. He's no better than the terrorists. This saying that he doesn't speak for the IRA is a load of bullshit.'

Theresa shook her head. 'Now don't start, Frank. These diaries come from a very different time. The War of Independence was a national revolution. Anyway, she doesn't carry on about this. The next few entries deal with fairly trivial things although Richard appears more and more in them. She doesn't seem to have confided any of her grief after the funeral to the diaries.'

I shrugged. 'She was probably trying to put the whole thing out of her mind.'

'Anyway, I've looked ahead a bit and she wasn't contacted by the IRA until December. That's nearly three months. Here's the entry about that. I'll read this one.'

Monday, 1 December 1919

R gone home for a week. I do not know how I shall tolerate it. Half of my mind continues to mourn for A and G, while the remainder clings to thoughts of dear R. This is the first time we have been apart. He said that he would write every day. In addition, I am feeling very ill. The doctor has given me a horribly bitter mixture, but it has had no apparent result. I have told him of F's treatment but he insists that if I wish for this to continue, I must commit myself to F's care. Every doctor to his own methods. Everything is the same as last month. F has told me on many occasions that it is a woman's lot. Oh, to be a man.

In the middle of my dreadful day, a strange thing happened. I received a telephone call in the office. I was mortified. During working hours! As usual, E took me to task for encouraging my friends by allowing them my telephone number. A man spoke to me. He did not give his name. He sounded dreadfully Irish in the worst sense. He said that he knew F. Would I like to meet him at a time and place of my choice? I declined. Then came the strangest part. F has given him permission to press the meeting on me. I should receive a letter from him today. It would explain all and he, the man, would telephone me tonight. I came home and it was as he had said. A long letter from F was awaiting me. I took it to my room to read. He repeated the reasons which he had given me after the funerals for deciding to assist the IRA. Lord Martindale, incensed by the murders, had taken the trouble to travel to Dublin to present the facts, in person, to the Lord Lieutenant. To his astonishment, his complaint had been met with laughter and derision. He left with the impression that the Army are operating with a carte blanche. They were accountable only to London. The Irish were to be brought to heel once and for all in such a way that would ensure that they would never again consider rebellion. This course would regrettably cause pain and injury, even death, to some innocent people. However, the Irish, as a race, were incapable of understanding anything but force, so force they would get in full measure. LM returned home convinced that a great evil has come upon the country. He spoke to F and told him to assure the families living on the estate that they would have the full support of the Manor House in any self-protective measures which they might feel obliged to take. F writes that the men who approached him earlier were now in a position to make full use of such aid as I could give. They know of my work in Dublin Castle and wished to know whether I would be prepared to help them. In return for their promise that I would not be exposed to any personal danger, F supplied them with my address and telephone number. These people are said by F to be on the more peaceful side of the IRA. Their object is Irish independence with a minimum of violence. If I co-operate with them, F believes that the country will be saved from needless bloodshed. I am very doubtful about our family becoming involved in Irish politics, with all that the expression entails. However, as it is F's wish that I should meet the men, I will, of course, do so. I resume this entry two hours later. The man telephoned me as he had promised. He said that LM and F are fine men. This sounded like the basest flattery to me, but nevertheless, I agreed to meet him during my luncheon period tomorrow. I am to wait outside the main gate of Trinity College. He knows my appearance and will approach me. He stressed that I should not discuss the meeting with anyone. I have a premonition that this is the start of something both dangerous and foolish, but I will play my part for F and my darling brothers.

'It all sounds like an Irish James Bond thing. They clearly wanted her to get information from the Castle. She doesn't sound any too pleased about it. Whatever Father asks, the good daughter will deliver, regardless.'

Theresa frowned. My flippancy did not suit her mood. 'You're not really being fair to her. She obviously felt the deaths of the boys very deeply. And, she said at the time that she was angry over the murders. No, her father might have pointed her in the right direction but she was quite deliberate in her move to take some action against the men who had killed her brothers. I think we've found the beginning of a part of Mrs Perry's life that has been her closely guarded secret. I'm tempted to skip through the books looking for the next stage but I think I'd better take them in sequence. Now, are you ready to help me?'

'All right, I suppose I'll have no peace until I do.' I looked at the cover of the book which I had been reading. 'This is number eleven. You find the next one and read. I'll listen.'

Three

The doorbell rang. We looked at each other and at the box on the table. I whispered urgently. 'I'll get rid of these. Don't answer the door until I tell you.'

I threw the book I had been reading into the box and carried it to the cupboard. I sat in a chair, picked up a newspaper and nodded to Theresa.

I heard her open the door and speak. A deep voice answered and after a moment she came into the kitchen, followed by a tall, spare man. He wore a black overcoat and carried a trilby hat in his hand. His head was completely free of hair, the scalp gleaming as if it had been polished. 'Frank, this is Inspector Ryan from Broomstown Garda Station. He wants to talk to us about the fire.'

I stood and took the outstretched hand. The grip was dry and firm, the blue eyes appraising.

'How do you do, Mr Doorly. As your wife says, I'd like a few words.'

'No problem. Have a chair. Cup of tea?'

'Thank you, that would be nice. If you don't mind, Mrs Doorly?'

Theresa smiled and crossed to the sink where she filled the kettle. While we waited for her to return to the table, I saw Ryan's eyes take in the room in a quick sweep.

'Right, Inspector, fire ahead.'

'As Garda Culligan told you on the night, the fire next door seems to have been deliberately set. In such cases, we usually find that the reason is to cover the signs of robbery. It seems, however, that this was not a possible motive here.'

He paused and Theresa, in her 'womanly innocent' tone, asked, 'But are you sure the fire was deliberate, Inspector? It hardly seems worth anyone's time. The place was empty, hardly any furniture, even.'

The pink head nodded slowly. 'Exactly. We have to accept the Brigade's advice about the fire and concentrate on the reason. The first point to be cleared up is the occupant.' He took a black covered notebook from his inside pocket and opened it. 'Mrs Mary Perry, deceased. She was taken ill the morning before. You, Mrs Doorly, called the ambulance and our people. Tell me about that.'

Theresa related the events of the Friday and Saturday up to the time that Mrs Perry died. She did not mention the staff nurse or her comments, for which I was glad.

'Neither of you had any conversation with her between the time that you discovered her on the floor and her removal to hospital?'

I took the ball. 'She was unconscious as far as I could tell. Anyway, she did not open her eyes at all. And before that, she was inside the house and we were outside.'

'Yes, that's clear. Now, what about in the hospital? I believe you visited twice during the day?'

'We called during the morning and later we were sent for. We were there when she died.'

'Did you speak to her on either occasion and did she speak to you?' Theresa replied in her level voice. I could have told the policeman to beware. 'I spoke briefly to her the first time, telling her that we would sit with her. This we did, for more than an hour. She was getting weaker by the minute. We were the only halfway familiar faces there. It is hardly surprising that she welcomed our presence. Her nearest neighbours.'

'Mrs Doorly, I would not dream of criticising your motives. You and your husband behaved absolutely correctly, even more so considering that you hardly knew her.'

Theresa nodded in acknowledgement and Ryan continued, 'Did she give you anything while you were at her bedside?'

I sensed rather than saw Theresa's watchfulness and decided to bluff it out. 'No, Inspector. The woman was dying. Hardly the time for exchanging mementos.'

'My information is that Mrs Doorly removed a ribbon from around the neck of Mrs Perry. If you had forgotten the incident, perhaps you could now remember if anything was attached to the ribbon? Perhaps a key?'

The final word was left floating in the air. I could almost see the burning letters above Ryan's head. It was a time for quick thought. Theresa rose to the challenge.

'Oh, of course, the key. Remember, Frank? She asked me to take her front-door key from around her neck. I untied the ribbon, it was pink. Yes, Inspector, it's on the dressing table upstairs. Would you like me to get it?'

Before he had a chance to reply, she had risen and hurried out of the kitchen. I heard her footsteps running up the stairs. The keys were on my bedside table and I prayed that she would be able to untie the knot in the ribbon and remove the one for the cupboard.

I need not have worried. Within seconds she reappeared, the ribbon coiled in her hand, the latchkey attached. Handing them to Ryan, she smiled rather ruefully. 'I'm very sorry, Inspector. It slipped my mind in all the fuss at the time. We didn't get much sleep, you know.'

He stared at her for a few seconds, plainly wondering whether she was being altogether frank with him. Taking the key, he asked, 'Did you try it in the front door, at all?'

'Never got a chance. The place was gone before we could. Mrs Perry gave it to me in case she needed anything from the house. Nightdresses, toiletries, that sort of thing.'

I broke in. 'Inspector, as you may know, I undertook the payment of Mrs Perry's funeral expenses and a few other items. When the demolition men arrived I started to try to find out about the house. I found that she owned it, it was insured by Trident Insurances and that you informed them of the fire. Could I ask how you knew who to report to?'

'I presume the same way that you got your information. The Fire Brigade informed us that the building was unsafe and we had our people do a search.'

I thought for a minute before going on. 'Do you happen to know whether there is a will?'

'I have no idea. Of course, one may be gathering dust in some solicitor's office. I'm afraid that this is very unwelcome news for you. A great shame after you both behaved so admirably over the whole affair.' He stood up. 'Thank you both. You have been most co-operative. If I need anything else, I'll get back to you. Don't come out. I can make my own way.'

We sat silently until the door closed. Theresa went out to the hall, I suppose to make sure that he was not hiding, waiting to take down everything we said. As she returned I pulled her close and kissed her.

'What's that for?' she giggled.

'You know, you're a natural at this sort of thing. Lying to the police, I mean.'

'Don't be daft. It's nobody's business except ours. Mrs Perry, God rest her, trusted us. And what harm are we doing?'

'Oh, I agree with you a hundred per cent. That bitch of a Sister didn't miss much, did she? Anyway, now that Sherlock is gone we can get on with reading "The Papers".'

'Of course. Bring back the box. Sounds like a TV game show, doesn't it?'

As I carried in the box, I remarked, 'It's a bit thick, our being stuck for two grand, all the same. I haven't a clue where to start looking for our money.'

'Ah well sure, if we haven't got it we won't miss it. Let's concentrate on the diaries for now.'

In my mind the words 'it's not your money' formed but never saw the light of day. Such a remark at this time could well send Theresa into one of her rages.

When we were once again sitting at the table, she found the book and turned to the page following the entry of 1st December.

Tuesday, 2 December 1919

This has been an amazing day. I waited as arranged and I was immediately approached by a well-dressed man. He was in his early thirties, as far as I could judge. He raised his hat to me and addressed me in a most cultured accent containing only the faintest trace of rural Ireland, probably County Cork. I quickly realised that he was not the man to whom I had spoken on the telephone. He was extremely courteous throughout. He addressed me as Miss Stewart. He suggested that we might go to Bewley's Café and talk there. I agreed. We sat in a back booth where we could be both unobserved and unheard. He said that his name was unimportant, but when I protested that he knew mine, he agreed that I might call him Mr C. This is what he said.

'The government in London has devised a plan, under the control of Mr Churchill, to bolster the RIC. A force of demobilised ex-servicemen is to be recruited and sent here. They will be ostensibly under the command of the police, but in reality will be answerable only to Mr Churchill. They will be actively encouraged to instil terror into the population. Even the most loyal citizens are not to be spared. In order to combat such widespread injustice, groups of men throughout the country have joined forces.' Their object is to be prepared in advance to organise resistance. To do this, they need what Mr C called intelligence. I, with my unique position in the Castle, am ideally situated to obtain intelligence. I spend each day taking down and typing letters concerning security. Mr C asked me to make private notes of AC's correspondence. Things which he wants to know are troop movements, future targets, numbers of new arrivals for the force and the names of all officers. When I asked to what use such information will be put, he said that I would be safer if I did not know.

I must state at this point that he is a most persuasive man. At no time did he speak about violence, merely defence of the people against the excesses of the Crown Forces. His tone and the content of his words seemed far removed from the ruffians who brought such destruction upon Dublin three and a half years ago. I asked if he had been a part of that foolish rebellion and he laughed. I thought that he sounded quite charming when he confessed that he had been refused permission to take part because he was unable to fire a gun. He admitted that hindsight had made him thankful. I observed him keenly when I asked him if he was a loyal subject of His Majesty. His reply, with a small bow from his chair, was 'And what else?' I had to be satisfied with this, but in reality, I trust Mr C, even on such short and bizarre acquaintance. He said with great seriousness that the King would never lend his name to the cold-blooded murder of my brothers. The decision had been taken in London by a group which, Mr C believes, has anti-Irish sentiments. Reassured, I then proceeded to ask how I would be expected to pass on any information. He told me not to worry. The plan is a simple one. When I have something of interest to impart, I will telephone a certain number in the Dublin area that night. Mr C will meet me the next day at the same time and place as today. The hour for my reappearance in the office being near, the

> meeting ended. I left Bewley's with much to ponder.
>
> This man whom I have never seen before today has left me with a strange feeling of excitement. He completely won me to his cause by dint of his soothingly friendly voice and the apparent reasonableness of his words.

Theresa stopped reading, causing me to open my eyes which I had closed to help my concentration. 'Don't stop there, for God's sake. I want to know when she passed over the first information.'

'No. That's enough for now. A while ago you were asking for your dinner and now I'm going to cook something. I'm quite hungry myself.'

'OK, I suppose you're right. One thing is starting to stick out a mile from those diaries, though.'

'And what's that?'

'The identity of Mr C, that's what.' I probably sounded quite smug. I don't often out-think Theresa.

'It's obvious it's Michael Collins,' she said. 'Any fool could see that.'

When she saw my face showing how it felt to be 'any fool', she came to me, curling her arms around my neck. Her breath was hot on my cheek. 'Sorry darling. I didn't mean you. It just came out. I was as surprised as you. Come on now. Let's not fight.' She placed her mouth on mine in one of those kisses which put all thought of hurt pride up the chimney. Sometimes I can't help feeling...To hell with it. Enjoy the kiss whatever the motive.

We sat down to eat and neither of us had much to say. I looked at her face to see an expression of deep thought. I knew that any question about it would not bring her back to the table. I felt excluded. There were times when she was a closed book to me. I give her all the comforts of a fairly good life and she rarely complains, but these little silences, taking her who knew where, were becoming more frequent of late.

The short meal finished, we cleared away the

dishes and as Theresa washed, I dried. A look at my watch brought me up with a jerk. 'It's after twelve. Let's leave this until tomorrow. I have to get up in the morning.'

She shrugged and we replaced the box under the stairs.

I hurried home the next night, Wednesday. We bolted our meal and started where we had left off.

Friday, 5 December 1919

A lovely letter from R. Three pages full of his love. He misses me terribly, as I do him. He will return on Sunday night and promises to telephone me. I must go to morning service in order to have the evening free.

Today I was given a letter by AC for PM in London. It concerned the reaction of the Irish to the RIC and their reinforcements. AC wrote that the people are horrified by IRA attacks and roundly condemn them. Actions by the military are, however, seen as intolerably cruel and indiscriminate. Very many of the victims are wholly innocent of any anti-government leanings. Their only crime has been to be in the wrong place at the wrong time. An example of this was the attack on the village of Danielstown in Tipperary. The local RIC station had been fired upon during Saturday night. On Sunday, as the people were in church, a detachment of Essex Light Infantry drove into the village in an armoured car. Eyewitnesses say that the men were drunk and they interrupted the Mass. They behaved disgracefully towards the priest and from the altar called on the congregation to hand over those who had attacked the station. When no reply was received, they selected three young men from the pews and brought them into the street. They were lined up against the wall of the church and shot. The entire village was then set alight and the officer in charge announced that any person attempting to fight the fires would be killed. Many shots were fired into the air and, as the armoured car was leaving, a child was run down and subsequently died. AC is adamant that conduct like this will only result in the population turning to the IRA for protection. He strongly recommended that the new forces planned to back up the police be disbanded. When I brought the letter to be signed he looked very troubled. I will wait a few days before deciding whether to relate the matter to Mr C.

Sunday, 7 December 1919

I must sit down and write of tonight's events. My head is light, my heart pounding. I have never... No, I will start at the beginning. At seven o' clock I was alone in the house. AB was at church and intended calling on friends. R telephoned and we talked for a while. I do not know what made me tell him that I was alone in the house, but I did. He immediately announced his intention to walk from the harbour and in ten minutes he was ringing the bell. When I answered the door he stepped into the hall, closed the door with his foot and took me in his arms. That kiss was unlike any other I have received. It affected me powerfully in a manner which frightened me at first. We went into the drawing room and sat together on the sofa. I attempted to talk but he would have none of it. Again he kissed me. He said that he had been unable to keep thoughts of me from his mind every moment he had been at home. I replied in a similar vein. This seemed to effect him strongly. He said that he wanted me to be his wife. As I was endeavouring to frame an answer he continued. He cannot possibly afford to marry on his lieutenant's salary and besides, he is certain that he would be refused permission such a short time after receiving his commission. He could not, would not wait. I held him tightly, whispering that I would wait forever. He seized me roughly and pressing me to his chest, said the words which I will never forget. 'Molly dearest, we must be together now. Say that it is your wish also.' I said that it was so, but that we must try to think of a way to get married soon. 'No, no. I cannot wait. We are alone now.'

He pushed me down on to the cushions, kissing me the while. He started to behave most improperly and to my surprise, I did not try to stop him. In fact, I joined in and in a trice the deed was done. We lay there afterwards and, for myself, the pain forgotten, with a feeling of happiness that was all-consuming. R attempted to apologise but I cut him short. I told him that I had no regrets and did not want to hear any from him. Eventually, we set about resuming our usual posture. He said that he had to leave as he was due in barracks at ten o'clock. With much embracing and many more kisses, he tore himself away. I went to my room to examine my feelings. Certainly I have not planned or expected this, but I am truly happy. I can write no more. My hand is shaking.

Theresa paused, a strange light in her eyes. 'The little fool. Imagine, giving him what he wanted with no guarantees. He must have been laughing all the way home.'

'Oh, come on now. I would have thought that you approved. It sounds to me like a great gesture. Don't forget, this is over seventy years ago. It meant much more than it does today, with everyone hopping in and out of bed when they feel like it.'

'There are times, Frank, when you sound just like one of those female novelists you hate so much.'

'This is no novel. These are real people. One of them lived next door, for God's sake.'

She stared at me, a look of speculation on her face. 'Answer me honestly. If I had let you into my bed before we married, what would you have thought of me?'

'That's hypothetical. I could never know my reaction to something that never happened.'

'You see. You're stalling already. Men treat sex differently.'

'I'm not stalling. OK, I'll try to answer you. If we had...I think I'd have been more certain that you loved me. More sure of myself.'

'Sure of yourself. My God, the number of times I had to stop you pulling off my knickers. You seemed perfectly sure of yourself when you made me rub you. Frank Doorly, you were the randiest man I ever went out with. Even when I had my period, I had to wrestle you off.'

I found a bitter taste drying my mouth. 'You make it sound calculating and sordid, Theresa. I admit that I got carried away a few times. So did you, if I remember.'

'That's a lousy thing to say. I wasn't made of steel. Of course I got a bit...wound up sometimes. But it was left to me to draw the lines. I had that responsibility. You were only interested in going a bit further every night. If you'd had your way, I would have been six months pregnant at the altar.'

The retort shot from my mouth before I could stop it. 'Pregnant. You? Chance'd be a fine thing.'

Her face paled, her eyes rounded. Her lips disappeared as she drew a sharp breath.

'You bastard. You fucking bastard.'

Four

She turned and walked from the room, leaving me with a sick feeling. This was serious. I knew that I had gone too far.

Her failure to become pregnant had not been mentioned for many years but I knew that it simmered below the surface, perhaps waiting for the arrival of some volcanic convulsion to spew it out over us.

In the early years of our marriage we had rowed regularly because I had refused to consult a doctor to find out if the fault lay in me. I was still certain that I was a hundred per cent right. No other consideration ever stood a chance with me. Maybe I was now afraid to investigate the matter. I knew that I could not tolerate such a failure in myself.

My mind, however had begun to accept the fact that we would be childless. A bit over-dramatic probably, even after fourteen years. Still, I felt strangely certain.

I rose and went upstairs to try mending a few fences. Our bedroom door was closed and when I tried the handle it would not budge. I put my ear to the door but could hear nothing. I had half expected crying. 'Theresa, love, I'm sorry. I didn't mean to hurt you. It slipped out. You know the way it does.'

Silence. I rattled the handle. 'Open the door, love. Let me in. I want to show you how sorry I am. Come on, Theresa. Open up.' After a wait in silence, I slowly returned downstairs. I wandered into the kitchen. The exercise book she had been reading was lying open on the table. Listlessly I picked it up.

Monday, 8 December 1919

This is really a continuation of yesterday's entry. I awoke to a glorious feeling of completion. I have dwelt on last night's events all day. As I dressed, I could not suppress a fervent wish that R was watching. I took a longer time than usual, unable to stop myself looking at my reflection in the mirror. My body seems, somehow, to be much more important to me. I suppose that I am of average build and passably attractive. Undoubtedly, certain features take on a new meaning. If I am to believe R's words, the touch of his hand on my skin makes him lose all self-control. I would never admit it, but I am not entirely unaffected myself.

Enough of this. Back to my ordinary world. Having given much thought to the matter, I have decided to pass on the contents of AC's letter to Mr C. I telephoned this afternoon when E was out of the office, making a show of talking to a cousin and arranging to meet him tomorrow. Not ten minutes after I had finished I overheard General Macready talking to AC. He said that Sinn Fein were taking total political control of the country. They were enabled to do this by the dreadful behaviour of the Army. The IRA factions now find themselves cast in the guise of protectors of the people, rather than mere rebels resisting the Crown. In the north, Mr Carson seems prepared, as always, to fight the Government to prove loyalty to the King. What a typically Irish situation.

It was no good. I did not want to take in any of it. The whole thing seemed to my numbed mind to be particularly irrelevant when read in conjunction with all the fuss at home and abroad over whether the IRA would accept the Downing Street Declaration and declare a ceasefire. My inbuilt cynicism concerning anything bearing the mantle of the IRA or Sinn Fein killed optimism stone dead. The thought that these lunatics would even contemplate voting themselves out of existence was to me a stupid hope.

I shook myself back to the kitchen, my words to

Theresa repeating themselves over and over in my brain. I knew how I would be feeling if she had said them to me.

Again I went up and listened at the door. Nothing. I called softly, 'Theresa, darling, can I come in? Please, love, don't punish me like this. I want to talk to you.'

I was standing there, dully searching for my next move, when the door suddenly opened. She came out on to the landing. She was dressed in her best suit, the make-up was faultless, her hair was hanging loose in the style which she had not used for a long time.

Her eyes were neutral as she looked at me. 'I'm going out. I don't know what time I'll be back.'

I looked at my watch. 'It's nearly nine. Where will you go at this time?'

'Oh, I'll think of somewhere. I'm taking the car. Don't wait up.'

She brushed past me and ran down the stairs. I heard the front door open and slam. The sound of the car starting coincided with the glare of the headlights piercing the glass of the front door.

With the feeling of dread which came with the knowledge that events were no longer under my control, I returned once again to the kitchen. Would I go to the pub? I knew that I would be trying to punish Theresa because we only ever went there together. If she did not know I was there, the point would be lost.

The room was usually bright and the centre of the house, but not now. It seemed as desolate as when we had spoken to the policeman after the fire in the pre-dawn hours.

I kicked moodily at the fender. My eyes suddenly filled with tears.

I knew the signs only too well. Self-pity was taking over. In an attempt to deflect it I took Mrs

Perry's exercise book and started to flick ahead from where I had stopped earlier.

The time span between the entries varied enormously. There could be five or six in one week, and a gap of a fortnight before the next one.

The whole thing resembled a novel rather than a personal journal. Once I had identified the characters concealed in the initials, the narrative took on a flow. After a while, Mrs Perry began to emerge in a way far removed from the frail woman who had died.

She had obviously been a girl of strong will, but broadly ready to do what her father wanted. Her initial decision to pass information to the IRA seemed to run contrary to her own opinion of the organisation. Had not her father put them in touch, they would have been the last people whom she would have helped. However, her deep anger at her brothers' murder was a powerful motivator.

There is no mention of the words 'treason' or 'spying' as far as I could tell. Certainly she never confided to her diary any fear she might have had of the outcome should she be caught.

Her relationship with the handsome young lieutenant was a strong sub-plot. Her frank words after he had seduced her were probably bold in the extreme, in the context of the time. She did not seem to have suffered from any feeling of guilt, regret or even doubt. He was the man for her and she joined in his obvious delight in having her body for himself.

Sunday, 21 December 1919.
Home for Christmas. F and M kissed and embraced me at the station tonight. I longed to tell them about R but I have promised him that I will say nothing for the moment. The house is bright with balloons, holly, mistletoe, paper decorations and of course the tree. It was cut by the farm foreman and it reaches to the ceiling of the drawing room. M has done all the decorating herself. She never trusts the servants to do

it. I think it is rather charming. Of course we are still in mourning, but F decided that some show of Christmas cheer would not go amiss. Angeline and Martha are also home. They are full of questions about my life in Dublin. Angeline asked me whether I have met any gentlemen. I replied that *all* the men whom I have met are gentlemen.

After dinner F called me into his study. This is the first time that we have spoken about recent events. He is most anxious that I should be aware of the reason for his request that I help Mr C. Though Protestant, we are truly Irish, as much as the most fervent nationalist. In view of the excesses being carried out in the name of the Government, we must decide whether independence is not the best path for our country to follow. Self-rule, with the calming influence which continued membership of the Empire would bring, seems to F to be the right aim. He detests many of the methods being used by Sinn Fein and the IRA. Temporary alignment with them is necessary to achieve independence. London has always taken a sledge-hammer to crack the kernel of the Irish problem. After speaking in this vein, he asked me if I agreed with him. Never before have I heard F ask such a question of anyone. I kissed him and said that he could rely upon me.

Later we were all having supper when Mr Stenson and his son, Harry called. H asked me to sit in the conservatory with him. Knowing him only too well, I was reluctant to agree but M insisted. As soon as we were alone he tried to kiss me, the very thing I had feared. I turned away from him and he became quite angry. He accused me of deserting him for the city gentlemen of Dublin. Despite my denial, he continued to press me and in an effort to stop his tirade I mentioned that I had met an officer who, far from being from Dublin, was English. This had the worst effect upon him and he caught my arms painfully. Pushing me against the wall he once more attempted to kiss me. He pulled at my blouse, tearing the neck. I did not want to cause a major incident by crying out. Finally, left with no alternative, I brought my knee up and with a gasp he released me, bending over in pain. I told him that I would say nothing on this occasion but that a repetition of such conduct would bring F into the matter. He begged me not to say anything. Mr S is beholden to F for his employment and the consequences for H if I should tell of tonight's happenings would be catastrophic. I rather think that this problem had been well and truly laid to rest. I will finish this now as I must write to R. I have much to tell him that is for his eyes only.

God, how ridiculous other people's problems seem. Even at a distance of seventy-five years. I sat by the fire, unable to concentrate any longer on the ramblings of a girl in her diary.

I thought back to earlier fights between Theresa and me. Before our marriage, we often disagreed about absurd things.

I remembered the time we fought over whether we would send our sons to a Jesuit or Christian Brothers' school.

I had been educated by the Brothers without damage to my mind or body, but her brother Gerry had suffered at the hands of one of those sadists who seem to be thrown up by any collection of celibate men from time to time.

'No twisted bastard is going to take his sexual frustrations out on my son.'

I pointed out that Jesuits were equally celibate, but she said it was not the same. Her parents had ignored Gerry's complaints until the day he came home with a broken wrist, the result of an accurately thrown board wiper.

Since then, all members of that particular order were anathema to the entire Whelan clan. They could do no right.

Theresa's vehement argument on the matter had looked rather silly, in the light of subsequent happenings. Or should I say non-happenings. I looked at my watch. Half-past eleven. No word from Theresa.

Maybe she intended staying out all night. Where would she sleep? Better not try to answer that. What I didn't know wouldn't hurt me. Should I go to bed? No point. Alone, I would have no chance of sleep.

A car door banged shut. A key in the door. I went to the hall to meet her. Without even putting down her bag, she ran to me with a cry and threw her arms around me. The kiss was open-mouthed, her fingers digging into my shoulders. I immediately smelt the gin on her breath. Anger flared. While I had been sitting here worrying, she had been off drinking. It wasn't fair.

I could not speak. She pressed herself against me, turning her head from side to side as if trying to bore her mouth through mine. Small sounds of passion came from her. I was lost in her arms. Anger vanished, lust flourished. Like Clark Gable in so many of his films, I bent and with my hand behind her knees, lifted her, carrying her easily upstairs.

I had not seen her so aroused before. She usually seemed to hold some part of herself back. Not now. We quickly adjusted ourselves to the situation and in minutes were being carried on the rising tide of our search for release.

My breathing became laboured. She began to moan, at first softly, then more loudly, insistently. The sounds came from the back of her throat, 'Ah, ah, aaah, yes, God, God, Frank, go on, don't ever stop.' Her breath was hot, the fumes of the gin rolling down my throat. I slumped against her, sweat pouring over my face. I had never experienced anything like this before. I tried to roll off her but she held me fast. Looking down at her I was surprised to see tears running unchecked over her cheeks. She saw my look and pulled my head against her. I kissed the tears, then licked them. Her grip tightened around my neck uncomfortably.

'Have a heart, love. I'm whacked. Let me go.'

She sighed and released her hold. I rolled sideways and we lay facing each other. When I tried to speak, she placed her finger to my lips, shaking her head. Her huge eyes stared into mine.

'Frank, do you love me?'

I nodded.

'Not just this...bed and all? I mean really love me?'

'Of course I do. Surely you don't doubt that after all this time, Theresa. I've always been crazy about you. Right from the very first time I saw you.'

This much was true. I had been invited to a twenty-first birthday party by a girl I knew vaguely. It was actually Brendan Archer's party, but I did not know him. When we arrived at the house the first person I saw was this dark girl holding hands with the host. Within an hour, I had dumped my date and gone upstairs with her. That night I lost my heart and Theresa Whelan came within an ace of losing her virginity. Only by struggling madly had she held me off, but I had the feeling that she wanted me as much as I wanted her.

That set the pace of our 'courtship' and within a year we were engaged.

Back in the present, I lay on my back, drawing in gulps of air. She had turned to face away from me and I was puzzled to see her shoulders shake. She was crying softly. I turned to her and put my arm around her. Without speaking, she pushed my hand away and pulled the duvet around her shoulders. Whatever was causing this sadness, I was not wanted any more. I closed my eyes, but knew that sleep would not be easy tonight.

A funny woman, my wife.

Five

The alarm woke me at seven o'clock. I rolled on to my back and looked at Theresa. Her head lay on the pillow, long hair spread like an autumn sunset. The curled eyelashes were barely touching the smooth cheek. The bedclothes rose and fell in a slow, smooth rhythm.

My heart lurched. She was so beautiful that I wondered how I had won her and kept her for so long.

I washed and dressed before going down to the kitchen, where I prepared breakfast. Putting the food on a tray, I retraced my steps. I placed it on the bedside table and bent to kiss her forehead gently. 'Wakey wakey. Come on, beautiful. Breakfast.'

The eyelids opened and her deep blue irises looked at me. As memory returned her cheeks pinkened. She was beginning to look embarrassed and I quickly placed my lips on hers. Her hand found my face and she gently cupped my chin.

She eased me away and sat up. I put the tray across her legs and smiled at her. I sensed that she would not welcome any comment on last night.

'Have a cup of coffee. It'll wake you up.'

Gratefully she set about the morning ritual, the automatic movements bridging the moment. 'Mm. That's good. I need it. I slept like a log.'

'Me too. Never stirred.'

She had regained her usual morning humour. 'Any post?'

'Yes, as a matter of fact. A letter for you. I'll go down and get it.' I returned and passed her the white envelope with the handwritten address. She tore the flap and extracted a single sheet of white paper. As she read it, a frown creased her forehead. She turned it to look at the back and, picking up the envelope, glanced at the postmark. Without comment, she handed me the letter.

There was no address of origin or date. The writing, untidy ball-point, was childish in form but easy to read.

> Dear Mrs Doorly,
> I have learnt of the death of my aunt, Mary Perry. I will call to your house on Thursday to collect anything you have belonging to her.
> Yours faithfully,
> Andrew Valentine.

I felt as if someone had emptied a bucket of cold water over me. The knowledge that we were the only people caring about, or even aware of, Mrs Perry's death had become strangely comfortable to me. The letter showed that this man had much more right to grieve than we had.

Theresa spoke slowly. 'How did he hear, for God's sake? We didn't put it in the papers.'

'Search me. When he calls do we give him the books?'

'I suppose we've no choice. If he really is her nephew.'

'How the hell do we know if he's genuine?'

'I'll have to ask for identification.'

'Bloody embarrassing if he gets on his high horse.'

'He can't possibly object to me making sure that he is her relative, can he?'

I shrugged, gathered up the breakfast things and started down with the tray. I left the dishes in the sink and put on my coat. Upstairs, I kissed her and then I went out to the car for the hour's drive to the office. I had only been at my desk a few moments when the phone buzzed.

'Mr Doorly, my office please.'

Mr Craddock is my boss. He is the Assistant Secretary of the Department and, as such, is not to be kept waiting, so I hurried up the two flights of stairs.

I was fairly certain of the reason for the summons. Six weeks earlier I had appeared before an Appointments Board. I was trying to reach the next grade and felt that I had done well. The result had probably come through. The fact that Craddock was personally informing me pointed to success. He was not the sort of man to bother with failures.

I checked my tie knot and knocked. A distant voice called unintelligibly and, with a deep breath, I went in.

Like all civil service offices of the older kind, the room had an ornate, high ceiling. The single window looked out on the car park. The floor was carpeted and a huge desk stood diagonally across one corner. Robert Craddock had a big head on a spare frame. It was covered with thick silver hair. A pair of black horn-rimmed glasses perched on the tip of his red-veined nose. The eyes were pale and watery. A gold fáinne gleamed on his beautifully cut lapel.

'Mr Doorly.' His voice was rough, with strong traces of his native Cavan. 'Take a seat. Take a seat.'

I did so and waited.

'I have had a visit from the police, Mr Doorly. An Inspector Ryan questioned me about you.'

I was so taken aback that I could not think of anything to say.

He continued, his tone hardening. 'I am not accustomed to being quizzed about senior members of my staff.'

'I'm very sorry, sir. I really have no idea...'

He interrupted me. 'Apparently you were involved with a neighbour. A fire, next door to you.'

'Oh I was. But why did he call on you? He has spoken to my wife and me. We have not heard from him since.'

'He wanted to know whether I had any knowledge of your political leanings.'

'Sir, I know of no reason why you should be questioned like this. I will certainly call on the man on my way home tonight to ask for an explanation.'

'What *are* your politics, Mr Doorly?'

'Really, sir, I don't think that's relevant. The incident of the fire was considered suspicious, but the house was empty. There was nothing for anyone to steal. I told the man as much.'

'Well, I don't know. It all sounds very queer to me. I do not like my staff's private lives being brought across this desk.'

I sat silently. He dropped his eyes to a document on the desk. 'All right then. That's all.'

For the rest of the day I found concentration almost impossible. The coincidence of the letter and Craddock's complaint would not go away. Finally, at a quarter to five, I gave up and headed for home. Broomstown Garda Station was a short distance from the house, and I parked outside between two Garda cars. They could hardly give me a ticket here.

Inside, a sergeant presided over a hatch. 'Could I see Inspector Ryan please?'

'What's the name, please?'

I gave him my name and address, neither of which seemed to interest him.

'What do you want to see the Inspector about?'

'Well, it's really a personal matter.'

'He's out at the moment.'

'If he won't be long, perhaps I can wait?'

'I've no idea when he'll be back, and the waiting room is full. You could ring him or call again.' It was clear that he did not care whether I did either. I left it at that and went home.

Theresa was sitting in the kitchen reading one of the exercise books. She acknowledged my kiss in a distracted sort of way. I shrugged, and hung my coat under the stairs.

'Any dinner, love?'

'It's in the fridge. Just needs heating in the microwave. Spaghetti and sauce.'

'Find anything interesting in the diaries today?'

'Oh yes. There's some great stuff here. Our Mrs Perry was some girl.'

I frowned. 'Incidentally, how do we know that it's about her? There's no name on it and her name was Perry. Not Lincoln, Richard's name. I'm presuming that she married him in the end.'

She shook her head. 'You're right, of course. But all the same I have a feeling that it's her. She was so insistent that we found the stuff and kept it secret. Besides, her Christian name was Mary or Molly.'

'What would she say if she found that nice Mr and Mrs Doorly were reading her private papers that she wanted destroyed?'

I heated my dinner and hurried through it. I was anxious to get on with the reading. Before I started, however, I told her about Craddock and Ryan. Her face flamed in anger.

'The bloody cheek of him. Calling your boss like that. He could have got you into trouble.'

I nodded. 'Craddock was far from pleased and I can't say that I blame him. I intend giving Inspector bloody Ryan a piece of my mind.'

'Phone the station later.'

'OK, let's get to it. Where should I start?'

'You left it just before Christmas 1919. The next interesting bit is about a month later.'

'Is it about IRA activities or her love life?'

'Both. Here's the place. Read out from there.'

Monday, 26 January 1920
I write this after a ghastly day. My monthly time is with me and I have been quite miserable. The bottle from the doctor does not seem to have any effect. The awful cramp and headache are as bad as ever. I do not

relish another visit to Doctor Bruton. He asks me such intimate questions. If only M were here, we could go together and she could deal with that side of things. That is enough. Now to the day itself.

A letter from R this morning. He is free tonight. We meet in the foyer of the Gresham at eight o' clock. I can hardly contain my thoughts. Even though I am feeling ill, our meeting fills me with joy.

At one o'clock I met Mr C. In Bewley's I gave him the information. He professed himself satisfied. He asked me, quite hesitantly, if I would like to be more deeply involved. I replied that I did not understand him. He said that I had been taking great risks and that I was entitled to know how my information was being used. He spoke for the first time about Irish freedom, as he called it. Because of my background, the work which I do for him is even more important to his people. I said that his word was enough for me. He thanked me but pressed me to become more politically involved. I am afraid that I became angry. My involvement has always been for the greater good of my country, not to encourage any group of extremists. Because the Army have murdered my brothers I am prepared to fight against them. In his turn, he became agitated. I have never seen him so intense before. He said that I must come in on one side or the other. When freedom is won, those who participated in the struggle will be the people upon whom the new Ireland will be built. The greater the number of my class, the better. We do not want to fight among ourselves after we gain our independence. After his astonishing statement, I asked him to explain precisely what he wanted of me. He smiled at me in his charming way. Tomorrow night, at half-past seven, I am to stand at the corner of Sackville Street and Henry Street. He will be driving a motor car and will take me to a meeting. I do not know the place or the purpose of the meeting. Despite myself, I have a feeling of great excitement. Mr C's very being seems to light up in a curious way when he speaks of Ireland and independence.I must stop now as I need to prepare for tonight's appointment with R.

It is after midnight as I resume. I met R as arranged

in the Gresham Hotel. He was dressed in civilian clothes and looked impossibly handsome. We went into the lounge and he bought drinks. Mine was sherry and I had to force myself to drink it as my stomach was feeling ill. R sat very close to me and whispered in my ear. He had taken a room upstairs in the names of Mr and Mrs Evans. He had already deposited two suitcases in the room to give credence to his story that we had just arrived from the country. I admitted to being upset at the thought of his lying. He responded warmly that for a night of my company, he would lie to God Himself. Where I should have been angry at such loose talk, I was in fact flattered that he showed his true feelings so. He asked me to finish the sherry in order that we could go up. From his pocket he took a gold ring. I was to wear it as a wedding ring in case we were approached by any member of the hotel staff. When we reached the room and were alone, he took me in his arms and kissed me deeply. Suddenly I realised that I had forgotten to make allowance for my condition. I could not possibly allow R to come near me tonight. With mounting embarrassment, I tried to dissuade him. The more I tried, the worse things became. How does one tell this most beastly thing to one's love? I feared that he would surmise that I no longer loved him. And I was right. He said that unless I consented to spend the night with him, he would not see me again. As he spoke, I realised that R knew nothing of a woman's time. I held his hands in mine, closed my eyes and started to tell him. The longer I spoke, the more dismayed he became. When he finally accepted that we could not be together tonight, he began to weep. I held his head on my shoulder and tried to reassure him. The result of all was that we parted and went our ways. R said that he would telephone but I fear that he will not. As I write, my eyes are full of tears. I can do no more.

Theresa smiled. 'She was a real lady. Imagine having to tell a young man who knew nothing that she had her period. It must have been like being stripped naked in public.'

'What about Collins? He seems to have started the heavy stuff with her.'

'It's obvious that so few Protestants were involved that he wanted to have a person like her on the inside. A very shrewd man, our Mr Collins.'

I tossed the book on the table. 'Let's skip ahead. I'm getting tired of this eternal talk about nothing from her. It might have been earth-shattering in those days, but not now.'

Theresa sucked in her lips. I had said the wrong thing. 'No way, Frank. We either do this in order or I'll burn the lot like Mrs Perry wanted. Anyway, I find it fascinating. The times come alive when I read it. As I said before, I don't mind if you give up, but I'm going on.'

I sighed and shrugged. 'OK, you read this time.'

Tuesday, 27 January 1920
The day passed slowly in the office. Last night's events preyed on my mind and the meeting tonight filled me with foreboding. I ate no luncheon. I had told Aunt Beatrice that I was meeting a friend and would not be home until late in the evening. I had only arrived at the meeting point, when Mr C drove up in a splendid motor car. I got in and expressed my admiration for the vehicle. He laughed and confessed that he had borrowed it for the night. Apparently he usually travels around the city on a bicycle. He drove calmly, talking little, which was just as well. The number of motor cars and trams on the streets amazed me. Several times Mr C was forced to sound the horn, so slow-moving was the traffic. On one occasion the delay was caused by two constables standing in the road. When we stopped, one of them approached Mr C and asked him where we were going. His tone was respectful and when Mr C replied that he was taking me, his niece, home to visit my aunt, the constable saluted and stood aside. Mr C was highly amused by the incident and continued to laugh quietly to himself for some time.

I noticed that we were in Drumcondra, a part of the city which was new to me. We turned several corners before Mr C brought the motor car to a stop. He led me to a house which had no lights showing. He produced a key and we entered. In a room at the back of the house a group of four men were waiting. Mr C introduced me by name but did not give the names of the men, which I thought strange. He was addressed throughout as Mick. He related the incident with the constable and they all laughed. The mood continued in this light vein for some moments. Mr C then said that he had invited me here to meet what he called the leadership of the organisation which received my information, or intelligence. I should know the high regard in which I was held by all who know of my work. Before proceeding further, he invited me to ask any questions which I had. I felt rather nervous, the only woman among five men. Nevertheless, I emboldened myself and said that as far as I could judge from the reports in the newspapers, the resistance to England was actually a religious affair. The Roman Catholic faith is held by the nationalists and I find that this is the major cause of doubt to me. The men deferred to Mr C and he addressed my remarks.

It is true that the majority of those who fight for Irish freedom are Roman Catholics. This is so because the majority of the Irish people are of that persuasion. It is important that the Protestant community should be represented and I am, hopefully, the forerunner of many. I said that I understood. The other men were quite young and the smallest of them, a man with a round face and of portly build who wore spectacles, spoke to me. In a soft voice he said that the organisation (its name was not spoken at this time) wanted me to assume a more active part in the struggle. With this in mind, I was now invited to join them, officially as it were. I asked what would be required of me. He said that I must swear an oath of loyalty to the Irish Republic. Further, I will from now onwards be under the command of Mr C. I said that I was already, in a sense, working for him. The small man replied sharply that things were different now. We are fighting a war and this makes us soldiers. Military law applies and this carries severe penalties for failure to obey one's orders. The atmosphere in the badly lit room changed. I felt a sense of threat. In what was I becoming involved?

I was not long in doubt. Another man, dark haired and handsome, told me that I had to decide my loyalties tonight. I had seen the faces of those present and could not be allowed to walk out with this knowledge. The police and military were looking for all these men, Mr C included. Somewhat frightened but angry, I asked if these words meant that I would be murdered should I find it impossible to join them. Mr C leaned over and touched my hair gently. As his hand rested there, he whispered that they had no alternative. How long have I got to decide? Fifteen minutes. I have obviously been in great danger since I first met Mr C. Perhaps I have known this all along. Now I must face the fact that I am required to really join these men's fight. I try to visualise F's reaction. I am almost sure that he would advise me to join. His commitment to independence, now that he has grown to his present state of mind, is total.

I spoke to them. I will take your oath but reserve my right to fight for more than a Roman Catholic state. Each of them came and shook my hand. Mr C was clearly relieved. Perhaps he was the one chosen to pull the trigger should I have decided otherwise. With great solemnity a Bible was produced and a card placed in front of me. The words were in Gaelic. I confessed that I knew nothing of the language. This caused some amusement among the men and it took a few moments to find a copy in English. This is the wording as far as I can recall it. 'I solemnly swear that I will give allegiance to the Irish Republic and to its flag. As a member of the Irish Republican Army I will obey all orders given to me by officers and carry them out to the best of my abilities. God bless the Irish Republic.'

After I was sworn, Mr C said that he would drive me home. He will be my immediate superior and our arrangements will continue. I was silent during the lengthy journey, having much to think on. My companion did not attempt to draw me into conversation. I arrived home at a quarter past eleven. I am deathly tired.

Six

'I told you, Frank. It's getting exciting now, isn't it?' Her face glowed with enthusiasm.

I felt myself caught up in the mood. 'I think we're getting somewhere, all right.'

'I've been thinking. If this Andrew Valentine knows of the books, Mrs Perry can't have told him. She didn't actually say that she had no relatives alive, but I got that impression. She would have mentioned him, surely?'

'Who else could he be?'

She shook her head. 'I don't know, but with the fire and Ryan calling on Craddock, and this man's letter out of the blue, well, I'm getting a bit suspicious. Besides, there's still what that nurse said about Mrs Perry. I'm beginning to believe that the old lady could have been, well, abused in some way. I know she was only a minor sort of spy, but you never know.'

I laughed shortly. 'I think we're reading too much of Mrs Perry's adventures. Incidentally, I'm going to ring Ryan before it goes out of my mind again.'

I was dialling the number when the door-bell rang. Theresa signalled that she would deal with it and went out.

'Could I speak to Inspector Ryan, please?'

A disinterested voice replied. 'He's not in.' It was probably the sergeant I'd spoken to earlier.

'When can I get him?'

'Tomorrow.'

I was about to become insulting when Theresa came back. She put her finger to her lips and moved her hand in a fast circle. I took this to mean that I should hang up, so I did. I would definitely talk to Ryan tomorrow.

Theresa whispered, 'It's Andrew Valentine. I put him in the sitting room.'

I was puzzled at his appearance until it dawned on me: it was Thursday. I had assumed that he meant next week. 'OK, let's go in.'

She led the way. In the centre of the carpet was standing a small, stout man. He was wearing a dreadful blue anorak over a black sweater and jeans. His sparse hair struggled to cover the advance of complete baldness.

He took my outstretched hand with the tips of his fingers. They were icy cold.

'Mr Valentine?' On occasions like this, I am always tempted to add, 'I believe', but here was no Doctor Livingstone.

'Mr Doorly.' The accent, even in two short words, was pure Liverpool.

'We were not expecting you until next Thursday. Your letter only arrived this morning. Nevertheless, I am delighted to see you. I incurred rather a lot of expense over the death of your aunt. The funeral expenses mostly. Perhaps you would like to see the papers?'

He ignored my remarks. 'Mrs Perry was my aunt. I've come for her things.'

'Her things? I know of no things. Except of course the house. Not much of that left.'

'I'm more interested in her papers. Diaries and such.'

Theresa intervened. 'But Mr Valentine, we would not have anything of Mrs...your aunt's. We only got to know her when...at the end.'

'I was given to understand that you had her stuff.'

I was getting annoyed at this refusal to take our

word. I knew we were lying, but he did not. 'Really, Mr Valentine, if Mrs Perry had any papers they must have gone up in the fire.'

'She gave you a key before she died. It was for the cupboard where she kept her diaries.'

I switched to attack. 'All this might sound more convincing if Mrs Perry had not told my wife that she had no family, no relatives of any kind.'

His eyes, cold to start with, seemed about to sprout icicles. 'Are you calling me a liar?'

'I can answer that better when I see proof of your identity.'

All trace of courtesy went overboard. 'Look, Mr Doorly, you and your wife are playing a dangerous game here. My people want those diaries. They can be of no use to you.'

'Tell you what, Mr Valentine, why don't I call Inspector Ryan from the local Garda station? You can hardly object to showing him that you're who you say you are.'

His lower lip disappeared into his mouth as he bit on it. It was plain that I had scored a telling point. Whoever he was, he clearly did not relish the thought of meeting the police. He blew out his cheeks noisily and walked past us to the door. He looked at me. 'I'll be back.'

He was no Arnold whatshisname, but I believed him.

The front door slammed and Theresa caught my arm. 'I don't like that man. He's no more her nephew than I am. He seems to know about the books. I wonder how?'

I shook my head, frowning. 'Search me. I'm beginning to think that Mrs Perry's diaries must be quite famous. Ryan asked Craddock about my politics. If he knows who Mrs Perry really was, then maybe he's looking for the diaries too. Now this chancer. What would an Englishman want with them? Ah, I give up. Let's hit the sack. Tomorrow's another day.'

On Friday, I once again felt that Theresa had earned her breakfast in bed. Our unspoken decision to hang on to the diaries remained just that. I did not feel that anything would be served by talking about it now. Theresa did not mention it either.

I stood with my coat on. 'Ring Craddock, love. Tell him I might be a bit late. I'm going after Ryan, and I intend to sit there all day if necessary.'

To my surprise, the sergeant remembered me. 'Inspector Ryan was asking about you, sir. I'll just tell him you're here.'

Ryan was sitting in a small office at a desk which was bare of any paper. He was in uniform this time and I thought that he looked much more imposing for it.

He remained seated, looking up as I entered. His face showed no emotion.

'Mr Doorly, I've been expecting you.'

I decided to drop my marker right at the start. 'Inspector Ryan, I want to know why you went to my boss about me.'

'I'll come to that later. First I want to talk about Mrs Perry.'

'What about her?'

'She had a series of journals or diaries. They were not destroyed in the fire. I believe you have them.'

'Hold on, hold on. I came here to complain in the strongest terms. You interviewed myself and my wife in our home. Despite the fact that we answered every one of your questions, you then saw fit to approach Mr Craddock, a senior official in the Department of Education. He did not enjoy the experience and I did not enjoy hearing about it from him. I think you've got a damned nerve.'

I sat back breathing hard. Hopefully, I had diverted him from the question of the diaries. Some hope.

'I don't have to explain anything to you. I will follow my enquiries wherever they lead.' He leaned forward and brought the flat of his hand down on the desk top. 'In this case, I have reason to believe that you and your wife are withholding evidence.'

Well, I tried. I waited for him to resume.

'Mrs Mary Perry, also known as Molly Perry, died in Beaumont Hospital nearly three weeks ago. The only non-hospital people present at her death were you and your wife, her next-door neighbours. On your own admission, you received from her before she died a ribbon holding a latch key. I think that there was another key on the ribbon and it is reasonable to suppose that it too came into your possession.'

My brain was racing. It seemed more important than ever that we hold on to the diaries. I don't know why, but Mrs Perry had stressed that she did not want them to be read. OK, Theresa and I were reading them, but only because the old lady's house had been deliberately destroyed. I felt strongly that our motives were almost blameless. I tried to defuse Ryan's obvious anger.

'Inspector, who exactly was Mrs Perry?'

'I don't follow you.'

'Well, this old woman lives alone, has no money for coal, no electricity, little food as far as I know, no relatives of any kind. She dies, and what happens? The police start looking for her diaries. If they exist, why are they so important? What's in them, for God's sake?'

'I think they could tell us why the house was fired. Someone went to a lot trouble to destroy them. I want to know why.'

'And you've no idea what's in them?'

'None. To get back to yourself and your wife, you still have not answered my remarks about the second key.'

'My wife told you about the ribbon and the latch key. She gave it to you.'

'Only after I admitted that I knew of it. Before that, both of you denied that Mrs Perry had given you anything.'

'That was an oversight and you know it. What possible reason would we have to lie about a thing like that, for God's sake?'

'My very point, Mr Doorly. I came to the conclusion, after thinking about it, that you had another key, and to hide this from me, you denied knowledge of the latch key. Oh, you surrendered it readily enough. Tell me straight, have you another key?'

'No.' The denial was out before I could consider its consequences.

We would definitely be for it now, if Ryan really knew. Perhaps he was guessing?

He sat back in his chair and his threatening behaviour fell from him. He actually smiled at me.

'All right, Mr Doorly, we'll leave it there for now. If my approach to your superior caused any difficulty for you, I'm sorry. I am willing to phone the gentleman if you think that necessary.'

'No, thank you, Inspector. One approach is quite enough.' I rose to leave.

Ryan stood and extended his hand. As I shook it he smiled. 'Mr Craddock thinks very highly of you, you know.'

I was over an hour late, but Theresa had called and Craddock seemed mollified. I told him that he would not be hearing from the police again, and that obviously helped.

When I was settled in I rang Theresa and brought her up to date. Hearing of my direct denial to Ryan about the second key, she squealed with delight. 'Oh, Frank, that's marvellous. Now we can get on with the diaries.'

'I don't know, love. Ryan doesn't strike me as a man who gives up easily. I've been doing a bit of thinking. How about moving the box down to Rosslare?'

We have a mobile home in a caravan park there which is let out every July and August on our behalf. The income just about pays the site fees. Outside these months, the place is only half full and we spend many weekends there. A lot of overtime in the Department recently had meant that this year, we had not yet been down.

'That's a good idea, Frank. I'll ring the park to see if the van is let or not. We could bring the stuff down tomorrow and stay over. We'd definitely not be disturbed.'

'OK then. I'll get away as early as I can. You can throw a few things in a bag. We'll set off about eight. That way, we'll be there for lunch and we can start reading immediately afterwards.'

We left it at that and when I got home, she confirmed that the van was free until Monday morning.

I smiled when I remembered my 'few things in a bag'. Theresa was physically incapable of heading for Rosslare without packing clothes for every eventuality, from equatorial heat to Arctic blizzard. The car would be bulging at the seams in the morning.

And so it was. The box was in the boot under a pile of plastic bags. The rear seat was invisible for the same reason. I knew that most of what was in those bags would come back to Dublin on Sunday night without having been disturbed.

The journey is exactly a hundred miles from our door to the mobile.

Usually I allow three hours, which avoids rushing and impatience in traffic. Today, however, I felt a need to hurry and with an eight-thirty start, my watch said ten-forty as I drew up at the door.

I do not like conversation on a long journey, so Theresa kept the tape deck fed with her favourite cassettes. The strangled tones of Tom Jones, the enthusiasm of Abba, and the piano of Richard Clayderman played on while I concentrated on driving. Theresa sang along and swayed in her seat.

The mobile home is not mobile at all. It is firmly fixed to the ground and I would need a transporter to bring it anywhere. However, it is a home in every way. I pay steep rental to keep it here and in return I get water and flushing toilet, a shower, geyser and electricity. Cable television is also laid on.

Theresa keeps a complete set of everything needed for a home here.

Bright throw cushions litter the lounge area. Attractive net curtains hang on the doors and windows. Two beautiful lampshades stand in the corners. I often jokingly say to her that the standard of our lives is better in Rosslare than in Broomstown.

She had brought plenty of food and we had chicken and chips for lunch. After an unpromising start, the day had turned out fine.

We settled down. I sat with my feet on a coffee table and Theresa leaned comfortably against my shoulder. She had kicked off her shoes and her legs were curled under her. I could smell the freshness of her hair. I had to struggle to concentrate. She would not approve of interruption at this time.

Thursday, 29 January 1920

Mr C called to the office this morning. He told A that he was my uncle and that he must see me on urgent business. When I came in he doffed his hat and kissed me on the cheek. At that moment R walked in. I was confused but Mr C carried it off immaculately. R apologised to him for interrupting a family matter and left saying that he would come back later. I caught sight of E's face. She looked terribly angry. Mr C told me that he had to see me today at the usual place. On the stroke of one he arrived and we went to Bewley's café. His attitude has changed since Tuesday night. He seems much more stern. For the first time since we met, I knew fear. He spoke to me in the form of orders rather than requests. Do I know General Macready's movements? I do not. My business is with AC. I must find out if GM will be driving to the Lodge this week. This is impossible. He moves about in a random way. His whereabouts are kept a strict secret, even from his personal staff. If I were to start asking questions I would immediately come under suspicion. Who is closest to him, nonmilitary? After some thought, I know more of AC's staff. A detective named Mr Broy is very involved in implementing his orders. I do not know his Christian name. Mr C then asked me about General Crozier. What is his position? Officially he is second in command to GM. A recent letter from AC described him as Officer Commanding the Auxiliary Police Force which will soon be sent over from England. I am to keep my ears alert for stray gossip about any of the Castle senior people. Now Mr C changed his style from the almost hectoring one to an easier one. Have I ever fired a firearm? I have used a shotgun on occasions. It is essential that as a serving member I should attain competence with a handgun. I must find a way to leave the house for the weekend. I will be met at the General Post Office at ten o'clock on Saturday morning. I must bring warm clothing. Water and basic food will be available. I shall be uncomfortable but so shall everyone else. Where am I going? The Wicklow mountains. Before he left he told me that in the future I would be called Volunteer Stewart. I must address him as Sir.

When I returned to the office, I called upon R. We had arranged to meet on Sunday and I had been looking forward to it. I am afraid that I had to lie to him for the first time. How I loathe falsehood. We parted in pain, as we could not discuss our true feelings in public.

Sunday, 1 February 1920

I am so tired and am finding it very difficult to keep

my eyes open. I told Aunt Beatrice that I was spending the weekend with friends in Wicklow. I waited under the canopy of the General Post Office. At twenty past ten a covered lorry drove up and stopped. A young man alighted and approached. He asked whether I was Volunteer Stewart. When I tried to climb into the back, a hand came from under the canvas and gripped mine. I was pulled bodily into the dim interior and the lorry started with a great roar. I was told to sit on the floor and almost sat on a man. There was much laughter at this. I finally made out that there were six men. They were very young and dressed roughly. I had worn my oldest dress but I felt quite embarrassed being the only woman present. The man who had helped me to reach the inside leaned over very closely. He put his mouth against my ear and spoke. I felt a fine spray enter my ear and he smelt of fish. He asked me for my 'given name'. I did not understand what he meant until he whispered that his name was Jack. I tried to ignore his question but he persisted and I told him that I was Mary. I felt that Molly was much too familiar for the circumstances. He asked if he could use the name when we were not on duty. I had to nod my head. It would have been rude to have refused his request. After a lengthy period, I was horrified to feel his arm go around my shoulders. Thankfully the lorry stopped soon afterwards. The road had become bumpy some distance back.

I climbed down to find that we were in mountainous country. The driver called out strange words which I could not understand. The men formed a line and stood stiffly. The driver became angry and shouted at me. Again I could not understand him. Jack raised his hand and when asked why he did so, replied that I did not understand Irish. At last I realised that the men were speaking Gaelic. I told the driver that the language was unknown to me. He seemed puzzled by this and scratched his head. Jack spoke again. If I stood beside him, he would translate the words quietly for me. This was agreed and I went and stood beside him. We were then marched up the mountain at a very fast pace. I was quite breathless after a few yards.

Eventually we were told to stop, or halt as Jack called it. We were told to sit on the ground and wait until our names were called. I moved a little way in order to be alone but Jack followed and sat beside me. He seemed to think that his intervention on my behalf entitled him to speak in a forward manner. I did not disabuse him. He was very young and quite handsome. He works on his father's trawler out of Howth. He is eighteen years of age. Could he see me alone during the week? I replied that this would be impossible as my aunt did not allow me to go out in the evening alone. Could I not tell her that I was working late? I acted as if I were angry at the suggestion and told him that I could not lie. I felt quite a hypocrite, but at least, he no longer pressed me.

The driver and an older man who had been here before us were clearing a space in the dense undergrowth. They then fixed a piece of paper to a tree at one end of the clearing. The older man, who seemed to be senior, paced out a distance from the tree and at a place where he stopped, fastened a white cloth to a bush. To my surprise my name was called out first. I rose and went to where they were standing. The driver told me that the older man was Captain Murphy and he then walked away, leaving us alone. CM produced a revolver from his pocket. Had I ever seen a gun like this? No. I must hold the gun in my right hand. I told him that I was left-handed. He smiled and said what sounded like 'kithoge'. I took the weapon. It was surprisingly heavy but after a few moments, became quite comfortable. I had to hold my left arm with my right hand in order to stop the gun moving. He made me practise bringing it up to the aiming point. He took a small box of brass-coloured bullets from his inside pocket and showed me how to load them into the gun. Then he stepped back and told me to fire at the piece of paper on the tree. It seemed like a great distance but I looked along the barrel and fired. The gun almost fell out of my hand. CM said that I must try again. This time I was ready for the jump of the weapon and had no difficulty in retaining my grip. CM used a telescope to look at the paper which he called the target. He instructed me to fire until the gun was empty and I discharged four further bullets. He took the gun from me and invited me to walk with him to the target which he removed from the tree. He looked at it for some time and handed it to me without comment. It had six holes, one near the top and five almost together in the centre. He asked me whether I was sure that I had never used such a weapon before. I insisted. He took the target from me and looked at it again. Once could be luck. Have another try. So I did it all again at another target on the same tree. This time he recovered it himself and examined it as he walked back. He shook his head and I thought that I had failed this time. When he rejoined me he said that he had heard of people like me but that I was the first he had met. I was at a loss to understand but when he showed me the second target, I saw that the six holes were all concentrated into a very small area in the centre. He shook my hand and told me to go back and sit down. Jack again joined me and asked to see my target. I showed it to him and he gave a curious whistle from between his teeth. He said that it was brilliant. I began to feel rather proud of myself. Jack called the others to see my target and after that I was treated with a great deal more respect.

The remainder of the day passed in further shooting and my results continued to draw applause. At about four o'clock the evening began to draw in and we were told to gather around CM. He spoke for some time about how to care for a gun, demonstrating how to clean and apply oil to a revolver. A great fire was lit under a tree and the men were each given a time to keep watch. I was excluded from this task, thankfully. We sat around the fire eating our food and drinking the tea which had been made for us. CM called me aside. He said that he was old enough to be my father and as such could broach a difficult subject. I was mortified to discover that he wished to tell me of the toilet arrangements. A place was pointed out to me and he assured me that none of the men would be allowed to approach it. I could feel my face aflame but thankfully the gathering darkness hid this from him. At least, I hoped this was the case. We all slept on the ground with blankets over us. I slept badly, finding the cold pervasive, the ground hard and uneven. In addition, I was conscious of the men lying beside me. Thank heavens that they left me unharmed.

The following morning CM called me aside. My prowess with the gun is truly remarkable. I am evidently what he called 'a natural shot'. This means that I have the skill and accuracy of the best marksmen without their experience. He told me that he had set up a separate practice area for me alone. The others would fire on the targets in the place which I had used yesterday. He gave me a number of different shaped targets. They were three feet in length and two feet in width. He explained that this is the rough shape of a human form. At the top of each target, a circle had been roughly drawn to represent a head, and lower down a mark indicated where the heart would be. I was instructed to practice assiduously shooting at these shapes. To start with, I should concentrate my fire upon the body shape, particularly the heart. When I had reached proficiency, I should then attempt to hit the head outline. The proper method is to discharge two shots in quick succession, pause and fire two more. After each six shots, I looked at the target and entered the placement of the rounds on a piece of paper containing a number of body outlines. This was my task for most of the day. Whenever any of the others were free, they approached my area and continued to express their admiration. Several times during the day, CM made me load a revolver as quickly as I could. This aspect of my work requires much practice. I must learn to load the weapon with my eyes closed.

The food provided for the two days was basic, to say the least. Thick slices of rough bread with salty butter is not to my liking. However, it was made clear to me that no other food would be available and my hunger was such that I found myself consuming the bread with a great deal of relish. Large pots of strong sweet tea were available at all times and I found that the drink helped me to remain warm. Overall, the men treated me very well, due in no small measure, I fancy, to my marksmanship. Eventually, extremely tired, yet strangely satisfied, I joined the others aboard the lorry. As we were driven back to the city, it occurred to me that I had hardly spared a single thought for my dear R.

I was dropped off at the General Post Office. A tram took me home and apart from having to invent weekend activities for Aunt Beatrice, that is my account of an interesting time which I had approached with much trepidation. I must stop now or I shall fall asleep on my chair.

Seven

Monday, 2 February 1920

As I write this, a dreadful feeling creeps over me. Mr C telephoned and ordered me to our meeting point at one o'clock. He told me that he had received a report on the weekend's activities. My marksmanship is of the highest standard. I must take every opportunity to practise. He is thinking of changing my role but until he decides on this, I will continue with my present work. Then came the shock. Do I know an English officer named Lincoln? He is ADC to GM. I felt that it would be unwise to publish our friendship, so I shook my head. I am to get to know this officer, become his friend. I must find out his political views on Ireland. Is he sympathetic to the Government's position? Does he really want to be here risking his life for a cause which does not matter to him? Mr C left early with a warning that the affair is of vital importance.

This afternoon, R came to the office. E was absent and we were able to talk briefly. He is on duty every evening until the weekend. He insists that we meet on Saturday. With a boldness which I did not feel, I asked him if I would be going home that night. He grasped my elbow and whispered that he would never allow me out of his sight again. Sitting here now, my orders from Mr C ring out in my head. How can I spy on the man I love? I dare not tell R of my membership of the IRA. Neither can I disobey Mr C. The future looks very black. I fear that I will be unable to sleep tonight.

Sunday, 8 February 1920

Home again after an exquisite two days. I am more sure than ever that I love R and that he reciprocates. I feel the words of this entry boiling in my mind, far faster than I can write them. I will try to describe the events in a detached manner although this will be very difficult. I an becoming adept at telling lies to Aunt Beatrice. Again I said that one of the ladies in the Castle had invited me to her home for the weekend. Yesterday (Saturday) morning I went to the Main Gate of Phoenix Park. R was waiting for me. He took my hand and his eyes seemed to bore into my brain. I felt quite weak and was forced to lean heavily on his arm, which pleased him. He said that he had borrowed his friend's motor for the weekend. The machine was standing at the pathway and I put my suitcase on the back seat. The vehicle was small but very comfortable and R proved to be an accomplished driver. I asked where we were going but he smiled and said that he had a surprise for me. I had to be content with that and sat back to enjoy the trip.

We descended the hill and went towards Chapelizod. The river looked very calm in the winter sun. After an hour, we turned into a driveway and I saw a small house among the trees. It was quite hidden from the roadway. R produced a key and we entered. The house was simply furnished but beautifully clean. It too belonged to R's friend and we could remain there until Sunday evening. R carried in the luggage and told me that the servant woman who looks after the house for his friend would not be back until Monday morning. When he had deposited the suitcases, we walked through the rooms. A fire was laid in the main room and flamed at the touch of a taper. We finally sat on a sofa and he took me in his arms. Was I certain that I wanted to be here with him, alone? Did I realise the implications of spending a night with a man? My life would be ruined if it were ever to be revealed. I forestalled further questions by kissing him and pressing him to me. He returned the kiss and as we sat there, he whispered that we should go into the bedroom and undress. We held hands as we walked.

At the door he said that he would wait for me to call him when I was ready. I said no. We should prepare together like man and wife. He tried to argue, but I refused to listen. And so it was. He pulled the curtains closed and in the dimmer light, I reached behind me to open my dress. He stood there and moved away my hands. I felt his fingers opening the buttons and he gently slid the garment from my shoulders. It fell to the floor and I stepped out of it. I turned to him and removed his coat. He kissed me and his fingers shook as they untied my bodice. He looked down at me with great tenderness. He tried to speak but I closed his lips with mine. His shirt opened easily but the cuff-links were more difficult and he removed them himself. Before he could stop me I had pushed his braces off his shoulders and unbuttoned his trousers. At the same time he removed my petticoat. Without looking at his eyes I discarded my undergarment and stockings. When I stood up after this, he too was naked. With a cry he embraced me and I felt his body burning mine. I struggled from his grasp and stood back. I wanted to look at him. His body was the most beautiful thing I have ever seen. His face reddened at my gaze and I laughed aloud. I made him look at me in the same manner and I felt no embarrassment. Only the hope that he found the moment as wonderful as I. I do not know how long we stood thus, but finally he lifted me and carried me to the bed. Laying me down with great gentleness, he settled himself beside me. I circled his neck with my arm. To my surprise, I felt him tremble strongly. What is the matter, Richard? He shook his head silently and placed his finger across my mouth. He gazed into my eyes as if trying to see my soul. For some moments, we lay thus. Despite his clear desire that I remain silent, I nudged him. Are you going to lie looking at me all day? If so, we could just as easily have sat on the pier at Kingstown. Is it that you do not find me as attractive as you expected? He pulled me wordlessly to him and stroked my back. I could not see his expression. Gradually, I became aware of a change taking place in his body. He sighed and kissed my hair, his body beginning to move against mine. I felt the burning point of his longing and struggled free of his grasp. With some instinct, I arranged my limbs in a way which gave him freedom to do what he now so clearly desired. What followed was very beautiful and very private. I do not possess the words to describe it. I have become, in the true sense, a woman and will carry the secrets of my love for the remainder of my life.

When I first returned to Kingstown, I stood in front of my mirror, observing my reflection. It seems completely unbelievable that I appear unchanged by the experience through which I have passed. My face is the same one which greets me each morning. My body, up to this point, I have taken for granted. It has become something of sure delight and I will never treat it in the old off-hand way again. Richard taught me to recognise the pleasure which can be gained from it. I find it difficult to explain myself accurately. What a night and two days in the house have demonstrated is that there are several planes of sensation. The great pleasure of the joining of my body to that of the man I love. I have learned the secrets of my womanhood, until now hidden from me. In the many acts of love which we performed, I found that certain areas of my body respond to touch differently from others. For instance, the sensation of indescribable pleasure which I experienced when Richard kissed and caressed the back of my neck. Merely by this act, he reduced me to a trembling girl, my body aflame with new and incredible desire. I found his special secret. The touch of my lips on the inside of his ears can cause a shudder to run through him which brings about his premature arrival at the moment of release. This is indeed something of such depth as beggars my ability to describe it. The second, and much more lasting, feeling is the purely spiritual dimension of my love. I know with a certainty which is almost frightening that we have done no wrong. Rather, we have given each other the most enduring proof of love. I can write no more tonight. Sleep will not come easily to me.

I realised that my palms were wet as I put the book on the table.

My mouth felt dry and my breathing was uneven. I looked at Theresa. Her eyes were shining and her upper lip was trembling slightly. Without lifting her face she murmured, 'Wow! What a girl.'

'She certainly has a way with words, I'll give her that. Without going into the nuts and bolts, she managed to imply a great deal.' Theresa moved a little way from me. Her blue eyes challenged. 'Tell the truth, Frank. Did you get turned on, reading that?'

I was unwilling to admit to such weakness. 'Ah no. It's over seventy years since all this happened. It doesn't affect me that way.'

A little smile hovered on her lips. 'You're an awful liar, Frank Doorly. I could see your hard-on through your trousers. Look at you, for God's sake. Your face is scarlet and you're pouring with sweat.'

I raised my eyebrows in an effort to bridge the moment. I could not think what to say.

A look showing equal parts of anger and hurt came to her face. Her voice held a plaintive note. 'Come on now, Frank. Tell me why you have to lie like that. It's not as if it's something important, for God's sake. It's not a reflection on your manhood or anything.' A single tear trickled from the corner of each eye and I could see that she was fighting others. 'Surely I'm entitled to the truth from you after all this time? If you lie so blatantly about this nonsense, how can I trust you over something big?'

I sank deeper into the pit of my own digging. 'Don't be stupid. Why should I lie about a thing like that?'

'That's my whole point. I hate it when you lie to me. Maybe if it was over something important, I might see your reason. But this...'

'Can we drop the subject now, Theresa? I'm going to make a cup of tea. Will you have one?'

She shrugged. 'Oh yes, I'll have a cup. But try to see my side. We can talk about anything you like, but I'll remember that you were not honest enough to admit that reading that diary excited you. For your information, it got me going. I was leading up to asking you to lie on the bed with me.'

I hesitated for a second and rose to make the tea. Nothing knocks the balls out of a man like telling him that if he had been good, his wife would have let him fuck her. Shit, shit, shit.

When I put the tray on the table, she said in a neutral voice, 'I'm dying to find out how she handles the order about Richard. If she refuses or tries to invent things about him, she will be in the soup.'

'Mm. I imagine that all that about him and Macready was to try and set up an assassination attempt. She must have realised that.'

'She realised it all right, but she can't win no matter what she does.'

I nibbled at a biscuit. 'I suppose that we should get on with it.'

'Right. This time I'll read. I wouldn't like to put you under that sort of pressure again.'

'Theresa, for God's sake. We came down here to read these things in peace. If you can't agree to do that, maybe we should forget it and go home.'

'You do whatever you want,' she snapped at me. 'I'm staying until tomorrow and so is the car. I can drive you to the train if you like.'

I drew a breath for my reply but ended up shrugging, and I handed her the book.

Wednesday, 11 February 1920

I was ordered to the meeting place today by a telephone call. I did not recognise the voice and when I arrived I was met by CM from the shooting weekend in Wicklow. I asked him why Mr C was not there and he replied rather sharply that Mr C had no time to deal with every Volunteer. In future CM will be my officer. He said that 'they' were very pleased with me. Spending the weekend with Lieutenant Lincoln was an excellent move. Did he talk about his work? I was shocked that he knew of the matter. How did you find out? Intelligence. Despite my consternation I said that no conversation about either of our positions took place. He said something very vulgar which I refuse to write. I must 'cultivate the affair' by pressing R to spend more time with me. If all the women Volunteers had my approach to their duty his task would be a great deal easier. Now the reason for the meeting. I am to be taken off intelligence gathering. I will be transferred to 'an active service unit'. When I said that I did not know what the term meant, he laughed and replied that I would find out soon enough.

I have developed a strong dislike for CM. He is no gentleman, certainly. I find that he stares at me in a most offensive way, making no effort to hide his interest in my form. Were he not my superior, I would have no hesitation in telling him of my feelings. He handed me a piece of paper with an address written on it, 47 Bentare Avenue, North Circular Road. I must memorise the address and destroy the paper. I am ordered to call to the address at half-past six tomorrow night. He bent close to me and whispered in my ear. Take the number ten tram. It stops at the top of the Avenue. The password is 'Wolf' and the reply will be 'Hound'. This will tell me that I have arrived at the correct house and that it is safe for me to enter. He forced me to repeat his instructions several times until he was certain that I was accurate. He further ordered me to meet him this evening when he will take me to a place where I can practise my marksmanship.

When I returned to the office, I found myself unable to concentrate on my work. The knowledge that 'they' had been aware of my activities at the weekend was a severe blow. When I thought of the intimate moments R and I had shared, that knowledge seemed to expose our love to the broad light of day. I felt continuous shivers run over my skin and a ghastly sickness settled in my throat. AC called me to his office to take down a letter. I made errors on three occasions in the first paragraph and he spoke angrily to me. I could hardly tell him what truly caused my failures. I apologised and determined to do better. He consented to dictate the words again and I managed to write the correct symbols on this occasion. The letter was to the Home Secretary. The arrival of the most recent members of the Auxiliary Police (known locally as Black and Tans) must be kept from the Press. Their strength is now close to the fifteen hundred men envisaged at the planning stage. The fact remains that the RIC is now seriously under strength. Great pressure is being experienced by them and their families, and resignations from the body are increasing apace.

While I was typing the letter, it occurred to me that its contents would make an interesting report to the IRA. Why is it that I am unable to refer to the organisation as 'we' or 'us'? The truth is that I do not yet feel that I am really a member. More and more, it is born out upon me that I am not a free agent in this matter. It has been made very clear that should I decide to sever my connection, I shall be shot. Fear is a stronger binding than so-called patriotism.

After my work, I was taken by motor to the Dublin mountains, past a village called Rathfarnham. On a small farm, a barn had been prepared with targets. I spent two hours firing in the light cast by several oil lamps. The farmer said that he had never seen such shooting from a woman. I returned home, tired but pleased.

Friday, 13 February 1920

I have had the most horrible experience of my life. I called to the address as ordered. The password and reply occurred in the manner expected. I was admitted into the cold, damp house and confronted by two men. I was told that I was now a member of Special Unit Number Three attached to the North Dublin Brigade. We had been given a task to perform by Headquarters. I was ordered to sit at a table with the two men. One stated that his name was Diarmud, presumably a derivation of Dermot. The second man indicated that I should call him Turlough (pronounced Turlock). The true surprise was yet to come. From that moment I will use the name Gráinne (pronounced Grawnya). I enquired the provenance of the name, never having heard it before. T said that it was an old Gaelic name.

With a smile, he related the story of an ancient Irish pirate queen called Granuaile (Grawnya Wail), whose English name was Grace O'Malley. I asked the nature of our task. D, who seemed to be senior, removed a roll of paper from his pocket and passed it to me. It was a map of some sort. Street names were written on it but none was familiar to me. A point on the map was marked with a red star. I put it on the table, saying that I did not know the area. I do not think it is in Dublin? Very good, G. It is not Dublin. It relates to the town of Skerries. I know that Skerries is to the north but I have never been there. T told me that it did not matter as both he and D were familiar with the town. The star indicates the home of a man in whom we are interested. We will travel by motor car with T driving. I will sit in the front with him. At this point he opened a drawer and handed me a gun. It was exactly similar to the weapon which I had used recently. I was ordered to check that it was fully loaded. He then gave me a box of bullets, 'spares' he called them, which I should carry in my pocket. He told me to ensure that the safety catch was engaged on the revolver. I had become familiar with this on the previous occasions. We left the house and took our places in the motor. T drove out of the city and we were soon travelling in the dark with only our lights to guide us. He appeared to know the way and we made good time, not stopping until we were on the outskirts of what I presumed was Skerries.

D gave me details of the task before us. The man, who was now referred to as the target, was known to have association with people linked with the police. It had been proved beyond doubt that he was an informer. We are to 'mark' him. I asked what the term meant, but already a horrible certainty was dawning. I was to be a witness to murder. My fears were confirmed. The target was to be shot down as he came home from a public house. I was about to protest when the blow fell. This is your big chance, G. Do it with one shot. Make sure that he is killed.

My head spun and I felt ill. Perspiration broke out on my forehead and I began to tremble. Unwittingly, I wept. T leaned towards me and without warning gave me a heavy blow on my cheek. The tears stopped and I became angry. I fear that I attempted to strike him but, with a laugh, he easily caught my wrist. D spoke sharply, saying that if I had succeeded in striking a superior officer, I should have been shot immediately. T then started the motor and drove slowly through the dark streets of the town. We came to a stop opposite a row of small houses. I was ordered to look at the second one, the door of which was about thirty yards away. This was the home of the target. We must wait. It was extremely cold and I pulled my coat around me. D said that I should put my hands in my pockets as I must keep the fingers on my 'firing hand' warm. We sat there in silence for a considerable time. I was unable to see my watch. Eventually, T murmured in a low voice. Target. He pointed his finger and I saw a lone man walking slowly along the pathway opposite the motor. Take aim. I reluctantly withdrew the revolver from my pocket. As I hesitated, I felt something hard and cold pressing against my neck. D whispered that if I did not fire or missed the target, his orders were to mark me. He would then mark the target himself. I knew that I must do what he ordered. With shaking hand, I raised the weapon and looked along the barrel. I had never fired at a moving object but nevertheless I pressed the trigger. The target jerked upright for a second and slumped to the footpath without a sound. He was falling before the sound of the shot echoed inside the motor. D slapped T on the shoulder and, with a roar, the motor sped away from the awful sight.

I opened the window and put my head out. I was weeping uncontrollably and my stomach emptied itself into the wind rushing past the window. I remained thus for a long time. Eventually, D leaned forward and, catching my shoulders, pulled me gently on to my seat. I stared blindly into the darkness. I could only think of F and what he would say. I, in all my nineteen years, have never harmed another person. Now I am a murderess. I pray that God will forgive me, for I cannot forgive myself.

T drove until he was in sight of home. Before I alighted, D said that I must in future carry the gun at all times. Should I be faced with capture I must be prepared to sell my life dearly. It would be better for me to die rather than fall into the hands of the BTs.

I slowly walked the short distance to the house and went immediately to my room. I cannot possibly face AB tonight. I fear that sleep will not come.

I continue this entry at half-past seven in the morning. As I feared, I did not close my eyes. The memories of the horrible deed swept over me again and again. Through all my tears, I decided on one course of action. I shall tell R everything and throw myself on his mercy. This may be the last entry in my journal, as I am sure the very least that I can expect from the authorities when they hear of my perfidy is a lengthy prison sentence. Perhaps it will be the mercy of an early death.

Eight

Theresa closed the book and threw it on the table. 'That's the end of that one anyway. She certainly didn't stop there.'

'The whole thing sounds so cold-blooded. She says that she was sick but she still went ahead and shot the poor bastard.'

'Oh, I don't know. She hadn't much choice. Your man was ready to kill her if she refused.'

'He could have been bluffing.'

'Would you take a chance like that? No, she knew that he wasn't bluffing. This was his poker game. He had all the aces.'

I rose and stretched. Unconsciously, I had been holding my neck stiffly and now the muscles were protesting. As I stood moving my head from side to side, she came behind me and began to massage the hard ridges with strong probings of her fingers. This was a skill which she had shown in the early days.

I tried to relax as she manipulated the muscles. Soon I felt the pain disappear and the wonderful flow of ease crept down my back. Without speaking, she moved close to me and I could feel her body soft but insistent the whole way to my hips. I reached back and found her buttocks, pulling her hard against me.

Her lips began to worry at my neck and her right hand slid down inside my trousers. Her fingers closed on my penis. As I surrendered myself to the sensation she suddenly gripped me hard. Her nails dug into the tender flesh and I jumped away from her with a half shout.

I whirled, my temper boiling, to find her grinning. Her eyes danced as she giggled slightly. 'Got you, didn't I? Now you know how I felt the last time.'

'Jesus Christ, Theresa. That's diabolical. I could thump you this minute and maybe I will. I never thought you were a prickteaser.'

'Language, language. Keep your hair on. It was only a little nick.'

'Little my arse. You've gone over the top this time. I can take a joke as well as the next man, but that was deliberate.'

To my fury, she continued to smile. 'All right. I'm sorry. Now get down off your high horse. I'll make something to eat. What d'you fancy?'

'Don't try to change the subject. What you did was depraved. Maybe a bit of SM would suit you?'

'Jesus, Frank, hang on now.' Her eyes narrowed. 'Don't turn a little joke into a big deal. You can't handle that sort of thing and you know it. Cool down, can't you?'

I no longer cared what she said. She was close to home when she said that I was no good at the big fights. However, I had come too far to retreat. And besides, maybe I was looking for a beating.

I grabbed my jacket and walked out of the caravan. I thought I heard her say something but didn't go back to check. The gears screamed in protest as the car shot backwards and with a curse I pushed home first. My right foot had the engine racing when I released the brakes and, with a squeal from the tyres, I was off.

I came straight out of the entrance which is on a blind bend in the road. A mud-spattered tractor slid towards me as the driver desperately tried to brake on the uneven, crumbling surface. The last I saw of him he was standing in his seat, waving his arms at me. Who cares.

I took the back road and was lucky not to meet any traffic. There are places where passing is only possible by the vehicles edging onto the grass verge. After four miles I swung on to the trunk road from the ferry port and put my foot to the floor. Wexford is another eight miles, but I was speeding through its outskirts in five minutes. I slowed and found that I had been enjoying the risks I was taking. I almost dared anyone else on the road to hit me.

It was mid-afternoon and the warm summer was in the air.

The streets were thronged with holidaymakers, many clearly overseas visitors. I pulled into the car park opposite the Talbot Hotel. I had intended to go in for a drink, but the thought of any company made me walk on.

As I strode along the sea wall, the rail tracks gleamed in the sunshine. The usual row of mussel boats rested on their mooring ropes, the unloading arms swaying slowly in the slight swell running ahead of a balmy off-shore breeze.

On impulse, I turned into one of the narrow streets which thread their way up to the town centre. Halfway along was a pub. It was a small establishment, the single window hiding under a thick coating of grime. The door badly needed painting and the legend above it was a barely legible 'Thos. Peters. Fine Stout'.

Inside, the light took no help from the sun. A single fly-stained bulb hung from the centre of the brown ceiling. The bar was of almost-black wood, the pump handles adding just a little colour. A stringy old man stood on duty. I was the only customer. 'Paddy, please. Make it a double.'

Without greeting of any sort he held a glass under the optic, pressed it home twice and planted it in front of me.

I poured it straight down my throat and replaced

the glass. 'Single this time.'

I took my drink to one of the small tables along the wall. I put my back against the cushion and cradled the glass between my hands.

So here you are. What now? You've made your big gesture and where does it get you? No bloody where. She's sitting back there eating her dinner and looking forward to reading some more entries. I'm sure she hasn't given you a thought since you left.

I remembered the first time I had really taken Theresa on. It was three months before we were married. I had been particularly insistent that evening in the sitting room of her parents' house. I had wrestled with her on the settee and despite her resistance, had managed to pull her knickers off and open her brassière. My tongue was in her mouth and my fingers moved in her vagina. She became more excited than usual and, unasked, opened my fly.

She held my penis in her fist and pumped her hand back and forth. She moaned and pressed herself on my fingers as they found the spot. Suddenly she tore her mouth from mine. Gasping for breath she said, 'Yes, darling Frank. Come on. I don't want to stop. Go ahead. It's all right.'

I felt as if a bucket of cold water had been poured over me. My penis collapsed and I pulled away from her. She grabbed my hand and tried to return it under her skirt. I wasn't having any. Her decision to go for the big ride took me completely by surprise. All that I could think about was the possible result of 'going all the way'. She pushed me off her and stood up. Looking me straight in the eye, she slowly stepped into her knickers and pulled them up. Just as deliberately, she rolled up her sweater and fastened the brassière. When she was satisfied, she picked up her hand bag and began to tidy her hair and repair her make-up.

Finally she turned to me, her eyes wet, her voice

low. 'That's it, Frank. I've never before asked anyone to do that to me. I'm so mad at myself for acting like that. It's plain to see now that you only get excited as long as I fight against you. And all this time, here was I afraid that you might get carried away some night. Well, you had your chance. It's marriage or nothing for you, my boy.'

And I sat there and heard the words. What was my reaction? Relief, blessed relief.

I had never faced the situation of a woman wanting to have sex, 'all the way' sex, that is. Theresa was nearer the truth than she could possibly know. For me, the whole business lost its appeal as soon as resistance stopped.

I downed the last of the whiskey and called for another. When that was gone I ordered a fourth. The drinks did not seem to be reaching the parts which needed them.

The man behind the bar called out, 'That'll be the time now, sir. There's only meself here and I have to close while I get me tea. If you'd like one more, you can step into the back.'

I did not need favours from this old fossil. I rose and walked to the door, a feeling of complete sobriety bringing smugness to the swagger of my shoulders. The air hit me and I almost fell over. Gripping the edge of the door, I struggled for balance. With a groan of surrender, the contents of my stomach spurted down the front of my shirt. I held on to the door and doubled over, more spasms wrenching my body.

I was grabbed from behind and pushed violently into the street, where I tripped and fell headlong. He shouted, 'Ye dirty bastard. I've a good mind to rub your face in your puke. If I see you around here again, I'll kick your head off.' The door slammed shut and I heard the sound of a bolt being shot home.

A few people were passing and each one stepped

daintily over me, making sure that they were not contaminated. As I pulled myself upright, I became aware of the smell of vomit. My shirt and jacket were coated and my shoes had changed colour.

I can't say that I walked back to the car. My progress was more of a lurching stumble, my legs refusing to obey the signals from my brain. I was brought to a shuddering halt twice as nausea struck again. I was deathly cold, yet sweat poured from me. The smell of myself was becoming more than I could bear. I could already hear Theresa's words of welcome.

I fumbled for the keys, looking everywhere but the one place I always use. They were fastened to my belt and it was only when my arm caught them and made them jangle that I remembered. I sat in the car trying to gather my wits. I was not too drunk to appreciate the risks of driving in this state. The last thing I needed was to be stopped for speeding. I would not have to blow into any little bag to convince a zealous Garda that I was pissed out of my mind. I rubbed my face vigorously, blinking my stinging eyes.

Right, that's the best I can do. Remember, don't drive fast. I settled in and kept close to the verge, not allowing my speed to rise above twenty miles per hour. I sat hunched forward over the wheel, desperately trying to focus my eyes.

When I finally arrived at the door of the caravan I had forgotten how badly I smelt and how filthy I looked. My balance had returned to normal although my stomach felt sick. I opened the door and walked in. The lounge was empty and clear of any signs of a meal. I looked into the bedroom. She was lying under the duvet, one of Mrs Perry's books in her hand. She was fast asleep.

I took a dressing gown from the wardrobe and softly closed the bedroom door. In the bathroom I stripped off and pushed my soiled clothes into a bucket of cold water. I turned on the geyser and stepped under the shower.

I let the hot water run over my body for five minutes before I used soap. I scrubbed the skin and tore at my hair until the last trace of the sour smell had been rinsed down the drain. I gradually reduced the heat of the water and when full cold was reached, somehow managed to stand silently under the icy spray.

I towelled vigorously, the skin pink and tingling. A quick rub dried my short hair. In the dressing gown I walked into the lounge and switched on the gas heater. Not only did I feel clean, but no after-effect of drink remained. I was settling down to a cup of tea when Theresa came out of the bedroom. She wore a long sweater and white ankle socks. I found myself looking at her legs which seemed to go on forever. She was yawning and her eyes were sleepy looking.

She smiled slowly. 'Hi darling. You look delicious. Come and give me a kiss.'

It never ceases to amaze me, the way that she can completely ignore what has gone before. There was no sign of anger or even acknowledgement that we had disagreed the last time we had spoken. I stood and she came lightly into my arms. She hugged me and inhaled deeply. 'Mm. I love your smell before you spoil it with sprays and things.'

The kiss was warm, soft and utterly Theresa. Her lips were slightly parted but her tongue stayed at home. The breath through her nose was gentle against my cheek. She broke her mouth away and smiled up at me. She looked incredibly young and trusting as I continued to hold her. The very childishness of the ankle socks and the bare legs were almost enough to set my motor running.

Moments like this more than made up for her

brittle moods. She eased out of my arms and wrinkled her nose at me.

'You're a fine one, I must say. Making a cup of tea for yourself. You might have brought one in to me.'

'I didn't want to wake you. You looked very comfortable.'

'Ah well, never mind. Feel like something to eat?'

I realised that I was starving. 'I'd love a big fry. Chips and all.'

'Sit down and I'll have it done in ten minutes.'

As good as her word, she put a plate before me. It was piled with sausages, pudding, rashers, eggs and chips, and piping hot. We wired into the food, too hungry to talk.

When we were drinking our second cups of tea she said, 'It took me a while to find the next entry. She didn't write anything for three months. I was just starting the new book when I dropped off.'

I nodded. 'I noticed you had a book out. Nothing startling?'

'No. Like I said, I can't remember how it starts. Let's clear away and get on with it.'

She began to read in her soft voice and once again, I found myself cast back seventy-four years to the life of an extraordinary girl of nineteen in an extraordinary time.

Sunday, 16 May 1920.

I have wrestled with my conscience for three months now. After vowing never to write my journal again, I have decided that I would be less than honest to abandon the work. Because my life has taken a very unhappy direction, it behoves me more than ever to record it. A journal based only on selected events is dishonest. I will attempt to relate the happenings which have taken place since February. In the days following my murder on behalf of the IRA, I was tortured beyond comfort. My resolve to tell R was strong, but before I could do so I was ordered to another meeting in the house. D and T were present as before. I was given a letter addressed to me. It was typewritten and the signature read, General Michael Collins. He congratulated me on the success of the 'mission' in Skerries. I had dealt a grievous blow to the enemies of the Republic. The man who had been shot was an informer for the Dublin Metropolitan Police and many brave soldiers in our cause had been betrayed by him. The word had gone out that anyone aiding the 'Crown Forces' would be dealt with by the 'official executioner' of the IRA. The name of this person was Gráinne. Dublin Castle Authorities have only now learnt of her existence and few members of our own organisation knew her true identity.

To say that I was horrified at this news does not adequately express my feelings. D told me that the Supreme Council were personally involved in publishing stories of the never-failing aim of Gráinne. It was essential that the Skerries 'job' be followed up immediately by a bold strike against someone of note. The name suggested was Alfred Cope, my immediate superior. I protested that this would be madness. Should the attack be successful, the authorities would immediately encourage the BTs to exact an awful revenge upon the population. D said forcefully that this was just the sort of reaction wished for. It would be a perfect recruiting campaign. T said that AC was due to travel to Newry on Wednesday morning and that a place of assassination was prepared between Dunleer and Drumcar. At this point I stood up. As I am the one to perform the murder, I must have the ultimate decision. Once and for all, I refuse to attempt this foolish task. I am prepared to carry out such an order on people who can be seen to betray the movement. I will have no part in purely political murder. As I sat down, I must confess that my words sounded more defiant than I felt. I had obviously reached a point where my companions could interpret my remarks as refusal to obey their orders. Should they do so, I had little doubt as to what their response would be. Indeed, D looked extremely angry. However, he did not speak for a moment. Then, 'Very well.' He would bow to my decision. I must suggest a reasonable alternative target. They sat silently, waiting for my reply.

I felt a growing sense of my power over these men. My attitude, far from giving them doubt about my commitment, seemed to impress them. Now I was to choose my own target. Of course this was not an easy choice. Whomsoever I named was condemned to death. Quickly I prepared to run through the names of people who satisfied my own criteria. It dawned upon me that I knew of no one so situated. I was about to admit as much when T spoke softly to me. How about Spencer? For a moment, the name meant nothing to me. Major Robert Spencer? Of course. He was a particularly cruel officer in the BTs. He had given the orders for reprisal executions after a party of BTs had been ambushed in Kerry. Their armoured car had been stopped by a fallen tree and when they had alighted they came under fire. None of them were hit but on Spencer's orders they had driven to Listowel where four young men and two women were shot dead after being beaten. The bodies had been hung naked from the spire of the local Roman Catholic church. Spencer had warned the people that he would return and if the bodies had been taken down a further six would be executed. F had written to me about the sorry affair. Such conduct, carried out under the Union flag, would drive thousands of young people into the IRA.

T told me to wait in the house until he returned. He was back within the hour. MS was actually in Dublin tonight. He is to report to GM in the morning. He is housed in the Castle but is at the moment calling upon friends in Bray. We have an hour to strike before he again comes under the protection of the Army.

We immediately hurry to the motor and T drives towards the South. As before, I sit alongside him with D in the back. The reason for this becomes evident when we are stopped by two constables. They approach and T introduces me as his wife. We are on our way home after attending a musical recital in Saint Anne's Church in Dawson Street. The constables salute and ask our pardon for the delay. As we drive off, I see that D has been lying on the floor under a rug. When he regains his seat, he and T laugh at the incident. Eventually, T brings the motor to a stop on a dark stretch of road. I have no idea where we are but am ordered to sit quietly. I will have very little time when the target appears and I must be prepared to shoot quickly and accurately. T then turns the motor around and extinguishes the lights. He walks into the darkness. D tells me that T is establishing contact with a local unit of the organisation. After some time T comes running fast and leaps into the motor. He starts the engine and within seconds another motor speeds past us. We set out in pursuit without showing our lights. We draw level with the other vehicle and D calls out for me to fire. I look across to see a man driving and he glances at our motor. His face shows alarm and he shouts but I am unable to hear his words. As I raise the gun he tries to bend below the door but I can see him clearly. I pause for a second and fire. The window between the driver and me dissolves into a million pieces of ice and a red mark grows from his temple. At the same time, our motor increases speed and we leave the second vehicle behind. I look through the back window and see it run off the road and overturn in the ditch.

I arrived home some time later. I was amazed at my feelings. When I murdered the man in Skerries I was plagued with guilt. This time I was only concerned that my shot achieved the required result. I had no doubt that Spencer fully deserved to die.

The next day's papers were full of reports of the incident, together with police statements that an arrest was imminent. I am now ordered to meet D in Bewley's café every day at one o'clock. Weekends are, of course, not included. He will pass on the names of possible targets for my approval or otherwise. It has been made clear to me that a further refusal to mark a target chosen by my superiors will bode ill for me.

In the twelve weeks afterwards I was given the names of three men. I knew nothing about them. I accepted the information from my superior on each occasion and carried out the tasks of shooting the men. All died and I was not troubled by any investigation. Each of the victims was shot after darkness had descended. I fired from the shadows of the interior of a motor. It seemed a very easy method of killing. The victim never knew from where the fatal shot was fired. For the first time the name G was used in the newspapers. Stories were published about the almost mystical powers of this woman. I began to be quite entertained by the guesswork surrounding the search for G. My companions in the office often spent time discussing the type of woman who could perform all these murders. The view was frequently advanced that she was in fact a man. No mere woman would have either the courage or coldbloodedness to kill so well.

At this time I was ordered to attend another weekend gathering. I travelled to Kilkenny by train where I was met by a young woman. She was dressed in shabby but clean clothes, as was I. She introduced herself as Volunteer O'Flaherty. I was forcibly struck by her easy demonstration of her authority. She addressed me initially as Volunteer Stewart, but at most times between us, she called me Mary, soon changed to Molly. Her name is Bridget. She is one of the few women having a particular closeness to 'The Big Fellow', a name for General Collins. She talked at length about him and it became clear to me that my Mr C is, in fact, he. I feel sure that Bridget is deeply in love with him.

She took me by horse-drawn cart some miles into the country. We reached a remote farmhouse and barn. In the latter were gathered about one hundred people. Bridget and I were among twenty women. A platform or stage had been erected at one end of the large building. Entry was by a small door in the wall and an armed man was on duty there. Chairs had been placed in rows inside. Bridget led me to a place in the two front rows where the women were seated together. Many eyes were turned upon us but no one spoke to us.

Presently, a group of ten men entered and mounted the platform. I was not particularly surprised to see that included amongst them were the men who had been present at my initiation into the organisation. Mr C took his place in the centre of the row. Absolute silence fell. A handsome, dark-haired man, who appeared to be only slightly below Mr C in importance, rose. Moving to the centre of the platform he began to speak. I could not understand one word. He was speaking in Gealic. I turned to Bridget and whispered that I knew nothing of the language. Initially she appeared incredulous but soon agreed to translate into English for me. I took a notebook and pencil from my handbag and wrote the words in Pitmans shorthand. This has enabled me to accurately transcribe the speeches which followed. The man's name was Sean Mac Eoin (Mac Keown). He is Chief of Staff.

'I hold this post in trust for those better qualified who are at present in English prisons. The Dáil has been declared an illegal body and those members who are at liberty are on the run from the Crown Forces here. This does not, and will not, prevent them from meeting and passing into Irish law all the measures required to prosecute the war against the English invaders. The English King may have emerged victorious in the Great War which has racked Europe recently. He shall not do so in the Irish Republic. The Irish Republican Army will not rest until every foreign soldier, every traitorous member of the so-called Royal Irish Constabulary and Dublin Metropolitan Police, every drink-sodden product of English prisons, shall disappear over the horizon of the Irish Sea, never to return. The only oath taken by Irishmen will be the oath of allegiance to the Irish Republic. The Irish tricolour, proud in its green, white and orange, will fly from every flag staff and building in our fair land. Never again will Ireland bend the knee to the symbol of British domination, the hated Union Jack.'

The entire assembly rose to its feet and cheered loudly, waving their fists in the air. The noise was deafening but the atmosphere was quite intoxicating. I found myself caught up in the moment. At that instant, I was proud to be a member of the IRA, and I did not mind who knew it. The noise eventually subsided and the man concluded in this manner.

'Two Irishmen stand above everyone in their loyalty to the cause of Irish freedom. One of them, a leading figure in the glorious rebellion of 1916, the most senior surviving officer of that proud week in Irish history, cannot be with us today. Instead of standing proudly before you, he is at present representing our country on a nationwide tour of the United States of America. I salute our absent comrade and leader, President Eamon DeValera.' Immense emotion seemed to be generated by this name and again the speaker was forced to wait until the commotion had died down before he could continue. In perfect silence, accompanied by almost palpable tension he went on. 'We have however, one in our midst who does not hide his face from the English. That face is well known and well-feared across the Irish Sea. He served with great distinction as ADC to the fallen martyr, Joseph Plunkett, in the General Post Office in 1916. He was taken prisoner by the enemy when that struggle was brutally crushed and the centre of our beautiful capital city was reduced to rubble. He was imprisoned in Frangoch.' His voice dropped to almost a whisper and sarcasm filled his words. 'And then they let him go. They said to themselves that he was not important.' At this, everywhere in the audience, laughter broke out and the speaker allowed it to die naturally, showing great skill. He resumed. 'This nobody, this unimportant reformed rebel, came back to the Ireland he loved. Did he lick his wounds? Did he hide in shame? Did he take it all lying down? The answers to these questions, as we are all aware, are, no, no, and no.' We again came to our feet and called out in a mighty roar. 'NO! NO! NO!' 'I give you, my fellow Volunteers, the Big Fellow, General Michael Collins.' He crossed to Collins and shook his hand warmly, while we, the onlookers, surpassed all previous noise in our welcome.

The General stood alone at the front of the platform, his hands behind his back, his eyes cast down. It was the first time that I had seen him without his coat. He had discarded it and it lay over the back of his chair. His broad face was open and serious. His fair hair was brushed neatly back. From my position, I had an excellent opportunity to observe the familiar grey eyes, alive with a touch of humour in them. He stood over six feet and was broadly built. Only when silence had once again descended did he lift his face and look at the audience. Slowly, he ran his gaze from side to side. I felt, at the moment when his look met mine, that he had eyes only for me. It was an extraordinary feeling. Bridget told me later that he had the same effect upon her. When he began to speak, he did not raise his voice above the conversational. His accent contained soft traces of the provincial, Munster, which is, of course, very familiar to me. He used few gestures to supplement his words, and seemed to need no notes or script. His hands remained behind his back. He spoke in beautiful English. During his speech, the audience appeared to hold its collective breath. This is what he said.

'We come together here today, not to congratulate ourselves, not to criticise ourselves. This is more in the nature of a spiritual stock-taking. Our enemy has at his command 10,000 RIC and 1500 BTs. In addition, he has a purely military presence of 100,000 troops with an option on any number of reinforcements which may be deemed necessary, from time to time. The main target for our actions is and will remain the RIC. The lower the morale of this force, the greater the difficulty Britain will have in governing the country. As I speak, the daily number of resignations from the RIC is growing at a far faster pace than can be replaced by recruiting. This is, of course, the reason behind the establishment of the quasi-police group, the BTs. In a way, their deployment has emerged as an advantage to us. So ferocious has been their response to our activities that our recruitment numbers have leapt ahead. Their cruelty towards the general population has led to a feeling throughout the land that the people may as well join the struggle. At least, then, they will be armed to resist the wholesale slaughter of their kin and destruction of their homes. By our tactic of ostracising the police, we have dried up the main source of their intelligence-gathering. If the people will not recognise, let alone talk to, the RIC, no information can reach them. With this one plan we have blinded the eyes of the British Empire. The greater the pressure we can apply to the RIC, a body which regards itself as a civil police force, not a military one, then the faster will be their withdrawal from the outlying areas of the country. They will concentrate themselves in large numbers in barracks which they feel they can defend. By default, the rest of the country will become ours.

'The biggest problem which we face is, undoubtedly, the shortage of arms and ammunition, particularly ammunition. Now the scattered units of our army are free to make war in whatever way suits the local conditions best. We, in Dublin, do not wish to tie you down with orders about this, and orders about that. As long as the struggle is being carried on, we are happy. But it is now of supreme importance that we capture arms. I ask every active unit commander to turn his attention to this. Revolvers and pistols are plentiful. It is a simple task to carry one in a pocket. Every time one of our people returns to Ireland after visiting another country, it is a racing certainty that he, or she, will carry a handgun for our troops. Rifles. And more rifles. Bullets and more bullets. Each time a Crown Forces unit sets out on the road, it will carry weapons. It is our task to capture these weapons, even our duty. While we are dependent on these methods of acquiring arms, we can never undertake a really decisive push against the enemy.'

He allowed the applause to last just a very few seconds before he silenced us again. This was the type of speech which found ready listeners aplenty among the audience.

'I have spoken enough for today. To finish, let me outline the real reason for this meeting. I know that your attendance here in Kilkenny is not without risk. Imagine the faces of the G-men if they were to walk in here now. All those so well-known faces in the one place. Never fear, I am joking, of course. The whole county is sealed off by our people. I ask each one of you, so carefully selected to come here, to share your knowledge of whatever particular subject you know best. Let us all go away better informed about ways to embarrass our enemy. Let us bring back to our brothers and sisters in our organisation the experiences of the best qualified amongst us.' He smiled broadly as he concluded his remarks. 'I will just tell you of the arrangements for your stay here. Food, drink and beds for the night are available in the farmhouse. I ask you all to go there and talk to each other about my words. Do not discuss present operations. The senior officers here on the platform will circulate among you and we hope to greet each one of you personally. I thank you for listening to me. God Bless The Irish Republic.'

He turned and sat down. There was loud and prolonged applause, which lasted for many minutes. I stood there in a state of great emotion, beating my hands together in unison with my fellow Volunteers. One outstanding thought came to me from the experience of listening to Gen today. The fate of our nation was here evident in this young man – for young he is to bear the responsibility he shoulders. I looked at the men seated around him and saw with newly wondering eyes their youth. Here were no senior people, no elders. These men, by their very freshness, called to the world that a new generation was taking up the torch of freedom.

When it was all over, Bridget and I made our way into the house through a narrow underground tunnel. Long tables had been set up in the kitchen, an enormous room. They were stacked with food, and jugs of hot, strong tea were everywhere. I realised that I was very hungry and helped myself to a plate of bacon and cabbage with two huge potatoes. It looked to be more than I could possibly eat, but I swallowed every last scrap. In the outer room, a woman was noting everybody's name and allocating beds upstairs or in the barn. The women all got beds in the house, which was a blessing.

Bridget and I had adjoining beds and we sat for many hours discussing the speeches which we had heard. She attempted to find out my position in the organisation, but I answered rather vaguely and made it clear to her that I considered such questions to be unwise. After this, we resumed our friendship and had no further trouble. It was quite late as we sat side by side on my bed, with no thought of retiring. I felt very excited about the speeches. It was my first exposure to such rhetoric and I loved every moment of it.

Then a soft voice sounded behind me. 'Ah, dear Molly. My favourite Volunteer. You are well, I hope?' I jumped up and turned. General Collins was smiling warmly at me. He took my hand and held it for a moment. 'Still as beautiful as ever, I see.' I was taken aback by his familiarity and Bridget was clearly put out by it also. I mumbled as bland a reply as I could think of and he left us. When we were alone, Bridget became angry, saying that I should have mentioned that I was a friend of the General. I replied warmly that I had only ever met him when I was on duty. This seemed to mollify her somewhat, and we lay on our beds and slept until morning.

The remainder of the weekend was taken up with more speeches and discussions on various aspects of the IRA. Small groups were formed and tactical matters considered. I was not really involved in the offerings on such matters as fields of fire, ambuscade, field dressing of wounds, or use of heavy weapons such as machine-guns. My main interest was in discussions of assassination methods. The weapon which I have used to greatest effect is the Webley revolver. It is rather heavy and unwieldy. When I disclosed the difficulty which I experience in carrying it, a young man with a pronounced Northern accent took me aside and showed me how to sew a pocket into the inside of my skirt at the back at waist level. He gave me a leather pouch which he called a holster. I will stitch this into place with strong thread and the gun will rest there. It will not encumber me and will be safely concealed beneath my coat.

Towards the end of the Sunday meetings an item arose which was of great interest to me. A group of a dozen people, four of them women, discussed the part which what they called 'the Protestant Ascendancy' could play in the new Ireland, when the British have gone and we are an independent state. I gave a summary of my background, without, of course, mentioning places or names. I asked whether it was possible to be a member of the organisation without being a Roman Catholic. A woman of about forty years of age answered. Not only was such a person welcome, he was absolutely vital. The people of the six north-eastern counties, overwhelmingly non-Catholic as they are, need the example of the Protestant minority in the remainder of the country taking their part in the process of government. They cannot then argue that they would be swallowed up and their culture and traditions lost. I was told to hold my head high and not to be ashamed of my participation in the birth of the new state.

I returned to Dublin and home, afire with eagerness to do my duty. I am a member of the IRA in heart as well as in body. For the first time, no threat plays a part in my involvement. The anger at the murder of my dear brothers has now focused upon the total removal of all things British from my country. I have written at great length about that weekend so that anyone reading these journals in the future will be left in no doubt concerning the total commitment of Molly Stewart in the war. I will now turn to my 'other' life.

Nine

Theresa, her voice sounding dry after the longest passage either of us had read, put the book on the table and walked across to the sink. 'I need a glass of water. My throat feels raw. You can take over in a minute.'

'That's a very indigestible piece, I must say. She really went to town on the speeches. She could have given a summary.'

Theresa came back. 'I don't know, though. This was the most important part of her indoctrination. She realised that herself. She's conscientious as a diarist, I'll give her that.'

'Well, if she was really wooed to the IRA side, she picked very high class men to do the wooing. You can't get much better than Mac Eoin and Collins.'

Theresa nodded in agreement, picking up the book again and tossing it to me. 'Carry on from where I left off. The same date. She was just about to start on her private life. Richard and all that.'

> I have not, after all, spoken to R about the matter which bothered me so much in February. My mind has settled upon a much more confident track, as described above. My thoughts about R have been of a different kind altogether. I have discovered that I am to have his child. The first suspicions filled me with panic. F has always treated me as an adult, particularly since I left home. His and M's reactions to this news do not bear thinking about. Several times, I have sat down to write but my courage has failed me. R, on the other hand, is ecstatic. He wants to approach GM and request his permission to marry me. In such circumstances, the

army insists that officers marry. I have serious doubts about the step. In my present position as G, there is always a possibility that I will be killed or captured. Should this occur, R's career and even life would be in serious jeopardy. Before I became aware of my condition, I had begun to realise that perhaps our paths might be forced by fate to part. My love for him is too great to allow him to suffer for me. For the moment, we have agreed not to speak to anyone about the child.

R has become quite protective towards me. I had to be very firm with him before he would agree to spend another night with me. He was of the opinion that it was not suitable for us to be together. I soon disabused him of this notion. Truth to tell, I have found our lovemaking even more wonderful. I have cradled his head against me in order that he can feel the life within. Such is the position at present. I will have to tell my parents within the next two weeks. Any later, and they will see for themselves, particularly F. The matter of R's name being on the interested list of the IRA has not been mentioned to me since I have been transferred to active service, for which I am extremely grateful.

Theresa looked at me. 'You know, Frank, Mrs Perry is...was a very complex character. On the one hand, she was the young girl in love, discovering the pleasures of sex, getting pregnant and afraid to tell her parents, all very normal. Then again, she was changed into an executioner, and beginning to enjoy it. It's hard to marry the two sides.'

My voice held scorn. 'If you want to know what I think, she was a psychopath. Once she discovered that she could shoot, it took very little persuasion to make her a murderer.'

'That's oversimplifying it a bit, I think. If she had refused the first time, she would have been shot herself. Collins and his lot didn't mess about.'

'I don't know. There doesn't seem to me to be a lot of difference between then and now. That shower in the north say the same things today. They think nothing of killing indiscriminately and say it's for freedom. If they are wrong now, they were wrong then. Besides, all this bullshit about peace and ceasefires that you see everywhere shows us to be so desperate that we'll latch on to any hope, no matter how unlikely. You can't open a paper but Adam's face stares out at you. John Hume seems a decent sort but he's got himself involved with Sinn Fein now. If he really believes that crowd are interested in peace, he's one gullible fool.

'My father always had that gang up there taped. He used to say that he'd rather be shot at by the worst Orangeman than have to sit down with a nationalist. I remember him when one of the crazy raids from Limerick or Tipperary ran into a posse of well-armed RUC on the other side of the border. One young fellow got killed and the papers here were making a fuss about the latest hero and martyr. Dad said at the tea table the next day that he believed the IRA arranged a killing like this from time to time. It helped recruiting no end. Peace my arse.'

'Ah come on. At least in the War of Independence, the people supported the IRA. The present-day lot speak for no one. Gráinne must have seemed like a gift from heaven to Collins. Terrorise the RIC with an unknown assassin. The thought that it was a woman must have made them wet themselves. They must have suspected every oul' wan walking towards them in the street.'

'That's true, I suppose. There are plenty of women and girls these days, but in 1920 it was an unknown situation. Women carrying messages in their bloomers was one thing, but a woman murdering anyone who strayed out of line was different. That's all changed now, of course. She sounds as if she'd murder her granny if Collins said the word. Ah well, let's leave it for tonight. I'm for bed. Coming?' She rose and stretched. She was still in the sweater and socks. When her arms were at full length above her head, I saw a flash of white beneath the hem of the sweater. I reached out and pulled her on to my lap. She grinned like a kid and circled my neck with her arms. As her lips covered mine, I slipped my hand up her leg to the soft panties. They felt slightly damp and warm. My forefinger wormed inside. Her hand clamped over my wrist.

She shook her head. 'Mm mm. Not tonight Frank. I'm due in the morning and I wouldn't like to take a chance.' She leaned her head against me and said softly, 'if you're desperate, maybe I can help.'

God, how this woman can take the romance out of me by putting the unspoken into words. Still, this was not the first time she had used these or similar words in recent times. For a woman who would not even mention the word 'period' when we married, it seemed to me that the term might be coming in quite handy nowadays.

Ah for fuck's sake Doorly, cop yourself on. You're becoming paranoid.

On Sunday morning we rose early and went to Mass in the local church. It was a small building of recent vintage. Circular, with a low ceiling, it was far more intimate than the older type. The priest was a young man and his homily was delivered in a matter-of-fact style. He did not hurry and yet seemed to cover all the relevant points in five minutes. When we went to receive Communion, it was made a personal experience by the warm smile on his face.

Kneeling afterwards, I found it easy to pray with my face in my hands. At home, I always felt slightly embarrassed in this position. As I finished and sat up, Theresa's hand touched my arm and when I looked at her, her eyes were moist.

The priest was outside when we emerged and came forward to greet us. I was surprised at this as we had never spoken to him before, usually going to

Saturday evening Mass during the season and hurrying away while the last prayers were being said. 'Mr and Mrs Doorly, how nice to see you. This must be your first visit this year?'

How he knew our name was a mystery to me.

Theresa spoke up. 'Thank you, Father. We came down for the weekend. It's nice and quiet after the bustle of Dublin.'

'Yes indeed. You are both looking well.'

I laughed. 'Ah, it's hard to kill a bad thing, Father. We'd be lost if it wasn't for Rosslare.'

'You've brought good weather with you anyway.'

He turned to leave us and then said over his shoulder, 'The English gentleman said that you would be down. He said that I should give you both his regards.'

I was about to reply, but Theresa gripped my arm and pushed me towards the car. When we were seated she turned to me. 'Bloody Andrew Valentine. How the hell did he know about the van?'

I shrugged. 'Probably the same way he knew about Mrs Perry dying. He certainly wanted us to know about him. Telling the priest to give us his regards. I suppose that it is him?'

'Who else? The English accent is a dead giveaway. I wonder if he's still around?'

'If he wants us to know that, he'll make sure that we see him. Anyway, we'll go back and have a cup of tea. I'm freezing.'

An hour later I was about to look for the book we had been reading the night before when Theresa forestalled me. 'Hold on a minute, Frank. I've been thinking. If Valentine knows that we are here, there doesn't seem much point in staying. The whole reason for coming down was to get away to where no one would know about the diaries.'

'My thoughts exactly. I think we might as well go home. How about taking off now?'

She thought for a minute and nodded. 'Right. I'll throw a few things into a bag. I won't be a minute.'

It actually took her twenty minutes to get ready, but as this constituted some sort of record, I did not complain. Off we went with all the same plastic bags full of clothes which had accompanied us down the day before. The cardboard box was in the same position.

Sunday morning is the ideal time to travel in Ireland, and I made good time. In two hours I was braking to turn into the drive. Theresa opened the deadlock with the brass key as I was unloading the first of the bags. They piled up in my arms above the height of my head and I walked slowly towards the porch.

When I got to the door I heard an exclamation from her. I let the bags fall on to the floor. She hurried from the kitchen towards me. 'Somebody's been here, Frank.'

'Here? You mean in the house?'

'The back door is unlocked and the drawers are emptied on to the floor. We've been burgled.'

'Shit. That's all we need. I'll go upstairs and have a look. You check the rest of downstairs.'

The whole place was a shambles. Drawers emptied on the floor, wardrobes stripped of their clothes, beds turned over, pictures thrown everywhere.

I ran downstairs. The same chaos. Theresa was standing in the middle of the kitchen muttering to herself. 'Bastards, bastards, bastards.' Her voice was low but hard and she was spitting out the words with a world of pent-up feelings in them.

I found myself laughing despite the anger that I felt. She looked so young and completely immersed in what she was saying. I went to her and put my arms around her. 'I can't see anything missing. Everything is tossed around but at least it's all here.

Let's be thankful for small mercies.'

'Small mercies my arse. Can't you see they were looking for the damned diaries? I suppose we're lucky they didn't burn the place down like Mrs Perry's.'

'You're right, of course. I'd better ring the Guards.'

I dialled the number of Broomstown Station which I had jotted in the margin of the pad. I gave the details to the desk sergeant. When I told him my name, he paused for a second before promising to send a man around.

Theresa was still standing there, the look on her face even more enraged. I put my hand on her arm. 'They're coming, love. He said not to touch anything.'

'Fuck that. I want a cup of tea. Put the kettle on for God's sake.'

I had only started the tap when the doorbell rang. Theresa went out to answer it. I was not entirely surprised to see Inspector Ryan follow her into the kitchen. This time he was in civilian clothes and could have passed for a shy retiring man of middle age. He carried a hat in his hand.

'Hello, Mr Doorly. We meet again.'

I raised my eyebrows. 'A bit strange to send someone of your rank to investigate a mere break-in, surely?'

'Oh, come now. I doubt if this is a mere break-in. You reported that you did not think that anything was taken. I think it's fair to assume that the burglar was looking for a particular thing,' he paused, 'or things.' The 's' seemed to hang in the air after he had stopped speaking. His eyes were fastened on mine as if he were trying to read my thoughts. I hoped that he could not.

Theresa broke in. 'What in God's name would anyone hope to find here? The only things of value are the television, video and stereo. They're all here.'

Ryan answered drily. 'I'm not sure that the burglar was looking for anything of commercial value, Mrs Doorly. The matter seems to refer back to the diaries of your late neighbour. I'm sure that you remember my previous visit. We spoke of Mrs Perry on that occasion.'

I cut in sharply. It was best to make my position clear as early as possible. Our previous denial of any knowledge of diaries made it imperative. 'Inspector, you are surely not going to go over all that again. We have not now, nor have we had at any time, anything belonging to Mrs Perry. Can we not let the old woman rest in peace?'

To my surprise he smiled. 'No, we do not need to cover that ground again. To change the subject for a moment, I gathered from your call that you have been away. Could I ask where?'

My voice showed the anger I felt. 'Are we to be questioned about our whereabouts now? Are we suspected of breaking the law?'

'Mr Doorly, please do not get upset. I was merely wondering where you had been, not for any official reason, believe me.'

'Let's say that we went away for a couple of days for a rest. Perhaps we could leave it at that.'

'If you wish.'

He rose and as he was making for the door, he said, ' I'll have my men call in a short while. Fingerprints and that sort of thing. Try not to disturb anything for the moment.'

Theresa looked at me and shook her head slightly. I was forbidden to interrupt her. 'Inspector, there is one thing.' She went to her bag and began to search it. In a moment she produced the letter from Valentine. Handing it to the Garda she explained, 'This arrived on Thursday morning. The man called on Thursday evening and said that he wanted Mrs Perry's diaries.

When we told him that we had no such things he became, well, threatening. He said that we would be hearing from what he called "his people".'

Ryan's eyes narrowed. 'Can you describe this man?'

She did so, adding, 'He was quite obviously English.'

'Well, that's very interesting. English, you say?'

'There's more. When we were in...away, we found out that a man with an English accent had been asking about us. He approached the local priest. As we did not decide to go away until Friday night, I wonder how he knew about it.'

Ryan rubbed his bottom lip with his forefinger. He drew a sharp breath and looked straight at me. 'Mr Doorly, in view of what your wife has just said, are you sure that you do not wish to say anything further to me? It is becoming clear that if anyone has possession of Mrs Perry's diaries, they could be in considerable danger. We, the Gardaí, cannot be expected to mount a guard over someone who denies the very existence of such documents.'

I stood up, not looking at Theresa. 'What else can I say? You've seen the result of the burglary. That's why I sent for the police.'

He seemed about to speak again, but shrugged his shoulders slightly and resumed his path to the door. Theresa saw him out and returned with a smile on her face. I made to say something but she got there first.

'I know, I know. I suppose I should have discussed it with you first, but there wasn't time. Anyway, I'm glad I told him.'

When the team of Gardaí arrived they began to comb the place for any clues. I could have told them that the people who burned down Mrs Perry's house so efficiently were not likely to have left their signatures here. They beavered away for over two hours and, naturally, we could not bring the diaries indoors while they were in residence. Finally, the senior officer among them came into the kitchen where we were drinking a much-needed cup of tea.

'We're finished now, ma'am.'

Theresa's face on hearing this title almost took my mind off the fact that our house had recently contained uninvited guests. Watching her, I saw for the first time what the term 'bridled' meant. Her head came up, her eyebrows almost disappeared into her hairline and her mouth tightened. For a moment, I feared for the safety of the Guard. With a supreme effort, she regained something like her composure.

'Have you found anything?'

'Not a scrap of a fingerprint. Sure, they wore gloves and every surface was wiped clean. A real professional job it was.' He said it as if we were to be congratulated on having such high-class burglars.

I escorted them to the front door.

'You can clean up now, sir. Inspector Ryan may be in contact later. He seems very interested in this case.'

They walked slowly to the blue car, perhaps hoping that I would give them an idea why Ryan was involved. I did not speak. When I returned to the kitchen, I smiled at Theresa. 'Are ye well then, ma'am?'

'Don't you start. I'll ma'am that gobshite. Still, I suppose it's better than missus.'

This particular reference was to the early days when she tried to get people to refer to her as Theresa rather than Mrs Doorly. At the time, I had attempted to make a fuss about her unwillingness to acknowledge the change in her name, but the issue had died a natural sort of death.

We spent the rest of Sunday getting the house back into something resembling normality. Theresa is one of those people who complain if she is left to do some unpleasant chore alone. I tried to help but she required me to stand beside her, looking on while she did the work. Holding a watching brief, I suppose.

The upshot of this arrangement was that we were overtired and it was too late when we finished to consider further readings. Actually, I thought it wise to wait until darkness had fallen before I furtively scurried to the car to bring in the box.

Monday morning is a lousy time. After our stay in Rosslare it felt more shitty than usual.

Theresa was wearing her dressing gown, a sure sign that she was going back to bed as soon as she could get me off to the office. I propped the paper between us to stop any small talk. The dreary day delivering one of those nasty June gales waited to be filled with the mindless routines that make up my job. A deep understanding of that French painter who, forsaking all things, took himself off to a Pacific island, seized me.

I was looking at the damn thing for ten minutes before it broke through to my brain. I read the *Irish Independent* which has on its second page small display ads. The sort of things which used to be called 'Social and Personal'. This one was almost hidden at the bottom of the third column.

> MARY PERRY, nee STEWART. Deceased.
> Anyone having claims against the estate of the above Mary (MOLLY) Perry, of 74 Greenview Road, Broomstown, Dublin 15, deceased Saturday 16th July 1994, is requested to forward details by post to the address below.
>
> The latest date for receipt of claims is Monday 12th September 1994 at 5 p.m.
>
> MARRINER and URQUART. Solicitors. 15 Holborn Lane, London WCI 4HF.
>
> Telephone (071) 845 1363.

I whistled through my teeth. 'Well, fuck me for a blind Chinaman.'

'Frank!'

It sounded like a high-velocity bullet and I fancied that I felt the wind of its passing.

'Sorry, but listen to this, for God's sake.'

'I hate that sort of talk at the table. And first thing in the morning too.'

'Yes, but listen. No, you'd better read it yourself. You'd think I was fooling, sure as not.'

Just before she launched her next missile, I handed the paper to her, indicating the notice with my finger.

She snatched it from me, tearing the corner in her temper. It took her a minute to find what I had read, but when she did, the reception was all that anyone could ask. Her forehead furrowed, her eyes widened and her lips formed a silent 'o'.

She looked over the top of the paper at me. 'Would you believe it? There must be a will, after all.'

'Will or not, I get my two grand back. I'm going to get a claim typed in the office and sent off today.'

'Yes, there's that too. I'd forgotten about the money.'

'You would. I wouldn't. That's the difference between us. One of them, anyway.'

She read it again and a third time. 'It's funny though. Now someone else knows of the death. Valentine or whatever his name is, was first. Now this crowd. They sound very posh.'

I swallowed the last of my tea and stood up. 'I'd better be off. I'll get that done as soon as I get in. I have the receipts in my wallet.'

She turned her cheek to take my kiss. I gathered in the briefcase and threw my coat over my arm.

The car started at the first try. That is, the first try after I remembered to turn off the disabling switch. I was soon moving along with the rest of the early morning traffic. It was no worse than usual. Nor better. I took the full hour to reach the office. My secretary, Belinda, was at her desk when I came out of the lift. She's not really mine, I share her with Alec Foley, the other Acting Sub-Secretary. Like me, he was waiting on the result of that Appointments Board. Only one of us could win. We were friends until the day after the interviews. I think Alec was afraid to be too close to the loser. Or the winner.

I wrote out a list of the expenses I had incurred over Mrs Perry and a letter to go along with it. When Belinda handed the sheets to me, I signed the letter. It lay on the desk in front of me and I sat there thinking. So much had happened since that Friday when I paid my only visit to my neighbour.

I made a decision. The directory gave me the code for London and I dialled the number.

It rang twice. A cultured female voice. 'Good morning. Marriner and Urquart. Ursula Salter speaking. How may I help you?'

'My name is Doorly. Frank Doorly. I'm phoning from Dublin. Your firm has a notice in this morning's paper. It concerns a Mrs Perry. Could I speak to whoever is handling the matter please?'

'One moment please, Mr Doorly.'

Clicks and buzzes. She was back. 'Mr Doorly, I'm sorry to have kept you waiting. The matter is in the hands of Mr Harold, Arthur, Urquart. The son of our Mr Harold, Robert, Urquart. I will connect you.'

'Yes?' The word was drawled and I got an immediate impression of being nothing more than an irritation to Urquart the Younger.

I went into my speech and there was not a sound from the other end of the line. I was about to start saying 'hello' and instituting enquiries.

'Excellent. We always get wonderful results from the *Indo*. Your *Times* is rather limited in its appeal. Just like ours.'

'I gather from this that there is a will?'

'Quite.'

I waited to be told quite what. Then I got the message. The expression meant that there was a will. 'Is the estate, er, large?'

'Hardly large. I would class it as adequate.' Before I could toss another question in his direction, he got one of his off at me. A touch of ice was plainly evident over the line. 'You seem rather anxious to learn of the matter?'

'I am. Very anxious. And I'll tell you why. I live, lived, next door to Mrs Perry. My wife and I were not more than passing friends with her, but we held her in high esteem. It came as a shock when I called on her one evening. I found her living in the dark. The electricity was cut off. There was no heating. She had no money to buy coal. She slept in the living room, fully clothed. She cooked on a spirit stove and her diet seemed to be baked beans. I have no idea how long this situation had lasted. She was an intensely private woman. Nevertheless, it was a great jolt to us to find real poverty so close at hand. I felt called upon to pay for a proper funeral. We still have feelings of guilt that we did not act sooner. Maybe you think that I am not entitled to make enquiries from you in these circumstances?'

'My dear Mr Doorly. I fully understand the distress of your wife and yourself. May I say that as soon as you informed me that you financed a full Christian burial for the lady without any guarantee of recompense, your motives became to me white as the driven snow.'

Somewhere in there, I suspected, was an apology. Another tack occurred to me. 'Mr Urquart, I have another question for you.'

Silence.

I ploughed on. 'Would you mind telling me how you heard of Mrs Perry's death? There was no notice in the papers here. I presumed that there were no relatives and it seemed pointless.'

'Ah yes.' A pause made me think, once again, that the line was dead. And I was paying for the call. All right, the Department was paying for the call. 'It was quite fortunate, I suppose. The hospital found Our Card' (I could clearly hear the capitals) 'in her handbag. Gave us a ring. When the case number on the card was read to me, I immediately knew that we had a special relationship with this client.'

'Special relationship?'

'Just a little system left over from my father's early days. He had several clients who had a more than usually close relationship with him. Won't go into details. All rather confidential. Suffice to say, I keyed in the code and the whole business was on the screen in seconds.'

At this point, I was getting a little bored with him. 'Be that as it may, Mr Urquart, if I call over the expenses to you and follow with a letter today, when could I expect payment?'

'Oh, soon after the final date. That's, let me see, 12th of September. Give us a fortnight to check all the claims, don't expect many of those, let me see. How would the week ending the 15th of October suit you?'

'That would be fine.'

'Righty oh then. Let's leave it at that, shall we?'

He did not wait for my answer or my list of expenses. I put the receiver down, thinking that all the gobshites were not in Dublin.

Ten

The morning wore on. It was almost noon when Craddock sent for me.

As usual, I saw the top of his head as I waited for him to acknowledge my presence.

'Mr Doorly, what's on your slate for the rest of the week?'

'The usual things, sir. Teacher placements, temporary appointments.'

'I want you to hand that over to Mr Foley. He can cope?'

'I should think so. There's nothing very awkward at the moment.' I was mystified. What had the old bugger got up his sleeve for me? I wasn't in the dark for long.

'I want you to go to Mullingar tomorrow. The new programme is ready to go. They must have it installed before the end of August. You spend a few weeks with them. Iron out any problems.'

'It's really rather short notice for a trip like this, sir. Is there any possibility of putting it off for another week or so?'

He continued to glare across the desk. I knew I was losing the exchange, but I made a last try. 'Well, sir, Mr Reidy might not be too pleased to have me coming down. He is quite capable of handling the changeover on his own.'

Michael Reidy was one of nature's bollocks. He was in temporary charge of the whole Mullingar project, which had come about as a result of some cute whoring by a local TD. It was envisaged that the whole Department would move to the Midlands town within the next five years. Reidy was sent there to get the show on the road and demonstrate that the idea could work. He had dug himself in like a sniper in South Armagh. Anyone horning in on his territory got nothing but hostility from him and his hand-picked staff. To date, not one Dublin-based officer had managed to disturb the dust of unchallenged ownership which he had spread over every aspect of the work.

Craddock snarled. 'Reidy will have to learn that he is not the Minister for Education. I expect you to exercise the authority of your rank, acting rank. The one thing I don't want is you coming complaining to me that he won't do what you tell him. It's your job to make him. Anyway, go down there and do the job. Look on it as an opportunity to prove your worth.

'Have your girl get you a place to stay. Make it an open-ended booking. Stay as long as it takes. And no running home for the weekends. Keep at it until you are satisfied that those idiots know all there is to know.'

As I left his office I was telling myself that the old fart had no right to order me to spend several weeks in Mullingar without coming home for weekends. Or anywhere else, for that matter. I was also telling myself that I hadn't the balls to stand up to him. I vowed silently that I would walk through Reidy like a paper wall and get the job done in the shortest possible time. I had to. Theresa would kill me if I left her alone for very long.

Belinda booked me into a fair hotel and I drew some cash for expenses.

I struggled through the rest of the day. Concentration was difficult because Mullingar and Michael Reidy loomed large. I was sure that Theresa would not be too pleased at my trip. I could see trouble ahead.

At six on the dot, I switched off the engine and

made for the hall door. My key had only opened it when my nostrils were filled with an unfamiliar smell.

No greeting sounded as I hung up my coat. I pushed open the kitchen door and walked into a steam-filled room. The window was completely misted over and the extractor fan over the cooker was moaning at full power. Theresa stood with her back to me, working at the table. She didn't know I was there. She is not the sort who enjoys being grabbed from the rear, so I cleared my throat but the fan drowned the noise.

'Hello.' The first try was too weak so I gave the second one a bit more lung power. She straightened and looked over her shoulder. Her face showed no surprise at seeing me. Maybe she had heard my entry after all. Ah well.

'Don't come near me. I'm covered in flour.'

She held her hands up for my inspection. Now I recognised the smell. Spice. To be more exact, spices. A large mixing bowl stood on the table, filled to overflowing with what I knew to be the makings of the latest batch of cakes for the freezer cabinet in the garage.

Last year, Theresa had talked me into buying an enormous monster which appeared to me to be capable of holding enough food for a fair-sized army. Every three months or so she set to with a will to stock the damn thing with things which we both knew she would press upon her unfortunate family and friends whether they wanted them or not.

I had walked in on the cooking part of the operation. Experience told me that within the week we would have delivered to us the best parts of a cow, a pig and a lamb. When that happened, she would carve the meat into appropriately-sized cuts as quickly and efficiently as any master butcher.

I looked at her. Her face, as well as having spots

of flour, was perspiring. Her forehead was wet and as I stood there, she wiped it with her forearm, leaving another streak of floury mixture.

On the cooker, a huge pot was standing, steam squirting from under the lid, which was held in place by the electric iron.

This contained the first of half-a-dozen Christmas puddings which she always produced before the end of summer. Her mother had taught her that the longer a pudding was stored, the better the taste.

As for me, I loathe Christmas pudding whatever its age.

I was just about to ask after my dinner when her face took on a guilty look. 'Oh God. I never watched the time.' The voice became that of a little girl confessing to a playroom misdemeanour, the eyes wide. 'I forgot all about the dinner. I'm awful, aren't I?'

To tell the truth, she did not look really concerned at all. In fact, I could see that she did not give a single damn.

I smiled with a warmth I was not feeling. This is the stock response to Theresa when she puts on that small voice.

'Never mind, love. I can have a sandwich.' The lie slid smoothly past my inner anger at being forgotten. I mentally added this to the growing number of times when she neglected me of late. One of these days I would take out that list and examine it more thoroughly.

She shrugged. 'I've been at this since I got up. I haven't stopped for as much as a single cup of tea. The pudding has been on for three hours. I've four batches of cakes and bread done. This is the last of it. Another hour will see it finished.'

Despite her talk of working all day, something struck me. There was a look of, what can I call it, energy about her. Her eyes were bright and she worked smoothly, seeming to be well within herself. In a nutshell, my wife looked a knockout, flour and all. I had a feeling that as soon as I started talking about Mullingar, the knockout might be heading my way, in spades.

I put the kettle on and managed to construct a couple of ham sandwiches without interrupting her too much. I retired to the living room with my 'dinner' and turned on the television. I ate the tasteless food and watched one of the seemingly endless interviews with John Hume on RTE. The BBC had Gerry Adams, complete with a not-quite-synchronised actor's voice. Of all the asinine laws passed by the British Parliament, the one which, having banned Sinn Fein from the airwaves, allowed this shabby stunt must be the worst.

I came across *Coronation Street* on RTE2 and tried to watch that. We had been fans some years before, but new characters seemed to have taken over the Rover's Return, and I quickly became bogged down trying to follow the storyline. It struck me that everyone seemed to have troubles which would turn the hair of real-live people grey with depression.

I was flicking through the other channels looking for something to take my mind off Mullingar when Theresa came in.

'The cakes are in. They'll be finished at half-seven. Anything on worth looking at?'

'Usual bloody rubbish. What we pay that licence fee for is more than I know. The way a man like Hume can allow himself to be used and manipulated by Sinn Féin is beyond me. And bloody Reynolds and Major are playing straight into their hands. Can they not see, for Christ's sake? All this is a blind to allow the IRA to bring in a few more tons of Semtex and train the latest bunch of recruits.'

'Well, turn it off if you feel like that. No one's making you look at it. Anyway, I can do with a chat after all that work on my own. How was your day? All OK in the office?'

This was as good a chance as I could hope for. 'Yes, everything's fine.' I paused for effect. 'That is until bloody Craddock called me in.'

'Oh, what did he want? Not the promotion, was it?'

'Not the promotion. I wouldn't have minded that. He wants me to go to Mullingar tomorrow. I'll be away for a couple of weeks. No weekends either, I'm afraid.' I waited for the explosion.

'Oh? What's this in aid of?'

'I have to transfer them on to the new programme. Reidy could do it just as well, but I think Craddock wants to pull him down a peg or two. I got the message that Craddock won't mind if I have to get rough with him.'

'Will you do it? Get rough, I mean?'

'I've no choice. Anyway, Reidy has been making life miserable for anyone from Dublin for too long. His time has come, I suppose. I wish it was someone else who had to do it, though.'

'Come on. I think it's a great chance for you to prove yourself. Go in with all guns blazing. Show them that you'll take no shit.'

I looked at her in surprise. 'That's more or less what Craddock said. You really don't mind me going?'

'Of course I mind. But if you have to go, you might as well have a positive attitude. It wouldn't help if I started throwing a fit now, would it?'

I got out of my chair and sat on the arm of hers. She craned her neck back and accepted the kiss.

Mm. Tonight might have possibilities.

Like nearly all pleasant thoughts, this one was followed by a less welcome one. Why was she not annoyed? She always had been in the past. From there, it was just a short step to thinking that she was actually pleased about my going. Why? Don't even think that. The answer would probably be so unpalatable as to ruin my night's sleep.

She half-pushed me away. 'Now then, Frank. Behave yourself. Get the diaries out and we'll have a go at them.'

I dutifully did as I was told. She said that she was much too tired to read, so it fell to me.

Thursday, 20 May 1920.
I am feeling quite light-headed at the news which I have. R met me during my luncheon break. He has arranged leave for the weekend of 28th May. I must confess that my first emotion was delight at the thought of another chance for us to be together for a night. But this was not his motive in applying for leave. He has reserved passage for us on the steam-packet departing Kingstown at eight o'clock on the Friday night. We are to visit his parents. I asked him to tell me truthfully whether he could guess at my condition, or not. I know that I would be unable to face his parents if they could observe that I was expecting a child. I fear these unknown people even more than my own family. R assured me that our secret was safe. I thought him quite charming when he said that I looked like any young, healthy girl except that I happened to be the most beautiful girl in the world. I found it difficult to restrain myself from throwing myself into his arms. The moment passed and I returned to the office.

When I was in the cloakroom combing my hair, A entered. She came to me and put her arms around me. She said that I should cherish the love which R and I clearly share. She envied me the happiness which is evident in my every movement. She laid great stress on her next words, her eyes filling with tears as she spoke. R and I must ignore what the world might say about us. Our devotion must be, and here, I use A's actual words, 'tempered in the furnace of life. It will come through this experience, a stronger, longer lasting and more certain love.' Initially, I did not understand the import of her words. A is usually a very light-hearted companion, not given to serious discussion. When I saw tears flowing down her face, I realised that she knew of, or had guessed at, my condition. Coming so soon after R's reassurances in the matter, I cried out, asking whether everyone could tell the truth. She laughed and said that she had not based her words on my outer appearance, but on what she called 'the glow of perfect happiness' which follows me around like a beautiful veil of lace.

I finally regained my desk to find that AC had been calling for me. I hastened to his office and apologised for my tardiness. He graciously told me not to be concerned. I took a seat and he began to dictate a large number of letters which he required me to type. The remainder of the day passed quickly as I worked and I found myself humming a happy tune quietly as I sat in the tram.

I looked up from the book. Theresa's head was resting against the chair back. She was fast asleep. I put the diary away and gently shook her shoulder. Her eyes opened, heavy with sleep.

I whispered, 'The cakes, love. I thought you wouldn't want them to burn.'

She muttered something unintelligible and stamped out to the kitchen. As we made our way up to bed later that night, I had a definite feeling of unease. My goodnight kiss produced nothing more than a smile and a remark that she was bushed after her busy day.

Nevertheless, I turned towards her, looking at her from the angle of my arm and shoulder.

Five minutes later I lay on my back, my stomach churning in the way that was becoming familiar.

She spoke softly. 'Look, don't worry about it. You're probably too tired. It must happen to everyone from time to time. Let's go to sleep. You have an early start in the morning.'

Eleven

My inner alarm woke me half an hour before the clock-radio was due to come on. I slid out of bed quietly. Theresa looked her usual childlike self and I decided that, despite the previous night's disaster, I would bring her breakfast up.

After my shower I dressed and carried the small bag down to the hall. It had taken me about a minute and a half to fill it with my needs the night before. Not a great deal of adventure about Mullingar.

I was just starting to climb the stairs with the tray when she appeared above me. She was fully and attractively dressed. Before I could speak, she said, 'Thanks for the thought, but I'd prefer to come down.'

I reversed and we sat at the table in silence.

So! Is not minding my having to go away much different from welcoming the trip? Or, worse still, not caring, one way or another. Oh for Christ's sake Doorly, eat your breakfast, kiss your wife and leave. Any more of this bleeding heart crap and you'll throw up all over the table.

'Frank. You know that I don't like the orange-juice carton on the table. If you had to open a new one, you should have poured it into the jug. How many times have I said that to you?'

I felt like saying a thousand. This niggling little futility had spoiled many a breakfast in 76 Greenview Road.

She had received a hideous glass jug with a plastic lid and pouring spout from her sister-in-law the previous Christmas. Since then, she had insisted on pouring the orange juice from the carton into it.

'I've told you that when we use the jug, the juice is just coloured water until the last few days. Then you can't drink it. The carton can be shaken every morning.'

'You always use the same childish argument. Why can't you use a big spoon to stir the juice in the jug?'

'I'll tell you why. *It's too much fucking trouble.*'

Isn't this the most ridiculous reason in the world for a row? Nevertheless, possibly because of its stupidity, it regularly formed the battleground where early-morning incivility blows up into war. This morning, I was feeling very dodgy about going away and I suppose I seized on this infantile subject to shout at Theresa and to throw my male weight around. I should have known better.

She rose from her chair, cheeks flushed. When she spoke, her tone carried none of the anger which I had shown. 'That's it. You can go to hell. It's only a mile beyond Mullingar. Stay there, for all I care.' She did not stamp out. She walked calmly to the stairs and as she went up, I thought I detected the first sounds of crying.

As for me, I banged the cup on to the table, slopping cold tea everywhere. I picked up the bag, threw my coat over my arm, slammed the hall door and nearly took the tip of my index finger off in the process.

I quickly left the city behind, glad to have the driving to keep my mind off other things. I made good time, deciding early not to stop for coffee. I was very calm when I pulled into the car park in the forecourt of the big granite pile which is a living monument to decentralisation.

I walked straight past Reception, where a busty redhead tried to interest me in telling her what I wanted. I had been here several times before and knew the geography.

A fast lift brought me to the top floor. I turned

right and stopped at the first door. I rapped my knuckles on it and pushed it open, not waiting for a reply.

It was a big airy room with a modern steel desk parked facing the door. The walls were painted pale yellow and a couple of paintings which looked as if they had come from the local kindergarten hung on them. Two enormous plants flanked the high window.

There were two people in the room. One was a young girl, quite pretty in a *Top of the Pops* way. She was standing in front of the desk, a sheaf of paper in her hand. She looked nervous.

Behind the desk, leaning back in a beautiful leather-covered chair, was Michael Reidy. He was short, stout and moon-faced. Younger than me, he nevertheless presented an air of ownership. I don't mean of the office. That was his. He looked as if he owned Mullingar.

He wore a grey pinstripe suit, a gleaming white shirt and the tie of a Jesuit college.

His head jerked up as I entered, a look of anger on his face. The girl looked over her shoulder.

I kicked off. 'Hello, Michael. You've had the fax from Mr Craddock?'

'What the devil do you mean barging into my office when I'm in conference?'

'I barged in because I have no time to wait on niceties. I'm here to do a job and I want to start as soon as possible. As for your conference, I'm sure the young lady will excuse us.'

She giggled. It was plainly a new experience to hear her lord and master addressed like this. And in his own office, too. She started towards the door. 'Oh yes. I mean no. Of course. Not important. I'll go.'

This she did, leaving me alone with a clearly incandescent Michael Reidy. He seemed to be having trouble with his vocal cords. While he was struggling, I spoke again. 'Well, Michael, did you get the fax or not?'

He blew a hard breath, inflating his cheeks. 'What fax? I got no fax. Why are you here? Why are you acting...as if you are in charge?'

Good old Craddock. I had a shrewd suspicion that he had deliberately refrained from telling Reidy that I was on my way.

'Oh well, if you didn't get it, no harm done. I'll just fill you in, shall I?'

He nodded, his eyes fixed on mine with a murderous look.

I continued breezily. It seemed to be working. After all, he was not Theresa. I can be very forceful with people who are not Theresa. 'I've come down to install the new programme. I have all the bumf. I'll start with you. Always best to get the gaffer set up from the start.'

'Now look, Doorly. I don't give a solitary damn what you lot get up to in Marlborough Street, but you're not going to shove your spoke in here. I have everything under tight control and I don't need you to tell me how to do my job.'

I sat on the chair, unasked. I was fed up standing. I let a moment pass in silence, then leaned towards him and spoke in a half-whisper. 'You couldn't run a chip shop, Reidy. This place is a monument to your incompetence. However, that's just my opinion and I don't want to waste my time arguing about it. Can I start giving you the dope on the new programme now please?'

His face had paled with anger. His lips parted to speak and the words were accompanied by a fine shower of spittle. I moved the chair back to avoid the spray.

'Don't you ever forget, Doorly, that you are exactly the same grade as me, and that it took you two years longer to get there.'

I had him now. Obviously, news from the smoke

had never reached the frontier. I was glad. 'Wrong, wrong, wrong and wrong again. Your lines of communication have let you down, Michael.' I emphasised the name. 'Since we last met, there have been some changes. You see before you Acting Sub-Secretary Doorly and I would appreciate it if you could remember that when addressing me.'

Now his mouth fell open like a fish which has just realised that there is a dangerous world waiting on dry land. Where before, his face had been a greyish pale, now it carried two spots of bright red on the cheeks.

He tried to rally. 'Acting grades carry no seniority with them. You're still a seven, as far as I'm concerned, and junior to me by reason of later appointment.'

It was weak, and he knew it, but I spelled it out for him anyway. 'My grade as ASS,' an unfortunate selection of initials, which, at any other time, he might have remarked on, 'comes straight from Mr Craddock. In view of your attitude, Mr Reidy, I intend to return to Dublin at once. I will explain to Mr Craddock that you found it impossible to accept my presence here. I'm sure he'll want to talk to you about that. Probably tomorrow.'

I rose from the chair. Of course, I had no intention of leaving. Had I done so, Craddock would have had my balls for dinner.

Reidy put out his hand as if warding off a blow. 'Wait. For God's sake sit down. I did not know of your appointment. Congratulations.' The smile looked as if it had been hurriedly painted in place. He swallowed several times. 'Tell me what you want to do.'

And there it ended. I was in charge and did not have any further trouble from this little shit.

I outlined my needs and emphasised that I wanted to leave, with everything finished, in two weeks at the outside. If this proved to be impossible without overtime, then overtime it would be. For him as well as me.

The job took eleven days and twenty hours overtime to complete.

Reidy's pallor grew increasingly pale and sickly with each of those hours as he saw his budget slipping away like sand through his fingers.

Personally, I did not give two pence about his feelings. With each passing day, I felt my separation from Theresa more keenly. Of course, I phoned her every night, but eighty miles of cable is a poor substitute for an armful of living woman. Besides, from the very first call, I thought I detected an increasingly clear note of less than perfect mourning on her part.

It was not what she said or did not say. The words were all that I could have hoped for, but she never quite managed to convey a sense of deprivation such as the one I was feeling.

In the main, our conversations were confined to the diaries which she was reading. She gave me a resumé of the entries she had read each night and we discussed them at some length. I told her that while this system was OK as far as it went, I would want to read the books myself when I got home.

To tell the truth, I found it difficult if not impossible to retain my interest at this second-hand account of Gráinne's activities. One particular passage dealt with a mission for which she was sent to Belfast, her only sortie outside the Dublin area so far. I particularly wanted to see the written words in this case.

The main result of all this was to make my dealings with Reidy go steeply downhill from our initial joust. I vented my spleen and frustration on him in ever increasing spadefuls and he gradually sank into a seething mass of hostility. Naturally, being Reidy, he could not allow his feelings to appear *en claire*, but I was in no doubt as to their malevolent content. I caught him looking at me on several occasions with wistful longing as if wondering whether he could get away with murdering me.

The digital clock on the dashboard showed 5:01 when I turned on to the Dublin road that Friday. The length of the June day should have made the journey quite easy except that driving rain had been falling since morning.

The rush-hour traffic, even in Mullingar, was reduced to a stop-start crawl and it was almost half an hour before I found myself free of the town. Not that the road was empty. Far from it. I had plenty of company, the Friday migration to Dublin setting new low standards in how to drive in the rain.

The wipers were set at fast and I followed the bright blobs of red which were the tail lights ahead. It really was an abominable evening. The prospect of three hours of this did nothing to calm my nerves after the final meeting with Reidy.

He had been particularly obnoxious today. I was leaving when he commented that the Department could not function without Mullingar, and Mullingar would be useless without him.

'I wouldn't bet on it. In two years, we'll all be down here, and if there are vacancies as floor sweepers, your chance of even an interview will be odds-on against.'

Not very appropriate language from one in line for a higher post within the Service. But, in my defence, the one thing Reidy was adept at was bringing his opponents down to his level.

Enough of this shit. Forget him and think about home. Theresa. The thought of a passionate reunion, with me tearing the clothes from her trembling and willing body, brought sweat from me as if I was a fountain. I expected – well, I hoped that Theresa was missing me as much as I was her. The thrum of the tyres on the road seemed to be beating out an erotic samba in my head.

A screaming klaxon brought me back to the car. A huge truck was roaring towards me through the rain. He was on the wrong side of the road. No, he wasn't. I was. I twisted the wheel and the power steering swung me from under the nose of the monster. With a terrifying howl the truck swept past as I wrestled for control of the almost runaway car.

My mouth filled with bile as I realised how near that had been. Another tenth of a second and Theresa would have been shopping for black. Or was it white, these days?

For the rest of the trip, I drove as if taking my driving test. It made for a dull journey, but I finally got home in one piece.

My key in the door brought no hail or other call. Not even a single light shone from a window. Mary Robinson, bless her soul, has nothing to fear from Theresa Doorly.

The note was on the mantelpiece in the kitchen.

'Hi love. Your dinner is in the fridge. Microwave it for six minutes. Visiting Sharon in Donnybrook. I'll be back by eleven. See you then.' A burning anger and hurt. The bitch. Going out like that. And to see Sharon fucking Magowan, of all people. That cow had been her bridesmaid and ever since, had been asking in her innocent 'Dublin 4' voice whether a baby was ever coming. She wants to be a godmother, so badly.

I ran upstairs and unpacked the bag. In the bedroom, I found one of the exercise books under Theresa's pillow. I came down, cooked the dinner, threw it in the waste bin and made a strong cup of black coffee. I took particular pleasure in adding a generous measure of whiskey to it. That'll teach her, about sums up how I felt.

Twelve

I stirred up the fire, pulled a chair close and began to search through the book for the entry which had interested me when Theresa told me about it.

Monday, May 24 1920.
I have had a singular experience. On Friday when I met D, he said that I was required for a 'special mission' during the weekend. I was to meet him at Amiens Street Railway Station at eight the next morning, Saturday. He refused to give me any further information, so it was with a faint sense of unease that I waited outside the station. This feeling increased when he arrived and told me that we were bound for Belfast. I have never been outside the environs of Dublin on duty except when I attended the marksmanship weekend in Wicklow and the meeting in Kilkenny. D purchased first-class tickets and we travelled alone, eating breakfast en route. The journey took several hours and I found the time heavy upon my hands, my companion looking out of the window for the greatest part. Before our arrival in Belfast, a city which I have visited several times with my parents, D said that we must leave the train separately. He instructed me to take a hackney cab and proceed to an address on the northern side where I would be 'taken care of'. This I did and was shown into a small sitting room in the house where D joined me a little later. He proceeded to inform me of the reason for our journey.

Although IRA strength is greatest in the areas outside the North Eastern part of the country, we have Volunteers organised into units in the counties of Down, Londonderry, Armagh, Antrim, Tyrone and Fermanagh. Of necessity they must act covertly and their rights of passage do not include the larger part of the countryside. IRA is continually attempting to win Protestant supporters and with this in mind, the behaviour of our men is subject to rigorous examination. It has come to the notice of Headquarters that one of our officers in the Belfast area has taken part in a series of criminal acts where robbery, threats and even violence have been carried out under the IRA name. Several attempts to persuade this man to stop his activities have failed and it has been decided that he will be court-martialled and, if convicted, executed in front of his men. To show that Headquarters considers the affair to be of the greatest importance, they decree that Gráinne must carry out the sentence. This news was not welcome to me, but I had no choice but to play my part. D made it clear that a refusal would be viewed in the most serious light by Headquarters.

We left the house, again separately. I was accompanied by a woman whose name was Rosemary and we boarded a horse tram which took us through the streets to the outskirts of the city. I was led to a large house set apart from its fellows and we entered through a door at the back of the building. Rosemary said that she would remain with me until what she referred to as 'the business' was about to commence. She brought me down a steep flight of stairs to a large basement where a table had been placed at one end and many chairs arranged in rows facing it. The place was empty and my companion said that proceedings would be starting in half an hour. I would wait in a small room behind where the table stood. At this point I asked her what weapon I would be expected to use. On Friday, D had ordered me not to carry my gun or ammunition as police activity was much more extensive in Belfast and the risk of discovery was greater. Rosemary answered that I would be provided with the necessary equipment by D who had been issued with it.

At exactly half-past two on my wrist-watch D arrived and Rosemary left. I broached the subject of the gun with him and from a bag he produced a weapon the likes of which I had never seen. It was a pistol with a straight butt and a long slender barrel, called, he informed me, a Luger. I took it in my hand and was surprised to find it considerably lighter in weight than my Browning. D showed me that the gun was loaded with a clip of bullets, ten in number, which was pushed upwards into the butt. I said that I was nervous at the prospect of firing a new weapon without rehearsal of any kind but he replied that I would only be called upon to fire one round, and that from point-blank range. He was attempting to reassure me when we heard footsteps descending from above. He bade me to remain quiet and listen to what was about to take place. He showed me a small hole on the door of the room which we occupied and said that I could observe proceedings from there. He stood at a similar hole higher on the wood.

From my vantage point I saw many men occupying the chairs. I began counting the number and had reached twenty-five when they fell silent and five newcomers came to the table and took their places behind it. One of these spoke. 'Are you ready?' The others at the table nodded. 'Bring him down.' Steps sounded on the stairs again and a further five men descended. Four made up the main group walking two by two. In their midst came a single man whose hands were tied behind his back. The five stopped in front of the table, two on either side of the fifth. The man who had spoken earlier resumed. 'We have here the members of the Belfast Brigade.' He raised his voice and addressed the assembled onlookers. 'You have come here on the order of Headquarters to see justice being done towards your Commanding Officer, Captain Sean Mulligan. It has been reported that he carried out criminal acts using the name of the Irish Republican Army. The five of us seated at this table shall listen to what Captain Mulligan has to say and reach a verdict together.' Here he turned to the bound man. 'You are free to say anything you like in your defence of the charges.'

The accused spoke in a loud voice. 'What difference will it make what I say here? Headquarters has decided that I am guilty.' He bowed his head.

From the front row of chairs a hand was raised and a man rose to his feet. 'I'm not much for speeches but I say that Sean Mulligan is a fine soldier and a fine Irishman. Here in Belfast, things are different from Dublin. We have few friends, few houses where we can hide when the RIC are after us. The people mostly are Protestant, Loyal and Orange. If they get a chance, they can't wait to call the Bobbies. They're not interested in Ireland. They're more English than the English.' He sat down and a smattering of applause broke out which was quickly taken up until the room resounded with it.

The officer at the table waited until the noise had completely died away before he spoke again. 'Well said, Finbar Martin, well said. Sean Mulligan is truly a fine man. No one at this table will deny that. But he did things in our name, robbed and stole, and not a penny piece of what he got came to Dublin for fighting the war. He does not deny any of the charges against him. Therefore, we on this court-martial have only one job to do.' He resumed his seat. His companions pulled their chairs closer together and the five began to talk earnestly amongst themselves. After a short time the men in the body of the room spoke to each other in low voices.

Suddenly the officer rose again and a stillness spread over all. 'The officers making up this court martial are unanimous in their decision. Captain Sean Mulligan, we are convinced of your guilt. You are sentenced to death by shooting. The sentence will be carried out forthwith by a Volunteer sent from Dublin especially for the purpose.' He paused before calling loudly, 'Gráinne will show herself.'

I looked at D in disbelief. 'I am to shoot this poor man in front of an audience? You must be mad. I cannot show my face like this.' D replied quickly, 'You are in no danger here. These are all brave men who will never reveal what took place here today outside the IRA. However, if it makes you feel better, I have here a mask which you can wear.' From his pocket he took a black hood with holes for eyes cut from it. He placed it on my head and pulled it down to my neck. I could see quite perfectly and nodded to him.

Immediately before I emerged into the basement I

asked, 'What happens now? How must I proceed?' D took my elbow and led me out before the watchers. He stopped in front of the table. 'I am the escort officer for Gráinne. We have heard the result of the court-martial. Before she carries out the sentence, has the accused anything else to say?' Mulligan smiled a little. 'Well, at least I won't feel anything. Make a good job of it, Gráinne, your usual perfect job.' D nodded to the officer in charge and this man walked forward and tied a cloth over Mulligan's eyes. He then touched my elbow again and positioned me facing Mulligan with my back to the room. I managed to stop my hand trembling and drew the pistol. I raised it and took aim. Behind me, someone cleared his throat, the sound seeming thunderous in the silence. Not a breath was drawn. I fired. Mulligan crashed to the floor. A low sigh came from many throats. D took my hand and led me from the scene. As he helped me to remove the mask he smiled. 'Mick knows what he's doing all right, Molly. The men in this part of the country have learned a hard lesson today. And I suppose everywhere else too. The news of this will spread like wildfire. The British will hear of it and realise that if Gráinne is sent to kill one of our own, what will she do to the enemy?'

I have no wish to dwell any longer on these events. I returned home safely. My sole consolation is that I will be with R on Friday when we travel to meet his family. I ask myself what he would say of me if he knew my secret life.

I slowly closed the book. This was the best, or worst, entry so far, depending on your point of view. The execution described by this girl from all those years ago in such detail made me cold. I feel that Molly/Gráinne has moved to a new plane. This was no ambush from inside a dark car, no firing from concealment. This was a staged and witnessed execution for the sole purpose of keeping the troops in line, what would be called today a punishment for anti-social behaviour.

My mouth was dry with a tension that had built

up while I was reading. Another quick cup of coffee, and I opened the book again.

Tuesday, June 1 1920.
Despair threatens to overcome me as I sit down to write these words. I will attempt to be as factual as possible, keeping emotions under control. On Friday evening, I walked to the harbour with my suitcase. R was waiting at the boatside. We boarded and he brought me to my cabin. I was surprised and a little hurt to discover that we were not sharing a cabin. I saw that the accommodation for those travelling alone was the same size as for couples. The only difference was that in the double cabins, the second berth was directly above the first. R explained quietly to me that, should I be unwell from the motion of the vessel, I would be more comfortable alone. He is so wise in matters of this kind. I must mention here that the day had been fine and warm in Dublin. The heat had at times been too great for comfort. As we stood on deck prior to sailing, I noticed that a strong wind had sprung up. A great bank of black cloud had turned the waters outside the harbour to an unpleasant dark-grey colour.

We sailed promptly at eight o'clock, and the ship was quite crowded. R suggested that we should go to the restaurant for a good meal. He is of the view that this is the best method of avoiding motion sickness. I was feeling well and had done so all day. Our plans were thwarted because when the vessel left the shelter of the harbour it proceeded to pitch and roll in a most unpleasant way. The crew were forced to close the restaurant. As we made our way below, I saw that the surface of the sea was covered with large areas of white foam. The considerable swell was causing the waves to break over the bow. I began to feel unwell at this point and R walked me to my cabin. I discovered how right he had been. I wished above all things to be alone. I soon became violently sick in the basin provided for the purpose. I will not detail the repeated attacks which racked me during the eight-hour crossing. When we finally docked, I was barely able to stand, so severe was the pain which I was experiencing in my abdomen. R almost carried me from boat to train where we thankfully had a first-class compartment to ourselves. He insisted upon my lying horizontally along the seats on one side. I was feeling really dreadful, but slept fitfully during the five-hour journey.

We left the train at Watford and after a lengthy wait, caught a connection to Guildford. We were met by the family chauffeur. The final stage of the journey, in a beautiful Rolls Royce, took another ninety minutes. Outside the lovely village of Trency, we finally reached Trency Hall in a state of great weariness. The time was three o'clock, our passage taking a total of nineteen hours.

We were met by R's mother, Lady Patricia Lincoln, a beautiful woman with no sign that she could be of an age to be so. She embraced me warmly and insisted that I go to my room and lie down until I should feel strong enough to join them. I enjoyed a wonderful bath, during which the pain vanished. I slept soundly until R brought a cup of tea to me at half-past seven. Dinner was at eight and I assured him that I was quite well enough to attend. After he left, I dressed, donning my blue dress, the only formal wear which I had brought with me. I descended to the large dining room where LP introduced me to R's father, Sir Montague Lincoln. He was an intimidating figure at first sight. Tall and erect, he had an almost bald head, bushy eyebrows and keen eyes. He wore a thick moustache on his rather florid face. In a loud and deep voice, he welcomed me to the house. I soon discerned that he was a little deaf, and, no doubt, this contributed to the volume of his remarks.

When we took our places, there were just the four of us, he began to ask me about my family. Upon hearing that F is a doctor, his eyebrows rose in surprise. I think that he was quite unable to understand R having a friend whose father works for a living. The moment passed and the meal proceeded enjoyably. Then, Sir Montague asked me about conditions in Ireland. Before I could answer, he said that the only way to treat what he called 'the Irish Matter' was to use military force to the maximum degree against the entire population. England is tired trying to teach those drunkards how to live their lives in something approaching civilisation. He asked me what the Irish view of 'that Collins fellow' was. When I tried to explain that General Collins is a much-loved man, I'm afraid that SM became angry. His voice became louder and his face deepened in colour. 'The man's a gangster. Should be shot like a dog. Only thing the Irish understand.' Had he been speaking about almost any other Irish figure, I would probably have sat and listened in silence. Something within forced me to take up the argument and I departed upon a long speech in favour of Irish independence. R's face became white as I spoke. I have never expressed these views to him. LP clapped her hands in delight and came to kiss me. She laughed as she said that not even the Prime Minister had spoken to her husband in such a bold fashion. I became quite embarrassed and took some wine to cover the moment.

Just then, a searing pain gripped me and I cried out, dropping the wine glass. I knew no more, and have to depend on the later accounts of R and LP to explain what had occurred. The next memory which I had was finding myself lying in a bed, in great pain. LP was sitting in a chair beside the bed. When she saw that I had awakened, she leaned over and took my hand with tenderness. When she asked me how I was feeling, I confessed to much pain and weakness. She told me not to worry. She had guessed at my condition upon my arrival and had been in two minds whether she should mention it, or wait for me to tell her. When I had cried out, I had fallen to the floor. She immediately saw that I was haemorrhaging and sent the men from the room. She called two maids, and together, all three had carried me to my room. She sent for her doctor and he confirmed her fears. I had suffered a miscarriage in the twelfth week. He suggested hospital, but LP said that I must decide that.

R had been walking the corridor for two hours, his face pale, tears in his eyes. She said softly to me that we must be very much in love. She said that he thought that I would die. She then knelt close to me and said that R must marry me without delay. I told her that I wished to see R alone. He entered the room and stood wordlessly, looking at me with fear in his eyes. Gently, I told him that the child had died. I would be ready to return to Dublin tomorrow, Sunday. He gave me the details of the journey which faced us. The boat sails at three p.m. We must catch the nine o'clock train from Guildford which calls for a seven o'clock start. He protested, but I told him that I was sufficiently recovered to undertake the trip, promising to visit my own doctor on Monday.

I am afraid that the entire return journey passed for me in a cloud of pain. I can recollect no details and though R assures me that the crossing was calm, I lay in my cabin, weak and tearful. We finally docked at seven on Sunday evening and R hired a taxi-cab to take us the short distance to my home. He was forced to come to the door with me as I was unable to stand alone. AB cried with concern when she saw me. She asked R, whom she had not met, to help her to carry me upstairs, which he did. She asked him in a most kind tone if he wished to stay with me. Before he could reply, I said that he must leave as I was aware that he was due back in quarters at half-past nine. He held my hand tightly and then turned and departed without speaking. I almost succumbed to tears, such was the look of suffering upon his face. AB removed my clothing and helped me into bed. Without a word to me, she telephoned her doctor, Doctor O'Brien, and he called within minutes. He proved to be a charming man with a friendly smile which is never far from his lips.

The sound of the hall door opening. My watch showed a quarter to eleven. I sat still, the book open on my knees. I did not turn my head as she walked in.

There was a silence, just too long to be natural. Her footsteps approached the chair from the back.

'That must be a good one. The diary.'

I half-turned. 'Oh hi, love. I didn't hear you come in.'

'Balls.' The word was short and bald. 'You're not reading. Just sitting there, waiting.'

I stood up fast and swung around. She was wearing the navy woollen dress that I liked. Her hair was in a bun, earrings, fancy stainless-steel drops. As she smiled, her red mouth seemed very wide. My hands twitched at my sides. I had never been nearer to hitting her. Maybe some day.

'I don't think it's funny coming back to an empty house, Theresa. You didn't have to go out tonight.'

'Ah, come on. Mullingar is not exactly China. Besides I've been stuck here on my own every night. Sometimes you're a very selfish man, Frank.'

Dozens of words wrestled for selection on my tongue. What came out was not exactly dynamic. 'OK. Good to see you, anyway. Give us a kiss.' It wasn't warm. It wasn't passionate. It was a kiss. Barely.

She came back after hanging up her coat. 'I see you've been catching up.' Her head nodded towards the book.

'Yes. I've read a bit. I found it under your pillow. How far have you got with it?'

'Only a page or two since the last one I told you about. I fell asleep with it last night.'

'I've caught up on her Belfast trip. That was some performance, I must say. I think it was a turning point for her. After that, she could never pretend, even to her diary, that she was being forced to carry out orders she didn't agree with.'

'I suppose you're right. The word probably flew around about the public execution of a backslider. Very powerful stuff. Anyway, to change the subject, notice anything about the house?'

I shook my head.

'I might have known. You never even noticed.

I've cleaned the place from top to bottom. Walls, paintwork, windows, the lot.'

'Give us a break. It's night and I've had a long drive. I'm not in the mood for an inspection tour.'

She sighed in a resigned sort of way. 'I'll put the kettle on. You can bring me up to date on the diary and we'll go on from there.' It turned out that she had stopped just short of where I had reached. I filled in the details. The entry for the first of June continued.

> He examined me very gently and immediately said that I should be in hospital. I have lost a great deal of blood. I declined. It is beyond thinking that my family should visit me in hospital, particularly the Rotunda. It is an establishment associated in people's minds only as a place for giving birth. Both my parents would know immediately what had occurred, F by professional observation, M by instinct. Dr O'B wrote a prescription for pills and a tonic. He also penned a letter to AC, excusing me from the office for a week. He stated that I was suffering from exhaustion, following a chill. He did these things with a good grace, accepting my decision not to enter hospital.
>
> When he had departed, AB came to my room and began to weep. I pressed for the reason. She confessed that she feared the wrath of M. My friendship with R and my subsequent condition both occurred while I was under her care. She had given her promise to treat me as a daughter. I endeavoured to put her mind at rest. I will take full responsibility for everything. I will inform my parents, should the need arise, that I have lied to her and that she knew nothing of R. After a time she ceased to weep and spoke to me as if she were, indeed, my mother. How have I met this man? Who is he? Does he come from a good family? Is he now prepared to announce our engagement? Despite my illness, I laughed at the questions. I explained about R and his family in Hampshire, which seemed to mollify her to some degree. However, when I stated that I could not marry him, she stared at me, incredulously. Am I of sound mind? Do I know what I am saying? I

said that R continues to press me to marry him. I have a perfectly good reason to refuse him, which must remain private to me. I asked for her trust in the matter. She replied, rather tartly, that it was through trusting me that she now found herself in this situation. I kissed her and said that I love her very much and that it brings me great distress to upset her so. As I was deathly tired by now, we left the matter and she departed. My strength is only enough to finish this entry.

As I closed the book, Theresa sighed. 'God, that's tough. All that's happened and she loses the baby.'

'I would have thought it best, all told. I know a miscarriage is a blow, but surely she couldn't have gone to full term? In those days, with a family like hers, cosy to the Lord of the Manor, they would have all been destroyed by her having a bastard.'

'That word makes me see red and always has. Why should the child be labelled?'

'Sorry, sorry. But that's what they called them.'

'I know. It was so unfair. Anyway, you're probably right about it being the handiest solution, although, if I know Molly, she'll be trying for a repeat asap.'

'Randy little thing, wasn't she? Couldn't get enough of our Richard. It's obvious that they slept together on a fairly regular basis.'

'Oh, I agree. Thank God she was too sensible to cover page after page with descriptions. Since that first weekend, sex hasn't really been mentioned.'

I did not reply for a minute. Then, I stabbed the air with my forefinger. 'Know what I think?'

'No.'

'I think Mrs Perry has the hots for Michael Collins.'

Her eyebrows rose and she drew a breath for reply. But it did not come. Instead, she blew out a silent whistle. 'Now that would be one for the books.

It's possible. Maybe more than possible.'

I was annoyed and let it show. 'Yeah. Imagine poor stupid Frank getting an original idea.'

She stood up. 'It's too late to start that now, Frank. Give it a rest. I'm for bed. Don't wake me when you come up.'

That was all she said, but she might as well have held up a notice. After nearly two weeks away, I should have been disappointed. But no, I'll be truthful. I was glad. Despite my thoughts of a passionate reunion, the realisation that it might – probably would – turn into another fiasco quickly dampened my powder.

Thirteen

I lay with eyes closed, allowing Saturday morning to creep gradually up on me. I was neither awake nor asleep but in that womb between. The doorbell clanged. I did not move. Again, this time on the double. Shit. I eyed the clock. Ten past fucking ten. If I stay here, they'll go away.

At the same second as the third peal, I got a sharp elbow in the back. 'Frank. The door.'

I hauled myself up, dragged on the dressing gown and went down the stairs, unsuccessfully trying to pull the heel of my left slipper from under my foot. The deadlock clicked loudly, the chain rattled like a milkman's crate of empties.

He stood outside the porch, speaking, like a large cod mouthing through a glass bowl. I slid back the door in time to catch, 'If you would not mind.'

I minded. I minded like hell. Whatever it was, I did not want any part of it. My head ached, my mouth was dry and sour-tasting. He was waiting for an answer, clearly under the impression that I had read his lips. If he had been George Bush saying 'no more taxes', I would not have cared. All I wanted was my bed.

'Sorry to bother you, old man. Hope it's not an awkward time?'

Old man. He looked twenty years older than me. Bollocks.

'What do you want?' I meant it to sound unfriendly.

'Ah yes. Well, it's like this.' He paused. 'I represent the owners of the, em, site adjoining yours.

My card.'

It came out of his pocket as if he was Tommy Cooper, on a bad night. I took it gingerly. 'Trident Insurances. Represented by PJC Walters.'

I waited. He was a medium-sized man wearing a check suit with an open red anorak over it. On his head he wore a narrow-brimmed trilby with a small green feather in the band. In his hand, he held a clipboard. 'Next door, you see.'

I did not see. I told him so.

'Sorry old man. Thought you'd got the message. Start again, shall I?'

Oh God. Go away, little man. He stayed.

'We, that is us, that is...'

I looked at the card again. 'Trident Insurances?'

'Yes. Absolutely. We start on Tuesday. Thought it only civil to tell you, old man.'

If he calls me that again...

'Start what on Tuesday?'

'Ah. Building. Rebuilding, as it were.'

I blinked. Through the haze, something was beginning to emerge. 'Trident Insurances insure the property that used to be joined to mine. When it went up in flames, you never came near me. When the wrecking crew moved in, you didn't think it only civil to warn or even tell me. Now, you are about to commence rebuilding. I will make a note of that. Thank you.'

I closed the door. Theresa often calls me pompous. Wonder why? Remembering her as I walked towards the kitchen, I thought, damned if you're getting breakfast in bed this morning. I heard her feet above and the bang of the bathroom door closing.

As I waited for the kettle to boil, she came in. To my surprise, she was dressed, and here was me in my dressing gown. Over the years, I had let her know that I did not approve of anyone appearing for breakfast, unless fully dressed.

'Make the tea, love. I'm off to get my clothes on.'

She called after me, 'Who was at the door?'

I raised my voice. 'Some idiot telling me that they're starting rebuilding next door on Tuesday.'

'Oh hell. The bloody house'll be covered in dirt and dust. Just after I've half-killed myself cleaning the windows. God, and Christmas only around the corner, too.'

The subject re-emerged at regular intervals thereafter. During breakfast. Driving to the supermarket. Pushing the trolley around. Waiting at the checkout. Loading the car. Driving home. Putting away the shopping.

After lunch, I intended watching tennis on television but rain in the south of England ruled that out. As an alternative, and to forestall any further comment about builders, I suggested that we press on with the diaries. Theresa chose to read to me.

Thursday, June 3 1920.
I am feeling much stronger and have no pain. AB insists that I rest all day, either in bed or stretched on a chaise in the drawing room. I am taking the pills and tonic as directed and Dr O calls twice each day to see me. He is very pleased with my progress.

During my hours of idleness, I have taken to reading a number of newspapers which are delivered each morning. The Irish ones are the best for daily news, and the serious English publications have learned articles on the situation in Ireland. The *Freeman's Journal*, the *Irish Times*, the *Irish Independent* and the *Cork Examiner* are the Irish newspapers which seem to me to keep a sense of proportion when reporting on the happenings around the country. Each of these, however, print some heavily biased editorial pieces. Although my loyalty to our cause is complete, I find that to ignore the other side of the struggle is childish. All loyalists are not anti-Irish, just as all nationalists are not anti-British.

The *Examiner* keeps me in touch with events in Munster and carries much news of Tipperary in general and Thurles in particular. The number of incidents involving the new recruits to the RIC (BTs) is growing daily. The frequency of IRA raids and skirmishes is also on the increase. As I read the reports, it becomes clear to me that the IRA is mainly employed in stealing guns and ammunition. Hardly a day goes by without a report of yet another bold action in which the Crown Forces (CF) are relieved of their weapons. Unless resistance is offered, they do not appear to want to injure the police or troops. In remote country areas, IRA is forming what are called 'Flying Columns', numbers of armed men who hide themselves in hedgerows, waiting for a formation of CFs. When scouts report that CFs are approaching, the road is blocked, either by felling a tree, or placing a vehicle across the carriageway. The CFs dismount from their vehicle and are called upon to surrender, when they find that they are surrounded. It is a simple and obviously effective method of gathering arms. The IRA scatter throughout the countryside, most having bicycles hidden nearby. They are also afforded shelter by the many sympathetic householders and farmers.

A sinister trait is now appearing in the reports from such incidents. It is becoming common for a detachment of BTs to return to the area of an attack and visit brutal reprisals upon the local people. The police do not appear to attempt to protect the population from such action. Over a period of four days within the last week, IRA attacks took place near the following places in Munster: Fermoy, Macroom, Nenagh, Cashel and Listowel. Nenagh was the only town not visited later by BTs. Eight innocent people were killed, in one case a man being stabbed to death with bayonets on the side of the road, and in the presence of his wife and three small children. My loss of Arthur and George seems quite civilised when compared to such savagery.

Most of Munster is still designated as a 'Special Military Area' and because of this, CFs are permitted, even encouraged, by their senior officers to carry out sudden and terrifying raids upon houses at dead of night. They expel the families from their homes, giving them no opportunity to dress properly against the cold or rain. They practically tear the houses apart and when nothing of a compromising nature is found, as is usually the case, the unfortunate householders are faced with the task of restoring the dwellings to a state where their families can re-enter them.

In Dublin, a curfew comes into force tonight. It is forbidden for any civilian to be on the streets between eight p.m. and five a.m. To ignore this order carries the danger of being shot out of hand. This will place new problems in the path of Gráinne. The police in the capital (DMP), on the other hand operate a tacit agreement with IRA that they will not work on any 'political' matters in return for their safe passage about the streets. This, of course, does not apply to the men of 'G' Division. These are intelligence officers and, as such, are a real danger to IRA. Several of them have been shot recently. Gráinne carried out one of these operations.

The *Times* published today a letter from Sir Henry Wilson, Chief of the Imperial General Staff. He writes that the whole future of the Empire hangs on the solution of 'The Irish Question'. The murderers must be apprehended without delay, appear before military tribunals and when convicted, be despatched the following day. The treatment of those found helping the criminals, carrying guns or ammunition, making seditious speeches, or gathering in groups of more than three should be the same. Those suspected of any connection with so-called freedom fighters, but against whom it is impossible to obtain evidence which would be admissible in the military courts, must immediately be interned in England. All Irish prisoners, must, in future, serve their sentences in English prisons. To this end, the Government should embark upon a programme to increase the number of prison places available. If Ireland is allowed to break free from the Empire, the word will go around the world that England is no longer master of its own destiny. Every part of the Empire will throw up people similar to De Valera and Collins, prepared to urge their fellow countrymen to flout the law of the Empire. Strife will break out on all sides. Further, Sir Henry warns that the ports and seas of Ireland provide an historical barrier to England against attack from the Atlantic, and to surrender them to these fanatical Roman Catholics would be both a great folly and an act of the basest treason.

The *Manchester Guardian* prints a leading article in a completely different vein. The writer asks whether it is either possible or morally right to continue to govern a people who will have nothing to do with the government. More and more of the Irish population are turning to the parallel administration appointed by their properly elected representatives. Ireland is, in fact if not in law, self-governing now. Surely we should encourage rather than militarily resist this unstoppable trend.

AB has just brought me a letter. It is from General Collins (Gen). He writes that he is sorry to hear of my illness. Probably D or T informed him that I was not in the office. He asks if he may call to see me here. If I agree to receive him, he will introduce himself to AB as a colleague from the Castle. Should I wish to decline, I am instructed to place a vase of flowers in the window of my bedroom before nine o'clock tomorrow morning. I will, of course, allow him to call. It is a great honour to be singled out in this manner and I am aware of the many calls upon his time.

Friday, June 4 1920

A great sense of confusion grips me. Events today have plunged me ever deeper into a situation which is not of my own making. I have often found that, when something is troubling my mind, the exercise of writing it down will help me to face the matter. I will start at the beginning. Gen called this morning and introduced himself to AB as Mr Green from the office of the Under-Secretary (AC). He was his usual charming self and quickly won her over. She served us tea and withdrew. We sat drinking tea, and he remarked upon its excellence. I promised to inform my aunt of his commendation.

When he was sure that we would not be interrupted and could not be overheard, he began to speak about 'the campaign'. Until now, we have been fighting with a view to acquiring arms and ammunition from the enemy, mainly RIC. We have such control over the Postal Service that the authorities are attempting to set up an alternative system. The rail embargo is damaging the army and police equally. It is expected that the embargo will be total within two weeks. No military or police supplies will be moved on the railways. In the provinces, RIC have retreated from hundreds of isolated barracks into more easily defended ones in the bigger towns. Patrols now operate only in numbers of twenty men or more. Even then, they dare not leave their quarters without a full military escort. In these circumstances, many troops are engaged on non-operational duties, thereby diluting the strength available to fight us. Vast areas of the country are now free of Crown Forces. We, the Volunteers, or IRA as we are better known, have established Land Tribunals in many places. The people are not alone bringing their cases to be decided by these courts, they are accepting the judgements handed down there. A number of properly qualified magistrates are sitting on such courts. Local events, such as horse racing or football games, are now being policed by Volunteers, many of them unarmed. Again, the spectators are accepting our men and give no trouble. RIC is now a completely discredited force. Morale is non-existent. They have been ostracised by the people of Ireland, a much more difficult thing to accept than being opposed with arms. That they could fight. One cannot fight silence. The constables are the loneliest men in Ireland. A consequence of this is that there is now no intelligence-gathering outside Dublin. Resignations from RIC are increasing every day. The newly arrived reinforcements from England, now officially known by the name given them in Limerick, Black and Tans (BTs), will make things more difficult for us but, on the other hand, any brutality against the people will send them into our ranks.

I had been sitting listening closely to his words. As

he paused momentarily, I ventured to interject. Why are you taking this time to instruct me, a very junior Volunteer, in such weighty matters? For a moment, I feared that I had angered him. He looked at me with those eyes which seem to burn with an inner fire. He nodded his head several times, saying 'Yes, yes, yes.' I clearly recall the words he used then and I will put them down here. 'It is true, Molly, that you are a single Volunteer in our movement, and as such, are not involved in forming policy matters. The future will show you that this will not always be the case. Listen very closely to what I now say to you. There exists in Ireland another revolutionary body besides IRA. Very few people know of its existence, and indeed, it has few members. But it is of great importance to Ireland, even greater than IRA. The name of this organisation is the Irish Republican Brotherhood (IRB). It is a secret body, where IRA is well known and acknowledged. The difference between the two bodies is that IRB is involved with secret political planning, while IRA is engaged in fighting. When freedom is won, and do not doubt that it will be won, the new nation of the Irish Republic will need a strong government. The role of IRB is to prepare for that day. I am President of the Supreme Council of IRB. We are a government in waiting. When the time is ripe, we will reveal ourselves. Our freedom, now being fought for with such bravery by our colleagues, will be placed in the hands of people who carry on the true spirit of the Fenians. IRB organised the Easter Rising and the Proclamation of Independence. It is our sworn duty to bring Ireland into the community of nations, not as a socalled democracy. The only true democracy is the Democracy of the People. Like our brothers and sisters in Russia, we will set up a truly socialist state here. I call on you, Molly, to join IRB. This is not the same as when you joined IRA. You will become a member of a 'secret society' with all that the term implies. Society does not like such bodies as ours. We are few, but, working from inside the existing state, we bring about changes out of all proportion to our size.'

He paused again and sat back in his chair, his eyes

upon my face, perhaps looking for clues as to how I was receiving his words. His voice had been low during his address to me but his sincerity shone through each and every word. I must confess that I was extremely confused. My only motive in taking part in the fighting is anger at the murder of my brothers, and a desire to act for F in resisting British rule. I have given little or no thought to my position, should I survive should England leave Ireland. The words of Gen seem to point to a longer and deeper involvement in affairs. I am twenty years of age and love a man who returns my feelings. My horizon is filled with these things. What more can anyone want from life?

Gen, as I have often said, is a most persuasive man. Whenever I listen to him speaking, be it at a rally, or, as in this instance, face to face, I am ready to do his bidding. I did so on this occasion. I nodded to him and he took my hand in his. 'I will swear you in. No Bible is needed and no witnesses are necessary. Neither is it necessary to sign anything. You swear to me and only I will know of your membership. Repeat after me. 'I swear that I willingly become a member of the Irish Republican Brotherhood. I know that my membership is for life, ended only by my death, and is irrevocable. I swear loyalty and obedience to IRB and will be bound from this moment to carry out orders of the Supreme Council and any person who may from time to time be a member of that Council. I will never reveal my membership or any details of IRB, under pain of death.' I repeated his words and as I listened to my voice, I realised that I was making a lifelong commitment, from which only death could release me. Gen smiled at the manner in which my voice trembled and retained my hand in his throughout. He resumed his remarks to me.

'Now that you are sworn in, I will give you your first task. You will continue to act as Gráinne whenever your superiors decide. Apart from these occasions, Gráinne will become my personal hand, within IRB, striking out where I require it. This arrangement will be known to us alone and must not be discussed with any other person. This, Molly, is the secret bond which binds us.' His voice fell silent and it was several seconds before I realised that he had finished. To my complete surprise, he lowered his lips to the back of my hand and kissed it for a long moment. He stared into my eyes and said, 'The future is ours, Molly. We will, together, write the next glorious chapter in the history of Ireland.'

He rose quickly, and without looking at me said that my arrangements for contact have been changed. I am ordered to go, each day, between one and two o'clock, to the Public Library in Capel Street. If he is not present, the librarian, Mr Guy, will deal with me. He is completely trustworthy. These arrangements do not apply to Saturday or Sunday, when the telephone number which I have been using until now will be in operation.

Before I could speak, Gen left the room and I heard the hall door close. AB came running. She was most disappointed that my visitor had departed without seeing her again. I said that he had a great deal of work to perform.

When the cobwebs of sleep drifted away, I saw that it was almost ten. Sunday! I heaved myself out of bed. Theresa's voice came from under the duvet.

'Frank? I'm not feeling great. I'm going to stay here.'

'What's the matter? Brewing a cold?'

'My stomach is sick.'

'Something you ate?'

A trace of irritation showed. 'I don't know, for God's sake. I was up at six, getting sick. You never budged.' The tone had depths of criticism for a husband who had slept soundly through it all.

'OK, love. I'll bring up your breakfast.'

'I don't want anything.'

'Nothing at all?'

'All right, a cup of tea. Not too strong. Go on down, Frank. I'm really not in the mood for a chat.'

I shrugged, made for the bathroom and washed my face. I pulled on a sweater and trousers. Mass could wait. Probably until evening. If at all.

When I carried up the tea, she was in the bathroom. I could hear her retching. 'God love, you don't sound so good. You're a bit green around the gills, all right.'

She wordlessly slipped under the duvet and took the cup. Her eyes had black circles under them and her face was the colour of putty. I left her and went for my own breakfast.

A shave later, I felt better myself. I tidied up, peeled a few potatoes for dinner, carpet-swept downstairs and reported. She was asleep.

I did the obvious. Took the diary down and settled in the kitchen.

Tuesday, June 8 1920.

On Saturday, I ventured a short walk, the first time I have left the house. I made my way to Dr O'Bs surgery. He expressed himself well pleased with my progress. After a thorough examination, during which he managed to put me at my ease – not an easy task, in the circumstances – he recommended a further week's convalescence. He wrote another letter to AC, detailing his prognosis. I shall, with luck, be fit to return to the office on Monday, 14th June.

I called to the Public Library which is a short distance from home, and looked through books in the section devoted to Irish history. Alas, there was nothing relating to IRB or the Fenian movement. I must remain dependent on Gen to instruct me in the origins of the organisation in which I now find myself.

I returned home, feeling rather tired. AB made me some tea, and I lay on my bed, resting. A notion with which I have been struggling ever since Gen left me on Friday, once more attempted to force itself into my mind. I cannot continue to pretend that it is not present, so I will consider it now. This may appear fanciful, but I think that Gen is interested in me, not only as a Volunteer and IRB member, but also as a woman. I have come to this conclusion as a result of his attitude towards me, rather than any words which he has spoken. The manner in which he looked at me, held my hand and finally kissed it, impressed me powerfully. I feel almost traitorous towards R by merely writing this, but the situation exists and I must confront it. I am in love with R. Of this there can be no doubt. I cherish our moments together and I will always regret losing his child from my body. He is kind and gentle, ever seeking to please me, whether in some small matter, or in our most intimate times. An emotion of a different kind awakens in me when I think of Gen. When I am in his presence, he seems to fill the entire world. I want to do anything which I can to please him. He has broad shoulders, it is true, but they carry awesome responsibility. I want to lighten this burden. I shock myself by even considering that I could offer him the comfort of my arms. If I really felt that he needed me in that way, could I resist? Do I wish to? Do I intend to? R, my love, how can I allow such thoughts to intrude upon my mind? I do not wish them to, but I cannot deny them. Please forgive me.

A laugh escaped me as I closed the book. So I was right. This would show her ladyship. When I went upstairs with the diary, she was sitting in front of the dressing table making up her face.

She put down the lip-brush and smiled at my reflection. I smiled back.

'You must be feeling better. Up and about, I see.'

'About what?' She winked, a thing which she can do very effectively.

'Come on, Theresa. Earlier on, you were puking your guts up. I'm just glad to see you better, that's all.'

'I know, love. I'm an awful tease, aren't I? The tummy's settled down OK. Put the kettle on, there's a pet. I'm starving.'

That was how I ended up cooking a fry for her. She ploughed into it with a will. It vanished in five minutes. She was good enough to let me wash up, as well. What a wife.

She looked across the table at me. 'I never asked you last night. How did Mullingar go? Any trouble with Reidy?'

'It worked out as well as it could. I had to put him in his place several times. Eleven days is not bad considering.'

She paused for a moment, watching my face. Her eyes held a strange expression. 'How is it, Frank, that you can handle a man like Michael Reidy so well, when you're completely the other way at home with me?'

I was cautious, seeing several traps yawning in my path. 'I'm not sure what you mean. I'm not any different at home than I am in the office. I suppose I'm more relaxed with you.'

Her head shook. 'I don't think so. Quite the opposite, in fact. At work, you seem to take things in your stride. With me, you're always...well... defensive, I suppose I mean. Taking offence all the time, starting rows but not able to carry them through. You know what I mean?'

I was getting exasperated. 'No, I don't know what you mean. Are you saying that I'm hard to live with?'

She spoke slowly, drawing her words out. 'Not hard to live with, no. If it was anyone else I was talking about, I'd know what to say. But with you, well to tell the truth, I'm half-afraid to say anything. You get narky so easily these days.'

I was not far from getting narky now, which I suppose, proved her point. 'Let's forget it for now. Sunday morning is no time for deep discussions like this. Tell you what. Why don't I pour a Bailey's for us? Then we can sit down and look at the diaries again.'

Half an hour later, we were sitting silently, each full of our own thoughts. I told her about Collins and Molly.

She shook her head in wonder. 'Now that's something I never knew about Collins. His women. I suppose he must have had some. Unless he was gay, of course.'

This was, I knew, a dart at my irritability. I could never use that term. Men of that sort were either queer, or homosexual. This time, I did not rise to the bait. She lifted the book and started to read the entry. I glanced through the paper while waiting for her to get to where I had stopped.

'Wow, this is getting very heavy. It would make a good mini-series. It has everything, murder, heroism, love, sex. Let's see where it goes from here.'

Fourteen

Wednesday, 16 June 1920
I am alone in the house. AB is visiting friends and R is on duty. I have much to occupy my mind. Since Gen's visit, I have been prey to a mass of contradictory emotions. His feelings for me, my thoughts of him and the love which R and I have for each other, pull me first one way and then the other. Nothing is to be gained by useless dwelling on matters which cannot be altered.

And so to my other life. I returned to the Castle on Monday. AC welcomed me back and was most kind in his enquiries concerning my health. I am very well. I was pleased to take up the routines of the office once again. AC called me to his office and showed me his desk. It was completely covered with papers and files. It was these latter which were causing him concern. During my absence, he drew files every day from Registry. He was however, unable to find the time to return them to their proper place. This he now requested me to do, with an unnecessary apology for the trouble which he was causing to me. I set to with a will and succeeded in clearing a great many files in a relatively short time.

At eleven o'clock, I was carrying a number of files to Registry. The one on the top of the bundle was coloured red, a signal that the contents were for the attention of AC alone. What gave me pause is more than I can tell. I slipped into an empty room off the corridor and quickly opened the red file. On its cover was the letter 'G'. As I leafed through the documents, there being many sheets, I realised that this was the file of secret communications between AC and DMP G Division.

My heart almost missed a beat as I read. The Deputy Commissioner had written to AC, outlining a plan to enable the police to capture Gen. The details are as follows. Two men in the employ of Detective Inspector Ruane are to play the pivotal roles in the scheme. They are John O'Leary, of Sackville Place, and Terence Doyle, of Prussia Street. These men are members of IRA, having joined the organisation three months earlier. Their comrades suspect nothing. On Monday, they will report to Gen that they have captured a man suspected of informing. He has been sought by us for some time. He is being held captive in a house in Clontarf. Gen is invited to take part in his interrogation, as the man is thought to have much valuable information. As soon as Gen arrives in the house, a massive force of troops and police will seal the area. They will close upon the house and capture him, dead or alive. AC prefers the former state. He has pencilled a remark in the margin of the top document. 'A dead man cannot be rescued.'

The treachery of the two spies almost caused me to become weak. A great anger, similar to the emotion which had assailed me after the murder of Arthur and George, swept through me. I consulted my watch. The break for luncheon would begin in less than two hours. The time for the operation was shown as three p.m. I had enough time.

As soon as I left the Castle, I hastened across the river to Capel Street. The Library is at the Mary Street section, on the left-hand side. I entered and thought that I was the only person present. After I had waited in puzzlement for some sign that I had come to the correct place, a tall thin man emerged from behind a book shelf. He approached me, a kindly smile upon his face. I asked if he had a book of poems by W. B. Yeats. He enquired whether the volume which I was seeking had been published by 'Freedom Press'. This being the pre-arranged sequence of words, he shook my hand and led me to a door at the rear of the library. He knocked twice in rapid succession, opened the door and closed it after I had entered.

Gen was seated at a table, speaking with two men whom I did not know. He glanced up and signalled that I should sit down and wait. His face showed no sign of welcome and his whole demeanour was curt. The men continued to speak in undertones for some minutes. They eventually rose and left the room. Gen looked at me and nodded for me to approach. I stood in front of the table. 'You have a report, Volunteer Stewart?' I said that I had and he asked me to elaborate. Instead of doing so, I asked, 'Have you an arrangement to visit a house in Clontarf today?' His eyes narrowed and I felt a great tension gather within him. 'What do you know of this?' I replied that it was a trap. He did not speak, clearly waiting for me to continue. I related the facts which I had gleaned from the file. His expression showed no surprise. In fact, he smiled broadly as I finished my story. 'Good work, Volunteer. The movement is in your debt.' I said that I was doing my duty and he nodded in dismissal.

As I left the library and walked back across the bridge, it occurred to me that Gen's attitude towards me when on duty was very different to his manner on more personal occasions. The remainder of the day passed very quickly in normal duties. I felt quite fatigued when it was over. Dr O'B has warned me that it would be so until I have regained my full strength.

Again, on Tuesday, yesterday, I visited the library as ordered. I went directly to the room at the back, the librarian giving no sign that he had seen me. Gen was absent, the table being occupied by D and T. They welcomed me, asking after my health. T said that the English had enjoyed an easy time during my absence and that it was time to 'stir them up again'. D said that they had a job for me that evening. I asked whether it could be carried out before eight o'clock and both men laughed. They reassured me that I would be 'tucked up with a book' long before curfew. D gave me the address of a house in Camden Street. The place is above a shop. I will call there at six o'clock and T will admit me. I am to ensure that I carry my revolver with me.

I carried out the instructions and at the correct time, I was admitted to the premises by T. He signalled that I must avoid making unnecessary noise. He led me into a darkened room in which I could scarcely see anything. After some moments however, I could make out a floor-length curtain covering an entrance to a second room. A chair was placed close to the curtain and I was ordered to sit there. T placed his lips close to my ear and whispered that I was to remain there, unless or until I was asked to move. I must listen to whatever takes place behind the curtain, while giving no sign that I am there. He left me and I heard the sounds of footsteps. I was reminded of that dreadful day in Belfast.

A sharp voice rang out. 'Prisoners stand. This court-martial is convened today, Tuesday 15th June 1920. It consists of three officers of the Irish Republican Army, properly appointed to act. The accused are John O' Leary and Terence Doyle.' Upon hearing this, I sat up in the chair. These were the men who had plotted to capture Gen. The voice continued. 'You are each charged that on or before today, Tuesday 15th June 1920, you did conspire with members of the traitorous, so-called Dublin Metropolitan Police and agents of the occupying forces of the British Crown, to cause, or attempt to cause, the capture, wounding or death of members of the Irish Republican Army, such conspiracy being in breach of the oath taken by you on your induction into the Irish Republican Army. How do you plead, John O' Leary?' There was a short silence and something was said which I was unable to hear clearly. 'Louder.' This time, a weak voice replied, 'Guilty.' 'Terence Doyle?' 'Guilty.'

Further murmurs proceeded through the curtain. A different voice now spoke. 'You have each pleaded guilty, as charged. There is only one sentence which the court-martial can pass in such cases. You will be shot to death by an agent or agents of the Irish Republican Army, at a time and place to be decided by others. May God have mercy on your souls. This court-martial is dismissed. God Bless the Irish Republic.'

Listening to the proceedings, I reflected that this court-martial was undoubtedly conducted in a more formal way than that in Belfast, where words from the attendance were allowed without causing any disturbance. I rather fancied that any interruptions here would be severely dealt with.

A door opened and I heard the movement of feet. After some time, T returned. Still speaking in a whisper, he asked if I had heard the proceedings. I nodded. He said that I had been appointed to carry out the sentences. I asked when this would be done and he replied, 'Now.' He pulled aside the curtain, revealing the other room. It held a wooden table and two chairs. Two men were sitting in the chairs, secured by ropes. Their heads were covered in black hoods, and they were facing away from me.

T picked up a cushion from the floor and placed it against the back of the head of one man. He nodded to me and I pushed the muzzle of the gun against the cushion and fired one shot. The sound was muffled and the body slumped in the chair, still held by the rope. The second man began to weep and plead for mercy. T repeated his action with the cushion and nodded. Again, the sound was not loud.

I did not look at the bodies and T led me from the room. He appeared to expect that I would exhibit some signs of shock at what I had just done. Such was not the case. I am fighting a war and everything which I have done has been towards this end. As had been promised to me, I arrived home no later than a quarter past seven.

Today I received another task at the Library. Again T and D were the only ones present. The plan was explained to me in detail and events occurred in exactly the way I was instructed. We are to 'mark' a man called Thomas Ruane. I remembered the surname from the 'G' file which I had seen on Monday. I enquired if this was the same man, and I was told that it was. He lives at number 11 Sinnot Street, behind Blessington Street.

At a quarter-past six, I arrived at a café called O'Dowd's on the corner of Blessington Street and Dorset Street. T and D were sitting at a table where I joined them. I made a show of drinking a cup of tea and we left at half-past six. T and I walked along Blessington Street together, with D walking alone, some yards behind us. At the corner of the laneway leading to Sinnot Street, T dropped back to join D. They made a play of being friends, talking animatedly. I proceeded to number 11 and rang the bell.

After a moment, a young woman opened the door. I asked if Mr Ruane was in, and when she assured me that he was, further enquired whether I could see him. I said that I was from his office and that some minor matter which needed his attention had arisen. She asked me to wait. From the corner of my eye, I observed D and T moving close to the house. At that moment, a very tall man appeared at the door. He was heavily built with a large friendly face and wore spectacles. He was not wearing a coat or jacket, being dressed in a shirt, trousers and braces. As soon as he saw me, he obviously smelt a rat and endeavoured to push the door closed, at the same time calling urgently, 'The gun, Jane. Bring the gun.'

D and T hurled themselves at the door, forcing it open further and propelling me forward into the hallway. Ruane staggered backwards and fell to the floor. T produced a gun and pointed it at him. D stood aside, allowing me to stand directly in front of Ruane as he rose from the floor. At that moment, the young woman, whose name was presumably Jane, rushed from the inside room, a gun in her hand. Ruane, who could be none other than her father, called, 'Put the gun on the floor, Jane, and go back inside. Pull the door after you.' His tone betrayed neither fear nor anger. Slowly she did as she had been told, tearfully speaking in a low voice. 'Don't shoot Daddy. He's all I have. Mammy died last year. Please don't hurt him.'

Her father looked at T with eyebrows raised, a question in his gaze. T nodded slightly and the policeman went to the woman, although I now saw that she was no more than a girl. He put his arms around her and whispered in her ear. She began to weep and her body trembled uncontrollably. Her father gently turned her around and moved her out of the hallway, closing the door. He turned and rejoined us near the hall door.

'So you have come for me, then? I know you well, Diarmuid, and you, Turlough. The lady...?'

D said softly, 'Tom, I'd like you to meet Gráinne.'

Ruane's eyes grew round. He whispered, as if to

himself, 'So young. So beautiful.' He addressed me directly for the first time. 'I'll tell you this much, Miss. Your name causes more naked fear than Mick himself.' He pulled himself erect and removed the spectacles, placing them in his pocket. He looked into my eyes and said gently, 'Don't worry yourself, my dear. I know you don't bear me any grudge. Like all of us, you have to do what you're told.' Speaking to the men, he added, 'I could never admit it before, lads, but I think you're going to win this time. The people are with you. Well, let's get it over with.' To me, 'Where would you like me to stand?'

I swallowed and whispered, 'Where you are, sir. I'm sorry to do this.' I took my gun from my handbag, aimed it at his head and fired one shot. The sound echoed around the little hallway and before it had died away, Ruane lay dead, a thick ooze of red spreading around his shattered head. The door of the room flew open and the girl rushed out. She stopped as if struck. Her eyes moved between the gun in my hand and her father's fallen form. For a moment, the hallway was quiet, then a strange high-pitched moaning sound arose from her.

D turned. 'That is how gentlemen die, Gráinne. Always remember this moment. It may stop you turning into the killing machine they want.' His voice became urgent. 'Let's be on our way. If we're here much longer, we'll be at the funeral.' The words galvanised us and we ran from the house. Our paths divided, with D running down a small laneway towards Mountjoy Street and a tram to the Phoenix Park, T making for Dorset Street, and I walking along Blessington Street. I caught a tram for Kingstown at Nelson's Pillar.

The memory of the dead man will remain with me for a very long time. It is the first time that I have actually spoken to any of my targets, and the experience has affected me powerfully. I will, of course, continue to carry out orders, but I will approach the resulting deaths with much more reflection. Truthfully, I shall never forget Thomas Ruane.

Thursday, June 17 1920

When I arrived home this evening, a letter awaited me. I recognised F's hand on the envelope. This is a very disturbing communication. The situation in Thurles had worsened considerably. The RIC barracks now houses a party of some twenty BTs. They patrol the streets in groups of five or more. The people have taken to crossing the street when a patrol is seen. It is best to keep one's eyes fixed upon the ground. Anyone, be they man, woman or child, who is seen openly looking in the direction of a BT is immediately stopped and searched. Men appear to cope with this procedure quite well, but it is terrifying for children and ignominious for women. The person being searched must raise his hands in the air while one BT stands directly behind him pressing the muzzle of his pistol against the back of his head. The searcher, his weapon holstered, runs his hands over the entire body of the suspect. In the case of girls or women, the watching BTs cry aloud vulgar observations while their colleague allows his hands to linger on certain parts of the body. Many of those searched, despite the searches proving futile, are then marched at gunpoint to the barracks and taken inside. They are usually released after an hour or so, but none will speak of their treatment while inside. It is clear that they are warned that any such talk will result in even worse treatment for themselves and their families.

The town is further terrorised by the habit of BTs discharging their weapons into the air and emitting fierce cries as they do so. The people are openly referred to as 'Fenians' , or, more frequently, 'Shinners', a term derived from the name Sinn Féin.

F continues that his real reason for writing to me is because a party of BTs called to the house on Friday night last, at ten o'clock in the evening. They drove up the drive in an armoured car, threatening to knock the door down unless it was opened immediately. F came to the door to ask for an explanation. The officer in charge said that the police records for the area show that his two sons had attacked an army patrol. As a result, they, the BTs, wished to search the house and all inside must assemble on the grass. As luck would have it, the girls are still at school. F and M, together with Anna, the cook, and Patricia and Susan, the maids, were forced to watch the band of drunken louts marauding through the house, breaking windows, emptying drawers on to the ground outside and overturning cupboards. The two horses which F keeps at the rear, with the permission of LM, naturally, were brought out and sent fleeing in terror as the men discharged their rifles above the animals' heads. As the party of BTs left, the officer told F that the Stewart family was well known in the town as Shinners. Any further resistance to the Crown Forces in the townland of Thurles will result in his arrest and the eviction of M and the servants from the house. I quote his final words. 'Molly dear, if anything happens to me, carry on the fight. Perhaps you should mention the matter to someone who should know of it.'

I reported the contents of the letter to Gen in the library today. He said that he would ask local units to 'keep an eye on things'. A deep fear holds me in its grasp. I am unable to weep, so strong is my foreboding. Should I travel to Thurles to be with them at this dangerous time? I am unable to write anything further tonight.

Fifteen

With the usual faultless timing shown by such things, a one-day flu bug found me during Sunday night and I was unable to go to the office on Monday. The worst symptom from the medical perspective was the high temperature which caused me to change my pyjamas four times during the day.

However, from a purely personal standpoint, what made the day so very bad was the three hours of almost non-stop diarrhoea from the moment of my early wakening until noon. Theresa left me to handle the nuts and bolts of this alone. There can hardly be a more undignified human condition than one which causes the sufferer to spend three hours sitting on the lavatory.

I could not summon any interest in the diaries, and Theresa decided to devote herself to her computer during the day. She had been avoiding it for some time and a few of her clients were becoming a little annoyed.

In the event, her own dicky tummy returned during the later part of the day and she decided to call on Doctor Cullen on Tuesday. She asked me to leave her asleep when I got up that morning, so I carried my clothes into the bathroom where I shaved and dressed. I was feeling reasonably recovered by then, if a trifle fragile.

It was a fine summer morning as I tried to pull the door quietly closed behind me. I heard a sound as I unlocked the car. A big lorry was pulling into the kerb outside. I saw four men get down and gather at the tailgate. I walked over.

'Morning, men. You the builders?'

'Aye.' The Cavan accent was pronounced in that one word. If it is a word. Also pronounced was a clear dislike for approaches at this time of the morning.

I tried a smile. 'Just making sure you don't block me off. You're on the job early.'

Cavan was definitely in charge. 'Your gate is clear. As for the time, there's a power of things to be done before the building starts.'

'Oh, I'm sure. There is one thing, though. The wife is not too well. She's still asleep. Will there be much noise?'

'Divil the noise at all. We'll be cleaning the site.' He nodded towards a large covered shape on the back of the lorry. 'That's a shelter there. We'll be putting it in the garden. We'll have to rig a bit of a lock and chain for it. For minding the tools, like.'

He turned to his companions. The conversation was over as far as he was concerned.

As soon as I arrived in the office, I made a start on my report of the Mullingar trip. Craddock was sure to be shouting for it following my absence yesterday and if it was in progress, I could reasonably claim that I was doing my best. Despite the temptation to go to town on Reidy, I had decided to keep it purely factual.

As Belinda deposited the first two pages of the finished product, the tea trolley arrived. I sipped the tasteless, grey water, trying to make sure that the inevitable drops on the base of the cardboard cup did not find their way on to the virginal sheets. I searched for a telling phrase which would not reveal that the operators in Mullingar knew more about computers than I did.

The phone on my desk buzzed. The red light showed that Craddock was on the line.

'Good morning, Mr Doorly. I trust you have recovered. The trip was successful?'

'Good morning, sir. Sorry about yesterday. Everything went very well in Mullingar. I'm actually writing...'

He cut in. He was good at that because he got plenty of practice. 'Never mind the report. I can read that later.'

I was puzzled. If he was not chasing the report, why the call?

'I would like you to come up. One or two things to discuss.'

Oh oh. Bells rang in my brain. Something must have gone wrong while I was away. I felt a little peeved that no one had tipped me off.

As usual, he kept his head bent when I arrived and I had to wait the obligatory minute until he looked at me. To my surprise, he smiled. Actually, really smiled. There's a first time for everything.

'Ah, Mr Doorly. Frank. Sit down, sit down.'

My antennae were probing the air in alarm. It had to be a trap. Either that, or the old shit had finally gone bananas.

He looked at me like a spider watching a juicy fly walking towards the web. Anticipation was the word. I swallowed, prepared for a full frontal assault.

'I have some news for you, Frank.' God, if he was going to carry on like this, I might very well give him a hefty thump. On the other hand, I might not.

He slid open a drawer in his desk and lifted a folder out. It was thin and coloured green. A bit like me at the moment. He placed it on the blotter and slowly opened it. If he says 'Frank Doorly, this is your life', I swear I'll... Having read the top document, he smiled again. Other than a wild desire to shout, 'What the fuck do you want?', I could not think of a word to say.

'I have here,' he tapped the file with his knuckle and corrected himself. Another first. 'This is the notification of the result of the deliberations of the Interview Board.'

I waited. If he wanted to go on playing silly buggers, let him. I already knew the result. As I said before, Craddock does not concern himself with failures.

He half-left his chair and stretched his hand towards me. I rose and took it. The grip was, at best, limp.

He expelled air from his lungs, expanding his cheeks. He looked like a saxophone player searching for that high note.

'Well, heartiest congratulations, Frank.' His official look slipped for a second as he said, 'Thank God those fools got it right for once.'

'Very kind of you to say so, sir.'

'Now, about the position itself. It is a new post, so you cannot rely on the previous incumbent for guidelines. The Minister has asked for the services of a senior officer with, and I quote her, 'a hands-on knowledge of the Department'. I understand this term to mean an officer who can turn his hand to any aspect of education. We, like the other Departments of State, keep a strong staff in Brussels to assist the Minister in aspects of European legislation concerning education either directly or indirectly.'

As he paused for breath, I tried to discover exactly the meaning of what he had just said. I failed. Like cancer, an awful thought grew in my mind.

'Excuse me, sir. You are not suggesting that the post involves moving to Brussels?'

'No. I was informed that was made clear at the interview. You will be expected to travel over there, or to other destinations from time to time. Present policy relating to officers not actually seconded to EU encourages them to take their spouses, or, ah, partners when travelling abroad for longer than seventy-two hours.'

Jesus, wasn't Mrs Doorly going to lap that up. I could already hear the cries of 'But what will I wear, Frank? I haven't got a thing'.

Craddock rambled on for another twenty minutes. The sum of what he said was: based in Dublin, downstairs in a large office of my own, to be exact; I would be known as 'Sub-Secretary (European Union Liaison)'. My job will be to provide the Minister with the Dapartment's views on any projected or current European legislation. This is expected to call on me to travel over quite often. In most cases, it is envisaged that I will travel in the Government jet. When my presence is required in Brussels, 'up the sprout' in Departmental jargon, I will be given a minimum of forty-eight hours' notice. The official reasoning behind basing me in Dublin is that the Minister wishes to have me 'on her team and not a part of the Brussels coterie'.

When he had finished pontificating, Craddock produced another unheard-of surprise. 'Take a couple of days off, Frank. Give you time to get used to the idea. Great things are expected of you. The Minister is said to be 'delighted'. See you on, shall we say, Wednesday. Come in when you feel like it. No more clock-watching. Within reason, of course,' he finished, doing his usual job of covering his back from every angle.

I completed the report toute suite, read over the typescript and signed it. I gave Belinda instructions to give it to Craddock just before five.

I sang all the way home. Is that the title of a pop song?

When I stopped in the driveway, I noticed the men from the morning. They were standing on the concrete base of what I will always call Mrs Perry's house. Mary? Molly? Gráinne? The Cavan man nodded in greeting but remained where he was.

I got out of the car, eager to see Theresa. The

promotion. I knew that she would be walking on air about that. She never tried to interfere with the way I did my job, but I knew that she felt I did not push myself enough. This job would delight her, not for the extra money, or even the grand-sounding title. It would thrust me forward into the sight of the Minister. I could become one of her most influential advisers.

My arrival brought no response from inside. The house was empty. Tidy, but empty. The mantel clock said five past two. Where the hell was she? Of course. Cullen's surgery hours on a Monday were two until four. Or were they?

A cup of tea sounded nice while I waited. I slapped a slice of transparent ham between two thick slices of Saturday's bread. I took the food to the table, switching on the radio. Some genius was asking Marion Finucane why he kept getting parking tickets when he left his car daily on a double yellow line on a clearway. He said that it was a small car.

I went to the cupboard to get a diary. The Sunlight Soap carton was there, empty. I swore. Wait a minute though. She had been cleaning last week. Theresa was a menace when the bug hit her. Anything not nailed down could vanish for months. I had grown accustomed to her habits in this regard over the years. Things with no fixed place usually ended up in the attic.

Twenty minutes later, I stood on the landing below the trap. I was filthy, my clothes were covered in grime, but I had the diaries. She had put them into an old case, a survivor from the honeymoon. It had been wedged behind the water tank, low down in the roof space. I had glimpsed it by chance as I was about to abort the search. I was far from blessing Theresa as I wriggled on my chest across the joists until my outstretched fingers closed on the handle.

I stripped off, ran a quick shower and climbed

into jeans and a teeshirt. With a piece of rag I wiped most of the dirt off the case. I left it in the bedroom, pushed well under the bed, taking the next two books in sequence.

By a quick count of the remainder, I judged that we were well into the final phase, which made me think that maybe we did not have all the books. God, that would be a bummer. However, I would cope with the problem when I came up against it.

Monday, June 28 1920

F has been arrested. He has been held in Thurles RIC Barracks since Thursday night. The shattering news was given me by AB when I arrived home today. She had received a telephone message from Lady M this morning. She was, understandably, rather incoherent. Herself and LM have been attempting to contact me over the weekend. The telephones to both F's house and the Manor were not in working order until today. Efforts to send a telegram were fruitless, the post office clerk having been ordered not to serve anyone from the Estate. AB only pieced the story together during the day, when she placed several calls to the house, speaking to Anna.

The BTs arrived at three a.m. on Friday. They kicked in the door and four of them ran up the stairs. Moving from room to room, they discharged their guns repeatedly into the ceilings, doing a great deal of damage to them. M, F and the servants were pulled roughly from their beds and pushed and dragged to the hall. An officer addressed F. A constable had been shot three hours before in the town. F replied that all the members of the household were in bed long before that time. The officer then struck F across the face, drawing blood. He was told that silence was required from all. M and he were placed under arrest. They were bundled into the tender, still in their night attire, and driven off.

At the house, pandemonium reigned. Anna sent Susan up to the manor house. After some difficulty, she was granted access and related the events to His

Lordship. He instructed her to return to the house and secure it as best she could. She was to return to the manor house with Anna and Patricia, when shelter would be provided for them.

LM drove to the town and called to the barracks. According to his later account to AB, he demanded to see the officer in charge. A uniformed inspector emerged. Upon hearing of the arrests, he said that he knew nothing of the matter. He expressed regret, adding that the BTs are not under his command and do not recognise his rank. When asked what charges had been levelled, he retired inside the building. Returning, he said that no charges had been laid. The prisoners were helping with enquiries. He apologised to LM. No access to them was possible and LM should go home. If he returned in the morning, he, the inspector, would endeavour to obtain further information.

LM returned to the barracks at nine o'clock in the morning. He was seen by a BT officer. The matter was still under investigation. Once again, access was denied him. He endeavoured to protest and the officer warned him to be careful. They, the BTs, knew well that he, LM, had given shelter to Fenians and he should consider himself fortunate to have retained his liberty. Any further protest in this case could result in his own arrest.

Upon his return to the Manor House he placed a telephone call to Lord French, the Lord Lieutenant. LL was unavailable and an aide promised to relay the substance of LM's call to him as soon as possible. Two further calls were placed, to Mr Macpherson, the First Secretary, and to Lieutenant-General Shaw, General Officer Commanding, in Command, the highest military authority. In neither instance was he connected to the person whom he sought and he left similar messages to the one he had left for LL.

The remainder of the weekend passed in a series of attempts on his part, with great courage, to visit F and M. All failed. At six a.m. on Monday, a man called Michael Supple, one of the estate workers, arrived at our house in a horse-drawn cart. M was sitting beside him, clad only in a horse blanket. She was in a piteous state, weeping and laughing hysterically by turn. She had been released, naked, on to the street at dawn and Mr Supple, in town to collect a parcel from the station, had come upon her wandering about, quite unaware of her nakedness. Lady M immediately took her into her personal care, treating her with great kindness, for which I will always be grateful. M was unable to remain calm and the town's second doctor called on Lady M's instructions. He provided a sedative mixture and M is sleeping. I will travel to Thurles tomorrow. My heart is heavy.

Thursday, July 1 1920.

My darling father is dead. At ten this morning, a military tender arrived at the house. From it, a sealed coffin was unloaded and placed upon the ground outside the front door. The BT officer said to me that F had attempted to escape and had jumped from a second-storey window. His injuries were mortal. I was ordered to ensure that the coffin was not opened or interfered with in any way. The funeral must be confined to immediate family. Should any other persons attend, the BTs will look upon it as a demonstration against the Government and act accordingly. I asked when the inquest would take place. He said that Tipperary is a Special Military Area and among the restrictions accompanying such a title was the abolition of the Coroner's Courts. These have been replaced by Military Tribunals, whose sole task it is to decide on the cause of death. Nothing else lies in its remit. A post-mortem has been carried out upon F and I have been given a death certificate signed by a Captain Towers. The cause of death is described as 'injuries'. I asked the officer whether any avenues of appeal lay open to us. He laughed loudly. I should consider myself fortunate to have avoided arrest. Had I not done so, and at this point he looked insolently at me, 'We would have enjoyed good sport questioning a **** like you.'

Monday, July 5 1920.

I returned to Dublin today. It was a difficult decision to make, but I feel that I can do more here. The days since Thursday have been long, tear-filled ones. The tears were M's. The girls, at LM's suggestion, have remained in England. He correctly said that they would be safer. I must confess that I have not shed one tear. I have no place for tears. My entire being is consumed with rage and a desire for revenge.

In the stillness of Thursday night, when the house slept, I went to the dining room where the coffin rested upon a table. I forced myself to do that which I had been forbidden to do. By the light of a lamp. I removed the fastenings and lifted the lid aside. The corpse was covered by a stained, grey blanket which I removed. I could barely suppress the scream which trembled upon my lips. The body was unrecognisable. The face was covered in blood which had congealed, but it was immediately clear to me that the eyes had been put out and a great wound inflicted upon the head. I tore my eyes from this horror to examine the remainder of F's body. The skin was black over large areas and many marks which looked like burns covered the chest. The cruellest thing remains until the last. The male organ had been severed, obviously while F still lived, to judge by the quantity of blood upon the body and staining the wood of the coffin.

I do not know for how long a time I remained standing there, looking at the results of British justice. I did not kneel, for there can be no god where man commits such vile evils. Rather than praying, I repeated my oath taken when I joined IRA. I vowed, with all the passion which seethed within me, never to rest until the last British foot is removed forever from Ireland. My vocation as Gráinne seems to be all the more worthwhile and I am already impatient for my next task. Tomorrow, I will call to the Library.

I frowned as I threw the book on to the table. Almost three. I got Cullen's number from the directory. Two minutes later, I replaced the receiver. Theresa was not there. Monday surgery was from ten to twelve. She had telephoned this morning and had been given an appointment for eleven-thirty, but had not shown. Shit.

She could be anywhere. I did not want to start ringing around, giving a laugh to our friends, when she was probably sitting having her hair done. She might have left a note if she was going swanning off like this. So much for my few days off and promotion. Some celebration.

I kept rationalising her absence, but annoyance was turning to anger, the very last thing I wanted.

I thought of going ahead with the diary but, to tell the truth, it wasn't half as enjoyable to read it alone. Sitting together with one of us reading aloud had grown into a cosy habit. Anyway, the entries were obviously very important at the point I had reached. Theresa should catch up before we went on.

I consumed some time getting lunch, setting the table for two. A born optimist.

I remembered that I had left my briefcase in the car, so I went to get it. I was reaching into the boot when the Cavan voice sounded behind me.

'The lady. She seemed well enough?'

Lady? What lady?

'Oh yes. You, eh, saw her then?'

'Aye. She came out this morning. Asked if we'd be making much of a mess.'

I smiled, a fully paid-up member of the 'that's women for you' club.

'Oh, I told her.' He did not wait for my reply. 'I said straight out that you can't build a house without dirt. But sure it's clean dirt. I told her.'

'Did you, I wonder, notice if she went out? This morning, I mean?'

He lifted his shiny cap an inch and poked his finger up under the rim. 'See her? Oh yes, I saw her. Sure, didn't her and the man go off in the car?'

I did not want to hear this, but I'm a glutton for punishment.

'Any idea of the time? When they went off in the car?'

''Twas, let me see now, ten and thirty. Peter was just after calling us for the cup of tea. Ten and thirty.' He nodded to himself, evidently satisfied with the answer. I think he hoped that I would now go away, having helped him to pass a few minutes.

But I was not quite finished with him. 'Did she speak to you when she was going out?'

'Can't say she did. Can't say she didn't. We were just sitting down and the bin lorry was passing. Sure you wouldn't have heard a shout with that.'

I thought for a minute. I knew that there was a simple explanation to all this. Nevertheless, I said, 'The man? What was he like? Young, old, big, small, thin, fat?'

He laughed. 'Ah now, you're pulling my leg. Sure he couldn't be all them things.'

'But did you notice what he looked like? What he was wearing?'

A wary look crossed his lined face. He began to turn away, speaking to me over his shoulder as he moved to rejoin his mates. 'I've got more to do with my time than look at every Tom, Dick or Harry as goes in and out of a house. I'll bid you good day.'

He reached the others and all four spoke together. I could hear nothing, so I went indoors. Disconsolate, about summed it up.

I tried to run through a list of men with whom Theresa would go for a drive, missing an important doctor's consultation. There was not even one candidate.

The seed of anger threatened to fork into two branches. Full blooded, eye-bulging, sweat-starting rage was one. The other, not even poking above the soil yet, was fear. I closed my eyes tight and forced the rage to hold.

It worked until four-thirty. Then, I said to hell with sounding foolish, and began to ring around. When I boiled it down to fact, there were only three possibilities. None of them had seen her.

I sat in the kitchen, sipping a whiskey. Special circumstances deserve special treatment. What to do? It's a little, somehow, juvenile to call the police because I don't know where my wife is in the middle of the day. Like a pair of gloves. You own them. You thought they were in the drawer. The fact that they are not there does not mean that they are gone. You know they will turn up. Sometime.

A loud ring from the doorbell. I ran out. None of your casual saunters for Doorly. I stared through the porch at him. He was dressed in black, from head to toe. Even the crash helmet was black.

A big motor bike gleamed at me from the gate where it stood on its rest like a horse waiting outside a saloon in a Roy Rogers film from my childhood. Or was it my father's childhood?

As I opened the door, he raised the visor.

'Mr Frank Doorly?'

I nodded.

'Carryall Courier Service. Package for you. Sign here please.'

Sixteen

It was a small rectangular package wrapped in brown paper, with sticky tape binding the ends. My name and address were typed on a white label.

It was about the size of a video cassette. It was a video cassette. There was no accompanying letter. Just the black plastic box. To show my state of mind at the time, almost ten minutes passed before it occurred to me to play the damned thing.

Theresa sat at a table. It was made of some treated stuff, plastic, that sort of thing. A concrete block wall was behind her. Strong lights bathed the scene, making everything, even her hair, seem to shine. The film was in a grainy sort of colour. I recognised her red anorak. It looked pale pink at times, blue at others. I could not tell how she was looking, but at least, there was no sign of outward damage.

She was holding a copy of the *Irish Independent* facing the camera and the shot was close enough for me to read the date. Monday, 29 August 1994. Today.

Her voice sounded thin. Perhaps the equipment was unsophisticated. Perhaps her voice did not really hold a tremor.

A giant hand was squeezing my heart as I watched and listened. Her eyes looked slightly to her left, where she was clearly reading something beside the camera. Hardly a tele-prompter.

'Frank, please listen carefully. I am a prisoner of the Provisional Irish Republican Army. They know about the diaries and they want them. They say that they belong to their movement. You will receive a phone call tomorrow, telling you what to do. Don't say more than hello. The caller will do all the talking and will not repeat anything. Get it all down the first time. Do not tell the police. If you do, they will know and will kill me. Please Frank, I beg you. Do exactly as you are told. Otherwise, I will be killed. I love you.'

The final three words really got to me and I put my head in my hands and cried like a baby. The pictures ran on for about ten seconds after the message finished. As the tears dried up, the jumping silver streaks of the unused part of the tape sped through the machine. When it clicked to a stop, I rewound it and played it again. In fact, I played it six times, watching and re-watching. I timed it. There were forty seconds of film.

I did not even consider calling the police. Theresa's words of warning that 'they will know' frightened me badly. The house was probably being watched and any sign of blue would give a clear message to the kidnappers.

No, I had to face this alone. Except for the whiskey bottle which had suddenly acquired the status of a confidential adviser. I downed two measures quickly and then discarded the measure. The original 'four fingers of rye'.

Food was a non-starter. My stomach was tight, almost painful, my breathing more than a little unsteady. The hours stretched in front of me. They would call tomorrow. What time? God knows.

I knew there was something I should do, but it kept evading my haphazard mind. Then, all at once, a sort of calmness settled on me. The one thing I could do, to my possible advantage, was to read as much of the remaining diaries as I could between now, five forty-five, and the ring of the telephone tomorrow.

I did not expect to sleep a lot between times, so I

might as well try to bury my terror with the books and the whiskey. I carried the case down to the kitchen and laid it open on the floor beside my chair. I sorted the bundles of books into two piles, those we had read, and the rest. I leafed through the unread pile, trying to estimate how long it would take me to finish.

As with all the books, many of the entries were devoted to page after page of what I would call 'ordinary' stuff. The day-to-day world of a young Irish girl in the early twenties. We had, throughout the reading period, trawled the pages for unusual or seemingly important items. I continued this policy, running my eye over the pages, on the lookout for anything significant or memorable. Even Gráinne's descriptions of killing after killing palled with repetition. Her first kill was, clearly, significant. The public execution in Belfast shook her badly, even though she hardly referred to it in later entries. The shooting of the two informers after their 'court-martial' was important. Ruane's death made a big impression on her but there is only so much that can be written about shooting people dead.

Friday, July 9 1920.
Upon the advice of Lady M's doctor, who has been attending her every day, M has been admitted to the North Riding Hospital. It is a place for the treatment of mental illness. I am told that the authorities want M committed, a procedure which requires the permission of the next of kin. I hold that sad position but have not reached my majority, a state of affairs which disqualifies me. Lady M suggested to the doctor that she would be prepared to offer herself as a reliable person, who, with my consent, could give the necessary permission.

M's condition has deteriorated every day since her release from the police barracks. She no longer recognises those who look after her and visit. The nurses report that she never speaks, eats or drinks. She lies in bed, staring before her, a look of horror upon her face. If she does not show some improvement soon, the doctor will be faced with the task of feeding her by force. Otherwise, she will surely die. I suspect that, if she could express herself, she would declare that she did not wish to live without the man whom she loved.

To compound these sad events, my situation in Dublin has changed. When I returned to the office on Tuesday, I was astonished to find that the ladies, even my beloved A, were refusing to speak to me. I embarked on an account of F's death when E stopped me. I should not discuss such matters until I had been seen by AC. I hurried to his office and asked him for an explanation. He did not ask me to sit, which I found strange, he being at all times a perfect gentleman. He produced a document from a file upon his desk and proceeded to read aloud from it. It proved to be a report upon the happenings in Thurles written by a Captain Landy. My father, a well-known Republican agitator, had been arrested following the murder of a constable. In the course of his questioning, he had revealed that I was of a similar political persuasion to himself. The Captain concluded that he thought it highly improper for such 'a rebel' to be employed in the centre of government. Accordingly, he asked AC to discharge me. This he proceeded to do, without once looking at my face. I was ordered to leave the Castle at once. No member of the staff was allowed to have any conversation with me.

The initial shock was severe, but as I reflected upon my dismissal, I found myself more and more inclined to regard it as a boon. To continue to serve in the very heart of the government which has murdered F would be quite impossible. I took a decision to remain in the city until I could make a report to Gen in the Library. It was my hope that he would agree with my assessment of the situation. I have not been employed as an intelligence gatherer since Gráinne made her appearance.

I spent the intervening time walking through the streets, looking at the window displays in the shops. In the Library, Gen was present and alone. I related the events of the morning, without reference to F's death.

He replied gently that he had been advised of the sad news. He said that local people had informed him that F was a noble man. Upon hearing these words, I lost my composure completely. I began to weep as if my heart would break. He moved away, turning his back to allow me to grieve alone. These were the first tears which I had shed since the night of the murder. They flowed without cease for many moments. At some stage, I do not know when exactly, I felt Gen's powerful arms circle my shoulders. He drew me to him without speaking and I gratefully clung to him. My head rested against his chest. Gradually thereafter, a feeling of great peace came upon me. I found a wonderful freedom after my tears, which had now stopped. I stayed in this position, eyes closed, listening to the beat of his heart.

Finally, he raised my head by putting a finger under my chin and drawing it upwards. I found his grey eyes regarding me with a look of compassion. He then gently disengaged my arms and took a step backwards. Holding me at arm's length, he spoke softly. 'Oh Molly, Molly. What have we done to you? Is any cause worth turning you into what you have become?' I thought that he was about to weep. He stared at me for several moments, shook his frame and a look of determination settled upon his face.

When he spoke again, it was as Gen. We were on duty. I asked if I could return to Thurles to find the officer responsible for F's murder. After a moment's thought, he refused. I was too personally involved and could put my life and the lives of others in the area in danger. However, the matter would be dealt with on a local level. I could rely upon that. The officer in question was, in all probability, this Captain Landy who had demanded my dismissal. He then spoke about my position in the Castle. Perhaps it was just as well. If an operation went wrong and someone escaped from one of my 'marks', I might well be recognised subsequently by him on a casual visit to the office.

I was inordinately pleased that Gen had reached the same conclusion as I in this matter. However, I said that it would not be easy to report each day if I was in

Kingstown. I needed another position. He said that he had the very thing for me. He told me to come with him, and we walked along the quays and into Abbey Street. We came to a premises with the name George Moreland, Painters and Decorators, over the door, and entered.

A man came from the back through a door. Upon seeing Gen, he smiled and said, 'There you are, Mick. How are tricks?' I felt this to be very familiar but Gen did not object. He introduced me as Molly Stewart and said that I was coming to work here. The man, whom Gen addressed as Vincent, led us through the door into an office with a desk and typewriter. Three other men were sitting in chairs and they rose to greet Gen. I was again introduced, but I was not told the names of the men. Gen nodded to them and they retired, leaving us alone. He related to me the purpose of this place. Business is carried out from here on a perfectly proper basis. However, most requests for work are answered by the statement that the firm has so many orders that nothing can be done for many months. Records and books of account are maintained in good style and this will be my task.

I remained somewhat puzzled about this matter and told Gen as much. He then took me into his confidence. Gráinne was not the only executioner in Dublin. He has assembled a group of men who are just as expert as she. There are twelve of them and he laughed as he said that he called them his 'Apostles'. Now that I was here, he suggested that I might be, in future, referred to as his 'Virgin Mary'. I was taken aback by these remarks, but as he clearly found the entire matter to be amusing, I smiled in concert with him. Somewhat more seriously, he said that his team were known throughout the city as 'The Squad' and had amassed a considerable number of successful operations. I will work during normal business hours and my salary will be the same as heretofore. The business aspect will be explained to me by Vincent.

Gen left at that point and I was soon immersed in my new duties. Truth to tell, the work is rather light, but V says that I will be permitted to read when there is no work to be done.

I cannot finish this entry before writing about R and my feelings for him. The dreadful events in Thurles have left me with a deep loathing for everything English. How then, can I resolve my personal situation with regard to R? I have written a letter to him, merely setting out the details, without touching upon the emotional effect. I also referred to my dismissal from the Castle, pointing out that, perhaps, he is now compromised by virtue of our friendship. I await his reply with trepidation.

I threw the book into the case. Pouring myself a drink, I saw that the bottle was showing signs of wear and tear. A distant voice tried to get me interested in abstinence, but it didn't have a chance. I knew that Theresa had stored several bottles of booze in the bedroom against the possibility of unexpected guests. No need to go searching yet.

Molly seemed to have reached a very important part of her life. It was not so long ago that she was revelling in the arms of Richard. Now, her anti-English feelings had grown to outright hatred, not that I blamed her. The Brits got more than they bargained for when they killed her father. The Tribunal report that he had died of his injuries sounded a bit like the Steve Biko affair in South Africa. Amazing how many otherwise quiet prisoners try to escape by jumping from second-storey windows, sometimes getting through steel bars to do it.

With my glass replenished, I opened the next book.

Tuesday, July 20 1920.
Ten days since the last entry. My life has been far from dull during this time. I have had to postpone writing until now. The reason for this will become clear over the pages.

On Friday last, I was involved in a complex operation. This followed many days of rehearsals, by myself, and nine other Volunteers, after we had received an order to mark a high official who is heavily guarded. Intelligence reports showed that he was to travel to Belfast on Friday by train. Our dominance of the railways is almost complete, the embargo against moving military supplies or personnel total.

We boarded the train at Amiens Street Station separately, four to compartments in carriage number five on the seven-carriage train, the remainder to carriage number seven. I was the sole woman. Gen told the men that I was their good-luck charm. This resulted in my being treated splendidly by all. I was dressed in a dark-coloured travelling coat, with a wide-brimmed hat shadowing my face.

As soon as we got underway, the driver increased the speed as quickly as possible. One of the men in my carriage walked forward to the connecting tunnel and waited there. An attendant appeared, calling that breakfast was being served. He was pushing a trolley shrouded with a cloth. When those going for food had departed, the three of us remaining were given guns by the attendant. They had been concealed beneath the cloth.

Two furlongs from the Howth spur, when we were travelling very fast, our man uncoupled the chains and the locomotive accelerated away with four carriages. The remaining three carriages and the guard's van were switched on to the spur, taken on by momentum. Our team and the six in carriage seven burst into the guarded carriage at the same time from front and rear. The detectives, seeing our guns, had no appetite for a fight and surrendered to a man.

I appeared for the first time and went to the third compartment from the front. I removed my hat and entered. Three men were playing cards. I asked if Major-General Tudor was present. When they replied that he was not, I called my comrades to confirm this. It appeared that Tudor had been ready for the trip, having actually arrived at Amiens Street Station. At the last moment, he had suffered a severe attack of gout but had insisted that all the security procedures planned should go ahead.

I was now in a dilemma. These men had seen my

face and might well recognise me on future visits to the city. I could not take that chance. I asked my comrades to step outside. I informed the three that I was going to execute them and offered them time for prayer if they so desired. They remained looking at me. I ordered them to turn around and despatched each with a bullet in the back of the head.

I emerged from the compartment and V asked whether that had been necessary. I replied strongly that Gráinne has no mercy on her enemies. Several of our men crossed themselves.

The men scattered to three fishing boats moored in the harbour. I replaced my hat and walked to the tram terminus. In thirty-five minutes I was in Abbey Street. When I described my actions to Gen, he said that I had done more harm to the enemy than if I had succeeded in killing Tudor. The newspapers made great play of the fact that Tudor had outwitted the IRA, but the truth soon spread through the city causing him to be referred to thereafter as 'Gout Tudor'. Gen remarked that his, Tudor's, reputation as a ruthless, clever policeman would never truly recover. By continuing to live, he becomes a monument to Gráinne's ruthlessness.

Christ, shades of Jesse James. There's no doubt, Gráinne meant business. How come that I had never heard of her before?

I stretched and yawned. More out of tension than any desire, or even possibility of sleep. The room had become cold, probably as much from my lack of food as anything else.

I stirred up the slack-covered fire and threw a couple of pieces of coal on top. The result was a gratifying burst of yellow flame. I hitched my chair nearer and topped up my glass. The bottle was fast running out. I would soon have to go hunting for Theresa's secret store.

This thought pushed her again into the front of my mind. I looked at the clock. Almost eight. How was she passing this particular moment? Was she, perhaps, thinking of me? If you are, love, maybe you can pick up my vibes. Nothing in the world matters if I lose you. Of course, being in this mood brought into bold relief the recent occasions when I had caught her crying or near to it. As if the words were projected on to the wall in front of me, I thought, what if Theresa is unhappy with me. I didn't mean vaguely depressed. What I was thinking of was unhappy with a capital U, unable to bear much more of her life with me. God almighty Doorly, what the hell are you trying to do to yourself? Things are bad enough without this sort of shit.

The entry continued.

> My personal life has been rather uncertain of late. I received a reply from R, requesting a meeting at Nelson's Pillar one evening. I decided that I would meet him and at half-past five arrived at the rendezvous. For the first time during any of our meetings, he wore uniform. I asked why this was so and he replied that he had told GM of our friendship. GM had insisted that R wear uniform and that he remain in the sight of a colleague. I looked around and there he was. A captain stood not ten feet from us.
>
> We walked along Henry Street. R said that he was very concerned about the facts of F's death. My reference to it at my interview with AC as 'murder' was unfortunate. He had spoken to GM and had been advised that if I were to write to AC, apologising for F's conduct and disowning his 'rebel tendencies', it might be possible for me to redeem my tarnished reputation. I controlled my anger and asked calmly, if he, R, was in agreement with the phrase 'rebel tendencies'. His reply was that all the evidence confirmed it. My brothers had attacked a military patrol. F was known to have IRA sympathies. He had also attempted to escape from legal custody.
>
> I still continued calm. I told in pitiless detail what I had discovered in the coffin with which I had been ordered not to tamper. He then said that I could not

understand the reason for military decisions taken by officers. I am a mere woman. I turned to him and shook his hand, assuring him that he need not worry about me.

I left with my head held high. My sang-froid remained intact until I reached the ladies' room in the Gresham Hotel. There, I fear, I broke down, weeping uncontrollably. Our love was at an end, the love to which I had given myself, heart and soul. The memory of my recent visit to Hampshire and the kindness shown by his mother, the visit which ended in my miscarrying our child, came flooding back.

I remained there for thirty minutes and when I arrived home, AB asked if I was ill. My eyelids were swollen and my face was pale. I pleaded a headache and went to my room, where I lay awake during the long night.

The next morning, my appearance caused comment from Vincent. He said that I looked as if I had not slept well. He said that he hoped that I was not 'going soft'. I asked him what the phrase meant. He laughed and explained that it meant that he hoped that I was not losing my appetite for Gráinne's work. I reassured him on that point.

During the morning he asked me to deliver a message to Gen. The address was 4 Brunswick Street. As I was not familiar with the area, he gave me directions and I set off. I went by way of Blackhall Place, not the shortest route, but the one of which I had most knowledge. The buildings in Brunswick Street are residential houses, rather small and slightly dingy in appearance. I knocked upon the door of number 4 as ordered. After a short interval, a woman appeared at the door of number 6, next door. She said that Mr Brown of number 4 was not in. Would I care to leave a message with her? She would make sure that he got it. These were the words given me by V, and I gave the correct reply, 'I want Mr Brown. Mr Green will not do.'

The woman pulled me quickly inside her house and closed the door. She directed me upstairs, with instructions to knock upon the door facing the stairs. This I did and Gen opened the door and smiled. He said that he hoped that I would not mind that the entire affair was a ruse to see whether I could find the house. He had wagered five shillings with V that I would arrive and now he had won the wager. I felt that it was silly in the extreme to waste my time in such childish pursuits, and I said so.

He became very stern, and spoke to me harshly. The people in the movement who operate close to him are living in a continual state of alertness, ready to move quickly if in danger. They know that the next second could be their last. It is very natural that they should seek diversion in simple ways. He frowned ferociously at me as he concluded, 'It would do you good if you played silly, childish games occasionally.' With these words, he seized me in his arms and pressed his lips upon mine.

I was too surprised to resist, initially, but I soon gathered my senses. I began to struggle with all my strength, beating my clenched fists against his shoulders and head. This activity by me seemed to give him encouragement and he tightened his hold upon me. All at once, an astonishing thing occurred. His lips forced mine to part slightly and I felt something warm, soft and living dart into my mouth. The sensation was initially delicious until I realised that it was his tongue which was in my mouth. I attempted to bite it, but the force of his lips was too strong for me. At that moment, his hands, which had been holding me about my waist, slipped lower, much lower, and I felt his fingers moving disgracefully. My anger had now reached a peak and I kicked him with real force upon his shin. He cried out in pain and released me. He bent down, rubbing his leg the while. I attempted to regain my composure, a difficult feat. My heart was pounding, my face was aflame, my vision was blurred and I was having great difficulty in controlling my breathing. I turned from him and stood awaiting his inevitable apology.

There followed a silence, presumably while he gathered the courage to speak. Then I heard the most extraordinary sound. I could not identify it at once, but it continued, growing louder with each passing second. Suddenly, there was no doubt as to the nature of the sound. I was listening to Gen laughing. He seemed to be struggling to keep it under control, but now it was rising in volume. Now it was ear-splitting I whirled around, ready to confound this vulgar fellow. As I drew breath to speak, he ceased laughing for long enough to allow himself to splutter, 'Oh, for God's sake, don't be so serious. Crack your face and laugh, can't you?' I could scarcely believe my ears. And then, beginning deep within my body, an overwhelming desire to laugh came upon me. I attempted to quench it but failed. My lips opened and my laughter filled the room. Within seconds, Gen had resumed his own hilarity. Soon, we were both bent over, attempting to catch our breath. My eyes sent tears rolling down my face. I could no longer see Gen through my tears.

I felt his arms encircle my shoulders, pulling me close to his body. He pressed me against himself and now his laughter was taking on a new tone. It was no longer light, no longer amusing. As I heard this change, the sounds from my own throat began to go out of my control. I felt the convulsions of my body become more demanding. All at once, we were no longer laughing. His hands grasped my face and he brought his lips down hard upon my mouth. I felt my emotions running to catch up with his and at the same moment, I thought that I was hearing alarms sounding within my head.

This is not right. I must stop this before I allow myself to be carried into a dangerous situation. Gen lifted me from the floor and walked to where a small bed was standing. Still joined to his mouth, I felt myself being forced downwards on to it. His weight bore upon me and, once again, his tongue entered my mouth. It thrust itself demandingly at my tongue, and almost instinctively, I began to return the caress. I felt my resistance draining away and experienced a sensation of losing touch with reality.

From a long distance, I heard a sound which I could not identify. It came again, and again, and again. Gen lifted his mouth from mine and came to his feet, his eyes upon the door. Now I recognised the sound. Someone was knocking insistently upon the closed door. A woman's voice called. 'Patrol outside. May be coming in.'

'Right.' The word came from his mouth. Gone was any sign of laughter, or passion for that matter. He pulled me to my feet, saying urgently, 'Sorry Molly. We have to get out. Stand there.' He lifted a chair into the corner of the room and climbed on to it. He reached above his head, the palms of his hands flat against the ceiling. He strained upwards for a second and as I watched, a section of the ceiling rose. He shoved it to one side revealing a square opening. He swung his hips upwards until he was sitting in the opening, his legs dangling into the room. He reached down with his hand. 'Quickly, Molly. Stand on the chair. I'll pull you through.'

I did as he said and he hoisted me upwards until I was sitting beside him. I stood up in the darkness and when he too was standing, he replaced the panel. He placed his lips to my ear and whispered, 'Stand still. There is no light. Do not move your feet until I tell you. I have your hand.' Slowly, he guided me through the complete darkness, his voice never rising above the whisper. Finally, he whispered that I should sit. I felt with my free hand and found a chair. He sat beside me and said, 'Not a sound, Molly. They may come into the room. I'm beside you. Do not be afraid.' Had conditions been different, I might well have told him that I was not in the least afraid.

We remained there for some time but I could not see my watch. It felt like a very long time indeed. Our vigil ended when a tapping sound came from the panel. Gen took me gently back the way we had come and lifted the panel aside. He lowered me into the room and quickly joined me. As we dusted ourselves off, he laughed. 'You should be honoured, Molly. You're the first woman to have been in my den.'

'I could not see very much. What is up there?'

He explained that the row of houses in which we were has one long, common attic. The dividing walls between the houses only reach to the upstairs ceiling. Up there was stored enough food and water for a large party of people. They could comfortably remain there for a number of days. Separate trap doors (the panels), gave into each house, enabling him to ascend and descend wherever he wished. He often held important meetings there, and lamps are then provided.

At this point, I said that I had better be returning to the office. He came to me and looked into my eyes. 'Remember what I said about laughing, Molly. Even Gráinne needs a break, sometime.'

I have found myself dwelling upon these events over the following days. I have not seen Gen in that time. I am at once eager to do so, and afraid of the consequences if I do. The more I think about the moments before the alarm that sent us into the attic, the less certain am I that I could have stopped our conduct from turning on to a certain path. What is more worrying is a growing conviction that I would not have wanted to stop. With these confused thoughts turning in my brain, I rest my pen.

Seventeen

I was on my knees in the bedroom, my head buried in the wardrobe. I had just located the bottle when I leapt upright, enfolding myself in the skirts hanging above. Someone had placed a finger on the bell-push and was keeping it there. I called down a silent curse on all 'neighbourhood employment canvassers' as I hurried down the stairs, the bottle firmly in my left hand. A large piece of my mind was ready on my lips. I deliberately did not switch on the light in the hall. Let them stand in the dark.

No sooner had I turned the latch than the door was pushed open, forcing my fingers from their hold on it. A figure stepped past me, in the gloom, turned, and shoved the door closed. As I tried to recover, I caught a glimpse of someone going into the kitchen. A man's voice called out urgently, 'For Christ's sake get away from that door. Come in here.'

Well, it is my house. I think you could say that. I stormed from the hall and when I entered the kitchen, a hand swung the door shut.

'What the fuck...?' I looked, and not believing what I saw, looked again. Inspector Ryan was standing there, a smile on his face. Two things entered my mind immediately. His appearance put Theresa's life in greater danger than it already was. Secondly, just to show the bloody foolish thoughts that come to you when the pressure is strongest, he's going to see the diaries and won't half be annoyed that I lied about them.

Theresa came first by right. 'In the name of Jesus, you're the worst news I've had in a bad day. If you only knew, you've thrown a fucking spanner in the works.' I took a moment off to ask, 'Did you see anyone hanging around outside? Sitting in a car? Not going anywhere?'

His smile was a thing of the past. 'No, I saw no one, but that means nothing. They could be anywhere.'

'Leaving that for a minute, are you going to tell me what all that in the hall was about?'

'Can't you guess, Mr Doorly?'

'At the moment, I'm not in the mood for guessing games. Now you tell me, and it better be good. Something very important hangs on it.'

'Believe it or not, I've come to offer my help. About Mrs Doorly.'

'But...how the hell did...do you know where she is?'

He shook his head sadly. 'Now that would be a help. No, I'm afraid that I'm as wise as you are about it.'

Something struck me. Something he had said. Not once, but twice. Got it. 'Are you here in an official capacity? Am I talking to the Inspector? Or is it Mr Ryan?'

'Unofficial. Very unofficial. If my boss knew I was here, I'd be patrolling a beat in farthest Connemara.'

I was getting away from my biggest worry. My only worry. 'You seem to know that Ther...my wife is missing. How you know is for later. If you know about it, then it's reasonable to assume that you also know that I have been warned that she will be killed if the police become involved. So now, will you get the fuck out of my house. Every minute you're here increases the chance that those bastards will find out.'

I actually made a move in his direction. A small one, true, but a move. His eyes showed that he hadn't missed it. He raised his hand pacifically and his tone became reasonable.

'Hold on there, Mr Doorly. Not for a minute would I jeopardise the safety of your wife.'

As I made to speak, he stopped my interruption by hurrying on. 'I think I can help. Really help. Not Garda help. This is personal.'

He sounded sincere. But what good is sincerity if the kidnappers have no pity? Still...

'Look, you might as well sit down seeing as you're here. Drink?'

'I see you have Paddy there. The best whiskey in the world. A small one, please.'

I handed him the glass. I didn't offer to get water. Neat was good enough for me. 'Suppose you tell me first what you know? And how you know? I only found out a couple of hours ago.'

He took a small sip from his glass and held the liquor in his mouth for a few seconds, moving it from side to side. When he had swallowed it, he said, 'I, em, you might say that I found out today that Mrs Doorly had been abducted from here this morning.'

I sat wide-eyed, listening to this man who had come to me out of the blue. He hadn't really told me a thing.

He went on. 'The next thing of which I'm certain is that they contacted you. I don't know how, but that's irrelevant. What I do know is that they want Mrs Perry's journals.'

His eyes strayed to the floor beside my chair and a faint smile twisted his lips. 'And there, if I'm not mistaken, my dear Watson, they are. You know I've always wanted to do that Watson thing. It never fitted before.'

Him and his Watson. I'm afraid that I became terse at this point. My voice rose. 'Fuck you, Ryan. Fuck you and your fucking Watson. My wife's life is in danger and you want to play word games. Fuck off, fuck off, fuck off.'

He let my anger run down before speaking. 'I'm really sorry, Mr Doorly. That was unpardonable of me. You were quite right to react as you did.'

I shrugged, wagging my head wearily from side to side. The strain was getting to me. 'Don't mind me. I'm feeling a bit desperate. Anyway, you were right all along. Those are the diaries.' My voice soared again. 'I wish I'd never seen the fucking things.' I slumped back in the chair, closing my eyes. I wasn't trying to keep out the light, either.

He started to speak gently, like a skater not sure about the thickness of the ice. 'One thing I've never been able to understand is why you denied the existence of the diaries. I mean, it's not as if the old woman was related to you. Tell me why you kept them, Mr Doorly. I'm genuinely curious.'

'I...we...promised her that we would destroy them if she died. It seemed very important to her. We intended to do it too. But then the fire – obviously arson, professionally done. Well, it made us want to have a look ourselves. I thought it would be OK if we destroyed them afterwards without talking about them to anyone. Ever.'

'And was it worth the bother? Did you find anything that might explain the fuss?'

'I'll answer that with one of my own. Why are the police after them?' The smile made a return trip to his lips. Like that, with his hairless head, he looked like a six-foot gnome. 'Oh, but the police never wanted them. My enquiries have been purely personal all along. I have, well, contacts within certain groups. They keep me informed about anything of interest. I was advised that Mrs Perry's diaries could contain compromising information about...well... particular matters. I was asked to recover them. If they did not burn in the fire, you had to have them. You see, Mr Doorly, most police work is recognising that the obvious solution is usually the right one. I did not have to be a great detective to figure this one out.'

I sat back in my chair, frowning. The central issue remained Theresa's safety. Making up my mind, I told him about the tape and ran it for him. When the pictures faded, he asked me to replay them.

He nodded, apparently satisfied. 'I won't pretend that your wife is not in some danger. I think that I managed to get in here without being spotted. Can't be sure, of course, but I'm pretty experienced in this sort of thing. That being so, what are your plans? Look at some more of the diaries?'

Oh well. If he was here, he was here. I couldn't change that, so I nodded at him. 'It'll be better than sitting looking at the walls.'

'I agree. Will you tell me the story so far? If anything of importance comes up, I'll let you know. It's only by finding out why they want them that I, we'll have an idea how to proceed.'

'We, Theresa and I, only concentrated on what seemed to us to be important events in her life. We ignored the normal sort of thing like 'got up and went to work'. I'll give you a rundown of what we've found.'

He sat with his eyes closed, face impassive, as I built the picture of

Molly and her life. When I first mentioned the name Gráinne, he jerked erect. His eyes widened and he held up his hand to stop me. His words were not addressed to me. Rather he murmured them to himself. I had to strain to hear.

'Gráinne. Well I'm damned. So that's who she was.'

'You've heard of her then?'

'There's been rumours around since God knows when that there was a woman in the War of Independence called Gráinne. Not her real name. She was supposed to have been the executioner for the IRA.'

'Well, now you know who she was. Our little Mrs Perry. She certainly turned out to be a special kind of Volunteer, I'll give her that.'

'Maybe we're near the reason they want these things handed over. Go on with the story.'

An hour later, half-ten, to be exact, I had brought the story up to the latest entries I had read, including the train job looking for Tudor. When I mentioned the un-walled attics in Brunswick Street, Ryan laughed aloud.

'I used to hear my grandfather, God rest him, talking about those houses. He always thought there was something queer about them, suspicious characters hanging around. It was only after the Truce that he found out about the attics.' He ran his hand over his shining pate. 'You get a feeling of the times from an account like that. 'The Squad', for instance. Granda often mentioned them. He was DMP and they used to be frightened out of their lives that they'd get on Collins's list. Those fellows used to walk around Dublin like they owned it. I suppose they did in a way.'

As I listened to his reminiscences my eyes pricked and I wiped away a tear. I did not want to be sitting here in years to come remembering her. I was skating on the very limit of my tolerance, and I knew it. How I would stay together until morning was more than I knew. Despite my attitude to Ryan's arrival, I was glad that he was here. The night hours spent alone would have found me out.

Sunday, August 1 1920

I am very tired. Yesterday I travelled by train to Thurles. AB made the arrangements and LM's car was waiting. Kennedy, the chauffeur, advised me to lie upon the rear seat, with a rug concealing me. He apologised for this, but said that LM had instructed him to suggest this course to me. I agreed, at a loss to understand.

Upon reaching the manor house, Lady M made me welcome. LM explained that ever since F's death, the BTs had been watching our house. The townspeople were under instructions not to speak with any member of my family, under pain of arrest.

I was then forced to perform one of the most unpleasant tasks of my life. With F gone, M in hospital probably for the remainder of her life, the girls in England – they now live with Aunt Joan, M's younger sister – and myself in Dublin, the house is being closed by LM. He states that he will not allow anyone to live there as long as I am in the country. I have had to dismiss the staff. There were many tears, as the three ladies have been almost family members. I gave each of them a hundred pounds and wished them God's blessing.

I spoke to LM about the situation in Dublin, not, of course, my part in IRA. He is most pessimistic and feels that the government has lost touch with the people. The 'rebels' are stepping into the vacancy and are now seen by the majority as a credible alternative. He tells me that life in Thurles is most unpleasant. Almost nightly, BTs carry out searches, leaving the houses in a state of chaos, with damages that will take many thousands of pounds to repair.

I travelled to the North Riding Hospital to see M. It is a large grey building, forbidding in aspect. The windows are covered with iron bars and men guard the gates. My strongest impression was of a prison. I was taken through many long corridors, up several flights of steps until told to pause outside a door without a handle upon it. A small grille fitted into the door was drawn back and I was invited to look inside. The room into which I looked was hardly more than a cupboard in size. It was completely bare of furniture. I saw a thin woman sitting against the wall. She was naked. After a moment, I realised with horror that she was M. I spoke through the grille but she made no show of understanding or, indeed, recognising me. Her hair had been cut and only a short growth remained. Her state of filth was difficult to bear and the stench was overwhelming. I was forced to hold a handkerchief over my mouth and nose.

I asked indignantly why she was being treated this way. The woman accompanying me replied that M has no human feelings and is, in reality, an animal. I was about to take the matter further when a tall woman in a blue dress arrived. She introduced herself as the Matron, Mrs Stafford. When I spoke about the conditions under which M is being treated, she became extremely hostile. She said that the family, including me, have cast M on to the Riding for the remainder of her life. Having taken this step, it was hardly to be expected that she would be treated as if she were still in her own house. If I wish to remove M from the hospital, I must make an application to the court. For such an application to succeed, the doctors treating her will have to sign a declaration that she is not a danger to society or herself. It is her opinion that the application will fail upon the second of these conditions. She finished by saying that future visits to M will be a nuisance to patients and staff.

When she had departed, I allowed myself to be led away. Upon my return to the manor house, where I was staying, I related my experiences to Lady M. She confessed that she had encountered the Matron when she called to visit M. She had not wanted to distress me further by telling me of the hospital conditions. She was kind enough to summon the doctor who now carries on F's practice. He merely repeated the words of the Matron. M is beyond our aid, and the kindest act which I can undertake upon her behalf is to pray for her early death.

All this had a frightful effect upon me and I thereupon decided to return to Dublin by the first available train. I boarded it at six o'clock. As I slowly departed from Thurles, I was seized by a certainty that I will never see my home again. The journey was dolorous in the extreme.

This morning, to my great surprise, Gen called at the house. Once again, he became the delightful Mr Green for AB. He invited me to walk with him through the People's Gardens which are at their most beautiful at the moment. I was not afforded time to remark upon this. Gen said that he had not come to Kingstown to admire any ****ing flowers.

He has a task for me or, to be more accurate, for Gráinne. He has received disturbing intelligence. Some time ago, it appears that a meeting took place in, of all places, the city of Cairo, in Egypt. The meeting was convened by Sir Henry Wilson, Chief of the Imperial General Staff. Those attending were the most senior officers of British Intelligence. The agenda had only one subject upon it: how to wrest Ireland from Michael Collins. As a result of this, a slow but steady flow of intelligence officers into the country has been noticed by his men. They are all nominally members of real regiments, although none comes from any regiment serving here at the moment. As each man arrives, he takes lodgings in Dublin and pursues a life of business. No overt contact with the Castle is made. Gen has decided to strike at this group. I am ordered to meet T outside the Royal Dublin Showgrounds tomorrow at one o'clock. He will have the plan which we will follow.

Gen turned to another topic. He is 'getting fed up' coming out here each time he wishes to see me. I must move into the city. I asked what motive I can give AB for such a course. He shrugged carelessly and asked if it mattered. With no one living at home, there is no longer a need for me to stay in Kingstown. Upon my enquiry as to where I could obtain lodgings, he stated that he had taken care of this matter. I am to move into number 8 Brunswick Street. He will be able to 'keep an eye' on me. His closest associates live in these houses. A group of *bona fide* people are the registered occupiers but all the upstairs rooms are available for our purpose. I must move in on Tuesday morning.

After Gen's departure, I approached AB. She asked after 'that nice young officer'. Why has she not seen him since that night he accompanied me in my illness? She has already informed me that she was aware of the nature of my illness, and in the circumstances, has been expecting the man to call. I said that I was no longer seeing him. She appeared shocked by my words, and said I must tell her about Mr Green. He is clearly a gentleman of high standing, she said. Has he given sign of his intentions? I fear that I laughed at this and she became silent. I apologised immediately, explaining that my laughter was not at her but at the thought of Mr Green having intentions of that sort. I assured her that we were friends and colleagues, no more.

I seized the moment to tell her that I was leaving her home. She began to weep, saying that with M in hospital, she felt more than ever a mother to me. I put my arms around her, telling her that I would always look upon my time living with her as very precious to me. I attempted to reassure her that I merely wished to live nearer to my new position. I said that it was the wish of my employer, Mr Moreland. Weeping more tears, she gave her consent. I must visit her at every opportunity.

Eighteen

I threw the book violently on the floor. I practically screamed the words. 'What the fuck am I doing? Theresa in the hands of a bunch of psychopaths, and I'm sitting here, swigging whiskey and reading this shit. Why, why, why?'

Ryan had been listening with his eyes closed. He rose quickly and picked up the book. 'Hold on, Mr Doorly. We can only wait for the call in the morning. It's all we've got. Try another drink. Come on, Mr Doorly.'

'If you don't stop calling me Mr fucking Doorly, I'll swing for you. I swear. Call me Frank, can't you?'

'Sure. Right. Frank it is. I'm Bob, by the way.'

'Bob my arse. You'll always be fucking Ryan to me.'

He smiled and, despite myself, I did the same. Maybe not quite as steady as his, but a smile nevertheless. I sat there, twisting my head from side to side. I could have done with one of Theresa's massages. My head ached from the unaccustomed drink. I had eaten little that day. I was aware that my tirade to Ryan was hardly the words of a sane man. I was prepared to disagree with him, regardless of what he said.

He clearly knew this and spent a moment pouring himself another drink. I noticed that it was a small one. I could not remember the size of my last one, or the one before for that matter.

Ryan pulled his chair around until it was facing mine and only a couple of feet away. He leaned forward, his face close, a conciliatory look on it. 'Tell you what, Frank. Why don't I tell you a few things about myself? It might make you more confident about tomorrow.'

'Things? What do you mean things? What things, for Christ's sake?'

'I thought you might prefer that to reading.'

'What's wrong with my reading? It sounded fine to me. Well, just for that, you can read. Let's see how marvellously Inspector Ryan can fucking read.'

I knew that I was making no sense, but I didn't care. I was pissed off with the whole evening. A strong, healthy, feeling of guilt was flowering in my mind. Why should Theresa, not me, be the captive? If I was, you can bet your life that she would not have spent the time reading to Ryan. Or anyone else.

He opened the book, trying to find where I had stopped.

I knew that I had finished that one, but I was not about to tell that to a prick like him.

'This one is finished, I think. Where's the next one? Let's have a look. Ah, here it is. Will I run through it first? Like you have been doing? Concentrating on the important parts?'

I refilled my glass for the umpteenth time, nodding rather loosely.

He fished in his pocket and removed an ancient spectacle case from which the original covering had long since gone. Slowly, he took the spectacles out, closed the case and returned it to the pocket. As he fixed them on his nose, pushing them up to the bridge, I knew that I was looking at an oft-repeated routine. When he started to read, I was surprised at his voice. Somehow, I had expected a thin, reedy sound. Instead, I got a lusty baritone, with shades of bass.

Tuesday, 3 August 1920

I should have written last night, but I was completely

spent. Monday morning progressed at a leisurely pace. I left the office at noon, in order that I should be in time for my appointment in Ballsbridge. T was waiting and, to my surprise, suggested that we enter the Members' restaurant in the Society's buildings. That he was a frequent visitor was shown by the fact that he was recognised upon all sides. We sat near a window and he ordered tea and pastries. When we had been served and I had poured the tea, he proceeded to outline the plan for our approaching activities. The man to be marked was named Captain Ambrose Rowley, lodging at 19 Glenvore Terrace. The address is within ten minutes' walk. T and I would make our ways there separately. This was the first disturbing note struck. I have always had company at each stage of any mark. However, T is my superior, so I agreed to do what he said. I would walk to the end of the street where it joins Ailesbury Road and wait at the corner. T would approach from the opposite direction, pausing several houses from number nineteen. Rowley would leave the house between two o'clock and ten past, turning towards the spot where I would be waiting. T would be on the opposite pavement, clearly in my sight. He would signal, pointing out Rowley. This was an essential part of the plan. Only when I received that signal was I entitled to fire. T had me repeat the details over and over, until, in his words, 'they are burned into your brain'.

At the appointed time, I took up my position. My gun was in the left-hand pocket of my coat and I kept my hand upon it at all times. Suddenly I saw T in the expected position and at the same time a man emerged from a house on my side of the street. The man began to walk towards me. I saw T lift his hand in the manner arranged and I stepped out into the centre of the pavement, facing the oncoming figure. He was approximately twenty feet from me and I drew my gun from my pocket. Before I could bring it to the aim, I heard a shrill whistle from behind me. Rowley threw himself across a low garden wall and at the same time T called out loudly, 'Get down, Gráinne. It's a trap. Look behind you.' Instinctively I jumped to my right, into the next garden to that used by Rowley. I landed heavily and rolled as fast as I could manage under a hedge on the lawn. I heard two shots followed by at least six others. A man's voice cried out in pain and T shouted at me, 'There are two of them, Gráinne. See if you can draw their fire.' I crawled back to the wall and looked over it towards the corner of Ailesbury Road. There was no sign of Rowley but two men were crouched behind a motor which was standing a few yards away. One of them was attempting to fix a white handkerchief around the leg of the other, at the same time firing his pistol in the direction of T. He did not look in my direction.

I aimed my gun at him and fired two shots quickly, as I had been taught. Without a sound, he fell backwards, rolling into the roadway. Suddenly, I heard a slight sound behind me. I half-turned towards it to see Rowley, not five feet from me, a gun aimed directly at me. I thought, without much fear I must reveal, that I was about to die. I looked straight at him and a shot rang out. I was surprised that I could feel no pain. Then, T's welcome voice called to me from the wall. 'You owe me a favour now, Gráinne. I'll tell you what it is later. For the moment, let's get out of here.'

I jumped upright and over the wall. He led me across the road and along a narrow lane at the side of a house. This ended at another, running at right angles, and we raced very quickly until T stopped at a small gate. It opened to his touch and I saw that we were in a back garden. A few strides brought us to the door and it opened as we approached. A man stood there and signalled us to enter and run up the stairs. A door stood wide, and we were guided into a bedroom.

'Quickly now, get undressed. Into the bed, both of you. Not a sound mind. If they search here, give a good imitation of a married couple.' Without thinking, I began to remove my clothing and I hardly noticed that T was doing likewise. When I was wearing only my petticoat, stockings and undergarment, I climbed under the covers. Immediately, I was joined by my companion. As we lay there, he whispered, 'Now I can tell you the cost of that favour I did for you.' With this, he threw his arms around me and pulled me against his body. I became quickly aware that T was wearing less than I. As I was attempting to frame a strategy for extricating myself, a loud knocking came from downstairs. I heard men's voices shouting and the tramp of many feet running up the stairs. At that moment, T rolled over until he was lying on top of me. His lips descended on to mine with great force. What he attempted next was familiar to me from my time with R. Only on the purely physical plane, of course. I felt none of the gentleness with which my dearest one treats me on such occasions. Of course, I did not experience the compulsion to give myself, and proceeded to struggle with all my might. I was tensing my leg in order to bring my knee to my defence, when the door burst open.

T remained lying upon me, not turning his head towards the intruders. I saw two armed soldiers standing at the door, looking at us. What their impression was they clearly demonstrated by laughing coarsely and calling out expressions which I refuse to write. T was not neglecting anything which might give similitude to the ruse which we were hoping the soldiers would believe. To this end, he moved his body vigorously up and down. I realised very quickly that he did not intend to shirk his duty. Of course, he knew that I dare not struggle with the soldiers present. I was almost beyond saving when they left. They looked in other rooms but did not delay, and soon they had returned to the street.

Their departure was indeed speedy, but it was pedestrian compared with the speed of my leg as I brought my knee into the body of T. With a howl, he rolled from me and as I sprang from the bed he squirmed in agony, holding the injured part with both hands.

It was twenty minutes later when we left the house. T was silent and walked with a limp. I did not remark upon this but in reality felt a definite sense of having fought the good fight. We boarded a tram and were quickly in the city. It was not until we arrived at Abbey Street that my companion spoke. He whispered as we were about to enter the premises, 'A word about this to Mick and I'll make sure you don't come back from your next mark in one piece.'

Gen was indeed waiting for us. T gave an accurate description of events, and I described the manner in which he had saved my life. Gen appeared greatly troubled by what we said. He questioned T closely, asking him whether he was certain that we had walked into a prearranged trap. T nodded and a sombre mood came over the room.

Gen turned to me. 'Do you realise what this means?' Before I could frame an answer, he continued, 'You were betrayed, Molly. Someone wanted you captured. They would prefer that to killing you. I can think of a couple of men who would have a special welcome for you in the Castle.'

At that moment I realised the implications of what he was saying. A cold anger flooded my mind. 'When you discover the identity of the traitor, please allow me to deal with him.' He shook his head. 'No, Molly. You are too deeply involved in this. We have a system for handling such matters.' Despite my protests, he refused to be moved and left with the promise that he will advise me when the informer is unmasked.

When we were alone, T smiled at me. I confess to feeling some embarrassment in the moment, but he spoke quietly. He stated that he wished to apologise for his behaviour. It was unpardonable and far removed from his usual standards. I should realise that, coming so soon after the gunfight, he was in a state of high nervous excitement and completely forgot himself. If I wished Gen to know of it, he would be prepared to confess in person, saving me from the ordeal of discussing such a private matter. After a moment's thought, I returned his smile and said that I would find some way to reward him for his bravery. I think that he was surprised at my response – even more so when I came to him and kissed his cheek. We thereupon declared the matter to be our secret, never to be mentioned again.

I did not sleep well last night, a combination of reaction from the day's events and regret at the prospect of leaving AB. I packed my clothing and effects into my suitcase and it was ready for me when I came down for the last time this morning. I did not linger over breakfast, being determined to be upon my way at the earliest opportunity, thereby avoiding the distress of a protracted farewell.

The newspapers are full of what some call 'the Battle of Ballsbridge'. The reports state that Captain Rowley has been killed and two detectives from DMP wounded, one seriously, the other superficially.

At three o'clock, Gen arrived in the office and asked me to walk in the street with him. He said that he had discovered the identity of the traitor who had so nearly brought about the capture or death of T and me. I allowed him to continue without comment and he revealed that it is D. The shock was severe. I do not know him in the same way that I do T, but he has treated me well, always ready to listen to any remarks which I might make. I asked if there could be any doubt. Gen said that when confronted, D made a full confession. He continued by saying that no 'special measures' have been necessary. I take this to mean that no unpleasant treatment has been needed. I asked when the execution would be carried out, and he said softly that it had already taken place. A sad chapter has now been closed.

When I finished work for the day, I walked to Brunswick Street accompanied by T, who carried my suitcase. Number 8 proves to be the last house in the row and I have been allocated a small room upstairs, overlooking the back garden. I unpacked and placed my clothing in the wardrobe and chest of drawers. T assisted me in finding and operating the entrance to the attic. We climbed up and I was pleased to see that a lamp has been installed. The thought of mice being present in the darkness has been troubling me.

Back in the room, T left and, shortly thereafter, Gen paid me a visit. He asked if I am satisfied and comfortable. I requested a small table on which I can write. When he enquired the reason for this, I said that I keep a journal. He asked if I would permit him to see it, but I refused. I said that it was for my eyes alone. He asked what the result of my capture or death would be, in that case. I assured him that he will have sole possession of them should anything untoward occur. He expressed himself satisfied, provided that I gave him this right in writing. I tore a leaf from this book and inscribed the following. 'I, Mary (Molly) Stewart declare that, in the case of my death or capture by agents of the British Empire, my journals and diaries dated prior to such event shall become the property of General Michael Collins. Signed this 3rd day of August 1920.' He placed the paper in his pocket and left. Soon after, the woman who owns the house carried in a small table. I write at it now.

I looked at my watch. After midnight. I reached out my hand for the bottle. It was empty. I had consumed the best part of a bottle and a half of whiskey. Apart from a throbbing headache, I appeared unaffected. Ryan removed his glasses and stood.

'If you'd point the way, I'd like to use the toilet. When I come down, maybe I can brew up some tea?'

When I was alone, I went and stared into the mirror over the mantle piece in the living room. I may not have felt too bad, but the mirror told the truth. My eyes were bloodshot and my skin was pasty with an unpleasant-looking sheen to it. I put out my tongue, but quickly returned it. Some things are best not seen.

I heard Ryan filling the kettle and the clink of crockery. A cup of tea was a nice thought. Food was not. I returned to the kitchen just as he was wetting the tea.

'What about food, Frank? Will I make something?'

'No chance.'

He looked searchingly at me. 'You look awful. You should get some food into you. Otherwise, you'll be wrecked in the morning and that won't do your wife any good. You'll need to be alert then.'

I groaned. 'The sight of food would finish me. You're probably right, but I can't do it.'

'Look, why don't you pop upstairs and lie down on your bed for a while? I'll doze in the chair here.'

'If I lie down I'll probably pass out and wake up feeling a damn sight worse. We can both lie in the chairs. A break will do us good.'

He seemed to accept that, so we drank the tea and settled down. I pokered the fire and the flames gave a warmer feel to everything.

He said from his chair, not opening his eyes, 'You know what?'

I stayed silent and he went on. 'That piece of paper'd be worth a packet now. The thing about leaving the diaries to Collins.'

'I doubt if it'd stand up in court, even in those days.'

'Oh, why not?'

'No witness. She signed, but she never mentioned anyone else. I think they were there alone at the time, so no witness.'

He chuckled quietly. 'You're not as drunk as you look. I never spotted that and me a detective.'

I pulled a cushion under my head and closed my eyes. I had a feeling of floating above the chair. It was quite pleasant, in a disembodied sort of way. I remember thinking that I would lie like this for a few minutes.

I became aware of my own breathing. It was a comfortable sound and I did not want it to end. I felt no need to move. Then I heard a rustle. Paper.

I opened one eye. The room was dark, except for a pool of yellow light from a table lamp and the muted glow from the fire. Ryan was sitting under the lamp, his glasses on his nose, a book in his hand. He was turned side on to me and for the first time I noticed that his thin nose had a pronounced curve to it. I thought he looked like a bald pirate. He must have sensed my attention on him. Without moving from his position or lowering the book, his voice sounded softly in the warm darkness of my corner. 'You didn't waste any time, I must say.'

'How so?'

'It's after two. You've been out for over an hour. Feel any better?'

'Jesus Christ. Ten past two. Theresa could be dead by now. You should have wakened me.'

The last five words held more than a hint of accusation. In my guilt at sleeping, I was trying to blame him. Or someone. Anyone. But not me. Sensibly, he did not respond. Instead, he rose and said, in his deep voice, 'I'll make tea and a few sandwiches. I found some ham and half a chicken in the fridge.'

I sat up. Incredibly, my first sensation was one of hunger. 'Never mind the sandwiches. I want real food. I'm going to cook us a fry-up.'

'My God. The last time we spoke, you were like an overdue corpse. You must have a great stomach.'

'I don't know if it's great, but it's certainly empty. Just sit and watch this. I've always felt that there was a great chef lost in me.' Sure enough, we were sitting down to the meal inside fifteen minutes. Ryan, despite proclaiming loudly and often that he was not hungry, more than held his own.

When we were drinking our second cups of tea, he surprised me by offering me a cigarette. I was even more surprised to find myself accepting it. I had not smoked since I got married. That was one rule Theresa enforced right from the word go. Anyone, no matter who it was, who wanted a cigarette had to stand in the conservatory.

All this, of course, meant that the house was bare of ashtrays. We used saucers and I made a mental note to throw them in the bin before Theresa entered the house again. Always provided that she did enter the house again.

That brought me up with a jerk. The food I had just eaten seemed to call to me that, likely as not, she was hungry right now. Fuck it. Ryan saw the change in my mood and reacted fast. 'I had a good look through some of the older diaries. Ones that you had covered. Hope you don't mind?'

I shook my head. 'What do you think of her now?'

'Oh, I'm impressed. Very impressed indeed.'

'Considering that she was only twenty or so, I think she was a bloody marvel.'

'Mm. All the same, it's a pity that we don't get a better picture of Collins. It's all a bit 'he said, I said'. No real attempt to show his character.'

'I suppose you're right, but to me, the picture of Molly/Gráinne shows vividly the change from being a young girl, not long out of school, coming from a sheltered background, into one of the most cold-blooded killers I've ever read about. How does she compare with any you've met in your day?'

'Definitely the worst. Or best. Depends on your point of view. Of course, don't forget, she had a real cause to fight for. That makes a big difference. Any of the paramilitaries I've come across have that same ruthless streak. I suppose they can justify to themselves what they do. No guilty consciences to contend with.'

I cleared my throat. The unaccustomed cigarette made it feel on fire. I stubbed it out in the saucer, irritated that I had started it. 'My turn now. If you don't mind, I prefer the main light on.'

Wednesday, August 11 1920

Life has become extremely dangerous. Since the affair in Ballsbridge, the authorities have thrown a tight cordon around Dublin. All people entering or leaving the city by regular routes are subject to very strict examination. Vehicles are searched as a matter of rule, and on a more random scale, this is done to people. The curfew is being strictly enforced and almost nightly there are incidents of citizens being shot for no more reason than their presence on the street. After dark, the night is full of the sounds of armoured cars and tenders speeding through the city. House searches are now commonplace. More than ten thousand people have been arrested and, while most of them are freed within hours, there nevertheless prevails overall a sense of desperate danger. In Brunswick Street we sleep with the traps to the attic open and a chair positioned beneath ready for instant use. In my own case, my sleep has become no more than a light rest for fear of being caught by the searchers. We are now under orders to stay indoors unless we are on duty.

Another unwelcome development has lately appeared here. A senior RIC detective has gathered in Dublin a band of informers from the provinces who are familiar with Volunteers from their local areas. These men skulk around the streets, eager to recognise IRA people who have come to Dublin to report to Headquarters (GHQ). The name given to this group by us is the Igoe Gang, the detective's name being Sidney Igoe. Gen has embarked upon a concerted attack against them. I have been upon three such missions, each one completely successful.

On Monday last, Gen appeared in Abbey Street. He was furious and when asked the reason, related the story of a group of four Volunteers who came across a tender full of troops travelling along Camden Street. Our men opened fire and succeeded in keeping the soldiers pinned down for over an hour. Three soldiers were wounded and we suffered no casualties. I said that I thought that the outcome had been rather splendid, but Gen disagreed vehemently. He pointed out that the tactics of the enemy was to draw us out into the open. In this position, there can be but one outcome. IRA wastes valuable ammunition. What price delaying troops if in the process we expend hundreds of rounds of badly needed ammunition? Our strength is that we strike suddenly and briefly, withdrawing when the enemy has recovered sufficiently to take the fight to us. We can never win what Gen called 'a bullet war'. We have neither the personnel, the arms nor the ammunition, particularly the latter, to take part in this sort of flashy engagement. Gen stated that it is his intention to have the senior of the four hailed before a court martial at the earliest moment. Upon reflection, I realised that he was correct in his anger. We are forever being warned to save bullets. For myself, I do not think that I have failed to score a hit with any of my rounds. May this good fortune continue.

The overall feeling is one of great tension. This seems to affect some people more strangely than others. I have noticed among my comrades in Brunswick Street that petty disagreements are common. Men who are usually good friends can live together for days without speaking to each other. As so many Volunteers are now forbidden to leave the houses, overcrowding is becoming a problem. In this respect, I consider myself fortunate. As the sole woman on active service, I have a room to myself. The men are three or even four to a room no larger than mine. I have formed a pleasant friendship with the woman whose husband is the owner of number 8. Her name is Pauline Burke. She has told me that her husband is serving a sentence of five years' imprisonment in Dartmoor Prison. He attempted to set fire to a London police station while he was under the influence of drink. Rosemary is of the opinion that he would not 'harm a fly' when he is sober. She adds, 'provided it is not an English fly'. She is the cook for those of us at number 8. The food is good solid fare and I have noticed a welcome return of my appetite which has been rather bad since my illness.

I had to suspend this entry. Rosemary ran to my room to tell me that an armoured car had stopped outside. Heavily armed troops were conducting a search. In a flash, I was in the attic, in time to see many others scrambling up from the other traps. There followed a long wait. The searchers could be clearly heard below as they stormed from room to room with much banging of doors, breaking of glass, dreadful language. We were under orders to maintain absolute silence. A man close to where I was sitting whispered desperately that he could feel a sneeze building up in his nose. The man next to him attempted to stop the explosion by placing his finger beneath the victim's nose. This seemed to be satisfactory but very soon the urge to sneeze returned to the unfortunate man. Finally, his neighbour struck him upon the head with the butt of his gun, rendering him unconscious. Our silence thus assured, we remained in the attic for almost two hours.

When I finally climbed down into my room, I was covered from head to toe with dust and cobwebs. I was forced to wash and change, a small price for safety. The incident has illustrated the lesson which Gen constantly repeats to me. A secure hiding place can always be found if the person being pursued will look at his immediate surroundings. Who would guess that the most wanted fugitives from British justice in Ireland could hide in an attic directly above the heads of the searchers? He invariably finishes the lesson with the words, 'simple is best'.

Nineteen

Ryan produced the cigarettes again and I took one. The smoke invaded my clean lungs, bringing with it tar, nicotine, saltpetre and God knows what else. It also brought a sense of relaxation, the early forerunner of addiction.

I was once again aware of the absurdity of my situation. Surely I should be able to do something, anything, which would improve Theresa's plight? But what?

Ryan seemed to recognise the same thing. 'None of this is getting us any nearer to knowing why the diaries are so important.'

A feeling of utter helplessness came over me. 'What do these people really want? Surely you don't kidnap someone to get your hands on seventy-four-year-old diaries?'

'Well, they've done it. I still think the reason's somewhere in the books. Something they don't want known.'

'But seventy-four years ago? What could be in them that could affect anyone so long after? All the people mentioned must be well dead by now.'

He took the cigarette from his mouth and brought its tip close to his eyes, blowing lightly on it. His frown reached right across the bareness of his skull. Without looking at me he murmured, 'All but Mrs Perry. She only died recently, just over a month ago. What do we know about her?'

I considered this. 'Well, for starters, she was the only woman involved in what you might call the sharp end of things. At least that's what I gather from her writing. She always seemed to be the odd one out.'

He nodded slowly. 'Fair assumption. She was careful to write that she was the only woman. What does that tell us?'

'God knows.' I ground out the cigarette in the saucer with a growing sense of futility. 'But I don't fucking know. What's going on here? It's all crazy.' My voice rose to a scream and I leapt to my feet. Tears ran down my face and I could do nothing about them.

Hysteria was not far away. Ryan rose to his feet quickly and caught me by the shoulders, keeping me at arm's length. 'Easy. Easy now Frank. Come on, you're all right. You're not on your own in all this. I'm here to help you.'

'What can you do? No more than me, I'd say.'

'Look, Frank, they want the diaries and you can deliver them. They'd have no chance of getting their hands on them if they harmed your wife. You have to insist on that. They free her, no strings attached, before, and I mean before, you hand over anything.'

'That's all right, before I hand over anything, but if some bastard holds a gun to Theresa's head, I'd pass over my soul.'

'That's where you're wrong. You really hold the aces in this. They want the books so badly that they lifted her, but they get nothing unless and until she is safe. That's the bottom line.'

I was too tired to continue. I walked to the back door and opened it.

I revelled in the cool breeze as it took me over. I stepped into the garden. It was a black night, not a single star visible. The moon was in its first quarter and I could see the unruly threads of cloud racing across its tiny light.

I looked around at the darkened houses, envying the occupants their trouble-free sleep. If they only knew what was happening across their fences. If they only fucking knew.

I filled my lungs with the freezing air and opened my mouth. 'Fuck the lot of you,' I shouted.

Not a single light went on.

Ryan came to the door. 'Come in, Frank. You'll get your death out there.'

I felt drained as I sat down again. Ryan's face wore its usual expression of mild enquiry. I fancied that I could detect the beginning of bristles on his chin. Not on his head, though. That remained a smooth round shape.

He stood with his back to the fire, his hands clasped around each other. 'Let's go on and think about what we have learned from the diaries that might have some relevance today.'

I sighed and shrugged. 'Might as well do that as anything. Go ahead.'

'As I see it, unless there is something in the earlier books that you missed, the only thing we have is her signing them over to Collins. The words were... wait, it's here somewhere.' He leafed through the book, stopping when he found the entry he wanted. '"In the case of my death or capture". Well, suppose that, somehow, the IRA have that piece of paper. Mrs Perry has died. They could probably make a case for them being the heirs of Collins. Political heirs, anyway. So now, with her dead, the diaries become their property.'

His words hung at the entrance to my mind, while it considered whether to take them in or not. 'Even if you're right, there's nothing in the damn things for them to get excited about. It still doesn't make sense to me.'

'Granted there's nothing sticks out. But that's our opinion. We're not IRA people. How do we know that their reason for wanting the diaries will become obvious to us? We might not recognise it. For all we know, you could have passed it by weeks ago.'

I burst out again, nerves once more taking over. 'But that makes the whole thing fucking useless. I have to believe that they took Theresa for a logical reason. If not, she's probably dead already.'

He nodded. 'You're right, of course. If it's something we would not notice, then why worry about the books?'

'So.' I was trying to focus my mind. Slowly, the picture dissolved. We had to go on. 'My turn to read.'

As I opened the next book, I glanced at the clock. It was half past three. Despite us the night was passing. Or was it because of us?

Sunday, August 15 1920.
Gen brought us news from the provinces. There are brigades operating in Clare, Cork, Limerick, Longford, Monaghan, Tipperary and Waterford. Each brigade has 'flying columns' of Volunteers which strike at the enemy without warning. Army lorries and tenders are now fitted with metal mesh cages to ward off grenades and bombs. RIC units have been rearmed with rifles and Lewis guns to enable them the better to resist our attacks. Gen says that despite these measures, morale in RIC is lower than ever. Hundreds of resignations are being received each month. One of the results of this is the recruitment of a second group of demobilised men in England to reinforce the RIC. These are referred as 'Auxiliary Cadets'. They are drawn from the officer ranks and are in receipt of a wage of one pound per day, found. Their headquarters are at Beggars Bush Barracks here in Dublin but they roam the countryside in a random way. They are known as BTs but they are actually more dangerous than the original force of that name. I have seen photographs of them and they appear sinister in the extreme. They dress in the usual mixture of khaki and bottle-green uniforms but, in addition, sport almost-black tam-o'-shanters with a gold-coloured harp badge.

Many of our men have related how these Auxiliaries strike terror into the populace by their very appearance. Strapped to each leg, they carry a large pistol and in addition hold a rifle with a wicked bayonet attached. They wear a black webbing over their jackets with grenades attached to the front. We hear that they are not afraid to use any one of these weapons. Several men have been stabbed to death with the bayonets. They, rather than their forerunners, carry out savage reprisals whenever an attack is made upon the police or army. This force is nominally under the control of RIC. The reality is very different. They accept orders from no one outside their ranks and are responsible only to Mr Churchill in London. They are not afraid to put whole towns and villages to the torch. In their frequent searches, they regularly cause damage to property to the tune of thousands of pounds. Gen refers to them as a drunken band, but insists that they are more dangerous to us than the original BTs.

I dropped the book into the case and looked at it on the floor. 'How would it be if I put a match to the lot? I can tell them in the morning that the diaries are destroyed.'

'And how could you prove it? No. You have to hand them over. Don't think you can mess these people about, Frank. They might sound ridiculous, sometimes, but they're deadly serious. Believe me, I know.'

'The last thing I'd call them is ridiculous. Tell you the truth, they frighten the shit out of me.'

'All right then. As long as you understand that, you'll be fine. If you put the kettle on, we can have a cup of tea. Are you very tired?'

I got up, shaking my head. 'No. I think I've passed that point. Tiredness doesn't come into it. Anyway, I've had more sleep than you. I got a couple of hours, at least.'

When we had finished the latest batch of tea and sandwiches he found the book and opened it. He turned the pages slowly as he ran his eyes over them, looking for the next interesting one.

He looked across at me. 'This looks important. It's nearly two weeks after the last one we looked at.'

Saturday, August 28 1920
Freeman's Journal carries a leading article today about the hunger strike of Mr MacSwiney, Lord Mayor of Cork. He was arrested a week ago last Tuesday as a result of documents discovered in his house during an Auxiliaries' search. Having begun to refuse food as a protest against 'unnecessary arrests of political representatives', he was transferred to England last Sunday. He is now in Brixton Prison, London. The article points out that the main document upon which the charges are based is a draft of Mr MacSwiney's address upon his inauguration as Lord Mayor. The paper publishes, in parenthesis, the full text of the speech, reminding readers that the same words were carried by all the Irish papers and several of the English ones in their reports of the inauguration. Should not the editors of such newspapers be prosecuted? Or is there one law for Irish nationalists and another for the rest of the populace? The author of the piece calls upon the Government to answer this question either by arresting the journalists involved or by returning the Lord Mayor to his family in Cork.

Feelings are running very high at the moment. This is particularly apparent in Cork. Gen has compared Dublin to an armed camp. Curfew is rigorously enforced. The slightest shadow upon the streets brings instant fire from the weapons of the authorities.

I have received a long letter from Lady M. Life in Thurles remains unpleasant. BTs now control every yard of soil. They march into whatever place they desire with complete impunity. The priest has been forced to close his church during curfew hours and he has been told that the so called 'seal of the confessional' does not release him from the duty of reporting rebels to the authorities. I must stop here as I have come to the end of this volume. I go in search of writing paper.

If I am successful, I will continue this entry later.

The time by my wrist-watch is a quarter past three in the morning. I have been away for more than four hours. The discovery of this unused book has delighted me. I can now relate the details of a remarkable night.

Having called upon many of my comrades in my search for writing paper, V suggested that Gen would surely possess such a thing. I made my way to number 4 where his room is situated. I knocked upon the door and after a short interval Gen opened it to me, inviting me to enter. I asked for paper and he admitted that he had some books of the type he had seen me using. I waited for him to produce them but he seemed in the humour for a friendly talk. I took a seat upon his chair while he sat upon the bed. He looked closely at me and asked me 'How do you feel?' I replied that I felt well, thinking that he was referring to my illness. He laughed and said that he meant to ask my feelings about our position in Brunswick Street. I said that it was not pleasant but that we would make them pay for it later. He mentioned the matter of Terence MacSwiney. His situation is exercising the minds of the people to a considerable degree. Gen said that his fast from food was capturing headlines around the world. England is under great pressure for his release.

Gen was silent for a long period. I was at a loss for words myself, not knowing whether or not he wanted me to speak. Finally, he said that what he was about to say was not for the ears of others. Neither was it a matter for my journal. From the deepest recesses of his heart, Gen wished for the release of the Mayor. However, in his capacity as the one most responsible for the prosecution of the war, he had to confess that his hopes are different. If England wishes to present us with a weapon with which we can scourge her, she will allow MacSwiney to die. I was dumbfounded at his words and my face must have shown him this for he rose from the bed and caught my hands in his. As I looked into his eyes, I saw tears brimming in them. He whispered, 'Oh Molly, you must think that I am a monster. If he should die, think of what the world will say about England. If I was to toil for ten years, I could never achieve what the deaths of this brave soul will. No greater recruiting slogan for IRA could be penned than "Remember MacSwiney". Every man and woman, every boy and girl, will want to be a part of the fight against the people who killed our martyr. God forgive me Molly, but I pray that he will die.'

At this he was completely overcome with emotion. The tears now ran from his eyes. Instinctively, I put my arms around his shoulders and drew him into an embrace. His head rested upon my shoulder and I felt his body tremble. I stroked his hair, whispering the while, 'Do not fret. Do not punish yourself so. We all know that you must take difficult decisions every day. Every commander is faced with this sort of thing. If it makes you feel better, weep for as long as you must. Not a soul shall ever hear of it from me. I swear.'

And so we remained in this position, I sitting in the chair, he kneeling in front of me, his head upon my shoulder. Many minutes later, I felt him move, and I released my hold upon him, thinking that he wished to rise. Instead, he tightened his grasp upon me, whispering, 'Hold me Molly. Hold me in your arms. I never want to leave them. I love you, Molly. You must know that. I have loved you since I first saw you.'

A strange breathlessness swept over me. I cannot be hearing these words. This is the commander of the army to which I have pledged myself. I was still pondering my thoughts when he turned his head towards me and gently pulled my face to his. I could scarce feel the touch of his lips, so soft was the kiss. I allowed my head to remain there, my eyes closed, a thousand emotions churning within my heart. His lips felt soft and warm, dry and gentle. He gradually increased the pressure of his arms and I found my own returning around his shoulders. I thought that the kiss was never going to end. Slowly, his head drew back from mine while his arms retained their hold. As I opened my eyes, I found his searching them. They were free from tears now. His gaze was unblinking and I felt a swell of embarrassment sweep over me. I fancy that my face reddened, for I could feel its heat. He smiled at me, but it was not like any other smile that I had received from him before. He pulled my head towards him and allowed his lips to lightly touch the tip of my nose. Then he rose, pulling me to my feet also. He whispered, 'I can lock the door if you wish. Or you can leave. If you do, I swear that I will never mention this meeting to another soul'.

So saying, he released his hold upon me. For a moment, I looked at him. My embarrassment had fled. This time, it was I who whispered, 'If you lock the door, I cannot go on calling you General.' Again he smiled and reached over my shoulder. I heard the click of the lock as it went home.

Now he spoke again. 'My friends call me Mick. My dear ones use Michael. You can choose whichever one you prefer.'

For a moment, a thought rushed into my mind. The next seconds would decide the future of my happiness. 'I must tell you something before...'

'You do not have to tell me anything about yourself, Molly.'

'Ah but I do.'

'You look so serious. Don't be. It makes you frown.'

'Listen to me, Michael. You are not the first...'

This time, his laugh was loud. His eyes danced with mischief as he said, 'I thought you were going to tell me that you looked on me as a father.'

Now we both laughed. It was a wonderful moment, sharing our first sensation together. His smile faded and a sober look came into his eyes. 'Remember the day when you first came here? I did not behave very well. I hope you do not think that I carry on like that with all the women I meet.'

'What I do hope is that you do not invite them here. To your room.'

'Only one person alive has ever seen the inside of this room. Until now.' I waited but he did not continue. I gently kicked his ankle. Once more, the boyish smile lit his face. 'Vincent is the one. Now are you satisfied?'

In answer, I kissed him. There was little gentleness in this kiss, I remembered the day to which he had referred and wanted him to react as he had done then. I was not disappointed. His arms tightened and his mouth bore upon mine. His lips parted and I felt the flicker of his tongue. I propelled mine into his mouth and, with that, all pretence was gone. He edged me backwards and my legs struck the low bed.

Before I collapsed on to it, he took my weight and gently lowered me. When I was lying along the bed, he sat facing me, his feet still upon the floor. He bent to kiss me again and I felt his hands stroking my face. He began to caress me in a manner which I recognised as being a foretaste of things to come. I was filled with a longing to give him that which was mine to give. I must have conveyed this, for he brought matters to fulfilment with great haste. While I am not very experienced in this activity, I found a sensation of disappointment coming over me. I had felt none of the heady climb to release which had swept me to pleasure when R made love to me. At last I lay in his arms, a feeling of lassitude spreading throughout my body. My eyes grew heavy and I knew no more. Before I opened my eyes, I felt a sense of loss, remaining unaware of the reason. I moved my hand to find Michael and realised that he was no longer beside me. I was lying on the bed with a blanket thrown over me. I looked around for him and saw him standing before a small mirror. On the table before him was a bowl of water, heated, to judge from the steam climbing from it. I continued to watch in silence. His lower face and neck were covered in soap which he rubbed vigorously with a small brush. Satisfied, he then took a razor, its long blade gleaming in the light from the bulb overhead. Now he began to run the blade over one side of his face. I could see the great amount of concentration which he was giving the task. He used short rapid strokes, from time to time breaking off to clean the soap from the razor. When he had removed the soap from one side of his face, he ran the blade along a leather strap which was secured to the table. After half a dozen strokes, he lifted the blade and inspected it closely, its edge no more than an inch from his eyes. As he proceeded with the shave, and as I watched him, the entire operation began to effect me powerfully. I was a woman watching her man perform a wholly male act. I was excluded and I did not like the feeling. In an effort to partake even a little, I allowed my eyes to run over his body. For the first time, I became aware that he was still naked. He was standing to one side of the bed. His organ was limp, hardly visible in the mass of thick black hair which covered his thighs and abdomen. Something called for my attention but I knew not what. Ah, yes. I remembered the last time I had seen R naked, his organ visible to my gaze as it hung passively. The tip had been concealed within the wrinkled skin. This was a different picture. Michael's organ was no larger than R's but its head was clearly visible, the folds of skin resting like a soft ruff. Was such a difference in detail significant? I recalled looking at one of dear F's books which mentioned that males born with the skin too tight around the head of the organ are subjected to a surgical procedure. It is called circumcision. Michael had been circumcised as a child.

He had now finished his shave and stood looking at his reflection in the mirror. Slowly his sober look receded, to be replaced by a smile. It was a small smile, a private smile. I watched as he ran the tip of his tongue over his lips. My body stirred to see the folds of his organ start to fill, the head lift from its position against his thigh. I realised that his eyes were now upon my reflection. The longer he looked, the greater his organ became. I will not dwell upon the events which followed. Suffice to say that when I finally left his room it was with a light heart. I know that I have eased the weight of concerns upon his shoulders. At the same time, I have acquired a lover to whom I can give everything.

A silence occupied the air as his voice died. I looked over at him. His eyes were almost closed and I could see sweat beading his forehead. I waited for him to speak.

'You know, it's the extraordinary way she writes all this down so matter-of-factly.'

'Oh?'

'Well just remember it was seventy-four years

ago. She was from the upper-middle-class, Protestant, educated in England, sure of her membership of the elite in Ireland, before she fell into the arms of "The Boys". The very fact of her joining the IRA is strange enough. When you add the way she writes about the sexual things, I tell you, Frank, this lady's in a league of her own. That last bit is one of the most erotic passages I've come across.'

I laughed shortly. 'I agree. Theresa and I have thought along those lines reading about Richard and her. I'd say she was well ahead of her time. The ladylike way she describes everything adds a definite spice.' He fished a large red handkerchief from his pocket and blew his nose. In the early hours, it sounded like a bull elephant to me. He settled back in the chair. 'I'll sit and close my eyes for a bit. Not to sleep, just to rest them. You fire ahead.'

Twenty

Sunday, September 5 1920

The situation of our group in Brunswick Street has grown precarious. It appears that the authorities have suspicions about the houses. In the last eight days there have been five painstaking searches. The fact that the attic was not detected says more for the stupidity of the searchers than for our skill in remaining hidden without leaving clues to our whereabouts. Even I, a virtual novice in this area, can see that an officer who looks closely at the configuration of the buildings must realise before long that the roof spaces should have access from within the houses.

I continue this entry from new quarters in Rathmines on the south side of the city. Gen arrived in Brunswick Street shortly after I had started to write. A meeting of the Army Council of IRA has yielded the decision to despatch all residents to what are known as 'safe houses'. My companion here is F to whom I was introduced by Gen a few days ago. I asked him whether Gen would be visiting us in the near future. His reply was to remonstrate with me. The leader of our forces has more important matters to take his attention. He should not be expected to waste time visiting a message carrier, however comely she might be. I realised at that moment that F was not aware that I am Gráinne. I held my tongue. If Gen wants him to know, he will tell him. I have left him probably thinking that he was a shrewd judge to have spoken as he did.

To return to more important matters. From tomorrow, I will once again attend the Abbey Street premises of George Moreland. It has received no attention and is clearly considered by the police to be an authentic painting and decorating firm. The Squad will move around Dublin using Abbey Street as their headquarters.

The news of our comrade in the hands of the British is doleful. Terence MacSwiney is prepared to make the supreme sacrifice for the cause and his jailers show no sign of acceding to his demands. The Lord Mayor's case is receiving enormous publicity around the world, particularly in the Empire. Word has come from India that Mr Ghandi, the prominent agitator for freedom, has allied his cause to that of Mayor MacSwiney. The gentleman has said that fasting from food, as the Mayor continues to do, is a powerful and legitimate method of registering one's opposition. The *Manchester Guardian* has requested an opportunity to interview Mr MacSwiney in prison in order that the British people will know to what lengths this peaceful man is prepared to go to achieve justice.

Ryan drew a deep breath. His face had assumed a worn look. I didn't think it was tiredness and I was right. His voice, when he spoke, had a touch of awe in it. 'Jesus, you've got to hand it to MacSwiney though. To sit day after day, week after week, in that kip Brixton and slowly and deliberately starve himself.'

'I suppose it takes a certain kind of character to do that?'

'That it does. Take it from me.'

I looked at his bleak expression. He was showing his age, all right.

'You've seen it? Hunger strikers?'

He nodded slowly. 'Aye, I've seen it all right. Some of our crowd were secretly sent to the Maze towards the end of Bobby Sands's strike to see if we could appeal to him and to get experience in case it happened here. It wasn't a pretty sight, I can tell you. And don't forget, MacSwiney was force-fed. They don't do that any more, thank Christ.'

'It's been said that the force-feeding killed MacSwiney. Would that be true, do you think?'

'Absolutely. It was a terrible procedure. They'd

tie you up first and stuff the tube down your throat. As often as not, that killed you. Either by bursting your windpipe and drowning you in your own blood, or causing you to inhale your vomit.'

I shivered. 'For fuck's sake, I'm not in the mood for that. Let's get on. Will I keep going?'

'Yes. Carry on.'

Thursday, September 9 1920

It is seven a.m. I have just bade farewell to Michael. He arrived late last night and asked if he could stay. I am in my time at present and had some difficulty in framing my words. He kissed me gently and said that my company was all that he required. We lay together on the bed fully clothed. I have rarely seen him so calm. For the first time I saw him with a gun in his possession. He removed it from his overcoat and placed it within his reach on the table beside the bed. I revived the dying fire and the room was comfortably warm. He asked me to relate my life's details to him.

As I spoke of my parents and how much we, their children, had loved them, he was silent, listening with a look of sadness. I enquired the reason and he replied that he knew the ending of the story. I fear that I was overcome and began to weep copiously. He put his arm around me and gently pulled my head to rest upon his shoulder. He produced a handkerchief and wiped my tears as they fell. When I had recovered, I attempted to apologise but he stayed my words. If the day ever dawned when I could think of these sad events without tears, I would be a lesser woman in his eyes. I felt a great sense of comfort. Together we made a silent wish for peace in Ireland.

He said that he was tired from all the stresses of the war. He longs to put down his gun and govern Ireland in peace and prosperity. I asked him about his plans when peace comes. He seemed to recede from me a little at this. His eyes became grave, almost sad, his forehead taking a frown which made him look several years older. He did not speak for many moments but I did not press him. He was clearly in the grip of powerful, perhaps frightening, emotions. I merely squeezed his arm slightly and lay waiting for him to return to the warm room.

Finally, he turned his head to me and kissed my forehead. He looked deeply into my eyes and spoke so softly that I had to strain my ears to catch his words. 'To begin to make plans for a day which I, in all probability, will never see is to tempt providence. Every day I go about my business in and around Dublin and each moment of these days I am a hair's breadth from death. I hope that I will be ready for it when it comes, for I feel that come it will.' He seemed on the threshold of his own tears and I was prepared to comfort him as he had done for me earlier. To my surprise he asked me a question far removed from any internal sadness. 'Tell me what your views are of Eamon DeValera.'

The question took me completely unawares and I did not answer for several seconds. He appeared to take my silence as a refusal to reply and sat upright on the bed, looking down at me with an expression of annoyance.

'I do not think that I have any views on him. I only know what I read in the newspapers. I suppose that he is a brave man. If I remember what I have learned, he is the most senior officer to have survived from the Easter Rebellion. This obviously makes him an important figure in the war against England.'

'Surely you know that he is President of the Republic? He is not alone important, he is the perceived leader of Ireland abroad.'

I thought that I detected a note of criticism in his words. Not of me, rather Mr DeValera. I turned to him. 'Whatever people abroad may think, at home here, you are the one fighting the Empire. Mr DeValera strikes me as a politician. Am I correct in this view?'

He nodded. 'He is a politician all right, but much more than that. He views himself as the man to rule us after the English have left. I tell you, Molly, he is a dangerous man. I said months ago that the British were sending out signals through secret channels that they wanted to talk. And who do they want to talk to? Not me. Not to any of the people involved in the very struggle which has led to their asking for talks. The only man with whom they are interested in talking is DeValera.'

I asked about something that had been intriguing me. 'His name, where does it come from? Not Ireland, surely? It sounds rather Latin to me.'

He laughed shortly. 'The number of stories which I have heard giving reasons for his name makes me laugh. I asked him about the name once and he said that the Irish people could call him whatever they wanted as long as they supported his efforts to win independence. I ask you, Molly? His efforts? He spends his time running around America while we fire the guns and watch our people being killed every day. His efforts? He never even had to make an effort when Harry and I got him out of Lincoln. Come to think of it, I do not think that he even thanked us. He seemed to think that it was his right to be rescued for the country and for history.' His voice bore more than a trace of sarcasm as he spoke.

I smiled at him and said, 'I do not think that you like our President, Michael. Am I correct?'

'It is not a matter of my liking or disliking him. It is a matter of need. The country needs a figurehead who is recognised abroad. DeValera has support at home. Of that I have no doubt. But I think that he overestimates his popularity. I know in my heart that the Irish people see me as the cornerstone of this war.'

I confess that he had caught my interest by now. 'Tell me, Michael, in which capacity do you envisage him serving after the war?'

For a moment I thought that I saw fear in his eyes, but it disappeared in seconds. When he answered my question, his face assumed a rather bored look. 'President, of course. Sure what else is he fit for? But the Irish President will not be the same as the American President. The real power will rest within the Dáil, and above it, the Prime Minister. DeValera will spend his time meeting other heads of state and making speeches of welcome. He will be very good at that.'

I knew, instinctively, that he was lying. It was the

first time for this and caused a shiver to run along my spine. I know that I have no part to play in the leadership of the country, but I loathe falsehoods. As I am of such little importance, where is the point in lying to me? My feelings about such weighty matters are irrelevant. I remained silent but he did not continue the conversation.

After a few moments, I looked at him. His eyes were closed in sleep, his chest rising and falling in time with his breathing. His arm remained behind my head with his hand dangling across the front of my shoulders. Gently, not wishing to disturb his sleep, I took his hand and placed it upon my breast. I held it so until sleep captured me also.

Michael awoke first and when he made a movement to rise from the bed, I regained my senses. He told me in a whisper not to disturb myself. I watched him through sleep-leaden eyes as he splashed water upon his face. He used his hand to coax his hair into place and donned his coat, replacing the gun in his pocket. He came to the bed and kissed me tenderly, telling me to continue my rest. He promised to call again as soon as possible. With a last look around the room, he opened the door and left. The slightest noise of the latch was the only sign that he had been here.

I found that sleep was far off and settled down to write this. I think that I learned something very important this night, but I am at a loss to know what that is. I will turn my mind to it during the day. Perhaps it is merely my fancy.

When I stopped, Ryan was sitting straight in the chair. He was frowning, but a look, almost of triumph, was there.

'I think we're getting somewhere. Collins and Dev. I've always wondered at their feelings for each other. To his dying day, Dev never gave Collins the respect he deserved. It was almost as if he wanted to sweep Mick under the carpet once the Brits were gone.'

I raised my eyebrows sceptically. 'Hold your

horses for a minute. Dev might not have liked him, true, but he sent him to London to negotiate the Treaty. Doesn't that show that Dev considered him important?'

'Ah yes. The Treaty. Dev sent Collins to the talks despite Mick's objections. He knew that Collins was a fighting man at heart and that he would be out of his depth at the talks. No. Dev knew what he was doing alright. Don't forget that Collins was only about thirty at the time. Dev was sure that Lloyd George, with all his experience, would wipe the floor with him.'

I took a reflective sip from my glass. 'You know, it really was incredible that a man of thirty brought the British Empire, if not to her knees, then bloody damned close to it. And yet, all the revolutions that mattered in recent history were led by young men. Mao in China, Castro in Cuba and of course Che... The Hungarian uprising was led by students. And the Berlin Wall was toppled by the young people of Germany. It all must mean something.'

I realised that my mind was wandering from the main point and switched back a trifle abruptly. 'You think that's what the diaries are supposed to show? That the two of them hated each other's guts? A bit of an anti-climax, I'd say.'

His eyelids slid down in a slow blink and he rubbed a finger along the thin nose. 'I didn't say that at all. There's lots more to come out. I'm sure of that. But that last entry is what you might call a straw in the wind. I'll warrant that's not the last time Collins talked about Dev. I know there's got to be more. I think we should press on.'

I glanced at my watch. 'Jesus, it's half-five. We've been at this all night.' As I continued, my voice rose. I was feeling desperate. Whatever I had been expecting from the diaries, I was sure that we hadn't found it yet. 'We're getting nowhere fast. I can see myself tomorrow...today I suppose, talking to those bastards, bargaining for Theresa's life. So help me, if she's harmed I'll kill them. Every fucking one of them.'

His voice tried to bring reason back before hysteria took over again. 'We're nearly there, Frank. I know it. I can feel it in my water.'

Despite myself, I had to laugh. That expression. I had never heard it used in real conversation before. It kept cropping up in books, but I knew how far from reality they are. I subsided, as much from tiredness as any other reason.

'All right. If you think it's worth while. Do you mind if you read? I don't think I could hack it myself.'

He looked pleased as he opened the next book.

Saturday, September 11 1920
The pace of the war increases. Yesterday I attended a meeting of active service units in Cornmarket. Gen was there but the main speaker was General Mac Eoin. I have seen him previously. I think that it was in Kilkenny.

In the past three days, a series of savage reprisals have been carried out by BTs and As. I jotted the details upon a pad. County Clare has attracted special attention for no apparent reason. Kilrush, Kilkee, Lahinch and Lisdoonvarna are the towns which have suffered most severely. These reprisal raids are usually carried out following IRA activity in the area. Such is not the case in the Clare operations. Lisdoonvarna was the first community to be attacked. At noon on the 6th, two crowded Crossley Tenders approached and took up position, one at the western approach road and the other at the eastern road. The town being effectively sealed off, the As from both vehicles began a systematic series of attacks upon buildings on their courses, all the time moving towards the town centre and each other. Residents and shop customers were unceremoniously driven into the street and the buildings set alight.

Initially, some people made a series of complaints to the officer in command of the CFs. The horrible result of this was that three men were bayonetted to death in front of their wives and children. Many were beaten with rifle butts and kicked. The worst was still to come upon the unfortunate residents of this lovely town. Situated halfway along the main thoroughfare is the church. The parish priest, Father Trainor, came out to enquire as to the source of the noise, the As carrying out their invariable practice of discharging their guns in the air. He was immediately set upon by two members of the raiding party and beaten severely with their fists. He was stripped naked and dragged to the gate of the cemetery adjoining the church where he was tied to the gate. He was subjected to unmentionable abuse, physical and verbal. The final act was the shooting of the man as he hung from the gate. Eyewitnesses claim that his last words were prayers for his abusers. The other raids in the county were merely repetitions of this horror. Altogether, seven people were killed, forty-one injured, some seriously. Damage to homes and businesses is put at two hundred thousand pounds.

The counties of Galway, Dublin (outside the city boundary), Meath and Cork also witnessed terrible revenge for attacks upon RIC. General ME spoke of the need for the fighters in the city to deliver Ireland's answer to yet another list of English atrocities against our people.

I was in sombre mood as I left the meeting. I was making my way along the quays when a motor drew abreast of me. I heard a voice addressing me and for an instant thought that I had been discovered by the police. With my gun in my pocket I was doomed, but I was ready to sell my life dearly. I swung around, the gun half-drawn, only to see Michael smiling at me from the motor. It was a far from pleased Molly who entered the motor to be greeted by loud laughter. Michael threw his arms around me and, notwithstanding the driver's presence, proceeded to kiss me with great enthusiasm. My anger was not proof against such treatment and soon I was returning his kisses with my own. He said that he was delighted to see me. 'After the horrors described by Sean, it's like a breath of fresh air to see my beautiful Molly.' I remonstrated with him for the manner in which he had addressed me from the motor. This was just the sort of thing that the police did, something about which I and others like me have been repeatedly warned. He looked rather sheepish. I was reminded of a schoolboy being corrected by an overbearing teacher. In the face of this, I could not retain my anger for long and soon we were laughing together.

He then asked me whether I had eaten yet. When I said I had not, a sparkle came into his eyes. I should have been prepared for anything. The one thing which I would never have guessed was that we would go for lunch to the Kildare Street Club. This imposing premises at the corner of Nassau Street and Kildare Street is a stronghold of the most reactionary elements in Dublin society.

We alighted from the motor and he instructed the driver to meet us in one hour. In the great gloomy hall I was astonished to find that he is a member of the club. Not only that, however. He is registered as Mr Collins and addressed thus by the staff and members. I was very nervous to find myself in such a place. This state grew considerably worse when he leaned across the table and, in a whisper, drew my attention to a man sitting alone at a window table. Did I recognise him? I shook my head.

'Why, that is the man whom you went to so much trouble to shoot a short time ago. Major-General Hugh Tudor, Commander of Police.'

At this he summoned a waiter and directed that he, the waiter, bring to the Major-General, a double brandy with his, Gen's, compliments. I watched in amazement as the waiter carried out the task. Tudor looked around and the waiter pointed Gen out. Gen raised his hand in what I can only describe as a disdainful gesture. Tudor stood and bowed towards our table.

'The man's a complete fool. He thinks I am Maurice Collins, owner of a large drapery shop in Grafton Street. I had a drink with him last week and he spent the time complaining about the price of men's underwear. God help the police if he's the best they've got.'

I confess that I have no recollection of the food put in front of me. It was only when I was back in Abbey Street, among familiar faces, that my heart ceased to pound so painfully.

Ryan's laugh was tinged with admiration. 'What a man.'

'Collins?'

'Who else? A member of the Kildare Street Club, and using his own name.'

'Sure didn't he walk in and out of the Castle?'

'Aye. And never any attempt at disguise. It was extraordinary, really. Everyone knew him by sight, but I think it must have been the confident way he carried on. He sometimes stopped to pass the time of day with a policeman. The DMP and particularly 'G' Division were chasing their tails looking for him. They never got so much as a smell.'

He was shaking his head in wonderment as I resumed reading.

Twenty-One

Tuesday, September 21 1920
Bad news. The first Volunteer has been captured during an operation. A group ambushed a military patrol in King Street. They killed one soldier and inflicted some discomfort upon the rest. Another patrol who were in the area fell upon them from behind, cutting them off. With great courage and resource they managed to escape, all but one man. He was trapped under a motor car where he had taken cover and could not reach his comrades. There was nothing to be done but to abandon him in the interest of the escape of the remainder.

Gen is extremely low-spirited about the affair. He spoke to some of us this evening about the captive. He is a university student aged eighteen. His name is Kevin Barry. He was taken to the Castle where, after interrogation, he was charged with the murder of the soldier. This is a capital offence. He has been swiftly court-martialled and duly sentenced to hang. Gen is of the opinion that the British will never hang one so young. He is, nevertheless, convinced that Barry will be subjected to the most frightful treatment in an attempt to force him to betray his comrades. I asked if Barry would give them information. He replied forcefully and with considerable pride that all they would get from Kevin was his name.

The engagement in King Street was followed by a sweep of the area, when life was brought to a complete halt by a series of roadblocks. Every premises which could have provided a hiding place for our men was searched thoroughly. We, IRA, are unable to venture abroad as a result of this activity.

Ryan's voice broke the silence after I finished the

page. 'It's fascinating to read the words of someone who was alive when Barry was around. Somehow, he has always been more like a folklore personality than anyone real. Like Fionn MacCumhaill or Oisín. Is that how you see Kevin Barry?'

I shook my head. 'No, he was real enough to me. I've always thought of him as the only teenager of that time. Hero too, of course.'

He began to sing the tune very softly. His muted voice flowed gently into the kitchen at twenty to four in the morning.

In Mountjoy Jail one Monday morning,
High upon the gallows tree,
Kevin Barry gave his young life,
For the cause of liberty.

I let him sing the whole song without interruption. Its dreary cadence more than matched my mood.

I glanced at the book. 'Just a little more on Barry here. I'll read it.'

Tuesday, September 28 1920
The case of the youth Barry is very sad. For one so young to be in such a situation must be unbearably dreadful, both for himself and his family. I understand that he was studying medicine. Gen remarked that the lad's mother had approached his unit commander some time ago, with a request that he should be removed from active duty as it was inhibiting his studies. The commander had agreed to this course but Barry had pleaded with him to be allowed to go on one last operation. He was permitted to go and it was on this occasion that he was captured.

Tuesday, October 12 1920
I have spoken to Michael concerning Kevin Barry and Mayor MacSwiney. Our conversation took place in Abbey Street when we had the offices to ourselves. He said that his earlier remarks about the Mayor could just as aptly apply to Barry's case. The boy has become a

powerful symbol for the youth of Ireland. Should he be executed, which Michael doubts, another wave of outrage would sweep over the British Government. Michael is once again placed in the invidious position of requiring different outcomes for his divided loyalties. Should Barry be spared, the compassionate man would rejoice. If the lad is executed, the soldier obliged to plan and carry out the war will be given a clear weapon to wield against the enemy. Despite our surroundings and the possibility of interruption at any time, he took me in his arms. 'Molly, my love, I feel like a traitor, but I must consider the national good before any personal matters. If you pray, Molly, then for pity's sake, pray for me.' I was myself moved to tears.

I closed the book and stood up, stretching. 'God Almighty, this is driving me crazy. All the navel-gazing is a load of shit. I can't believe Collins suffered like this. From the little I've read of him, he seems to have been a single-minded bastard. Following the narrow line of a Republican goal without wavering. It's the only way he could have handled it, I'd say.'

Ryan nodded slowly several times then shook himself slightly. 'OK. I'll take over for a while. Give it here.'

Friday, October 15 1920

Michael told me that he would call last evening. 'Before eight' were the words he used, which brought a smile to my lips. I know, as he does, that if he was still here at eight o'clock, he would be unable to leave before five a.m. Such was the case. He stayed with me until this morning.

A singular event took place before he left. Having spent the night in my bed and having expressed the conviction that he did not expect to sleep for many of the moments of his presence, most of the night passed in a series of embraces. I tell no lie when I state that we loved on five occasions. I awoke with a sense of well-being and he seemed to be happy, humming as he shaved. This procedure of shaving has begun to play an important part in my life. I merely have to see him 'strop' his razor along the leather strap to feel a deep stirring of my flesh.

Ignoring this little aside, let me return to this morning. I experienced none of these feelings on this occasion and he dressed and kissed me goodbye. I walked to the hall door with him and closed the door when he had gone. Imagine my surprise when a knock sounded upon the door within seconds. I opened it and there he stood again. His face showed a rather strained look and, as he stepped into the hall, I closed the door and enquired if anything was amiss. For answer, he seized my shoulders and pressed me backwards against the wall. He brought his mouth down upon mine in a kiss which was almost painful in its intensity. The next thing which occurred was that I felt his fingers pulling at the tie of my negligee. He then pulled the garment above my hips, the nightgown with it. Keeping me pinned against the wall, he opened his clothing and within a second, we were joined, once more. He proceeded to thrust into my body, driving me painfully against the wall. His hands grasped my waist and lifted me until my feet had left the floor. During the proceedings he spoke not one word to me, the only sound being his laboured breathing and, at the end, a shuddering groan.

I confess to feeling a little ill at the manner in which he had used my body for his relief. He made no attempt to draw me into the act as a participant. I was a chattel. When it was over, he adjusted his clothing, leaving me to do the same for myself. He kissed my cheek as if the action was an afterthought. He left and I returned to my bedroom, to lie there in tears for many moments. When I had recovered, I went to the bathroom and drew a hot bath. I washed myself with a vigour which I have never before used. Only then did the feeling of being in some way soiled leave me. I do not know when Gen intends to return, if at all. I must formulate my feelings before then. My head aches and my hand trembles.

Wednesday, October 28 1920

I am deeply unhappy. I attempted to explain to Michael the depths of the revulsion which I felt as the result of his treatment of me. He has steadfastly refused to recognise that he has done any wrong. When I said that our lovemaking is an experience which we should share equally, he replied that while this is usually the case, there are times when it becomes a matter for him alone. To quote his words, 'I cannot always be expected to take time to be a great lover. Sometimes, completion is more important for me than your pleasure.'

In the face of this, I have refused him entry into my bed. He has become most unpleasant towards me, making comments of an intimate nature when third parties are present. An instance of this occurred today. He came into the office in Abbey Street. Two others were there, Charlie (C) and Paddy (P). He came to my desk and said that he wished to call upon me tonight. I replied that this was not acceptable to me. He then addressed the two men in a carrying voice. 'I hope you fellows pay our Molly every courtesy. She is very strict about that. Before she will talk to her friends, she insists on a recommendation from a school for etiquette. Even those she says she loves have to be on their best behaviour all the time.' He laughed loudly but I was relieved that C and P remained silent. They appeared embarrassed by his coarseness.

Thankfully, I have not been disturbed tonight. Away with such paltry matters.

Monday, November 1 1920

A deep depression has settled over everyone. Yesterday, Mayor MacSwiney was buried after succumbing in the seventy-fourth day of his heroic fast. Today, Kevin Barry was hanged in Mountjoy Jail. The end of these brave lives, although we were aware that the time was near, has nevertheless had a shattering effect in the finality of the announcements in the press. I have not seen Gen but he must be greatly saddened. I know that he told me the events were bound to gain recruits and publicity for us, but surely, now that they have come about, such thoughts will bring little solace to him. My own tears are falling freely and I can write no more.

Ryan drew his lips back, clicking his teeth together. 'Well, he got his martyrs. And he was right about them too. Barry and MacSwiney are two of our greatest patriots.'

'Yes. Actually, they are probably revered for the wrong reasons. The way they died is no longer relevant in these days.'

'Mm. In 1920, a teenage boy being hanged, and a young politician starving himself to death, must have made powerful propoganda, if such a thing existed at that time.'

He took up the book again. 'I'll go a while longer.'

Thursday, November 4 1920

I had the most frightening experience of my life yesterday. T called to see me. He had orders for a mark. The target lives in a room over a shop in South Great George's Street. We walked there after luncheon, waiting across the street as we examined the scene. All appeared well. In order to gain access to the rooms above, we had to enter the shop and walk to the back where a flight of stairs led upwards. The difficult aspect of the operation was that we had to avoid making noise. Our escape was through the shop and this would obviously be impossible if the sound of the shot had resounded there.

We arrived at the door of the room and T withdrew out of sight. I knocked and after a moment the door was opened by a woman. She smiled and enquired as to my business. I said that I wished to see Mr Norman. She asked me to step inside while she called him. He was in bed, having worked through the night. I produced my gun and told her not to make a sound. Had she screamed, I do not know what I would have done. I have never shot a woman. She stood there, a look of amazement upon her face. I called softly over my shoulder and T appeared. He also produced a gun and we forced the woman to allow us entry.

As I closed the door, a voice from inside called out. T thrust his weapon against the woman's body and held his finger to his mouth. I made an answer to the call in a muffled tone. A moment passed and as we were preparing to run into the bedroom where Norman was sleeping, the door of his room opened and he stood there, a gun in his hand. T reacted with great speed, jumping upon him and knocking the weapon to the floor. A struggle developed and for some moments, Norman more than held his own. At one point, he kicked T and bent to recover his gun. I stepped between them and said that if he moved again, I would shoot the woman. He appeared undecided until I said that my name was Gráinne, and that he knew that I would carry out my threat. This brought a remarkable change over him. His shoulders slumped and a look of resignation came to his face.

T stood back. The four of us stood in the doorway of the bedroom and I confess that I had no idea how to proceed. T again took command. He said to the woman that she should go into the room and close the door. She looked at Norman, her face ashen. She asked him if we were about to kill him. He nodded and kissed her gently, telling her that he would feel nothing. Gráinne never misses a shot. She took on a look of great dignity and said that we would have to shoot her also. Otherwise, she would raise the alarm as soon as we had left. Norman appealed to her not to be foolish, but she persisted. T moved to her and told her to turn her back. She held Norman's hand and turned. T immediately brought the butt of his gun down upon her head and she fell to the floor. Norman looked at her fallen form and thanked T for sparing her life. At this point, I interrupted to say that Gráinne does not kill innocent women.

T fetched a pillow from the bedroom and held it against the back of Norman's head. I fired a shot through the pillow and Norman fell. This is the first mark where I noticed blood in any quantity afterwards. Usually, I do not look at the mark after the shooting. A great red flood stained the wall behind his head and ran downwards like fingers pointing at the body.

We left the scene immediately and returned to the shop. T walked straight through to the street. I, in accordance with the plan, dallied and purchased some lace handkerchiefs. After a few moments, I walked slowly out the door and turned left in the direction of Dame Street. I had gone ten yards when a commotion broke out ahead. An armoured car sped around the corner and came to a stop. Two As ran past me to a distance of twenty yards, while a further two stood on the footpath twenty yards in front of me. I had walked into a flying roadblock. This is a tactic in daily use around the city where every person between the two teams of As is searched and questioned. I realised that my good fortune had come to an end. I was trapped in the block and unable to dispose of my gun. There was no garden wall over which I could throw it. I tightened my grip on it, determined to die rather than allow myself to be captured. I know only too well the treatment which would be mine in the hands of these beasts.

A line of people had formed on the footpath, waiting their turn to be questioned and searched. None spoke, looking at the ground rather than at their fellow citizens who were being 'dealt with'. I had reached a point where two men were ahead of me and was deciding which direction I would run after I had shot the two As. For shoot them I would.

An English voice rang out. 'I've got one, lads. A ****ing Fenian. Gather round.' With this the two As from behind me ran and took up position around the man being searched. A newspaper was waved in the air. I saw that it was a copy of the paper published by the Volunteers, *An t-Óglach* (Un Thoglock). Laughter ran among the uniformed men and the unfortunate owner of the paper was bundled into the armoured car. The others boarded and it sped away the way it had come. I was saved by the most extraordinary piece of luck. I was so shaken that I walked to Bewley's Café and ordered a cup of coffee. Eventually, I returned to Abbey Street to find T in a state of consternation. I was so late arriving that he had surmised that I had been arrested. I apologised for my lateness but did not mention the true reason.

He glanced at me over the tops of the glasses. 'That was a near one. She was not about to surrender.'

'I'm sure they all knew that anything was better than being captured. If what we hear is true, the Brits had a pretty fair line in torture.'

'No worse than today's lot, I can tell you. In Gráinne's case a bullet in the brain was preferable to the Castle dungeons. He opened the book again. 'Where to now, I wonder?'

Friday, November 5 1920

Gen called a meeting of active service units for today. We met in the same place as the last time, Cornmarket. We gathered around him, some on chairs, some standing behind them and myself sitting upon the floor at his feet. I counted the number present and found fourteen men and myself listening to Gen. No hint of any friendship passed between us. This was serious business. What he said was this.

'I mentioned to some of you a while ago that a group of top British intelligence officers met with Wilson in Cairo. The results of that meeting are now known to us. Over the last ten days, IOs have been arriving here in ones and twos. They are all regular officers, but none belongs to any unit stationed here. I need not mention that they are all in civvies. They have scattered throughout the city, taking lodgings under assumed names. Some have brought their wives along to avoid suspicion. We'll call them 'The Cairo Gang' for obvious reasons. We now know the reason for their presence here. On the orders of Churchill, they intend to carry out a programme of assassinations of leading Sinn Féin people, leaving evidence in each case which will point to us as the killers. I do not have to spell out for you the result of this plan if it succeeds even partially. It is sufficient to say that the country would be thrown into a civil war and would be an easy target for Britain. GHQ are putting together a plan to deal with these people. They must be stopped and I do not mean sent running. They will not run. This is the cream of British Intelligence. They must be killed. Each and every one of them.

And this is the tricky part. All the killings must take place at the same time. No matter where the targets are staying, you must find and kill them simultaneously. I do not want any possibility of reinforcements to persuade these people that they can escape by making a stand. The Castle must hear of all the killings at the same time. This will be by far the biggest operation of its kind in this war. To begin our reply, I am withdrawing every active service unit in Dublin from the field as and from this moment. All current or proposed activity is cancelled and I do not want any heroes going out and blowing some British soldiers to smithereens. Each of you go into hiding, outside the city if possible. If any of you have a difficulty about this let me know at the end and I'll see what I can do for you. Of course, that makes organisation of the plan a little difficult. To overcome this, we are dividing you into pairs. Each pair will be responsible for the agents at one address. There are at present fourteen British spies in Dublin lodging at seven addresses. The following are the pairs.'

He called out the names and I discovered that I was paired with T. I believed that Gen had finished speaking, but he continued, 'I want Volunteer Stewart and Captain Perry to remain behind after the rest have left.' He walked among the men and gave each pair a sheet of paper, with instructions to memorise the contents and destroy the paper. The room gradually emptied until only T and myself remained with Gen. He gestured us to chairs, remaining on his feet. He produced a sheet of paper from his pocket and held it aloft.

'This is your list. It is very special to you, unlike the ones I gave to the others. Headquarters are anxious that this action will have the greatest possible effect, not alone on the British Administration, but on the British public. Our best card at the moment is Gráinne, and the fear which that name generates.

Therefore, the main part in this operation must be played by her, that is you, Stewart. Among the addresses at which these spies are staying is an

Intelligence Centre. It is at 28 Pembroke Street and eight men are lodging there. From this address, the whole operation against us will be controlled. Both of you will have the job of taking that house and shooting the eight occupants. The actual killing will be by Grtinne, helped by you, T. It will not be easy. They will all be armed and probably ready to give you a good fight. Your aces are surprise and speed. I will have a plan of the house later today and you can study it. I want your proposals for the operation by next Friday at the latest. I have a place for you to stay. It is out at Swords, do either of you know the village?' T replied that he was familiar with it and Gen gave him instructions on how to find the farm where we would be staying. He ended by telling T that he would deliver the plan of the house in Pembroke Street later today. He dismissed us in a military sense and we left to find the motor of which T had use.

I am now in my room on the farm of Mr Bennet. I have some comfort with a bed and a chair upon which I am sitting. The farm is large and the farmhouse equally so. The Bennet family consists of Mr Bennet, his wife and seven small children, the eldest of whom is ten years old. The atmosphere of the house is one of continual noise and happiness. The children do not appear to need punishment and are encouraged to speak their minds at all times. After the first hour or so, I began to grow accustomed to the constant coming and going. Although T and I are here on deadly business, we are already being accepted as temporary family members. The children chatter endlessly and are forever asking questions. One little girl, who appears to be no more than five years, asked at the tea table this evening why T and his wife, by inference myself, were to sleep in separate rooms. She offered us the use of her bed if the ones we have are not large enough for the two of us. I must confess to laughing loudly at this, but T's face grew red in the extreme.

Gen called this afternoon and gave T the plan of the Pembroke Street house. It stands three storeys tall, with a basement. The back contains a small garden surrounded by a high wall into which a gate is set. This could provide an avenue of escape for the occupants of the house. We learn that the gate is kept locked and the key stored above the back door. Our first objective will be to find this key before our arrival becomes known. The rooms occupied by the spies are marked upon the plan. Four are on the first floor, four on the second. The basement is thought to be the Intelligence Centre, presumably manned at all times. T and I have spent the time since Gen's departure in attempts to devise a strategy which will give us access to the spies and at the same time provide us with the means of escape. I do not expect to have either the time or disposition to make entries for some time. When I resume, I will account for the time lost.

Ryan's voice sounded, soft, slow, not the definite tones of his reading. 'Have you been listening, Frank?' It dropped to a whisper. 'Or are you asleep?'

I replied without opening my eyes. 'Not a wink. Every bloody word. Why have you stopped? End of a book?'

'Yes.' He sounded as if he was excited, in a laid back sort of way. 'There's only one book left, as far as I can see. Number forty-seven.'

I sat up. 'Then they finish back in 1920. I wonder why. She started out to record her life and stopped after a year and a half. Doesn't make sense to me.'

'A lot of people start something like this and give it up fairly soon.'

'Maybe they do, maybe they don't. But if they do, they don't bother keeping the stuff for seventy-four years. And don't forget, her final wish was for the books to be destroyed. Without anyone reading them.'

He glanced at the clock. 'Five past eight. Fancy a shave? Are you an electric man?'

'I use a regular blade myself. I'll have first go, if you don't mind. I want to be ready for off when the call comes. You can put the kettle on. See if you can pick up anything important from that last book. You can read to me while I shave. I'll do as much for you.'

And that's the way we worked it. He set the table for breakfast. Not that either of us was hungry, it was something to do. He began to leaf through the book, running his eyes quickly over the pages.

'The next few entries are about the way they made their plans for Bloody Sunday.'

I stopped the path of the razor. 'Bloody Sunday? I thought that was in Belfast in the 70s. The Paras opened fire on an unarmed march.'

'This was the first and real Bloody Sunday. Twenty-first of November, 1920. That's the morning when the Squad went into houses all over Dublin and shot a crowd of Brits. I forget how many they got. The Tans went to Croke Park that afternoon and fired into the crowd watching a match. The books say that that was the day when England realised they were going to have to pull out of Ireland.'

'Skip ahead to that date and see if there's an entry.'

I continued to shave as he turned the pages. 'Ah yes. Here we are. Quite a long one too. Anyway, here goes.'

Monday, November 22 1920
The last two days have been the most exhausting days of my life. I have been here, in Aunt Beatrice's house in Kingstown, since yesterday afternoon. She does not know why I have returned but nevertheless agreed to my staying here, without explanation.

I will start my account with the remark that T and I have worked day and night. Gen has given us great support and supplied the extra personnel required to put our plan into action. All teams assembled in Brunswick Street on Saturday morning. Each pair was required to outline their intentions for Sunday. The final signal for the operation was given, the time of commencement, nine a.m. Gen stated that all operations must start at exactly nine and finish before nine-thirty. Everyone was to reassemble in Brunswick Street immediately afterwards, when details of arrangements for their conveyance to safe houses would be given to them.

During Saturday, each pair kept apart from the others. Tension was extremely high throughout the day and in my own case sleep was impossible during the night.

I was awakened at five a.m. on Sunday, and donned the habit of a Roman Catholic nun. T represented himself as a priest. Breakfast was provided for those who wanted it. We continued to sit around in our teams of two until Gen called us to attention. He did not attempt to deliver any words to bring us to the correct state of readiness. He merely wished us luck and shook every hand.

By prior arrangement with him, our team was reinforced with two other men, Brian (B) and Sean (S). We left Brunswick Street separately and made our individual ways to Pembroke Street, arriving there at a quarter to nine. B and S took up their positions in the lane way on to which the gate gives access. Their part in the operation was to prevent anyone from the house escaping through the gate. The remainder of the work fell to T and me.

At precisely one minute to nine, with T at my side, I rang the doorbell of number 28. It was opened immediately by a maid. I asked to see Mrs O'Kelly, the owner. The maid looked most respectfully at us and invited us to enter, closing the door behind us. She showed us into a drawing room on the ground floor. I asked her to tell Mrs O'Kelly that Father Murphy and Sister Geraldine were in rather a hurry and would not detain her for more than five minutes. She departed and almost at once a stout woman entered.

Before she could speak, T produced his gun and told her that she would not be harmed if she co-operated with us. She became very pale but agreed to do what we ordered.

T took possession of a thick cushion, mentioned the

name under which the first of our targets was posing and his room number, telling her to precede us to the door. She led us up the first flight of stairs, stopping outside a door directly beside the staircase. At T's signal, she knocked and called out her name. The door opened to reveal a man in pyjamas. I produced my gun which I had been holding inside my sleeve. T pushed the cushion against the man's head. I fired a shot which was muffled by the cushion, and as the man fell, I pulled the door closed. We ran to the next room and the procedure was followed again. The third door yielded no reply when the woman knocked. I added my knuckles and after an interval, a woman in night attire opened the door. I pushed her aside and T held her under his weapon. I ran into the room to find a man asleep in the bed. I called out to his companion whether this was the man I sought. She nodded and I placed a pillow over his head and shot him as he lay there. The last target on that floor was easily dealt with, opening the door to the knock, suspecting nothing. We had marked four and had another four to attend to on the next floor.

At this point, T shepherded Mrs O'Kelly into an empty bedroom and locked her in with the warning that she would be shot if she made a sound. Up the stairs we ran as fast as we could. Everything had progressed with gratifying smoothness, but I felt that our good fortune could not last. I was correct. The four men on the second floor, hearing the shots from below, had banded together and assembled in one room with the door barricaded. When we approached, we were met with a volley of bullets and were forced to leap for cover. I whispered to T that he must fire at the lock. He did this and the door opened slightly. I instructed him to keep firing through the door while I wormed my way forward on my forearms, not an easy undertaking dressed as I was. I lay against the bottom of the door and applied my strength to pushing aside the barricade. Inch by inch, I moved it. I could have done nothing without the magnificent behaviour of T. Eventually, I had opened up a field of fire which enabled me to commence firing. My first shot missed any target, my first failure of the morning. My next round brought forth a loud cry, followed by the sound of a body falling to the floor. T pulled himself to my side and placed his lips against my ear. I understood his whispered words and nodded my head. After a short interval, I fired again. An immediate volley answered. I cried aloud, as if in great pain. Simultaneously, T picked up a stuffed chair which was on the landing and threw it down the stairs. It sounded exactly like a body falling. We both tensed but remained perfectly still, uttering not a sound. The situation remained thus for many moments. At last, I heard a slight sound from the room, a shuffling noise. It seemed to be approaching the door. A man's foot slid outside and stopped momentarily, to be followed by a cautious head. The eyes were attempting to look around the door frame. I raised my weapon and fired a single round. An exclamation was cut off and the man's body toppled slowly on to the landing.

Two down, two remaining. I quickly reloaded. As I lay in the doorway, I looked at the space underneath a cabinet which had formed part of the barricade, I saw the foot of a man moving. I hit the foot with my next shot, bring forth a satisfying scream of pain. The victim, in his agony, rolled into my view and I despatched him with my next shot.

Now there remained only one. T called out for him to surrender. He made no reply. Again T called, saying that the man's situation was lost. We were four Volunteers and he had no chance against us. If he surrendered, he would be treated as a prisoner of war. A frightened voice asked if we would give our word as gentlemen. T replied that we would. A gun was thrown through the door and came to rest on the landing.

From behind a settee there arose a young man, his hands in the air. As he came forward, T moved to meet him. I called out for T to stop and shot the spy between the eyes. He fell silently. T appeared aggrieved in the extreme. 'I gave my word as a gentleman.' 'You kept your promise. I fired the shot. I was no part of your bargain. Neither am I a gentleman. We cannot take prisoners on a job such as this. You know that.'

The matter ended there and we made our way to the basement through the kitchen. The room was deserted and we knew that our comrades had made sure of this before a shot was fired. It contained what I now know to have been a radio receiving and sending set with a Morse key. T asked me to wait for a moment. He activated a switch on the side of the machine and within seconds, a humming sound could be heard. He then turned a knob, bringing forth strange sounds, not unlike birdsong.

He began to tap the object fastened to the machine (the Morse key). He did this repeatedly for some moments. I asked him what he was doing. 'I am sending a message to the British.' I asked what the message was and he replied, 'The word I have sent is Gráinne.' He instructed me to stand clear and emptied his revolver into the machine. Now he went into the back garden and blew a shrill blast upon a whistle. This was the pre-arranged signal to B and S that the operation was completed and successful. I looked at my watch. It showed twenty-one minutes after nine.

We, all four, arrived back in Brunswick Street before ten-thirty. All other groups returned also. Not one of our people was injured, much less killed, and we could report the killing of fifteen men, fourteen English spies and one 'G' man who had been previously warned to leave Dublin. It was a magnificent achievement. Operation 'Cairo' was over.

Gen asked that we disperse as quickly as possible and I thought of Kingstown and AB. And so, that is why I am here now. I must break off while I attempt to sleep. My eyes are tired and my mind insists on wandering.

I have abandoned any attempt at sleeping. My mind is too full of pictures of my activities of yesterday. I will proceed with my account of 'Cairo' and its aftermath. The papers this morning are full of news about the killing of the spies.

Another dreadful story also occupies many pages. At three p.m. yesterday, a party of As descended upon Croke Park, a football field in Dublin. A large crowd had gathered to watch a game of football. The As erected a machine-gun and fired into the crowd, also sweeping the field with bullets. In the ensuing panic, with people fleeing in their attempts to elude the fire, twelve people were killed. It is not yet clear whether all the deaths were caused by the panic or if any of the victims were shot. The exception is that one young man playing football at the time was found to have been shot in the head. The papers carry a statement by General Crozier, Commander of the As, in which he says that his men attended the game in a search for arms. He reasoned that all members of Dublin IRA, particularly those involved in 'the cowardly murder of so many unarmed officers' that morning, would be likely to have attended the game. When his men attempted to search those attending, they came under fire from the field and the grandstand. In the circumstances, they had no alternative but to return fire. The statement does not mention whether any arms were found in the search or whether any CFs were killed or wounded.

The English papers complain loudly that fourteen innocent men enjoying a quiet Sunday morning, some in the company of their wives, were murdered in cold blood. The name Gráinne does not appear in any paper that I have read. At the same time as the Croke Park incident, a military engagement was joined between a large force of As and a Flying Column of IRA under the command of General Tom Barry near the village of Kilmichael in County Cork. The splendid result was the killing of eighteen As. The Column lost three Volunteers. On the previous night in Dublin, three of our men were arrested in an illegal drinking den and taken to the Castle for questioning. It is announced in all the papers today that they were shot dead while attempting to escape from lawful custody. Their names are Volunteers McKee, Clancy and Clune.

I return to this entry after an interval of four hours. It is now eleven p.m. on Monday. AB came to my room while I was writing. I had had a caller, Mr Green, with whom I had worked in the Castle. Her face looked rather flushed when she came to my room. I suspect that 'Mr Green' has been weaving his magic spells upon her again. She looked in the mirror over the table and rearranged her hair. I could not prevent a wide smile from showing upon my face, which she ignored. Gen asked whether he could come to my room. I was forced to refuse. AB may consider him a charming man, but she would not hold such an opinion for very long should I entertain him in this fashion. We left the house and walked towards the harbour. The evening was fine but very cold. The moon was full, large in the sky. The stars glittered brightly and the waters of the harbour reflected them and the many lights showing on boats moored there. Gen said that he wanted to ask my pardon. When I asked for what, he said that he had behaved very badly towards me. He offered a reason but not an excuse. He has been carrying the burden of the 'Cairo' operation for a long time alone, unable to share it with anyone. I said that he could have told me. He said that such a course would have been unthinkable. I am the woman whom he loves, but only a Volunteer. If he heard of any member of IRA discussing operations with his wife or lover, he would hail him before a court-martial on a charge of treason. I know the penalty for such an offence.

I began to feel sorry for him and as a sign of this, I laid my hand upon his arm. He immediately took it in his and brought it to his lips. We stopped walking at this point and he gently propelled me into the lee of the harbour wall. We were hidden in shadows and he asked whether he could kiss me. I said that, while I was gratified by his apology, it would take me some time to recover my confidence in him. In the meantime, I would prefer to postpone any overt signs of affection between us. After a moment's thought, he agreed to this.

Now he changed the subject rather suddenly. Do I remember my admission by him into IRB? I said I did. The time has now come for my first task as a member. I remained silent as we stood beside the sea wall. The task before me is not difficult, particularly after my good performance in 'Cairo'. The place is the house in

Cornmarket where we have met previously. A meeting has been called for four p.m. tomorrow. I will travel to Dublin by tram and he will meet me outside the Gresham Hotel at a quarter to two. He will drive me to the house two hours before the meeting is due to begin. I will hide in the basement and he will fetch me when the moment is appropriate. I asked what the task is. He said that it was merely an extension of my present work as Gráinne. You want me to kill someone? Yes. Whom? After a pause, he said the name softly.

DeValera.

I was shocked beyond words. I endeavoured to protest but Gen interrupted brusquely. I have sworn to carry out all orders for my superiors. In the face of this, I lapsed into unhappy silence.

Twenty-Two

The shrill of the telephone exploded into the kitchen. We were sitting at the table drinking our second cups of tea. It was my spell to be reading and Ryan was smoking as he listened. The clock said twenty past nine.

I dropped the book and sent the chair crashing to the floor. As I started towards the phone, Ryan laid a cautioning hand on my sleeve. I shook it off wordlessly. The only thing that mattered was that phone which continued to ring. Each peal seemed louder than its predecessor.

My heart was pounding and my breathing laboured. I lifted the receiver and put it to my ear, desperately trying to rescue enough calm to speak.

'Mr Doorly?'

The accent was not Irish. I had programmed myself for a Belfast or Derry voice. Who the hell was this? I said, 'Yes.'

'You'll have received our little parcel, so you know the score. No talk from you. No questions. Just listen.' There was a momentary pause before he continued. 'You put the diaries in a case. Get into your car at half nine and drive to the Phoenix Park, the North Circular Road gate. That should take you no more than twenty-five minutes. Drive carefully now. It would be a shame if you got stopped for speeding. Or drunk driving, for that matter. Follow the road along to the old monument of the man on a horse. Go straight ahead. The road drops down into a dip and rises again.

'Drive at twenty miles an hour for point seven

miles. Get that, point seven miles, not seven miles. Be accurate. To your right, the grass will slope upwards and you will see a grey building. It's a bit derelict but it's the only building, so you won't miss it. It has a high wall around it.

'Carry the case to the wall. A yard to the right of the only gate, you stop. Look around there, Mr Doorly. Make sure that you are not seen.' He chuckled shortly. 'Except by us, of course. We'll be watching you from the time you leave your house. As soon as you are sure you are not being observed, throw the case over the wall. Then you get out of there. Fast. Very fast. You have to be back in your house not more than one hour after you leave it.

'I'll be in touch.'

The line went dead. I stood there, looking at the receiver. Nothing had gone the way I had imagined. Theresa wasn't even mentioned. I had fully intended to throw my weight around with a lot of 'unlesses', 'befores' and 'untils'. Instead, what had I done? Stood there like a stuffed bird without uttering so much as a syllable.

Jesus Christ, come on, Doorly. It's nearly twenty-five past. I was not dressed, having changed into my dressing gown after a shower.

Oh shit.

As I ran from the room, Ryan called out, 'Hold on Frank. I'm coming with you.'

I had forgotten his existence. I shouted over my shoulder. 'No, you're not. I'm going alone. I don't want any arguments, Ryan. Stay out of my hair. I mean it.' The last three words came from me in a drawn out scream. Frantically, I pulled on a track-suit and fumbled at the laces on my trainers. Bending over to tie them, floating spots drifted into my sight and out again. My head felt light. For a second, I thought I was going to pass out.

I charged back down the stairs. Ryan was sitting

at the table reading, another cigarette in his fingers.

I was in the car when he appeared at my window, tapping with his knuckles. I was about to give him the rocket of a lifetime and lowered the window to start. He held the suitcase in his hands. 'I imagine that you will need this.'

Without thanks, I tore it from him and flung it in the back. The car was reversing before it landed on the seat. I took off up the road with a roaring engine and squealing tyres.

I remember absolutely nothing about that drive. The first time I surfaced was as I was sweeping through the big silver-coloured gates. It had been so long since I had been here that I still remembered old Gough on his horse. He had an enormous scrotum. The horse, I mean.

My eyes would not focus as I tried to take a reading from the odometer. I slowed to a dead stop and reset the figures to zero. Point seven miles from here. Carefully I kept the needle on twenty. It was quite easy. When the numbers in the right-hand column reached seven, I pulled into the side of the road and braked.

I looked to my right. One building, grey, derelict, as ordered. Of course. The old Magazine Fort. The IRA had raided it, one Christmas long ago, and walked off with all the arms and ammunition in the place. Red-faced day for the Government. Everyone else laughed their balls off. Those were the days when it was considered sound to give tacit support to the IRA, a harmless crowd of lunatics.

I hefted the case and walked across the grass. The ground was soaked from a long period of rain and I found it tricky trying to keep my footing up the incline. My shoes were soon marked with muddy streaks.

The gate stood where I had been told it would. It was heavily chained and a roll of rusty barbed wire lay on top. I put the case on the ground at my feet and looked around. A hundred yards away, a seedy-looking old man was standing patiently, while his mongrel strained to deposit one more turd on the green slopes.

There wasn't another soul in sight. Maybe he was the IRA watcher. One way or another, I was not about to allow myself to be delayed by him, so I picked up the case and threw it over the wall as if I was spinning a large flat stone across the surface of a lake.

The drive home was uneventful and when I let myself in, there was Ryan, still smoking. He rose as I entered the kitchen. 'How did it go?'

I shrugged. 'How could it go? I threw the case over the wall and came home. What happens now?'

'I suppose they have a look at the diaries. If they are what they seem to think they are, I expect you'll get a call telling you where to find your wife.'

'And if I don't? Get a call, I mean?'

He stared at me for a second. 'Ah, I'm sure you will hear something today. Maybe even this morning.'

'So we sit here and wait for another thousand hours. Oh Christ, I don't think I can take any more of that. And this time, we have nothing to read to pass the time.'

'Try not to worry. You followed instructions to the letter. In my experience of ransom situations from this quarter, they keep their word.'

'Your experience? You've come across this before?'

'Oh yes. There are a lot more kidnappings than ever get into the papers. When the IRA are involved and the ransom paid, I've never known them not to come through.'

'That's all right, it's money. This time it's not so simple. We don't know. What are they after? There isn't chicken shit in those books.'

Suddenly he was not listening to me. A silence dangled in the air, fragile at first, then thickening. I looked at him. He was staring at me without seeing me.

He rose from the table and walked to the back door. He opened it but did not step through. Instead, he stood with his back to me and appeared to be breathing heavily.

The cold wind drove into the kitchen, bringing several miniature eruptions of smoke from the fire, where they fled to the corners of the room, before disappearing.

I sensed an important moment. I was about to ask him to shut the door when he did just that, walking back to his chair.

'Sit down, Frank. You're like a hen on a hot griddle, hopping from foot to foot like that. Sit down, can't you?'

'I'm for the toilet before I do anything. I've been bursting for a pee since I got back.'

I ran up the stairs. A certain peace stole over me as I stood directing the flow against the side of the bowl. I have always avoided the noise of the stream into the water. I remember one day when I was a nipper. A couple of pals were in the house with me and we clearly heard my father urinating into the water in the toilet bowl. One of them laughed and said that it sounded like a waterfall. I still get embarrassed at the thought.

I returned to the kitchen and took my chair opposite Ryan. 'Fire ahead, now. What's the matter that's new?'

For answer, he reached into his pocket and produced several sheets of white paper which he unfolded and placed on the table in front of him. As he was going through the routine of putting on his glasses, a monstrous suspicion burgeoned in my mind.

I slowly stood, my eyes on him, an empty ache in the pit of my stomach. I felt the sour taste of bile at the back of my tongue.

'Tell me I'm wrong. For fuck's sake, tell me I'm wrong.'

He remained busy with the prelude to reading, his eyes studiously avoiding mine.

I stepped forward, bringing him within range. Not since I was a hormonal boy of twelve had I struck another human being. My right hand flew out and my knuckles connected with his jaw. He did not react at first. I heard two sounds. The first and most important one was the thunk of my fist hitting him. The second was the click as my knuckle cracked, the skin splitting, blood flowing over my cuff and on to the floor.

When he did react, it was to grip my wrists with his hands. He never even rose from the chair, holding me at arm's length without apparent effort. His eyes remained tranquil, my only points the slight bruise forming on the side of his jaw. The tone of his voice did not change. 'That's your starter, Frank. The free one. If you ever lay a hand on me again, be ready to finish me off. Otherwise, I'll beat the bejaysus out of you with one hand.'

I pulled my wrists from his grasp, not through any sudden rush of strength, he just relaxed his grip. Tears welled and I turned from him towards the window. I tried to wipe them away, only to realise too late that I was using the damaged hand. It hurt like hell and probably left a smear of blood to mix with tears across my face.

I struggled for control and won, but only just. The precipice was agonisingly near.

I sensed him rising and his hand rested briefly on my shoulder. 'Why don't I put the kettle on while you see to that hand?'

I sniffed aggressively. 'Fuck the kettle. There's

another bottle of Paddy upstairs. I can drink tea anytime.'

Ten minutes later we were sitting opposite each other, glasses in hand, the bottle between us on the table. I had stopped the bleeding but the hand was swelling by the second. I didn't care. I intended drinking enough to drive pain from the picture.

The white paper was still there in front of Ryan. I gestured with my glass. 'What's all that then? I suppose you tore the pages from the back of the last book?'

'I may be a country copper but I wasn't born yesterday, Frank. If I had done that, they'd have spotted it a mile away. Sure the opposite pages would have fallen out.'

'Well, thank God for that anyway. I thought for a minute that you'd killed Theresa. What are those pages if they're not from the diaries?'

'They are from the diaries, but not the way you mean.'

I was about to explode when he hurried on.

'When you were asleep during the night, I went through the rest of the them. I used "court shorthand", a thing that is always handy for a copper. It saves time waiting for official transcripts. It's like ordinary shorthand, but a lot quicker.'

'And you wrote down the whole thing and then kept it quiet while we laboriously read it again? You're nuts, with a capital k as we say in my job.'

'Anyway, I'm going to read the stuff to you. Then I think you'll understand a little more why they went to such lengths to get the books.'

I sat back, took a sip of whiskey. 'It seems clear to me now. That bit about her orders to kill Dev. That's enough cat to put among any amount of pigeons.'

He nodded. 'Yes, you're right there. That's a real ball-breaker. But I can tell you that there is more to come. I won't spoil the story for you.' He looked down at the pages in front of him. 'This is exactly as she wrote it. In the first person.'

He cleared his throat.

Twenty-Three

Monday, November 29 1920

This is the most difficult entry I have ever written. Truth to tell, I am not certain whether I will be able to complete it. The purely physical effort involved in forcing my fingers to hold the pen is considerable. My hands give great pain, despite the excellent medical treatment I am now receiving. The only way in which I can tell of the last week is to begin on Tuesday, the 23rd of November. At eleven o'clock, I caught a tram in Kingstown and purchased a ticket to Dublin, as Gen had ordered. I was in a state of severe tension. I had no notion of what lay ahead, but some inner force seemed to tell me that my life was about to change in a drastic way. The weather was really foul, rain falling incessantly and a cold wind blowing in great gusts. I could see little through the window of the tram as it travelled along. I first knew that all was not as it should be when I realised that we had been stopped for longer than the usual time. I rubbed the glass to ascertain our position, to no avail. I was seated in the lower saloon directly behind the driver.

As I was about to look behind me, I heard the sound of running feet approaching from the back of the tram. I was seized roughly by the hair and my neck bent back painfully. A man with a pistol appeared into my vision and shouted loudly that I was under arrest and that if I resisted, I would be shot. I was pulled to my feet and only then realised that the other passengers had left the tram. I saw them gathered in a knot some distance away. When I was taken from the vehicle, I was immediately surrounded by armed soldiers, their rifles pointing at me. A large motor was standing beside the tram and I was propelled into its interior. Two men occupied the back seat with me, one on either side. Two others sat in the front. My arms were twisted behind my back and metal handcuffs fastened to my wrists. I was completely constrained from movement during the journey in the motor and none of the four men who travelled with me spoke at any stage.

I admit to being in a state of abject terror at this point. Everything had happened so quickly. My gun remained in its holster at the back of my skirt. I soon realised that we were driving towards the Castle, a route which I had followed every day during my employment there. We travelled at a high speed and, before long, the motor swung under the Castle gate. We came to a stop in the lower yard. I was pulled from the motor and taken at a run through a door. When the door was closed I saw that I was in an office with several desks against the walls. I had never had occasion to visit this area before. Again my head was pulled back by my hair and a uniformed policeman asked my name. I gave it, and my address in AB's house. I attempted to bluster, asking angrily why I was being treated in this manner. He said, 'You've come to the end of the line this time. A young lady on the tram recognised you and informed the driver.'

'What young lady? Recognised me as whom? This is ridiculous.'

'Does the name Ruane mean anything to you?'

I could not recall where I had heard the name before, but it was familiar in some way. Then the truth dawned. Ruane. The policeman who had died so admirably. His daughter had seen me clearly. My heart sank.

The policeman said that I would be held for the attention of Captain King. He asked the man who appeared to be in charge whether I had been searched. When answered in the negative, he swore dreadfully and proceeded to pass his hands over me roughly. I tried to ignore the manner in which he allowed his hands to dwell on certain parts of my body. Quickly, as I knew he would, he found my gun. With a cry of triumph he removed it and its holster. He pulled my coat from my shoulders and threw it into a corner.

I was then taken down a short flight of stone steps

into an unlit passageway. Several doors opened from it and one of them was unlocked as I was brought forward. I was violently pushed from behind and the door closed behind me. I stumbled forward, fell headlong, and collided with a wall in the darkness. The cell, for surely that is what it was, had no window and I could see nothing. I endeavoured to get to my feet, a difficult undertaking with my hands fastened as they were. I eventually managed to place my back against the wall and, moving in a sideways direction, began to attempt to discover the dimensions of my cell. I was near exhaustion when I found that I had travelled around the four sides, reaching the wooden door again. There appeared to be no furniture or fittings of any kind. I eventually found that I could take four steps in one direction and two in the other. Hardly a palace.

My initial fear was rapidly being replaced by anger. I did not have much time to attain such relief as this might have given, for the door was unlocked. A uniformed guard, holding a lamp, stood looking at me. I demanded that my hands be freed. He stepped forward and crashed his hand across my mouth. I felt as though several of my teeth had been loosened. A voice from beyond the range of the lamp laughed and a second man appeared, also carrying a lamp. He was dressed in the uniform of an army officer and I confess to a feeling of relief. At the very least, I would be treated properly by him. He surprised me by closing the door behind him. He placed the lamp upon the floor and asked me to turn around. When I complied, he opened and removed the handcuffs. His first words were, 'Hang on, I'll get a couple of chairs, shall I?' He opened the door and called aloud, 'Let's have a couple of chairs here. I'm not going to stand. I've been on my feet all day.' This produced immediate results and we were sitting opposite one another very quickly.

He was a small, slim man, thirtyish, with a red moustache. His eyes were almost colourless. I looked down at myself. My dress was streaked with dirt, my stockings torn at the knees and blood-spattered from wounds on my legs, caused, I surmised, when I fell into the cell.

'I am Captain King. I have charge of your case. I would like to ask you a few questions, if you would allow me.' His voice was rather quick, almost clipping the last syllables from the words. I said that I would answer as many questions as I could. 'Let's start with your name, shall we?' I noticed his habit of framing his questions as requests, rather than orders. He continued to do this throughout the time he spent with me. I rather welcomed it initially. I recited my name, adding my address for good measure. He wrote my answers in a small black-covered book with the stub of a pencil which he retained behind his ear.

'Why were you on the tram today?'

'I was travelling into town.'

'Why?'

'I wished to do some shopping.'

'Where were you going to shop?'

'Possibly in Henry Street, Grafton Street, even South Great George's Street.'

He took time writing each answer into the little book. I thought that his writing must be very small in form. 'What items were you intending to buy?'

'Nothing in particular. I intended to walk around the shops, and if I saw something which I wanted, then I would buy it.' All this seemed rather childish to me. How could such mundane subjects help him in his work?

He was writing when he asked the next question, almost casually. 'About the gun. I'll ask you about that now, shall I?'

I remained silent. He gave no indication of anger or any emotion, continuing to write. He bent his head downwards as he did so, as if he were shortsighted. 'I'll touch on the IRA now, shall I?' Again I remained silent. 'Which unit do you belong to?' No answer. 'Dublin Brigade, is it?' No answer. 'Put down North, shall I?'

As if I was answering every question, he continued. He did not repeat any one question, nor attempt to couch it in a different form. I was really quite bewildered by this time. I had realised even before I was removed from the tram that my life was forfeit. Of that, there could be no doubt. The circumstance being so, I found the questions of Captain King very strange. Overall, I came to the conclusion that he was asking the questions as a matter of form only. No answers were expected. I sat in the cell, knowing that I would die soon. I became resentful that I was being forced to spend my last hours in this absurd game.

Suddenly the inquisition ended. He stood and walked from the cell, leaving me sitting on my chair, his empty one opposite. The door had hardly closed when it opened again. He stood there, his little book and ridiculous remains of a pencil in his hands. He showed a semblance of a smile as he spoke. 'The clothes. Take them off, shall I?'

I was too taken aback to frame a reply. He stepped through the door and carefully laid the book and pencil on the chair so recently vacated by him. I rose to my feet, not yet understanding what he was about to do. His face continued to carry the rather pleasant look as he stepped towards me. Instinctively, I moved away from him until my back was against the wall and I could go no further. His hand darted forward and caught my hair. I was helpless as he pulled me closer and turned me around with my back against him. He reached across my body and, catching the neck of my dress, he tore the material down the front. I made an instinctive attempt to bring my hands across my body to cover myself. He bent my head so far back that I feared that my neck would break. 'You will keep your hands at your sides, I imagine?' Now he proceeded to tear the remainder of my clothing from me, leaving me naked. He bent and gathered the remnants together. As he straightened he said casually, 'Going home now. Wife and kiddies waiting. You'll be thinking of my enjoyment, I should imagine, yes?' He picked up the two chairs and carried them outside, then, returning, took the lamp. He was gone. The door banged shut and I heard a bolt being shot.

Darkness. Cold. Fear. Shame. Degradation. One by one these emotions and sensations visited me. Time ceased to have any meaning. What was a minute, an hour, a day, a year, a lifetime? At some stage, I sat on the floor because I was too weary to stand for a moment longer. After a time, I stopped feeling the coldness of the wall and floor against my skin. The need to relieve myself surfaced but I firmly banished it. That was one thing which I would not do. I remember now how I made that promise to myself.

How childish. How foolish. How ignorant. Particularly the last. I inflicted that suffering upon myself out of pure ignorance. I tried to induce tears, even of self-pity, but I could not. Anger refused to light its fuse within my mind. I wondered whether I would sleep from exhaustion.

Twenty-Four

I was just telling myself that I would never sleep here, like this, when I was awakened by the opening of the door. It crashed back against the wall, making me leap in terror. A bright light flooded the cell. It shone directly into my eyes. From behind it a voice came. This was a harsh voice, with none of the casual tones of Captain King.

'On your feet, whore.'

Dazed from sleep, the sudden light, the violent noise, I attempted to scramble erect. I was not quick enough. Out of the darkness, a fist thundered against the side of my head, momentarily robbing me of what little self-control remained. I was flung backwards by the force of the blow, my head hitting the wall cruelly, my naked back torn as I sank to my knees.

'Up, whore.'

This time, it was a foot. It caught me high up on the thigh and I screamed as the pain shot through me. I was grasped by my hair again and pulled upright. The light continued to shine into my eyes, blinding me to anything beyond its source. Then the beam slowly passed over my body, stopping here and there, as if wanting to confirm what had first been seen. It receded a little and I realised that it was now outside the cell.

'Out, whore.'

I moved slowly into the corridor. A hand grasped my shoulder and turned me to one side and I received a violent push between my shoulders. I staggered forward and saved myself from falling by finding the wall with my hands.

'Walk on.'

I remembered using that very command when I received my first pony, as a young child. I stumbled through the darkness until the voice commanded,

'Stop. Face right. Inside.' I followed these orders, unable to see anything.

Suddenly a light came on. I was dazzled by it, but soon saw that I was in a room, very much larger than the cell. It had a stone floor and was bare of furnishings, apart from a small table and one chair. I turned and saw my tormentor for the first time. He was very tall and thin. He wore an officer's uniform with lieutenant's pips on the shoulders. His face was quite red in appearance, his eyes darkest blue. His hair was black. He held a riding crop in his left hand. He removed his cap and placed it on the table. He stared at me searchingly for a moment.

Without warning the crop lashed forward and struck me across the cheek. I cried out and made to put my hand to the wound. Again the crop moved, making a whistling sound, landing on my hand. 'Move when you're told, whore.' Another moment's silent looking and he struck me again. This time the stroke landed across my breasts and a line of blood flowed over them. I cried out again, but somehow refrained from movement. He nodded his head. 'Better, whore, much better. My name is Hardy, Lieutenant Sidney Hardy. Repeat my name, whore.' As I did so, his hand tightened its grip on the crop, as if waiting for a reason to lash out again. The harsh tones sounded once more. 'You know my name, whore. Tell me yours.'

'Mary Stewart.'

The crop moved and again my breasts received the blow. He shook his head. 'Not that name, whore. The real name.'

I thought frantically, searching for what it was that he required. 'Whore. My name is whore.'

This blow landed on my shoulder and I almost fell, so dreadful was the pain. What did he want me to say? Then the answer came to me. A seed of resistance rooted deep within me. I knew with astonishing clarity that I could emerge from this treatment victorious. I would not say this one word. He could ask anything else of me and by his beatings force me to answer, but I vowed to reserve this one thing for myself, no matter what the cost.

Hardy put the crop on the table and took his cap off as he sat on the chair. He held a folder in his right hand and opened it. The top document appeared somehow familiar to me. He began to read and I remembered where I had seen it last. It was on the desk of Mr Cope when I had reported to him on my first day in the Castle. I remembered his words. 'Just a little something for you to sign, Miss Stewart. It states that you will never reveal anything which you learn during your time with us. Really a matter of form. The bods in Whitehall insist on it. Hope you don't mind.' Now that innocuous piece of paper was here, accusing me.

Hardy intercepted my glance. 'I see you recognise this, whore. I'll wager you never thought it would send you to the gallows. Well, it will. But before that event releases you from me, I intend to learn any little secrets Collins has let slip beneath the covers from time to time. That makes you think, doesn't it? No doubt you're wondering how much else I know. It will make your answers to my questions more interesting. Do you tell a lie and perhaps get away with it? Do you tell the truth and discover that I did not know the answer? Well, that's all ahead.'

At this point, he rose and removed his tunic, rolling up his sleeves. I noticed that his forearms were covered with thick, black hair. He carefully hung the tunic over the back of the chair. He walked a few paces from me and raised the hand again holding the crop above his head. He brought it through the air at great speed, causing that whistling noise.

'Right. Let's get down to it. The rules are very simple. I ask a question. You answer it. If you are not quick enough with your answer, you get a cut. If your answer does not satisfy me, you get a cut. If I catch you in a deliberate lie, you get a cut. If you move without my permission, you get a cut. Finally, if I feel like it, you get a cut. I'm really very accurate with this thing.' Once again, the crop whistled through the air. 'You are Collins's whore, correct?' The leather bit into the skin of my abdomen. He shook his head. 'Nothing like quick enough, whore. Let's try that again. You are Collins's whore?'

'Yes.'

'That's better. Now turn around. You will not be able to anticipate the cuts now. Next question. Collins's address?'

'He has no address.' I got the words out at the same time as the crop slashed across the skin of my buttocks. Never had I imagined such pain. Tears ran unchecked down my face, mucus streamed from my nose. Desperately, I tried not to move. I thought that I was successful until the whistle and the blow came simultaneously. I felt the warm blood running down my back from the shoulder.

'Well, where did he fuck you?'

I understood the vulgarity but it delayed the answer. I will not detail every stroke of the riding crop which landed on my back. At some stage, I passed through a barrier of agony, beyond which the pain ceased to register. I continued to feel the strokes, but in some strange way, pain no longer accompanied them. Eventually, I was taken back to the cell and the door locked. I found a corner in the blackness and lowered my body until I was sitting. I pulled my knees up and encircled them with my arms. In this position, I remained. I rested my flayed back against the wall, but when I tried to move, I found that I was stuck to the rough surface. The slightest movement reopened the wounds, caused more blood to flow, which in turn, caused the skin to adhere again. Amazingly, I slept.

The next thing of which I was aware was the door being thrown back. Captain King, preceded by a lamp, entered. He carried two chairs and ordered me to sit. He sat facing me, less than a pace away. The black-covered book and the worn pencil made their reappearance. As before, his manner was remote. The first question which gave me difficulty was when he asked for the names of 'the Squad'. I remained silent and for the first time he returned the pencil behind his ear and dropped the book to the floor.

He reached out and took my right hand in his. As he held it without pressure, his other hand disappeared into the inside of his tunic. It reappeared holding a metal tweezers similar to those used by ladies to dress their eyebrows. He brought my captured hand close to his eyes and gently grasped the nail on my little finger between the arms of the tweezers. I had not yet realised his intentions, and when he tightened the metal arms upon the nail and with one stroke, pulled it from its bed, I did not flinch for several seconds. I looked at the bloody finger in wonder before the pain struck with shattering intensity. I attempted to withdraw the hand, but his grip tightened. My scream of agony was the loudest I had uttered, the pain the deepest I had felt.

King continued to look at me with an almost uninterested expression on his face. 'Try that again, shall I?' He repeated the question and before I could have possibly replied, the nail was gone from the next finger. 'Take 'em all off, shall I?' I screamed my answer. 'I do not know their names.' A third nail. I would have cheerfully told him anything, but the truth was that I only knew many of my comrades by their Christian names. As I attempted to tell this to King, I lost another nail. There remained the thumbnail on the hand. Suddenly, he looked at his watch and rose, gathered the chairs and the book and left, closing the door firmly. The bolt slid home and I was alone in the darkness. I found my corner in my agony and cradled the mutilated hand, gently touching the fingertips with my tongue.

I have been as explicit as possible concerning these early tortures. During the following times which I spent with King and Hardy, the series of experiences through which they put me came together in my mind as one long repetition. I was never aware of the time, nor whether it was day or night. The only light I saw was from the lamps which they carried. Between their visits, I was left in the dark cell, confronting the demon of certainty that one or the other of them would return soon. I found that my mind reacted differently to the two men. Hardy was brutal in the extreme, lashing me with his eternal leather crop, calling me vile names, forcing me to tell him of my intimate times with Gen. But with all this, I preferred to be questioned by him. The very aloofness of King's manner, the way he had of couching his questions in the form of suggestions, as if he were inviting me to take tea with him, the very sight of his moustache, made my skin crawl as if confronted by a huge spider or garden slug. Even the writing of these words brings his colourless eyes back to haunt me.

At some time, I know not when, I was again taken to the room to confront Hardy and his leather crop. I no longer cared that I was naked, that he referred to intimate portions of my body in the basest way. I knew that he could not force one word from me against my will. I seemed to be standing apart from my body, watching this man mistreat it shamefully, feeling nothing. Now he asked me a new question. 'What is the name of the officer who fucked you first?'

I had not expected to feel any more fearful, but at these words my blood actually ran cold. I flinched, fully expecting the crop to pick out one of the few remaining areas of unbroken skin on my body. No blow landed. I opened my eyes. Hardy had taken a cigar from a case and was in the process of lighting it. He drew in the smoke and allowed it to re-emerge in a thin blue stream. Now his eyes returned to mine. He nodded his head, stood and left the room. I remained there, trying not to imagine what lay ahead when I refused to tell him about Richard. I heard his voice calling in the corridor and then he returned, leaving the door open. A uniformed policeman came in and approached me. He was holding a pair of handcuffs which he proceeded to fasten to my wrists at the front of my body. He led me to the wall and turned me to face the room. He then ordered me to raise my arms above my head. With an easy bend, he caught me around the waist and lifted me from the floor. The next thing I knew was that I was hanging from a metal hook fastened to the wall. My feet did not reach the floor. I could feel the cold roughness of the wall against the lacerated skin of my back.

Hardy walked to me. He stood in front of me, his eyes slightly lower than mine. Without a word, he drew on the cigar and when the end was glowing redly, placed it against the nipple of my left breast. A piercing scream escaped from me as the flesh began to burn. He replaced the cigar between his teeth and again caused the end to glow. This time he touched it to the other breast. He kept it in position until I could smell the acrid smoke rising from the spot. I screamed and screamed again. His face took on a dreadful smile. He was clearly enjoying the sport. He looked up into my face from a distance of two inches. I could smell his sour breath. His voice dropped to a whisper. 'Ready to talk now, whore?'

I think I whimpered a reply, but what its meaning was, I could not imagine. He took the cigar from his mouth. I lost sight of it. An exquisite shaft of pain flared as he touched the burning tip to my flesh. He removed the cigar instantly and held it between the finger and thumb of his right hand. 'The next time, the whole thing goes in, to stay. Now answer.'

'Richard, Richard.'

'Richard has a surname, I presume?'

'Lincoln.' I was defeated. I had betrayed the man whom I had loved, perhaps still loved. The tears were mainly of shame at my treachery. I deserved pain, wished for more pain, needed more pain to assuage the terrible guilt which threatened to engulf me.

I became aware that Hardy had walked to the door and opened it. I heard him call out. 'Prisoner, attention. Quick march. Left turn. Halt.' I looked down at a sight which will live in my memory for the remainder of my life.

Standing in front of me, at strict attention, was Richard. He was dressed in full dress uniform of his regiment. The only other time I had seen him thus clad was the night he had taken me to the reception in the Lodge. Our first time together. His eyes were fixed straight ahead, not moving a muscle. Hardy walked slowly round him, slapping the crop against the palm of his hand.

'Lieutenant Lincoln, do you know this woman?'

'Yes, sir.'

'Her name. Come along, man. The woman's name?'

'Stewart, sir.'

Hardy's voice again soared in fury. 'Full name, damn you.'

'Miss Mary Stewart, sir.'

'How well do you know her?'

'I do not understand the question, sir.'

'It's plain enough. What is the nature of you knowledge of this whore?'

'We are, were, friends sir.'

'Friends? I'll give you friends, you little toady. You will instantly relate to me the full circumstances of your knowledge of this whore.'

There was a pause. Richard was obviously searching for the correct words. I like to think that he was attempting to spare me the ordeal of hearing him describe our friendship and its intimacy. At that moment, a thought came unbidden. How could he have been waiting outside the room? Why was he so clearly prepared for this appearance? The answers gave me joy. They had known of Richard before I had spoken his name. It was not I who had betrayed him.

In a low voice he started to speak. He described our first meeting, our subsequent friendship and its development to the stage at which intimacy had occurred. He made no mention of our first weekend together, confining himself to relating the places we had visited in order to make love.

Hardy allowed him to complete his recital before speaking again. 'Lieutenant, you stand charged with the most serious offence in the military code. Treason. There can be but one sentence. However, you can influence the method to be used in carrying out this sentence. If you answer my questions to my satisfaction, I am ready to recommend to your court-martial presiding officer that your execution be carried out under military law. Do you understand this?'

Richard replied, 'Yes, sir.'

'Should you not satisfy me, I can arrange for your death to be a slow process, during which you will be conscious throughout and will very soon be pleading for death to release you. Such pleas will not be answered. Do you understand this?'

'Yes, sir.'

'Very well. Please relate the details of your rendezvous with this whore on the seventh of February in a house named Riverside, near Chapelizod.'

And so I hung there, listening to Richard describe in his own words that which had been so beautiful. Hardy interrupted frequently if some phrase or word did not meet with his approval. He insisted that Richard use the most gross words in describing our lovemaking. I closed my ears to it all, allowing my thoughts to dwell upon my dear father whom I would be joining soon. The charade finished finally and Richard was marched from the room. Hardy returned to torment me further, but it was to avail him nothing. No matter what he said or did, he had lost his power over me. He was no longer a figure of fear, rather a beast of the fields, not fit to appear in the same place as decent folk. He visited further ignominy on me, it is true, but he seemed to realise that I had passed beyond his power to inflict hurt. He called for King and for the first time, I was faced with both my tormentors simultaneously. King removed the last nail from my right hand, before starting on my left. They retired to the farthest corner of the room and spoke together in undertones. Finally, the policeman was recalled and instructed to lift me from the hook and remove the handcuffs. I almost collapsed, so weak was I, and the underling was forced to support me. I was taken out of doors for the first time and although it was raining steadily, my eyes were blinded by the unaccustomed brightness.

When I could see again, I realised that I was in a closed yard, some twenty feet square. A wooden pole was driven into the ground at the farthest point from where I stood. I think I realised immediately the play which was to be staged for my benefit. True enough, Richard was marched to the pole and tied securely to it, facing me in his dress uniform. He asked for a cloth to bind his eyes, but this was refused him.

Hardy and King stood with me, one on each side. King removed his revolver from his belt and handed it to me. 'There is one round in the breech, otherwise the gun is empty of ammunition. You will fire at Lieutenant Lincoln and kill him. Should you fail to kill him, you will be sending him to a far more painful death. He will be nursed back to health and then will spend an indeterminate period with us in the cells. We shall use all our considerable skills to make his stay as long and painful as possible.'

I asked, 'What is it you want to know?'

'Tell us who Gráinne is.'

I started to laugh, softly to begin with, but gathering volume and force as I continued. To think that all this suffering inflicted on Richard and me could be brought to an end so easily. Hardy stepped forward and struck my face with the back of his hand. I think that he was wearing a ring of some sort, as the skin under my eye split and I felt the warm trickle of blood. I looked at both these men and then at Richard, tied as he was, for his execution. I took the gun and almost dropped it. I steadied my hand and slowly raised the weapon to the aiming position. Richard was standing, his eyes fixed on me. I called out, 'I am Gráinne. I love you, Richard. We will be together soon,' and fired.

He slumped against the ropes. Hardy made a move to examine him, and I said, 'There is no need for that. He is dead.'

I will spend no further time in repeating the things done to me. Some details of a person's degradation are best left unwritten. The time passed, or I supposed that it did, for I had no way of knowing day or date, light or dark.

The next thing to impinge upon my mind was the sight of the policeman entering the cell with his lamp. He carried a bundle over his arm which he threw on the floor. 'Get those clothes on you. You're going for a trip.' He stood there as I tried to fasten buttons with bloody fingers which refused to answer my wishes. I determined that I would not ask for his help, so the process of dressing took many minutes. The clothes were not my own but fitted well enough. For sure, I did not care how they looked. I knew that I was being brought somewhere new where further torture would be performed on my broken body. I wished only for death.

Finally, I declared myself ready and I was taken out into a dark, rainy night. A motor was standing there, a driver at the wheel and two shadowy figures in the back. When I was seated, the motor started. We emerged from a back gate and drove along dark, rainswept streets. There were no other people or vehicles in sight. I could see little through the wet windows and, truth to tell, had the time been noon and the weather fine, I should not have been interested in our passage. In a surprisingly short time the motor came to a stop and the driver switched off the engine. There was complete silence in the interior, save for our breathing. I sat there for what seemed like an interminable length.

Suddenly, the back door was opened from outside. I could not see who stood there. A voice said, 'Get out. Out of the car. Hurry up. We haven't got all night.' It was a moment or so before I realised that the instructions were directed at me. I struggled out and stood on a wet road with not one light to be seen.

A figure appeared beside me. 'Wait here. A small light will come on straight in front of you, about a hundred yards away. When you see it, start walking towards it. Keep moving until a voice tells you to halt. You'll be taken care of.' He disappeared into the darkness. I tried to pierce the night with my eyes, but the incessant rain made this impossible.

Then I saw it. A light. A very small light. It seemed to be miles away. A hand pushed me forward gently, a voice whispered, 'Good luck. You're a brave little thing.'

I walked haltingly forward, not knowing what I was doing, where I was going, what diabolical people and things waited for me. The small light seemed to beckon, not moving, but not appearing to be any closer. I continued, listening to the sound of my feet against the roadway. Another noise impinged. What was it? Water. I could hear the sound of water. It came from directly below my feet. I was on a bridge. My strength was failing fast, I knew that I was close to collapse. My mind repeated over and over, do not fall, do not fall, keep going, keep going. It was no use. I had to stop. I must lie down. I felt myself falling. Hands held me, not cruel hands. These were kind hands, soft hands. The rush of the water grew to a crescendo and I knew no more.

Twenty-Five

My body was afire with an all-consuming agony. The cigar was burning its way slowly through the flesh covering the child which I was carrying. The child whose father was Captain King. Lieutenant Hardy laughed and the sound echoed around the great dark cavern. Richard called my name as he searched for me and I replied with the full force of my lungs. My voice was strong while it remained inside my body, but the moment the words reached outside they lost all sound. My mouth was wide open but Richard could not hear me although he was inches from me. Now I held an enormous revolver in my hand and aimed it at Hardy and King. The muzzle insisted on pointing at Richard's head and my finger pressed the trigger unbidden. I tried to rise but huge hands restrained me. I screamed silently in terror at this grasp of the devil. Through the fear a voice called from a great distance. It was repeating my name, but my name is Gráinne, not Molly.

The voice grew nearer, the words continued gentle. 'Wake up, Molly. Wake up. You're safe now, Molly. Don't be afraid. It's all over. Don't cry any more. Come on, Molly. No one's going to hurt you again.' The words reached into my mind despite the efforts of the pain to keep them at bay. The voice was very near now, soothing, easing, reassuring. I felt arms cradling me, rocking me with incredible gentleness. I opened my eyes and closed them immediately, so bright was the light. 'Open now, Molly. You'll get used to the light in a minute.'

I tried again and discovered that I could bear the brightness. A smiling face was suspended above me, a face that I knew but could not put a name to. I felt tears rising within my body at the unfairness of it all. The only face in the world, and I did not remember his name. I wept bitterly. I felt fingers lightly smoothing the tears away. 'Don't cry, Molly. Please don't cry.' Now I could see him properly. Who was this? What came to me was not a name. I thought of a letter of the alphabet. T. That was it. His name was T. Why he should be named a letter was quite beyond me, but I did not care. I wanted to say it over and over. T, T, T, T. Now I said it aloud. 'T.' His face creased into a smile, part pleasure, part relief. He lowered me on to a soft pillow.

It suddenly occurred to me that I was not wet and cold any more. Better still, I was comfortable, better again, I was in luxury. I made to move and cried out as a dart of agony sped through my body. I could not identify the source of the pain. It seemed to come from every inch of my flesh. T's face showed concern and he leaned over, placing his cool hand upon my forehead. 'Is the pain bad, Molly?' I nodded through the tears. 'I know, dear. It will take a while for it to ease. The doctor left a tablet for you if it became too bad. I have some water here.' He placed his arm underneath my shoulders and lifted me gently. He showed me a white pill and put it on my tongue. As he brought a glass close to my lips, I attempted to grasp it in my hands. I had no hands. At the end of each arm was a thick white wad of bandage. I cried in fear. He recognised the cause and reassured me. 'Don't worry, Molly. Your hands are not gone. They are badly injured but will recover. Swallow the pill with this water.' I did so and he lowered me again.

I brought my hands in front of my face, gazing at them in wonder. Then I remembered. The fingernails had all been removed by Hardy. I found that I could not remember the pain, only its existence. I transferred my gaze to the face above me. T. He must have a proper name. 'Why are you called T? I do not know of any other name.'

'Do not worry. T will suit me fine. At least you remember me. That's the main thing.'

By now, questions were flooding my mind, fighting with each other for preference. 'Where am I? How did I get here? How long have I been here?'

'So many questions, Molly. I'll try to answer them in time. For now, let me tell you what happened. When I've finished, if you have anything you still do not know, then you can ask away. How's that?' I nodded at his friendly face. It would be so much easier to listen than to talk.

'I will lie here with my eyes closed. I will not be asleep. You tell your story.'

And this is what T related to me. I will remember every word he spoke for the rest of my life. 'News of your capture on Tuesday reached us that afternoon. Apparently Mick was expecting you and when you failed to arrive, he started to make enquiries. He discovered that on the tram with you was the daughter of a detective named Ruane. You may not remember him, but I recall you saying that he died as you would hope to. Anyway, the girl recognised you as the woman who had shot her father. She reported to the conductor that a member of IRA was aboard the tram. He, in turn, alerted the driver and when the tram reached Blackrock, he stopped outside the police station. The other passengers were taken off and the police and their army guards arrested you. You were taken to the Castle. What happened to you over the following days until Friday night, we can only guess from your injuries. Mick took an immediate decision that you had to be saved at all practical costs. I have never seen him so agitated before. He walked up and down the room, talking under his breath all that evening and until dawn. He left the house, Brunswick Street, by the way, at seven in the morning after a night without sleep, cycling away. He refused to say where he was going. He took me aside and said that if he was not back by midnight, I was to assume command of all his people. He gave me a letter to be read to the Squad in that case.

'We waited all day for word. He arrived back at seven in the evening. He looked terrible, not only from lack of sleep, but his nerves seemed to be in tatters. When I spoke to him, he nearly took the top of my head off. Now that's not Mick at all. At half past eleven, a messenger arrived at the door with a letter for him. He went to his room, presumably to read it, came back looking even worse and rode off again. He left me the same instructions as before. During the night, we were wakened and sent to the attic. The city was full of patrols. They were searching everywhere, not just throwing everything out into the street as usual. They were looking for something definite. After a while of this, with reports coming in from all over the city, I began to guess that they were looking for someone in particular. I thought that they might have made you talk and that you had given them the addresses around Dublin. But they never came within an ass's roar of the attics. We all assumed that they were looking for Mick. But we didn't know where he was, never mind the Castle lot.

'Mick came back before breakfast, still looking like a corpse. You would have thought that he was over fifty to see him. He called me to his room. He lay on the bed as he talked. At times I could hardly hear him, he spoke so softly. He said that the loneliness of command sometimes put terrible strains on a man's loyalty. Things which he would not normally consider can become not only possible, but also necessary for the survival of all. He went on talking like that all day until four in the afternoon. He went off again. This time he came back in an hour. He called me in again. He seemed much calmer, even laughing like his old self. Then he got very serious. He had a job for me. It would be the last thing he would ever ask me to do. I was to take a car tomorrow night, Friday. No driver, no passenger. Just me by myself. I was to drive it to the junction of Capel Street and the north quays. I was to stop with the engine switched off facing across Capel Street Bridge, not showing any lights. I had to arrive at exactly ten. Not a minute before, not a minute after. The streets around and the bridge itself would be completely empty of traffic and people. The street lights in Capel Street and Parliament Street and on the bridge would not be lit. At five past ten, I would see a small light, like a torch light, from across the bridge. It would wink once and then stay steady. I was to walk towards it, keeping my hands above my head. In my pocket would be a sealed envelope. When I reached the light, I was to hand the envelope to the man waiting there. He would open it and read what was inside. He would say "right" and I would turn and come back to the car. I would find a small torch on the passenger seat. I would get out of the car again and stand beside it, pointing the torch back across the bridge, blink it once and put it on properly. I would stand there for ten minutes, during which you would walk to the car. I would put you into the car and drive down the north quays towards the sea. At the Point building, a ship would be moored with smoke showing that she was ready to sail. I would carry you aboard and hand you over to a doctor who would be waiting. I would then return by car to Brunswick Street, dumping the car near Christ Church Cathedral and walking the rest of the way.'

His soft voice fell silent and I opened my eyes. 'Please do not stop. You have not explained where I am now and how you got here.'

He looked rather shamefaced, rather like a small boy. I touched his hand with my bandaged one. He shrugged and smiled. 'Well, to tell you the truth, Molly, I disobeyed an order from Mick for the first time. When I carried you aboard the ship, she's Italian by the way, I found that I could not just walk away from you. I had to stay and tell you what had happened to you. The captain speaks good English, but he knows nothing about what went on before I brought you here.'

All at once, a thing which had been causing me much puzzlement, became clear to me. 'We are at sea. I thought that the movement I felt was in my mind. I did not want to ask you about it, in case you thought me mad.'

He laughed delightfully. 'I'm told that we are in the Mediterranean Sea, bound for Naples in Italy. We sailed from Dublin at ten-thirty on Friday night. It is now Sunday, just after six p.m. To complete your education, the ship is the SS *Michelangelo*, ten thousand tons, and the master is Captain Luigi Consetta.'

I frowned at him. He had left the strangest thing unexplained. 'Why did you stay with me? I am sure that the people aboard would have looked after me.'

'Ah yes, Molly. I really did want to explain things. But I must confess that when I decided to stay aboard in Dublin, it was my intention to leave the ship at Southampton. The Captain agreed to put me ashore for a few extra pounds. I changed my mind and decided to stay all the way to Naples.' He laughed again, a little self-consciously, I thought. 'And so, here I am.'

I lay back on the pillow. There was so much to think about. I was tired, deathly tired, and my body ached from head to toe. In several places there was real pain. Nevertheless, I wanted to know everything. 'The envelope. The one you handed over at the motor. What was in it?'

T shook his head. 'I have no idea. Mick was quite firm that I must not open it under any circumstances. Those were his actual words: "under any circumstances".'

I found my mind refusing to accept this. 'If he managed to persuade the police to release me, surely he gave them something in kind?'

T reached his finger forward and placed it gently against my lips. His eyes seemed to have grown to enormous size. I realised that he was near to tears. I opened my mouth to speak, but he shook his head and stood, turning his back to me. I raised myself upwards and touched his sleeve with my hand. He put his hand behind his back where I could rest mine against it. In silence we remained for many moments. Finally, he turned to me, traces of his tears showing on his cheeks. His voice was soft but insistent. 'Molly, you must put such things from your mind. Mick was, is, the leader of the Ireland we fought for. Whatever he had to do to get you away from those...animals, he did. He made the decision. I will never believe that he acted in anything but an honourable way. If you, if we, cannot believe that, then the whole fight has been for nothing. Ireland will win the freedom, not because we fought better than the British. We'll win because, in this world, right has a habit of coming out on top, and Ireland has had right on her side for eight hundred years.' He leaned down and, to my surprise, placed his lips on mine. The touch was so soft that I could barely feel it. He walked to the door, opened it, switched off the light, and closed it again.

I lay in the dark, my mind full of bewilderment. I did not, nor did I want to, think of the dreadful times in the dungeons. I tried to think of Mick, Gen as I have known him. The thought that would not retreat, which expelled all other thoughts and to which I finally gave full rein, was the presence on this ship of T. How should I regard his statement that he could not leave me here, had to disobey his beloved 'Big Fellow'? Note: I am writing this in a hard-bound ledger which T procured from the Captain. I hope to transcribe it into the usual type of book at some future date.

I awoke in the light of a beautiful morning. I find that I am in a small, well-appointed cabin. A nurse – she has no English – sat by my bed all night and showed great kindness. The first thing that I did after breakfast (which she had fed to me as if I were a small baby) was to insist that the bandages be removed from my hands. Initially, she refused, but when she realised that I would unbind them myself, she consented. My first sight of my hands reduced me to tears. They looked more like paws, as of an animal. The fingers were swollen into unrecognisable shapes. I asked whether I could wash. This I was forced to leave to the nurse. I cannot immerse my hands in water in their present state. However, Maria, the nurse, was gentle and efficient. My next demand was for clothing. I discovered that there was not one item of feminine clothing aboard. T has promised to purchase what I need when we reach Naples. I managed to borrow a dressing-gown from Maria, and wearing this, I have moved on deck, where a comfortable reclining chair has been placed for my use. The weather is wonderfully warm, with a light breeze blowing. T tells me that I was fortunate to be unconscious during our journey through the Bay of Biscay. The wind howled all day and the ship pitched and rolled in a most unpleasant manner.

The vessel is a fine one. She is a general cargo

steamer with six cabins for passengers. On this voyage, we are the only ones. The standard of appointments is of the highest quality. The Captain has visited me. His knowledge of English is minimal, but he makes himself understood by throwing his arms about like a dervish and smiling warmly. The only time the smile faltered was when he saw my hands. He spoke sternly to Maria and she fetched a pair of gloves for me. It was a painful operation putting them on for the first time, but I felt much more comfortable. I take them off only in the morning, in order that Maria may bathe my hands in salt water for half an hour. I have realised that I am playing a leading role in a farce. Here I am on a ship in the Mediterranean Sea with a man who states that he could not bear to be parted from me, and the only name I have for him is the letter T. I broached the subject. He admitted that his name is Turlough Perry. I said that I would call him Turlough, but he asked a special favour from me. He wishes to be known to me as Tee. To anyone else he is Turlough. To me he is Tee.

'For God's sake, Ryan. I don't want to hear any more of this. I have more on my mind than a sea voyage in 1920.'

He looked up, pushing the glasses onto his forehead. 'There's not much more now. We're nearly there. In fact there's only one more entry. She closed the journal on Sunday, 31 December, 1922.'

'You mean that she skipped from, when was it, November 1920, to December 1922 and then never wrote any more?'

He nodded. 'That's how it ends.'

I looked at my watch. Ten past twelve. The damn phone sat on its rest, mocking me. I was still no nearer finding out why Theresa had been kidnapped. I ran from the thought that she might already be dead.

Ryan held up a sheet of paper. This is the last bit. Since there's no news, we might as well finish it. OK?'

Sunday, December 31 1922.

I open this book for the last time. My life has undergone several transformations in the twenty-five months since I last wrote. The gap can be bridged briefly. I remained in Naples with Tee for over a year. My injuries healed, leaving much scarring, particularly on my hands. I have taken to wearing white gloves, even when I sleep. We learned to speak Italian quickly and Tee gained a position in a firm of accountants, his chosen profession prior to joining IRA. I gave classes in English at a local school. Let it be said immediately that Tee and I were married six weeks after arriving in Naples (Napoli to the natives). He proposed before the vessel docked, but I was not sure of my feelings. So soon after Richard and Michael. However, such was his eagerness that I consented.

I discovered that my treatment at the hands of King and Hardy had left me with a problem. The burns inflicted, particularly those inside my body, formed such thick scar tissue that the act of love was impossible. Penetration was agonising. Tee never put me under any pressure in this context, seemingly content with my friendship. For myself, possessed as I am of a healthy appetite, the position was far from ideal. I approached a Doctor Scalati, about whom I had heard good reports from my female colleagues in the school. I made it clear to him at our first meeting that I did not wish to discuss the circumstances that had led to the scarring. When he had examined me fully, he expressed himself as being prepared to undertake the removal of the offending obstruction. I entered hospital and the surgical procedure was performed. The pain in the affected area was severe for some weeks, but it finally disappeared. The result of Doctor Scalati's expertise was twofold. I was enabled to take a full and satisfying part in lovemaking, and, within two months, I had conceived. We were pleased beyond measure at the news. The pregnancy proceeded perfectly, no morning illness spoiling our delight. I went to term and gave birth to a girl on the eleventh of December, 1921. We named her Mary. Two weeks after birth, she contracted typhoid fever and, despite the best efforts of the doctors and nurses at the hospital, she died on Christmas Day. I was in a state of deep depression after the tragedy, but Tee became a changed man. He spoke to me not at all. He did not seem to be able to touch me. Even my presence in the same room affected him, reducing him to tears. In my unhappiness, I found an anchor to which I could hold. I joined the Roman Catholic Church. Over the long months of our grief, my prayers gave me courage. Before I took the final step, I talked at length to a Franciscan friar. I related candidly my undertakings as Gráinne to him. He said that if I was truly sorry for my acts, and determined not to offend in the future, God would understand. I received Confession before my First Communion and Confirmation. The peace of mind which flowed from my conversion was a powerful ally in my problems with Tee.

Twenty-Six

I had read in the newspapers – English ones were available in Naples only two days after publication – of the Truce signed in Ireland between the British Government and the Provisional Government of the Irish Republic. We decided to come home in March 1921, arriving in England on the 4th and crossing to Dublin the following day. Tee appeared to rally his spirits somewhat after our return. He found a small house in Drumcondra and we settled down there. He undertook employment similar to his Italian position in the city. Our intimate life had not recommenced.

There came a day when I was alone at home and a knock came to the door. Imagine my surprise when I found Vincent standing there. He asked to see Tee but I explained that he was at the office. I cannot pretend that he was more than strictly civil towards me. He refused to come in and did not leave a message for Tee. I could not understand his attitude. True, we had never been close friends, but we had shared many moments of danger. He had seemed to hold Gráinne in high regard. However, if the ending of hostilities caused him to distance himself from those with whom he had fought, so be it.

I told Tee of the matter. He said that he would visit some of the public houses where his friends used to forgather 'in the old days'. That evening he left home to do just that. He did not reappear for three days. I was so concerned that I reported his absence to the police. He arrived home in a state of drunkenness. Never before had I known him to overindulge in this manner. I had to undress him and put him to bed. He spoke in a slurred fashion and made no sense. However, as I was about to leave him, he sat up in bed and looked at me closely. I recall his words clearly. This is what he said.

'You're a fine woman, Molly. But that Gráinne, she deserved everything she got.'

I pressed for the meaning of these words. We had not mentioned Gráinne since getting married. I had tried to expel all thoughts of that part of my life from my memory, successfully until now. Tee continued, 'I found out what he did to get her out.' Hardly daring to breathe, I asked for the answer. This was the one question which I had always avoided.

'He threw Mallin to the wolves, that's what he did.'

Mallin? Who on earth was Mallin? I was about to question him further when my memory stirred. Mallin. There had been a detective called Mallin when I had worked in the Castle. I never knew his Christian name. His work had been to liaise between Military Intelligence and 'G' Division of DMP. I asked Tee to explain. He was sobering quickly now.

'Joe Mallin was our contact inside the Castle. Mick picked up his name from you. When he approached Mallin to work for us, he was only too glad to do it. He was a real Sinn Feiner. He kept us informed about goings-on inside. I reckon that Joe Mallin saved more IRA lives and ended more G-men's lives than anyone else.'

I asked him, 'What do you mean, Mick threw him to the wolves?'

'Just that. He gave them Mallin's name in return for them letting Gráinne go.' He spoke as if Gráinne was someone else, not me.

I could feel my world collapsing all around me. If this was true, my life had been bought at the expense of a dedicated Republican. Mick's motive can only have been personal. Not for a moment did I believe that he could not have produced another executioner to replace Gráinne. Another spy in the Castle was a different matter altogether. I had to ask, 'How did you find out about this? Was it from V?'

'Yes. I met Vincent in the Sackville Arms, in Abbey Street. There were about five of the old crowd there. They all feel the same about this.'

'What do they feel, Tee?'

'Collins is an informer and should be treated like we always dealt with informers.'

'You mean he should be killed?'

'Not just killed. He must be shot. He must be shot by Gráinne.'

I almost fell to the floor at these words. 'Gráinne is dead, Tee. You know that.'

'Not yet, Molly. There's one last job for her.'

'No, Tee. Never again. I cannot go back to that life. I cannot kill again.'

'You don't understand, Molly. There was a court-martial yesterday. Collins was found guilty of treason. He was sentenced to death and it was the ruling of the court-martial that he must be executed by Gráinne.'

'Court-martial? What are you saying? The war is over, Tee. There is no IRA or courts-martial or executions any more.'

He looked at me for a long moment. 'Gráinne, this is a direct order from me to you. You have no choice. If you disobey, you will be held in charge.' I could scarce believe my ears. 'What does held in charge mean?'

'I place you under arrest until a court-martial can sit on your case. I am responsible for the carrying-out of all sentences passed by a court-martial. I am now Adjutant-General of the Irish Republican Army. I was appointed yesterday.'

And so, the events in which I was to play such an important part were put in train. The war is not over, merely suspended while negotiations between Britain and Ireland take place. Nothing can happen while these talks are in progress. I did not say to my husband that I would carry out the order. Neither did I refuse. I held my counsel, hoping that whatever the result of the London talks, wiser counsels would prevail. If Gen returned with a treaty giving Ireland the independence for which she had fought, he would surely be regarded as a hero. The IRA could never contemplate murdering him. They would lose the support of the people overnight. Ireland had fought bravely. Now she wanted to enjoy the fruits of her sacrifice in peace. If the six north-eastern counties delayed joining us for a time, what of it? There was no doubt in anyone's mind that they would be asking for union within the year.

When the delegation returned from London with

the draft of a treaty, the Dáil passed it by an overwhelming majority. Mr DeValera led his supporters out, and the country found itself plunged into the barbarism of the worst of all possible wars. For nine months the legally elected Government were under attack by the so-called Republican side. IRA units which had battled valiantly against the British wasted themselves fighting each other. General Collins led the 'Free-State' side against the very people who had been at the forefront of his war machine.

There came the time when Gráinne was visited by men who professed to be her superior officers. She must decide which side she supported. When she said that she supported neither side, she was told that such a stance was not open to her. She had but one task to perform. The time and place were for her to decide. They left, and Molly mourned the events which took her husband into war again.

Gráinne honed the skills which would be necessary. She watched. She waited. She took the train to County Cork. From there she made her way to a place which did not appear on any map. She took up residence in a small white-washed cottage, the home of a farmer who loved Michael Collins and wished him in hell. A boy called to the cottage with a letter. Gráinne walked five miles across the fields in the rain and darkness until she reached the spot which she had chosen. Day dragged into evening, a bitterly cold evening. Men were crouched on both sides of her. A whistle shrilled, engines were heard in the gathering gloom. Several shots were fired and the convoy halted to give battle. Gráinne, dressed entirely in black, wormed her way towards the spot where the Government troops were crouched. The fire between the factions was no more than desultory. Now Gráinne had reached the hedgerow directly opposite the car. The darkness was defeating the efforts of a cloud streaked moon. She recognised a shadow. She had seen it on too many occasions to be mistaken. The military cap was new, but that line of determined jaw could only belong to one man. A whistle shrilled in the distance and there occurred a lull in the firing. A whisper said, 'Michael.'

A head raised itself without thinking. A volley came from the hill behind and masked the single shot. A man fell wordlessly.

Gráinne never returned from her journey to Cork. Two days later a man called upon Molly. He was very sorry to tell her that her husband had been killed in a gun battle in County Cork two days previously. He gave her a letter from the commander of the group in which he had served with such distinction. Molly threw the letter on the fire, unopened.

She made a short visit to London a few days later carrying these journals in the bottom of her suitcase. She had arranged an appointment with a young, struggling solicitor named Urquart. Her father had used his professional services on a number of occasions. When she returned to Dublin, the suitcase was lighter in weight and she felt a greater sense of security than heretofore. The journals would remain in London as long as men of ill will might seek to destroy them and their author. She prayed that the day would come when she could perhaps bring them back to Ireland. In her heart she knew that such peace as this demanded would take many generations to come.

Soon afterwards she was visited by Vincent. The Free Staters had won. They were looking for a few people who had led the fight against them. Not the politicians. Oh no. They wanted the soldiers. V said that he had heard that Molly kept a journal. If so, it must be destroyed. Molly had a short way with that sort of thing. She had indeed kept a detailed journal. She had but one volume in her possession. She would close it on the last day of this year. She had arranged with certain people to publish her journal if she came to any harm. V asked angrily who the 'certain people' were. Molly spoke three initial letters. IRB.

Ryan's voice died slowly, rather than coming to a sudden stop, but, before I could speak, he started again. 'There was a sort of postscript or something at the bottom of the last page. It was written with a ball-point. The handwriting was practically illegible, and obviously recent. I had a bit of a job making it out but I think I got it. It's quite short.'

I was on my feet, my mouth agape. 'Never mind that. Jesus Christ, she shot Collins. All this time the rumours have been around that one side or the other shot him. Now we know. And not only that. The bastard went against everything he had been preaching and bought her freedom by shopping an informer. For fuck's sake, how many poor johnnies did he have her knock off for that same thing?'

'Let me read this little bit. It finishes everything off.'

> *Wednesday, 13 July 1994*
> I take up my pen after 72 years. What I have to write will be brief. Even now, my hands find the task almost beyond them. A week ago, I wrote to Mr Urquart in London and asked him to return these journals to me. The talk of peace in Ireland at last has led me to hope that I may destroy them. Surely I am no longer in danger. The parcel was delivered this morning and I feel that this last entry will suffice. The day peace is declared I will burn the journals.

I said softly, 'Thirteenth of July. That's just before she died. Three days before. God, to go through all she went through and die before any ceasefire. I hope those bastards hurry up and say it's over. If only for this little old woman.' My attention swung back to my own position. I shouted aloud. 'What about Theresa? Surely they have verified that the books are all there by now. They should at least have phoned to tell me that she's all right. Do you think it's bad or good that we have heard nothing?'

'I'll be honest with you, Frank, I don't know. When you were out this morning, I phoned my people. If anything turns up I'll know soonest.'

'For God's sake man, if a crowd of cops go stamping their big feet all over the place, there's no knowing what might happen. Can't you call them off or something? At least until she's home safely.'

From somewhere, Ryan summoned a smile. 'Who said anything about cops and big feet?'

My eyebrows asked the question. He stopped smiling and said, 'I'm afraid that I haven't been entirely frank with you. I told you when I arrived last night that my interest has been purely personal all along.'

I frowned. 'Yes. Now that you mention it, I remember. It passed me by at the time. Tell the tale, Ryan. Who are you working for in this?'

'What I'm going to say to you now I will deny in any court of law. I have retained an interest in various fields since I was a lad of seventeen, and I thought it would be exciting to join a revolutionary group. Before I joined the force, of course.'

'You mean you're fucking IRA all the time. The lot holding Theresa? You can't be serious?'

'Hold hard, Frank. There are various strands to any political philosophy. Call them wings, if you will. I have never had much time for the death-or-glory lot.'

'Left wing, right wing. It's all a load of shit. And you're in it up to your inspector's neck. Get on the phone to your mad friends and get my wife back.'

'I don't blame you being upset. It's only natural. But let me explain. I joined the IRA in 1954. Even then, I was more interested in the political side than in going out on mad 'missions' where the chances of being shot were a lot greater than coming home 'in glory'. Ten years after joining I was sworn into the IRB, a group I thought, along with a lot of others, had lapsed after the Civil War. I found out that it still existed but was very small indeed. In those days, the man who swore me in was the only contact I had. Nowadays I get my orders by phone at home. If I want to deliver a report, I dictate it on to an answering machine.'

'What the hell has a group like that to do these days?'

He shrugged. 'I don't think you would really want to know that, Frank. Let's just say that I am rarely called upon. Apart from the man who swore me in, and now Mrs Perry, I have no idea who is or is not IRB. I swear to God.

'The republican movement has always suspected that somewhere, waiting to jump out and bite it, is a series of diaries or record books of some sort. I was given the task of locating them because of my position in the force. When I heard of Mrs Perry and her death, her house being torched by professionals, I had to try to find out what she had that was valuable. What put me on the alert was the hospital nurse's remarks about burns and torture marks on this harmless old lady. That's the same nurse who not only saw your wife taking the ribbon with the keys from Mrs Perry's neck, but overheard her telling you both about the cupboard and its contents.

I said sourly, 'I didn't like that bitch the minute I saw her. I should have known that she was trouble.'

Ryan allowed himself a slight smile. 'I put two and two together. Don't forget that we were always looking for any sign of the mysterious diaries. Unfortunately, another branch of what the Yanks might call 'the company' were a step ahead. They had been watching Mrs Perry's house for some time. I don't know what made them take an interest in the first place.

'One of their men, a little English git, called to the hospital and was told the same things as I was. He said he was a relative. I strongly suspect that he started the fire, ransacked your house and asked questions about you in Rosslare. Oh yes. I knew about your mobile home or caravan or whatever you call it.

'He is also the man who called here, using the name Valentine. He's a crazy bugger. Just because he was born and raised in England, he seems to think that he needs to be twice as fanatical as the rest of us. I have a shrewd suspicion that the boys up top in the Army will have a word or two to say to him about lifting your wife. Oh yes, he's behind that too.'

As I made to speak, he hurried on. 'I should tell you that the momentum for peace originated with the IRB. The Army have been told to call it off. Confidentially, it will be very soon.'

I controlled myself with great difficulty during the final words. I was looking at him with a far from friendly eye. Whatever he might say about different wings, he was tarred with the same brush as Valentine or whatever his name was.

I walked towards him until my eyes were staring up into his from an inch away. 'You told me earlier not to hit you unless I intended to finish the job. Either you make a phone call and get my wife back, or I'm going to take you up on that.'

It looked like a stand-off. Then he shrugged and went to pick up the phone. He had not touched it when it rang. He strangled the sound at birth. 'Yes. That's right. Where? When? You're sure about that? Really sure?'

When he turned to face me, I had no way of knowing whether the news was good or bad. He seemed to my terror-stricken mind to be standing there for a very long time.

I opened my mouth to scream at him but no sound emerged.

Suddenly a slight smile slid across his lips. 'The IRA have telephoned RTE in the last few minutes. Your wife has been left in the boot of a car in the area of Inchicore. They say that she is unharmed but refused to be more specific about where they have left her.'

A wild hope which had started to burgeon in me was snuffed out. 'But she'll die in the boot of a car. She can't bear to be in a confined space. She's claustrophobic as all hell.'

He stretched a hand towards me as if trying to physically take the panic from me. 'The message said she had been lightly sedated to make her release easier for their security. The guards are searching hard. Extra men have been brought in. My guess is that we'll have another call soon to tell us they've found her.'

As if on cue, the peals of the doorbell shattered the last vestige of calm to which I was hanging. I started to tremble violently and tears ran down my face. Ryan said urgently, 'Hang in there Frank. I'll get that. It's probably word.'

Of course it was. A juvenile uniformed Garda followed him into the kitchen. Seeing me, he made to remove his cap, but remembering that he was in the presence of a senior officer, merely stood with his fingers touching the brim. Ryan was brusque. 'For Christ's sake tell us. Have you found Mrs Doorly?'

'Yes sir. The wom... lady has been found in,' he glanced at a small piece of paper in his hand, 'Padre Pio Drive, Inchicore. Outside number 14.'

I burst out, 'Is she all right man? Is she hurt?'

'No sir, I'm not sure, sir. I was told to give you the message and to say that a car is on its way to bring you to the hospital.'

'Hospital!' Ryan and I shouted the word together.

At that moment, the doorbell rang again. I ran to open the door. Another guard stood there, this time older than me and wearing the stripes of a sergeant. 'Mr Frank Doorly?'

'Yes.'

'Sergeant Downes, sir. I have a car here to bring you to Beaumont Hospital.' He tried a reassuring smile. 'The word is that your wife is quite safe and unharmed in any way. I'm told that she swallowed half a dozen Valium and is sleeping like a... peacefully.'

Ryan appeared from the kitchen with the young copper in tow. At the sight of a senior officer, the sergeant sprang to attention, shooting a venomous glare at his junior.

Ryan turned to me. 'You go with them, Frank. I'll drive your car over so you can have it for later when you are coming back here.'

I threw him the keys and followed the sergeant out to the blue Granada waiting at the pavement. The driver switched on the roof lights and the siren, and we were drawing up outside the hospital door in ten minutes, having driven through a succession of red traffic lights as other vehicles pulled obligingly out of our path. At any other time, I would have relished the experience.

I entered the reception area at a run and a Garda who seemed to be waiting for me came over. 'Mr Doorly, if you will come with me I will take you to your wife. She's in a private room on the second floor. The lift is this way.'

I remembered the layout from the time I had visited Mrs Perry and, when the lift stopped, I discovered that the ward was the same one, the room being off the main corridor.

Another uniformed guard stood at the door, but I ignored him and thrust my way into the room.

She was lying in the white bed, the starched sheets pulled tightly across her chest. Her eyes were closed, her face pale and free from make-up. Her hair lay on the pillow. I thought, I've never seen her so...serene. Had a halo appeared above her head, she would have looked as many saints used to in the little booklets in the rack at the back of the church.

The rise and fall of her breathing barely moved the bedclothes. I could see that she was really all right.

Nobody could be sick or injured and look like that.

A sound behind me made me turn. A fat woman wearing a white coat came in. A stethoscope hung around her neck in the unmistakable badge of her profession. 'Mr Doorly?'

I nodded.

'I'm Doctor Mairéad Sweeney. Your wife is, as you can see, very well. She had been administered a mild sedative before coming here. We carried out a full physical examination to make sure she had not come to any harm. You'll be glad to know that the pregnancy is progressing quite normally. I'd guess at nine weeks. Does that tie in with your date?'

I nodded a second time. I did not trust myself to speak. Nine weeks and she never even mentioned it to me. What the hell was going on?

Now I found voice. 'When will she wake up?'

'Well, I would guess tomorrow morning. In view of what she has been through and her condition, I decided to boost the sedative. The sleep will do her good.'

I met Ryan in the hall and he returned my keys. He asked after Theresa. I brought him up to date.

He fixed a stern gaze on me. 'A word in season, if I may.'

I said nothing, and he resumed. 'Last night never happened, Mr Doorly. I arrived at your home after the IRA message this morning. Right?'

With difficulty, I focused on his words. His eyes stared straight into mine without a flicker of friendship.

I said, 'OK, if that's the way you want it. I'm Mr Doorly and you're Inspector Ryan.' I lowered my voice. 'If my wife had been harmed, I would have hung your bollocks from a flagpole. You and your fucking IRB.'

I left him standing there, a half-smile on his face.

Resolution

I slept little that night. I drank many cups of tea as I wrestled with my feelings. Theresa was safe. That was the main thing. However, clamouring for attention was the pregnancy. Why had she not told me? It was not her form to save it up as a surprise.

Having phoned the hospital early to be told that she was awake and had eaten a good breakfast, at eleven o'clock I was parking in the car park. I knocked on her door and went in without waiting for an answer.

She was sitting in an armchair looking out the window at the winter sunshine. When she swung her head to face me, I felt a breathless sensation. She looked stunning. Her hair was hidden under a white bandanna, and her face was almost childlike in its beauty.

She was wrapped in a white towelling robe and her feet were clad in mules.

Her eyes were clear as she looked at me. 'Hi, Frank.'

'Are you all right, love?'

A small smile appeared. 'I'm fine. I slept right through the night and woke at eight, starving. I've eaten an enormous breakfast.'

'Where did the dressing gown and things come from? It never dawned on me to bring anything in.'

'One of the nurses offered to lend me a few things. She saw that she was about my size.'

I moved to her and bent to kiss her. She turned slightly and my lips landed on her cheek.

I straightened, a bit put out, but she did not say

anything.

'Was it shitty, love? Did they treat you very badly?'

'Not really. After I was taken to the house, they made me make that video. They wrote out what I had to say. They never laid a finger on me. They were quite nice really, calling me Mrs Doorly all the time and bringing in food and cups of tea.'

I asked a question that had come to me during the night. 'Why didn't you give them the diaries when they came for you? Presumably that would have sent them off happy?'

She gave one of her giggles. 'When he, the one who took me away, rang the bell, he said that he was from the police. I asked him in, thinking it was about the burglary. He said that he wanted me to come down to the station for a few minutes. So I went with him – it never dawned on me that he wasn't police until he produced a gun and told me to lie along the back seat. By that time, I was too frightened to resist.'

'Did you tell him the diaries were at home?'

'Only when we got to where he was taking me. He got a right telling-off from the senior one. Guess who that was?'

I thought I already knew from Ryan but shook my head.

'Valentine. The Englishman who pretended to be Mrs Perry's nephew. Another man came and sort of took over soon after they had made me read the thing out to you.'

'Where did they keep you?'

She shook her head slightly. 'I promised not to say, Frank. When they said they were going to put me in the car boot, I got a bit panicky. One of them said he knew a chemist and got a few Valium. I took six of the yellow ones and the next thing I remember was waking up here late last night.'

I paused before speaking. 'Theresa, love, I saw a

doctor yesterday. She said you are pregnant. Nine weeks.'

'Oh yes. That would be about right.' Her face was expressionless.

I tried to keep the tremble from showing in my voice. 'Why didn't you say anything about it to me Theresa? Why keep it secret? You know how much I wanted a baby?'

Her shoulders rose as she took a deep breath. I knew I was not going to like this.

'No, Frank. I disagree. You don't really want a child. You just want to prove you can father one. Possibly to me, but definitely to yourself.' As I made to reply, she went on, 'You see Frank, I've known for a long time that if I wanted a baby, I would have to go to someone else.'

A bitterness filled my throat. 'Are you trying to tell me that you are having an affair?'

Now she laughed. 'An affair? Good God, no. That's the last thing I'd do. I decided about a year ago to get myself pregnant. I began plotting my periods and taking my temperature. All that sort of thing. At first it was hard for me to know the most fertile times. I went to a doctor and learned all about it. Of course, by this time I had been thoroughly checked out. The fault had to be with you. The upshot was that at the end of June, everything fell into place nicely. You were working for three nights running and the temperature thing was just right. So I rang Brendan. Brendan Archer. I told him I wanted to talk and we met in a pub in Rathmines. I came straight out with it. Said you were not able to father me a child and that we both agreed he would be the one to ask. Well, he said he would in a few seconds. I know Brendan has had a thing about me ever since I married you. He practically jumped on me there and then. He called on each of the nights you were working late. He would arrive at six and leave at eight.

'Of course, before we started I brought him to a solicitor and had him sign a disclaimer about ever seeing or supporting the child.

'Brendan had no problems about my insistence that everything would last only until I became pregnant. He had no desire for a relationship or anything.

'Anyway, he did the trick. A few weeks later I was sure. I went back to the doctor and he confirmed it. I'm due on the fifth of April, give or take.'

The room throbbed with a silence. I whispered, 'Just like that. You went out and offered yourself to that bastard. He's always wanted to get into your pants. But why? Jesus, Theresa, do you know what you're saying here?'

'Oh yes. I know what I'm saying all right. But be honest, Frank. You know we've been going downhill for the last few years. I'm not saying it was your fault. Not by any means. I don't really know the cause. Maybe it was just familiarity. It breeds contempt, they say.'

She hurried on before I could break in. 'No, contempt is the wrong word. I could never feel contempt for you, Frank. I can admit to myself that I still love you a little. We've had fourteen good, well fairly good, years. But I want a child. And more than that, I want my space. And most of all I want an end to the unhappiness I've been feeling for so long. I toyed with the idea of telling you that the baby was yours, but that was never really on. You could not do your bit in rearing a child. You would always be competing with it instead of loving it.

'Try to understand, Frank. And don't blame yourself. I know you're hurt and probably want to kill me. But that will pass. Just give it time. Then you'll find someone who's different from me and you'll both be happy.

She went on, 'The other night, when I was a

prisoner, I gave my life a lot of thought. I don't know what really made me decide. It was probably being away from you. But decide I did.'

She stood up and looked out the window, half-turned away from me. 'I'm leaving you, Frank. I'll be moving out as soon as they let me home from here.'

For a few seconds I was silent. My head was pounding and my eyes fought to keep back the tears forming behind them. Slowly, a surging rage took hold. 'You're nothing but a whore. And you have the nerve to lecture me about my being unfit to raise a child. You're insane. I'll have you committed and you'll never get out.'

She moved her head to look squarely at me again. 'Forget it, Frank. No chance. I thought you might try threats, so I had a doctor and solicitor sign papers that I was sound in mind and body. By the way, if you're interested, the other IRA man told me about the diaries. He said that the whole kidnapping was a bad mistake. So that I would understand why they wanted the diaries. Like I said, he told me the lot. About Gráinne being captured, how Collins got her out by giving the Brits an informer in the Castle. And how she killed Collins. I liked that ending. Molly Perry went out and did what she had to do. Now I'm doing what I have to do.'

Sometimes you know when you are beaten, that no amount of words will change things.

In the hospital front hall, I saw a newsstand and went to buy a paper. The first afternoon editions were just being unwrapped. I fancied the ink was still wet.

Funnily enough, it was not the headlines that drew my eyes initially. In a little box at the bottom of the page I saw that the IRA had admitted that kidnapping Theresa was a mistake and that the man responsible would be disciplined. A man's body had been found in Clontarf. His hands were tied, he was wearing a black hood and he had been shot in the head. Gardaí had identified him as Peter Synnot, a native of Liverpool who was known to be a member of the IRA.

Finally, my eyes moved to the screaming banner.

PEACE AT LAST.

I turned and walked out the door.